BROGAN'S PROMISE

Book Three of The Mackintoshes and McLarens

SUZAN TISDALE

Cover design by Wicked Smart Designs

Also by Suzan Tisdale

The Clan MacDougall Series

Laiden's Daughter

Findley's Lass

Wee William's Woman

McKenna's Honor

The Clan Graham Series

Rowan's Lady

Frederick's Queen

The Mackintoshes and McLarens Series

Ian's Rose

The Bowie Bride

Rodrick the Bold

Brogan's Promise

The Clan McDunnah Series

A Murmur of Providence

A Whisper of Fate

A Breath of Promise

Moirra's Heart Series

Stealing Moirra's Heart

Saving Moirra's Heart

Stand Alone Novels

Isle of the Blessed

For Gen, Laurie, Tara, Kate, and Sara.

Prologue

No one understood the depths of her grief. Despair and sorrow clung to her heart, weighing it down until Mairghread was no longer certain it beat any more. Her soul was empty, void of any good feelings. Only the pain, the sorrow, and heartache remained.

Even now, three long years after the deaths of her husband and only child, the pain was as real and as intense as if it had only happened moments ago.

In order to help pass the time, until she could once again be reunited with them in heaven, she drank. Aye, there was many a late night when she contemplated taking her own life in order to escape the deep suffering in her heart. The only thing that kept her from slicing through the tender flesh of her wrists, or wrapping a rope around her neck, or throwing herself off the parapet, was knowing that if she acted on those thoughts, she would never see either of them again. God would not allow her entry to heaven.

As it stood, there was a good chance He would not allow her entry anyway. Not if the rumors whispered behind her back were more than just cruel lies. Not if what her uncle hinted at but never really said was actually true.

There was a time when she would have demanded to know the whole ugly, sordid truth of what really happened that awful night when her world fell apart. The only things she remembered — for she herself nearly died that night — were told to her by her uncle and her maids. And rarely did any of their stories match up.

So horrific was that night, so horrible was her loss, she took up the flagon and bottle as soon as her outer wounds had healed.

After countless nights of drinking to the point where she could not have found her own hands with the help of guide and map, it was as natural as breathing. Now, after three long years of this, she doubted she *could* breathe or think without the aid of drink.

She cared not anymore what people thought of her. Cared not a whit about the whispers behind her back. Cared not for anything or anyone.

Were it not for her maid, Gertie — who had taken care of her from the day she came into this world — 'twas highly unlikely Mairghread would still be walking amongst the living. If one could even count the young woman amongst as such.

Once, before that dark night, Mairghread Mactavish had been a beautiful, vibrant woman who put the needs of her family and people ahead of her own. Aye, she had turned more than a few heads in her youth, what with her long, thick, auburn hair and dark, emerald green eyes. Mairghread was more than just a beautiful woman, however. She was a beautiful soul -- the kind of giving, loving woman that the world definitely needed more of. Or so her maid Gertie used to declare to anyone who would listen.

But now? Now, when Gertie looked upon her lady, she felt a profound sense of loss. Not just for the man and babe killed that dark night. As far as Gertie was concerned, the world lost more than two souls that ugly night. It had lost her sweet lady, too.

An empty a shell if ever there was one was Mairghread Mactavish.

And that was the saddest part of all.

Chapter One

Brogan Mackintosh was a sensible, logical thinking man. Whenever possible, he tried to see the good in people and all situations. It could also be said he was as honorable as he was generous -- the kind of man who would give you the tunic off his back if you needed it. There was naught he wouldn't do for the down-trodden or poor creatures of this earth.

Never, in the whole of his adult life, did he regret being such a man. Until now.

"Ye want me to do *what?*" He could not have been more surprised had the sun risen in the west that morn.

He sat at a long trestle table in the newly finished tower — a tower he had helped build with his own two hands. Across from him sat his sister-by-law, Rose Mackintosh, and two auld women he had met less than a quarter of an hour ago. Rose was a pretty, wee woman, whom he had always admired, adored, and respected.

Until now.

"Ye act as though I have just asked ye to kill the king," Rose replied.

To his way of thinking, the request was just as difficult, just as insane as killing the king. Nay, killing the king would have been easier.

He sat in dumbfounded silence as he tried to wrap understand her entreaty.

"She be a fine woman, m'laird," the old woman named Gertie said. She was seventy if she was a day. A short round woman with light blue eyes and hair the color of the blade of his sword.

"I do no' doubt that she is," Brogan said.

He was cut off from saying more by the one named Tilda, the mirror image of Gertie, save for her dark blue eyes and missing upper teeth. "Ye will ne'er find a lass more beautiful." With the missing teeth, she had a very distinct lisp whenever she spoke.

"Aye, as beautiful as the Highlands in springtime, I says," added Gertie as she looked at her friend.

"Aye, as beautiful as that. And kind! Och, m'laird, ye'll ne'er meet one as kind!"

"Or as givin'," added Gertie.

"Or as givin'," agreed Tilda, adding a nod of her silver-gray noggin.

At a loss for words, Brogan could only stare at the three women before him. Not a one of them understood the difficulty of their request.

Rose was studying him closely, undoubtedly looking for signs his resolve was waning. "Brogan, ye have been alone for far too long," she said. Her tone was soft and filled with warmth.

Brogan knew her intentions were sincere, born out of a sense of familial devotion. But really! Marriage? To a woman he'd never once laid eyes on? How could she ask such a thing when she knew how much he still loved and mourned the loss of his first wife?

"M'laird," Gertie said, drawing his attention away from Rose. "We ken we be askin' much of ye, me and Tilda. But we ask because we love our lady verra much."

"Aye, we do," Tilda agreed.

"If she be forced to marry that foul Frenchman, well, 'twill mean the end of our clan and the end of our lady," Gertie said. Her tone was forlorn, sorrowful and matched the sadness he saw in her eyes.

"Aye," Tilda said. "He beat his last wife to death, ye ken."

Gertie looked at her friend. "All because she gave him a daughter and no' a son."

"He be a bloody son of a whore if e'er there was one," Tilda said.

Brogan had heard enough. "Certainly, there be someone in yer clan who would be willin' to marry yer lady."

Gertie and Tilda exchanged conspiratorial glances with Rose before Gertie addressed his assertion. "Well, ye see, there might be a man or two willin' to do such ..."

He sensed a *but* coming.

"Ye see, she needs a strong man, m'laird," Tilda offered.

"Aye, a strong man," Gertie said.

"Are ye sayin' the men of yer clan are weak?" Brogan asked with a quirked brow.

Both women shook their heads, aghast at the notion. "Nay, m'laird!"

Brogan had had enough. Pushing away from the table, he glowered at Rose. "I shall have to politely decline," he said. Bowing to the three women, he bid them all a gruff good day, and quit the tower.

"Och!" cried Tilda. "Our poor lady! Now, she will be forced to marry the Frenchman!"

Gertie, the more devious-minded of the two, looked at Rose.

"Nay, all be no' lost yet," Rose said with a smile.

"What do ye mean, m'lady?" Tilda asked.

Gertie smiled deviously. "We need to introduce them."

ROSE KNEW HER HUSBAND HATED LEAVING THEIR KEEP — WHAT there was of it. 'Twas a work in progress with only one tower completely finished. The main keep, which would house a gathering room, a study for Ian, and fifteen bedchambers, was only partially built. This fine spring day, Ian and his men were working feverishly to finish enclosing the outside of their future home. If it were finished by winter, 'twould be a miracle.

Knowing her husband as she did — his penchant for working from dawn to dusk and his strong dislike of shopping — played to Rose's advantage this day. 'Twas less than a sennight since Brogan had *politely* refused to marry a woman desperately in need of a good, strong husband.

Knowing men as she did, she had to believe that Brogan was no different than all the rest. Lust and desire could be grand motivators. In most instances, Rose was not the meddling sort. However, she felt sorry for her brother-by-law and felt motivated to help him see that which he refused; he was lonely. He needed to move on with his life.

Thus, when there was a mysterious and sudden need for flour and other sundries, which required an immediate trip to *Camhanaich* - a small village a few hours north and east of their lands. Ian all too happily volunteered his unwitting brother to go in his stead. Brogan had as much of a liking for shopping as his brother, which was to say, he detested it. But adoring his sister-by-law, and being the kind, generous man that he was, agreed to act as her escort.

They took ten Mackintosh men with them, all well-trained and armed to the teeth. After the events of more than a year ago, when Rose had been kidnapped and held for ransom by Rutger Bowie — may he continue to burn in hell — Ian spared no expense at keeping the love of his life safe.

Brogan, as most men were, was completely oblivious and had not an inkling of what lay ahead for him.

They left before he had a chance to break his fast, for Rose insisted they needed to leave before all the 'good flour' was gone. Brogan's knowledge of such things was nonexistent; therefore, he was forced to believe her.

With her son, John, a sweet boy of nearly one, in the good and capable hands of two Mackintosh women, they set off for *Camhanaich* just after dawn. Intentionally, she nearly talked Brogan's ears off on the two-hour journey. 'Twas a purposeful ploy to frustrate and annoy so that by the time they reached the town, he would be all too eager to leave her to her shopping.

Unfortunately, being the honorable man that he was, he refused to leave her side. "If anythin' happened to ye, Ian would kill me."

On to a different plan, she decided. She intentionally took her time, lingering at each merchant stall. Just enough to annoy her brother-by-law.

"Brogan," she said as she was poring through fabrics at the wooler's stall, "I may be a while. If ye would like to, go on ahead and mayhap get a meat pie? I be certain I shall be safe with the rest of Ian's guards," she said with a nod in their direction.

'Twas after noontime and Brogan had not eaten so much as a crumb of bread since last eve. Starved, tired of his sister-by-law's incessant chatting and need to look at every item at every stall — none of which had yet to contain an ounce of the desperately needed flour — he could not wait to be away from her. He gave a few quick instructions to the men before leaving Rose in their capable hands.

Rose smiled an all-knowing smile as she watched her brother-by-law all but run away.

Lord, how he hated large crowds.

Were he not so hungry, Brogan would have declined Rose's suggestion. Instead, he would have politely insisted they hurry on with purchasing the 'good flour' and get back to their keep. He knew his pleas would fall on stubborn, deaf ears.

Making his way through the crowded street, he caught the scent of meat pies and freshly baked bread wafting through the air. His stomach growled and his mouth watered as he politely pushed his way through, motivated solely by hunger. Thankfully, he found the meat pie maker, made his purchase, and stepped away. The second pie was just as delicious as the first, both eaten in quick succession as he stood next to the stone wall of the ale house.

Though he was quite thirsty and the temptation to step inside and purchase *just one* ale was quite strong, he knew he could not. *Just one* would lead to *a second will not hurt,* which in turn would lead him to drinking an entire barrel. He had fought too hard and too long three years ago to become the sober man he was today. After the death of his wife, he had fallen so far into the abyss of drunkenness he nearly died. Had it not been for his parents — more specifically his father — chances were he would be rotting in the earth at this very moment.

He could have gone into the ale house and purchased a cider. But experience taught him that a man of his size and stature ordering cider, led to being taunted and ridiculed. The taunts and ridicule he could deal with. But nearly always, someone would challenge his manhood or call him a coward. It never ended well for the drunkard. A brawl would always ensue. And Brogan, being the sober man he was, would always win.

So thirsty as he was, he decided to stay outside and take his time returning to Rose. She was probably *still* looking at silks and wools. 'Twould be hours before they left this awful place overrun with people.

He decided, instead, to walk along the street, alone with his thoughts. 'Twas not often he had time to himself, so busy were they with building the keep and ensuring the clan was safe. Mayhap, he would find a quiet spot somewhere in this town, where he could sit and think without being interrupted. He had been here only once before, last autumn, and again with Rose.

Rose.

She *was* a good woman, with a good heart. His brother Ian loved her with all that he was. There were times when Brogan envied him. Ian had everything Brogan had at one time wanted. A wife, a child, a loving home. But fate intervened and took his sweet wife before he even had time to get her with child.

God, how he had loved Anna. She was much like Rose in many respects. Good and generous she had been. Not a day had gone by that she had not made him laugh, usually over something innocuous, and betimes, off-color.

He knew Rose had only good intentions in her heart when she had suggested he marry the Mactavish woman. But four years ago, he swore he would never marry again — even though he had promised his sweet Anna he would. The pain he had endured at losing her had nearly killed him. He refused to tempt fate a second time.

So he remained unmarried. And alone.

Brogan refused even to seek the comfort of bar wenches or whores. Not because he did not have any physical needs or desires. On the contrary, he had both. However, he refused the comfort of women because he felt he would be dishonoring the memory of his wife.

Down the street he went, passing by one merchant stall after another. 'Twas a nice spring day, with the sun shining brightly and just enough of a breeze to help take away some of the foul smells lingering in the street.

He was just passing by an alehouse, when someone stumbled and fell into him. Startled, he caught her before she could fall to the ground.

"Och!" she exclaimed as he was setting her onto her own feet. "I be terribly sorry!"

'Tis odd, at times, how God works. Or mayhap 'twas fate, or the stars had aligned perfectly. No matter what had caused the woman to stumble into him, Brogan would never be the same man after. He just didn't know it yet.

She was one of the most magnificent women he'd ever laid eyes on. Gloriously rich, auburn hair hung in riotous waves across her shoulders. A perfectly oval face framed big, green eyes, the color of emeralds. Auburn lashes, a straight nose, and full, pink lips; God's teeth, she was beautiful. A long moment passed before he realized she had stolen his breath away.

Someone bumped into her again, causing her to let out a yelp of surprise and cling to him even tighter.

They stood, these two oblivious souls, staring into one another's eyes while the rest of the world passed by. Brogan found it next to impossible to tear his eyes away from hers.

Another bump against her back, jostled him out of his current state of awe. Had he not been as tall and strong as he was, they would have both fallen to the ground.

"Gertie!" the auburn-haired woman exclaimed as she turned away from Brogan. "Stop that!"

Brogan blinked. His brow furrowed at the recognition of the name *Gertie.*

"Sorry, m'lady," came a scratchy voice he recognized from a sennight ago. "It be awful crowded here today."

Brogan finally tore his eyes away from the stunning woman in his arms. Standing next to her were Gertie and Tilda. Though they feigned innocence and refused to look at him, he knew better. Gertie was rocking back and forth on her heels, whistling as if she were as innocent as a newly born babe. Tilda was picking imaginary lint from her dark green shawl.

Stunned, he stood like a fool, looking at the old women and back to the woman he was still clinging to, and back again.

"Och!" Gertie finally exclaimed, as if she had just now realized 'twas *he* who had saved her lady from falling flat on her face. "'Tis ye! How be ye this fine day, Brogan Mackintosh?"

His stunned expression evaporated in the blink of an eye as he replaced it with a cold, hard stare. A stare that would have sent a grown man to quaking in his boots.

"Och! Ye be right," Tilda exclaimed as if she too, were only now realizing who he was.

Brogan glowered at her as a tic began to form in his lower jaw.

"What a surprise it is to be seein' ye here this day!" Tilda said with a wide, happy smile.

If he spoke a word now, he knew he would say something he might later — decades later — regret.

"Ye know him?" Mairghread asked rather perplexed.

"We have met, aye," Gertie replied. "When he came to the keep last year to purchase horses."

She lied.

Right to her lady's face.

Mairghread turned her attention back to Brogan. "I fear I do no' remember ye," she said, her voice but a whisper and her eyes filled with something akin to regret. Brogan found her response odd, if not a bit intriguing.

I would have remembered ye, he thought to himself.

"Come along, m'lady," Gertie said as she pulled on Mairghread's arm. "We still need to purchase flour, remember?"

Brogan's jaw dropped. *Flour?*

Aye, he knew then he'd been set up to meet Mairghread Mactavish. And there wasn't a doubt in his mind that Rose was involved. Up to her pretty little neck.

FOR THE REMAINDER OF THE DAY, BROGAN REMAINED SILENT, refusing to speak to Rose. He met every one of her questions and all her chatting with a cold-as-ice glower and even colder silence. After some time, she realized she was going to get nowhere with her brother-by-law and gave up trying. Even the men who travelled with them could tell he was in a black mood. Unlike Rose, they left him alone.

'Twas nearing the evening meal by the time they returned to the keep. Not quite ready yet to give up his frustration, he saw to it that Rose and the other guards were well within the walls of the keep before he left. One of the warriors had the audacity to ask where Brogan was off to. His reply was nothing more than a clenched jaw and a near murderous glare.

He had no real destination in mind. He simply needed to be away and alone. 'Twas doubtful he would be able to make it through the evening meal without saying something to Rose that would injure her tender feelings. Even if it was well-deserved.

Though he'd already ridden his mount to *Camhanaich* and back, they hadn't ridden fast or hard. Still, he was never a man to be cruel to anything, least of all a horse. So he kept a slow, unhurried pace.

Brogan took his mount south of the keep, along the little stream that ran through their lands. It led him away from all the construction and daily chaos that was the Mackintosh and McLaren clan.

The farther away he rode, the more at peace he began to feel. The sun still shone brightly against the pale blue sky. The spring grass danced in the cool breeze as birds flew noiselessly high above. The gentle sound of water rippling across stones and pebbles was just what he needed to calm his frayed nerves.

Then he thought of Mairghread.

The woman was beautiful. Damned beautiful.

He hadn't been so physically drawn to a woman since his sweet Anna had died.

But Mairghread? The moment he looked into those emerald green eyes, he felt an instant, visceral reaction. A need, a deep-seated need to keep touching her, to press his lips against the tender flesh at her neck and not stop. 'Twas as profound as a kick in his gut and nearly as painful.

Aye, Brogan had much to think about as he crossed the little stream.

What would his sweet Anna say to him? He shrugged for he already knew the answer. *"Do no' leave yerself alone in this world, Brogan Mackintosh. Do no' keep yer heart or yer life fer a dead woman."*

Those had been her exact words less than a sennight before she died.

That had been four years ago.

Aye, he had promised her he would not mourn her all the rest of his days, but the promise had been a lie. She had been so tremendously ill — with the wasting disease that took her from a beautiful vibrant woman to nothing more than skin and bones in less than two months — that he could have denied her nothing. Not even her simple request not to mourn her long. But his love for her had been so great. Anna and their love for one another had such a profound impact on him as a man, he could do nothing else but grieve and lament her loss. And drink.

Anna was everything good and right in his world. She was everything to him. Without her, he felt *less*. Less a man. Less alive. Less everything.

Losing her had left a tremendous, yawning wound to the very marrow of his soul. Brogan started drinking the day she died and did not put the bottle down for more than a full year. No matter how much he drank, he could not rid himself of the pain and loneliness he felt with her loss.

A dull throb began to pulse at the base of his neck. He pulled his horse to a stop and dismounted. Stretching his arms wide, he turned his head from side to side, his bones cracking loudly with the motion.

"Ye be an auld man, ye fool," he said aloud. Only his horse had heard him. "Yer bones crack and groan far too much for a man of only four and thirty." The horse had no opinion. Instead, he chose to lower his head and nibble at the grass.

"So what am I to do?" he asked God as he looked up at the clear sky.

It appeared God was no more interested in having a discussion with him than his horse was. Puffing out his cheeks, he let loose a quick breath, and gave a tug on the reins. The horse snickered once before complying.

Together, they walked leisurely across the open field. His thoughts kept turning back to Mairghread Mactavish. Their meeting had lasted only a few moments, but 'twas still far too long to suit him. He blamed the three she-devils: Rose, Gertie, and Tilda.

Had they not interfered with this ridiculous notion that *he* of all people marry the fair Mairghread, he wouldn't be feeling as low as horse dung on the bottom of a poor man's boot. He would not now be wandering aimlessly along the countryside, tired and hungry and confused. Nor would he be struggling with thoughts and memories that were best left in the past.

But alas, they had. The she-devils.

"Even if Rose be right — and I am no' admittin' to anythin' — it still be no' her place to interfere," he spoke to his horse as if he were an auld friend. "'Tis *my* life we be speakin' of, ye ken? No' hers."

Mayhap he *had* been living in the past for too long. Mayhap it *was* time to start thinking about his future. "It still does no' give her the right to do what she did," he said. "Even if it be the right time, it should be left to me to decide who my bride should be, aye?"

The horse snickered once and gave a great shake of his head, as if to disagree.

"What do ye ken?" Brogan said dismissively.

Across the small glen was a small thicket of trees. Brogan tossed the reins over the neck of his horse to allow the animal a little freedom to roam and graze. While the animal ignored him, Brogan picked a tree to lean against. Sliding down the trunk until he was seated comfortably on the grass, he stretched one long leg out and tossed his wrist over a raised knee.

He sat for a long while, struggling with his thoughts and feelings. 'Twas a heated debate betwixt heart and mind.

While he understood 'twas high time he left the past behind him, his heart was not quite as ready to give it up. His chest tightened when he thought of his sweet Anna. To this very day, it did not seem fair nor right that such a sweet, giving lass had died so young. As far as he was concerned, the world would have been much better off with a woman like her in it instead of a man such as he.

Or the kind of man he *had* been before he met her.

Nay, he was not the same man he had once been. Just as he was not the same after meeting her, after falling so hopelessly in love with her, he was also not the same since losing her. Some might believe a man incapable of change, but Brogan knew better.

Was he ready to move on? Was he ready to take another wife, to start a new life, mayhap be blessed with a bairn or two? Could he leave the memory of Anna behind and begin anew?

His heart ached still with missing her. He was not quite ready yet to let go. But now, he was willing at least to *think* about it. 'Twas a step in the right direction.

❦

BROGAN HAD SLEPT OUT OF DOORS UNDER A CANOPY OF SPARKLING stars with only his horse and his confused heart for company. Although he had come to the conclusion it might be time for him to move on with his life, he felt no better for it.

He walked his horse, rather than rode it, back to the keep, just after the break of dawn. Morning dew clung to everything around him. By the time he walked through the gate, his boots and trews were damp with it.

As was typical, everyone was already up and about. Several women were cooking over open fires whilst others were readying the long trestle tables inside the large gathering tent for the morning meal. He passed by a small group of men who were readying teams of horses to be used in the quarry. Other men were lined up to take bannocks and sausage with them, to eat as they headed either to fell trees in the forest or to work in the deep pits of the rock quarry. Children giggled happily as they chased one another around the encampment. All in all, 'twas as fine a morning as any.

So why did he feel such a strong sense of mourning?

He led his horse to the stables. The stable master, an older man named Ennis, volunteered to tend to his mount. Brogan politely declined his offer and tended to the animal himself.

He took his time rubbing the hobby down, making sure he had plenty of food and water. He ignored his own growling belly to take the time to clean the bridle and bit. Aye, he knew he was delaying the inevitable, like a child finds every conceivable delay when it is time to bathe or sleep.

Finally, his need to eat outweighed his desire to avoid Rose and Ian. He rubbed the back of his neck with his hand, took a deep breath, and left the stables.

He let out a relieved breath when he did not see Ian or Rose about. With a thankful heart, he happily took a trencher of food from one of the cooks and headed into the large tent. The tent was used as the clan's gathering room, until the rest of the keep could be built. Upon entering, he quickly perused the tables. No sign of Rose or Ian, which induced him to sigh in relief once more.

Mayhap this eve, he told himself as he took a seat at one of the tables. Mayhap he would pull Ian aside and ask for his guidance and advice.

Purposefully, he sat in the darkest corner with his back to the entrance. He hadn't taken his first bite yet when Rose sat down beside him. He shuddered and wondered if God was playing a cruel jest.

"Are ye through bein' angry with me?" she asked with a quirked brow.

"That depends," he answered drolly as he pulled off a hunk of brown bread. "Are ye done interferin' in me love life?" He popped the bread into his mouth.

Rose gave him a side-long glance. "I do no' ken why ye were so upset."

He chewed and swallowed before answering. "Because me life is me own, Rose."

Anger flared behind her bright eyes as she stood up from the table. "Then ye best start livin' it, Brogan Mackintosh. Else ye'll wake up some day and find yerself an auld man who is all alone in this world. And ye'll have no one to blame but yerself."

With grace reminiscent of a queen, Rose left him alone to simmer and think.

❧

FOR REASONS HE COULD NOT BEGIN TO UNDERSTAND LET ALONE explain to anyone, Brogan became angry. The more he thought on it, the angrier he became. So much so that he found he was unable now, to break his fast.

Mayhap his anger was born because he hadn't had a decent meal in two days. Mayhap 'twas because he had slept out of doors the night before.

Or mayhap, just mayhap, 'twas Rose's *I know what is best for you* attitude. Or more likely than not, 'twas the fact that she was right which he found so irksome. Either way, he pushed his trencher away, jumped to his feet and went in search of his sister-by-law.

He was fully prepared to give the woman a piece of his mind. *I will marry when I decide the time is right! I will choose me own wife, thank ye verra kindly!*

How on earth did his brother stand to be married to such a meddlesome woman?

It took a bit of searching and asking around before he learned that Rose was in her cottage, tending to her son. He knocked once, rather harshly. She had barely gotten out the words, "come in" before he shoved the door open.

He took only one step inside, seething mad. "'Tis *my* decision to make, Rose."

Pretending she had no idea to what he was referring, she lifted one fine brow lifted. "And what decision be that?" she asked before turning her attention back to her son. John was naked and cooing up at his mum as she changed his nappy and clothing.

Brogan growled deep in his throat. Aye, she was a meddlesome pain in his arse. But she was still his brother's wife. Without uttering a word, he turned around and slammed the door behind him.

He stood just a few steps away from the little cottage, his frustration building. Later, with a good deal of hindsight, he would realize he should have walked away. But he didn't. Instead, he turned around and threw open the door again. "Ye may be me brother's wife, but that does no' give ye the right to interfere in me life, Rose."

He gave her no opportunity to respond. Once again, he spun around abruptly and slammed the door behind him.

'Twas all he could do to keep from yelling at the top of his lungs. His hands, clenched tightly into fists, fair shook with his anger. He thought back to the day before when he had met Mairghread. Aye she was a beautiful woman. But to have the three she-devils lie to his face and force a meeting betwixt them? Nay, 'twas as wrong a thing as any.

Once again, he spun around and went back into the cottage. Rose was now sitting in a chair by the fire, nursing her son. Brogan did not care about the impropriety. "Ye lied to me and ye lied to Ian. 'Twas deceit and trickery ye used to get me to meet Mairghread Mactavish! Did ye think I would take one look at her and change me mind?"

Rose rolled her eyes. "Would ye have agreed to a meetin' with her had I asked nicely?"

Realizing he was on the precipice of losing his temper completely, he left again.

Lingering outside the door of his brother's cottage, Brogan fumed. *"Would ye have agreed to a meetin' with her had I asked nicely?"* Of course he wouldn't have! But that did not make her actions right or just.

And what of Mairghread? He could not be married to a woman who would be party to such a scheme, no matter how beautiful he found her to be. Was she in on the deception? 'Twas a good question, he supposed. So he marched back into the cottage. "Did Mairghread know about yer game?" he asked. His tone was harsh, his words clipped.

"Nay, she did no'," Rose replied. Her tone and expression were such that he had to believe her.

Some of his anger began to ease away. There was, he reckoned, no use in being so bloody angry he could bite his own sword in two. He offered Rose a curt nod before leaving. This time, he didn't slam the door behind him, nor did he thunder away only to return a moment later.

What truly has ye so angry? he asked himself as he stood in front of the cottage. Mayhap the number of things that were angering him at the moment were too long to list. He hung his head, rested his finger-tips on his hips and thought long and hard about his current situation.

What of Mairghread? If she did not know of yesterday's deception, he had to wonder if she had any knowledge at all of the plans the three she-devils had in store for them. What if he *did* agree to such a union only to find out Mairghread had no interest in marrying him? What then?

If he conceded — he was not quite ready to do that yet — and she turned him down, why, the ramifications would be significant. Rose would not rest until she had him well and duly wed.

He blew out a heavy breath and went back into the cottage. Rose was still sitting in the chair, still nursing her babe. 'Twas in that moment he realized *this* was what he wanted. A home, a wife, and bairns. The realization left him breathless and feeling as though he'd just been kicked by a horse.

"Is Mairghread for or against this union?" he asked, grinding his teeth together.

Rose looked at him for a long moment. He could not help but wonder what nefarious deed she was plotting now.

After a long moment, she blew out a breath and said, "I do no' ken."

He believed her, but felt there was something more she wasn't telling him. He did not have to wait long to find out what that 'something more' was.

"Mayhap ye should no' come to the evenin' meal," she said, her voice soft and low, as if she'd suddenly grown quite weary. There was something in her eyes that he could not quite describe. Mayhap she was tired of arguing with him.

"And why no'?" he asked, his own anger beginning to fade.

She let out another breath before answering. "We have invited Mairghread here to sup with us. Rowan and Arline Graham and Alec and Leona Bowie will be here as well."

Brogan's gut tightened. "When were ye plannin' on tellin' me?"

Rose shrugged one shoulder and ignored his question. "We —

Arline and Leona and me — are going to do our best to talk her out of marryin' the frenchman."

He scoffed at the word *frenchman*. "Pray, tell me, Rose, who be this frenchman?"

"Claude Courtemanche."

Claude Courtemanche? Nay, that can no' be. His eyes widened in horrified surprise as his heart seized. "The Frenchman," he muttered.

PIERRE CLAUDE COURTEMANCHE WAS THE FRENCHMAN. THE Frenchman Gertie and Tilda had spoken of a sennight ago, when they'd first approached Brogan with their plea. Had he known then to whom they referred ... aye, Brogan knew the man, knew him all too well. And he had no liking for the pompous, arrogant bastard.

The first time he had met the man had been more than ten years ago. Brogan had gone to Edinburgh with his father. They were there to welcome his eldest brother, Michael, home from Italy where he had been studying for the prior three years.

After greeting Michael, they decided to head to the nearest inn, where they would eat a good meal and consume vast amounts of ale. 'Twas at that inn where Brogan met Courtemanche for the first time.

Courtemanche had been nothing short of a whoreson. Ordering the barmaids around as if they were his personal slaves, making disparaging remarks about them, as well as Scotland as a whole.

At one point, he had pulled a young barmaid onto his lap and began to fondle her openly. She resisted vehemently, pleaded with tear-filled eyes for him to let her be — which apparently angered him. He ripped open the bodice of her dress, exposing her breasts to all the guests in the inn and laughed.

Brogan's father reached them first, with Michael and Brogan right behind him. John pulled the young woman out harm's way, handing her off to Michael.

"Frenchman," John growled as he pulled the man to his feet. "I do no' ken how ye treat yer barmaids in France, but here, we show them a bit of kindness."

Courtemanche scoffed and smirked. "Get your filthy Scottish hands off me," he demanded. "I am Claude Pierre Courtemanche and I am under the protection of your king."

John truly did not care who he was or whose protection he was under. "Under the king's protection or God's, I do no' care. I suggest ye leave now, while ye still can."

Michael chimed in then. "And apologize to the lass fer treatin' her so poorly."

Courtemanche smirked and looked directly at Michael. "I think not," he replied drolly before turning back to John. "And if you do not remove your hands from me, I shall tell your king. You will be arrested at once and hanged."

"I do no' take kindly to empty threats," John told him. "Especially from someone such as ye."

"Think you it is an empty threat?" Courtemanche challenged. "Above stairs is the king's chamberlain, Donald MacGregor. He probably has his cock buried in one of your Scottish whores as we speak."

John, typically a man of patience, turned purple with rage. "I will give ye one last chance to apologize to the lass and leave of your own accord," John told him.

Another sneer from the Frenchman nearly sent John over the edge. Before he could throw the first punch, Courtemanche had removed a dirk from his belt. He might have thought he was catching John unawares, but this was not John's first fight. Nor would it be his last.

With the flick of his wrist, John had disarmed the Frenchman and landed a hard blow to the arrogant man's face. Blood began to spurt from his nose, which anyone with a lick of sense could see was broken.

"You son of a whore!" Courtemanche had screamed as he writhed in pain on the floor.. "I will have ye hanged for this!"

Aye, he had been in Scotland as guest of the king. But what Courtemanche could not have known was that John was also quite close to David. And Donald MacGregor was a distant cousin.

Someone had summoned Donald MacGregor when the man had first attacked the barmaid. He had come racing down the stairs and into the main room. He took one look at Courtemanche, rolled his eyes and then turned to John. "Cousin," he said with a slight inclination of his head.

"Cousin," John returned his greeting.

"What did he do?"

"Attacked the barmaid," John said before returning to his seat.

"He attacked me!" Courtemanche cursed as he struggled to his feet. As he held his hand to his face, blood continued to spurt. Only one person came to his aid and he had been Courtemanche's own man.

"He broke my nose!" He growled. "I want him hanged!"

Donald laughed, shook his head and took a seat across from John. "Who here would like to stand as witness for the Frenchman?" he asked in a loud voice.

The room was deathly silent.

"And who here would like to stand as witness for John Mackintosh?"

Everyone in the room began to line up behind and around John.

Brogan was pulled back to the here and now by his nephew's loud burp.

"Ye jest," he said, disbelievingly.

Rose shook her head. "Nay, Brogan, on this I do no' jest. 'Tis true. Mairghread's uncle left a few days ago, for France. He plans to return in a few short months, with Courtemanche. And Mairghread will be forced to marry him."

A hundred questions raced in his mind. "Certainly, she does no' wish to marry him."

"I do no' think she understands the seriousness of it," Rose said with a sigh of resignation. "Gertie and Tilda have begged her to seek out someone else to marry. But she thinks the old women exaggerate about Courtemanche's reputation. Simply put, she does not know the man. And for whatever reason, she seems to hold her uncle in high regard. The woman does not believe he would ever try to match her with someone as awful as we ken him to be."

Brogan shook his head once again, as if doing so would bring more clarity to the conversation at hand. "But he *is* a bloody bastard," Brogan said.

"Aye, on that, ye and I can agree. 'Tis one of the reasons I invited

Mairghread here this night. Ian and I were goin' to talk to her, to try to get her to see reason."

He quirked a doubtful brow. "And try to convince her she should marry me."

"Nay, Brogan. To try to convince her she should marry *anyone else* but Courtemanche," Rose said as she glanced down at her now sleeping babe. "If you had no' agreed, I would have suggested Rodrick, or one of our other men. All 'twould take is one look at the beautiful woman to get them to agree."

Rodrick? He mused. The thought of Rodrick the Bold being married to such a beautiful woman as Mairghread was nearly laughable. Nearly.

"Then *why* did ye even ask me?"

"Because I thought the two of ye better suited to one another. Because I worry over ye bein' alone all the rest of yer days," she replied.

He realized then, that Rose's intentions were genuinely born out of the kind regard she had for him. Although her tactics left much to be desired, he could no longer fault her for her intentions.

Chapter Two

'Twas at times like these when Brogan wished he had not given up drinking. What he would not give to have just a dram.

There was much on his mind at the moment. He cursed himself for wanting to drink and shook away the urge. "'Twill solve nothin'," he mumbled under his breath as he crossed the courtyard heading for the armory.

"Och! Me wife has finally made ye addlepated." 'Twas Ian's voice coming from behind him. "She has ye talkin' to yerself now."

Brogan spun to face his younger brother. "I do no' ken how ye do it, Ian," he told him as he hung his head low. "She be enough to make a man want to drink, or strangle her. Or both."

Ian raised a brow. "Need I remind ye she be me wife?" 'Twas a rhetorical question, to be certain. But 'twas Ian's way of reminding him to show the woman some respect.

Brogan remained quiet as he raked a hand through his hair.

Ian smiled, a broad, knowing smile. "I defy ye to find a woman with a bigger heart."

Brogan gave a long, slow shake of his head. "Aye, she has heart all right. But her interferin' ways? Has she told ye of her devious plot to marry me off?"

"Aye, she has," Ian said as he slapped a hand on Brogan's back and began to walk with him.

"For the sake of Christ! Why did ye no' stop her!"

Ian threw his head back and laughed heartily. "Be we talkin' about the same woman?" he said playfully. "Me wife? Rose? The most stubborn women God ever set on this earth?"

Brogan puffed out his cheeks and expelled his breath in a rush. "I thought we were brothers?" he asked. "We are supposed to look out for one another. I have saved yer life more than once."

"And I, yers," Ian said. "Brother, no matter how frustratin' she can be at times, she always means well. She loves ye like a brother. And she wants only fer ye to be happy."

"I can be happy and *no'* be married," Brogan pointed out.

"True," Ian agreed. "But there be a difference between bein' happy and bein' blissfully happy. I tell ye true, I never thought to be married or to be a father of any legitimate bairns." He laughed at his own jest. "But Rose has changed me. She has made me a better, stronger man. And bein' a father?" A proud, warm smile lit up his eyes. "There be nothin' to make a man more proud. Nothin' more to make him feel as though he has a purpose in life."

A hearth and home, a wife, bairns. Those were things Brogan had, at one time, wanted more than anything. He wanted that life with Anna. But God had taken her far too soon. "I almost had that with Anna," he told him.

Ian turned quite serious then. "I ken, brother, I ken."

"Do ye think a man can have more than one chance at love in his lifetime?"

Ian quirked a brow. "I do no' ken. Mayhap we should ask our father?"

Brogan felt seven kinds a fool then. Their father, John, had lost two wives. Brogan's mother as well as Ian's. He was now married for a third time, to a lovely woman named Elsbeth.

Brogan felt his face grow warm from embarrassment. Not once, in all these years since losing Anna had he ever thought to look to his father as an example of what a man could have.

"Did Rose tell ye of Courtemanche?" Ian asked.

Anger bubbled up, deep in his belly. "Aye, she has." 'Twas not jealously he felt at the thought of Mairghread marrying the Frenchman. 'Twas abject anger. He knew all too well what the man was capable of.

"Poor Courtemanche," Ian said, feigning sympathy. "His nose never did set right." He was, of course, referring to the time their father had broken the man's nose.

Brogan laughed along with him. He rubbed his jaw, the memory of the one time in his life he felt the full weight of their father's fist. "Lord, above, our father can hit!"

Ian chuckled. "Aye, and I can tell ye, Frederick hits just as hard."

Brogan laughed, remembering how Frederick had quite literally beat sense in Ian's stubborn head when he had broken off his engagement to Rose.

"I still have nightmares," Ian admitted. "Of me makin' our older brother angry and him beating the bloody hell out of me again."

"If he hits like Da, I can no' blame ye," Brogan said.

Now the two men stood between the wooden wall and the stone wall that was still a work in progress. Stretching before them was the Mackintosh and McLaren Keep. Tiny huts, tents of varying sizes, and the newly finished tower filled up most of the space. Much progress had been made in the past year and a half, but there was still much to be done.

'Twas Ian who finally broke the silence. "I think marryin' Mairghread Mactavish is a good decision, Brogan. Rose loves ye. She'd no' play ye false or suggest a woman not well-suited to ye."

Brogan let out a heavy sigh. "I ken she would no' do such a thing on purpose," he replied. "But she does no' ken this woman well."

"Look at Frederick and Aggie," Ian said. "They knew each other no' at all when they wed. And look at them now. They have two children, and another on the way. They be verra much in love."

Brogan was not so naive to believe that arranged marriages ended in love matches. As far as he was concerned, his brother Frederick and his wife Aggie were the exception to the rule.

"If Frederick had no' taken that chance, he would never have found the love of his life," Ian added.

"I already had one love of me life," Brogan pointed out. There would or could never be a woman such as she. He felt it to his very marrow.

Ian chewed the inside of his lower lip before responding. "Aye, Anna was a good woman. But again, I say ye give our father's life a good long look. 'Tis possible for a man to love more than one good woman in his lifetime."

Brogan knew he was making perfectly good sense. Still, he was never one to take extreme chances, at least not without extreme and proper consideration.

"Besides," Ian said as he slapped Brogan's back. "Yer gettin' on in years. Ye do no' have much time to think on it."

Brogan grunted his disproval. "I be only four and thirty. I be no' dead yet."

"But I fear ye might be before ye make up yer mind to marry again," Ian said. "Besides, ye *would* be doin' an honorable thing by marryin' her. Ye'd be savin' her life, fer ye ken what a monster Courtemanche is."

Aye, there was *that*. Courtemanche. The Frenchman. Over the years since that first meeting, they'd all heard the stories told of the vile man. Brogan knew men could change, if they truly wished to. But Courtemanche? If anything, he'd grown worse over the years.

"He has been accused, once again, of rape," Ian told him. "Some young lass in Italy last summer."

Brogan expelled another heavy breath. He still could not quite grasp the fact that Mairghread's uncle would broker a marriage between the sweet and beautiful woman and that vile, cruel man.

"But this time, he chose the wrong young girl," Ian said. "She was of noble birth. Her father, one of the Italian king's chamberlains."

The thought of Courtemanche finally hanging for his misdeeds lightened Brogan's heart. But only slightly. There was still a good chance that Mairghread could be married off to the man before the Italian authorities could do anything with him.

In his heart, he knew what he must do.

ROSE FELT THAT IN ALL IT HAD BEEN A SUCCESSFUL EVE, SAVE FOR her stubborn brother-by-law, Brogan. He had not shown up to sup with them, which should not have surprised her. With the meal over, the foodstuffs cleared away, the tent was still filled near to bursting. But nowhere to be seen was Brogan.

Her husband, Ian, sat in a corner near the entrance, with Alec Bowie, Rowan Graham, and Reginald Mactavish, the steward of the Clan Mactavish. Just *what* the men were discussing, she did not know, nor did she care at the moment.

Rose drummed her fingers against the table as she pretended to not be as perturbed as she truly felt. *Blasted, stubborn men!* she all but screamed silently. Aye, that stubbornness proved useful on many occasion. However, on *this* particular occasion, 'twas proving to be as painful as a thorn in one's foot.

To her left, sitting between Arline Graham and Leona Bowie, was Mairghread Mactavish. She was such a lovely woman. It was difficult for Rose to believe she had a problem with strong drink. Mayhap Gertie and Tilda had exaggerated a bit, for Rose had not seen her take so much as a sip of wine this night.

Arline and Leona were well aware of Rose's plan to stop the Mactavish woman from being married off to Claude Courtemanche. Though none of the three women had known Mairghread before this day, they still felt it was their duty to protect her from such a fate. 'Twas good to have friends like that. Rose could only pray they would be able to talk her out of marrying the man.

Half tempted to leave the tent and go in search of Brogan, Rose sat with lips pursed and brow furrowed, secretly planning how best to torture him. She'd drag him in here by his nose if she must. With all her heart, she believed Brogan was the best man suited to marrying this poor young woman.

Just as she was ready to scoot away from the table, a group of men in the opposite corner began to play on their lutes and flutes. 'Twas a lively tune that propelled people to their feet to dance in the center of the tent.

She heard Mairghread and Leona giggle at something Arline had whispered. Too busy plotting her brother-by-law's death, Rose did not inquire as to what the women found so funny.

One of Ian's men, a young man named Thomas, approached the table and bowed to the women. "Mistress," he said to Rose before turning his attention to the other women. "M'lady, would ye care to dance with me?"

There was no mistaking which lady he was speaking to. The poor young man was staring intently at Mairghread with a wide, hopeful smile. Who could blame him? She was a stunning woman, with all that dark red hair and bright emerald green eyes. 'Twas the face of an angel, Rose believed.

Mairghread looked a bit surprised at his offer. But before she could accept or decline the young man, a deep voice broke through the silence.

"She has already promised this dance to me."

'Twas Brogan.

❧

BROGAN WAS MUCH LIKE THE OTHER MACKINTOSH MEN. ONCE HIS mind was made up on a thing, it usually took an act of divine intervention to get him to change it.

Refusing to even acknowledge Rose, Brogan came around the table, took Mairghread's hand in his, and escorted her out of the tent. Dumbfounded, Rose supposed, the poor woman did not even protest. She went willingly.

Rose, Arline, and Leona sat in stunned silence as they watched the two people leave.

Leona giggled softly. "It looks as though Brogan has made a decision."

"'Tis about time," Arline responded.

Rose remained silent, relieved and thankful he had finally come around.

"Are all Mackintosh men as stubborn as Brogan?" Arline asked.

Her question elicited another giggle from Leona. "I fear it be a trait all good men possess."

Rose sighed once again. "Unfortunately, Leona be right," she said as she watched Alec Bowie leave his group of men and head toward their table. "I have yet to meet a Mackintosh man who does no' suffer from the affliction."

The love shining in Alec Bowie's eyes when he looked at his wife was unmistakable. "Ladies," he said with a slight inclination of his head. "The hour grows late," he said to his wife. "Ye need yer rest."

Leona's eyes filled with warmth as she gazed at her husband. "Ye worry too much," she told him.

"I am only doing what our healer recommends," he reminded her. "In yer condition, ye are to rest as much as possible."

Rose recognized the looks exchanged between them. She and Ian had oft looked at one another the same way. It made her heart happy to know that Leona and Alec had finally realized how much they loved one another. Though it certainly had taken long enough for them to come to that realization.

If her assumption was correct, there would be little 'resting' going on this night betwixt the couple.

"I have four months before our babe arrives," Leona pointed out to her husband. "And I am enjoying the company of me friends."

Rose was quite proud of Leona. Per the advice she had given her months ago, no longer would she acquiesce easily. If Alec wanted something, he'd have to earn it.

"Aye, I see that," he said, raising a brow and offering Leona his most mischievous smile. "Mayhap it be I who needs the rest."

Aye, Rose was right. There would be little 'resting' this night. Alec had the look of a wolf about to devour a roe deer.

Leona rolled her eyes and smiled warmly at him. "And ye can no' rest without me?"

Alec placed a palm across his heart. "I could," he said with a bright grin. "But 'tis always more *restful* if ye are there."

A soft blush crept up Leona's neck. A heartbeat later, she was scooting away from the table and being led away by the aforementioned man-wolf.

"I think they love each other verra much," Arline said.

"Aye, they do."

Arline took a sip of wine and smiled. "Mayhap Brogan and Mairghread will be as happy as we someday?"

Rose, knowing Mairghread's secret as she did, could only pray her friend was right.

❦

THOUGH THE HOUR WAS LATE, THE SUN WAS JUST NOW MAKING ITS evening descent. At this time of year, the days were growing longer, and thankfully, warmer.

Brogan led Mairghread away from the noisy tent. Neither of them uttered a word as they crossed the yard, winding their way through tents and tables.

"I thought ye wished to dance," Mairghread said playfully as they made their way toward the outer wall.

Brogan grunted his reply. His mind was filled with a hundred questions and a hundred things he wanted to say. But in such close proximity to the beautiful woman, and with her hand still in his, he found he couldn't utter a word.

"I ken what Gertie and Tilda did," she told him. "Ye need no' be so kind, Brogan. Though I ken they mean well, ye should mayhap no' believe everythin' they say."

Brogan paused and turned to face her. God's bones, she was beautiful. And her voice? It felt like silk against his ears. He imagined he could never grow tired of listening to her speak. "What do ye mean?" he asked.

Mairghread rolled her eyes. "I ken what they be up to and I ken ye do as well. They wish fer ye and me to marry."

Blunt and to the point, Brogan thought. 'Twas an admirable trait. "Me sister-by-law is of the same mindset."

Mairghread nodded as she smiled up at him. "Aye, so I have been told."

"They tell me ye are to marry Claude Courtemanche," Brogan said as he found himself staring longingly at her hair. Strands had come loose from her braid, and were now dancing about her face in the evening breeze. It took all his willpower not to reach out and gently tuck it behind her ears. His fingers fair itched with desire to do just that. How long had it been since he had been so immediately and intensely attracted to a woman?

"Och!" she said with a smile. "For reasons I can no' begin to understand, they have an unnatural fear of the man. And we have yet to meet him."

Brogan studied her closely for a long moment. "Ye truly do no' ken the man, do ye?" 'Twas more a statement than a question.

"Nay," she replied. "But I can no' believe he be as bad as Gertie and Tilda claim."

Brogan shook his head. "I fear he be worse than even they ken."

Mairghread furrowed her brow. "Certainly ye do no' believe what those two have told ye?" she asked incredulously.

"Nay," he replied. "I do no' need two auld women to tell me about Courtemanche. I ken the man well."

His tone made her relief short-lived. She had only caught a fleeting glimpse of Courtemanche last year when he had visited their keep. Though she had seen him from a distance, and through wine-hazed eyes, she had seen enough to nearly make her ill. Much older than she, he was, and with greasy, slick, dark hair and scrawny legs that seemed to be strained and bowed with carrying the excess weight of his gut.

But Brogan? Brogan looked nothing at all like the Frenchman. Nay, Brogan was tall, and well-muscled. His stomach was flat, not bloated from gluttony like Courtemanche's. His ginger-colored hair hung well past his broad shoulders. With bright green eyes and full lips, he was a very handsome man. But 'twas his eyes and the deep timbre of his voice that made her unable to think clearly. He reminded her neither of Courtemanche or her deceased husband, which was either a blessing or a curse; she could not be certain at the moment.

'Twas impossible to think while looking at him. 'Twas also impossible to think without aid of drink.

"THE MAN IS EVEN WORSE THAN WHAT GERTIE AND TILDA BELIEVE.

I have met the man on more than one occasion. The stories ye hear, be true, lass."

She paled visibly.

"He did in fact kill his last wife, and aye, fer givin' him a daughter instead of a son. Though none in France are prepared to try to prove it before their king." In any other circumstance, he might not have been so direct. But Mairghread's life was literally on the line.

A moment later, she pulled her shoulders back and lifted her chin. "Nay," she said. "I can no' believe me uncle would ask me to marry anyone who was no' kind and generous."

"I fear I do no' ken yer uncle. But I *do* ken Courtemanche. He is as cruel as he is arrogant. The man is no' above anythin' to get what he wants. Whether that be power or money." The truth made Brogan ill. "And if ye do marry him, think ye he will stay in Scotland?" He paused, allowing time for that prospect to sink in. "Nay, lass, ye will no' . He will want to return to France where he has his king's ear and backing. There, he can do whatever he bloody well pleases. Ye would no' be safe."

With a slight shake of her head, she removed her hand from his and turned away. "Me uncle is a good man," she whispered. She was quiet for a long while, undoubtedly trying to make some sense of what Brogan was saying. "Nay," she said before turning back to him. "Me uncle would no' marry me off to such a man."

Brogan cocked his head to one side. "Mayhap yer uncle does no' ken the kind of man Courtemanche be," he suggested. Although he didn't believe it likely. According to Gertie and Tilda, Aymer Mactavish had met with Courtemanche at least twice in the past year. They had met in Edinburgh just a few months ago. It took only one encounter with the man for Brogan to understand Courtemanche was not someone you wanted as friend or foe. Either her uncle was a fool of the highest kind, or, he did not care. At the moment, he wasn't sure which thought upset him more.

Mairghread thought on that for a long moment. "If what ye say about Courtemanche be true, then I have to believe me uncle does no' ken him well. 'Tis the only thing that makes sense." It only made sense that he did not know Courtemanche well at all. That fact was disheartening. Lord, how she wanted a dram of whisky. But she had made a promise to Gertie that she would not drink this night. She was now regretting that promise. Her fingers were starting to tremble with need of it.

Brogan kept his thoughts on her uncle to himself. 'Twas apparent she held the man in high regard. "Has the betrothal been set then?" he asked.

Finally, she looked into his eyes. "Aye," she whispered. "Me uncle took the dowry with him."

Her emerald eyes fairly sparkled in the late evening light. "The bans? Have they been read?"

She shook her head slightly and swallowed hard. "Nay, they have no'."

Brogan smiled warmly at her. "Then there still be hope."

MAIRGHREAD LOOKED INTO HIS EYES, CERTAIN SHE WOULD FIND A hint of deception or treachery. Instead, she found something she had not felt nor seen in over three years: warmth and a sense of safety. She was too confused and taken aback to question the *why* of it.

She needed a drink or two. Her nerves were beginning to fray at the edges, the desire for wine or whisky growing stronger as the moments passed. Oh, why had she promised Gertie not to drink? Mayhap if she had a dram or two, his bright, warm eyes would not be having the effect on her person that they were now.

"Hope?" she dared ask aloud.

His smile was filled with warmth and aye, just a hint of something mischievous. "Aye," he replied. "Hope."

His voice was deep, smooth and rich, like good whisky, and had almost the same effect on her person. "Hope fer what?" she asked with a raised brow. The tremble in her fingers increased and her stomach felt strange, as if she'd just swallowed a sparrow and it was now trying to take flight.

"Hope to get ye out of yer betrothal with Courtemanche," he replied.

His words shook her out of her daze. "But me uncle is on his way to France as we speak. He has me dowry with him. I —"

Brogan cocked his head to one side. "So ye still wish to marry Courtemanche?"

She thought on the question for a moment. "Nay, I do no'," she replied. "But I can no' back out now. Nay, I must wait until my uncle returns and explain to him the error in his judgment."

"And what will ye do if yer uncle does no' believe ye? What if he still insists ye marry the Frenchman?"

There hadn't been much time in the last few moments to give much thought to the possibility. The fluttering sensation left in the blink of an eye. Now her stomach, her heart, were filled with nothing but dread. She loved her uncle, she truly did. But he did not always take her wishes, her concerns, into consideration. "I do no' ken." But she did. She knew, without a doubt, that she did not have the mental strength nor heart to go against him. He was the only living relative she had now, and for that reason alone, she felt she owed him and his ideas a good measure of respect.

A long length of silence stretched between them as Mairghread began to worry and her imagination ran amok. What if her uncle *did* insist she still marry Courtemanche? What if everything everyone told her about the man was true? What if she agreed to her uncle's wishes and married him? In her heart of hearts, she knew Brogan was telling her nothing but the cold hard truth. Courtemanche was a dangerous man and she would be forced to leave her home. Why had her uncle not given this more thought?

Dread turned to fear then, when she thought of her future and the future of her people. God, how she wanted a flagon of wine, or better yet, whisky. She could not think clearly without it.

Brogan's voice broke through the quiet and still night. 'Twas naught but a whisper, really, but she heard it with clarity. She felt the sincerity in his voice right down to her toes.

"Marry me."

❧

THERE WERE MANY REASONS WHY HE MADE THE PROPOSAL. THE main reason being he sincerely cared for this woman's safety and her future. Would he have cared as much were she not as beautiful or graceful? He wondered. The sense of duty, the need to protect those less fortunate souls, ran deep in his Mackintosh blood. Duty and honor had been instilled in him by his father since birth. Nay, 'twas only a blessing she *was* beautiful.

"Marry ye?" she asked breathlessly as she took a step away from him. Not for a moment had she thought he would agree with Gertie and Tilda's idea of a marriage between them. Up until this point, she thought his only purpose was to talk her out of a marriage to Courtemanche, not into one with him.

He could not be certain if it was fear or simply surprise that had garnered her reaction. "Aye, marry me, Mairghread."

"But why?" Her brow was furrowed, her eyes filled with more than just a hint of trepidation. "I do no' even ken ye."

He smiled thoughtfully. "I dare say ye ken me better than ye do the Frenchman, Courtemanche."

'Twas nothing short of the truth.

"Mairghread?" Brogan spoke her name softly, with much warmth. "I ken we do no' ken each other well. But I can promise ye, I am nothin' like Courtemanche."

She knew that already. So different in appearance were the two men, it took no great intellect to know they were as opposite as day and night. Whether 'twas instinct or lack of drink, she knew, deep down in her heart, that Courtemanche would end up hurting her, in more ways than a body could count. But Brogan? Nay, he would not hurt her, leastways not in the same manner as Courtemanche could or would.

"I would never hurt ye, Mairghread. I would rather have me arms cut off than bring harm to another living soul."

She snorted and shook her head. "But ye be a warrior. I have heard the stories told of the Mackintosh men and how ruthless ye all be."

Brogan chuckled softly. "That be on the field of battle, lass," he told her. "We are *only* ruthless on the field of battle."

The men of her clan were not warriors. They raised horses, fine, grand horses. People travelled far and wide to purchase the fine beasts. Mairghread was unaccustomed to living with warriors or men of that ilk. 'Twas why the attack on their keep had come so easily three years ago. They hadn't been outnumbered that night, nay, just the opposite. Whoever had attacked had been well-trained and just as ruthless. If only she could remember more of that night.

"Off the field of battle, we protect our own. We revere our women and love our children beyond measure. Ye can ask Rose if ye do no' believe me."

There was no need to ask Rose. Mairghread had witnessed the love between her and Ian. The way they looked at one another with such love and fondness. A woman could not look at a man the way Rose looked at Ian, or the way Leona looked at Alec, or Arline at Rowan, if they did not love their husbands. And a woman could not love a man in such a manner as that if those men were ruthless, cruel men.

"Will ye at least think on it?" Brogan asked.

Again, his voice felt as smooth as silk, warm, and with such tenderness and concern. It nearly brought tears to her eyes.

What was there to think on? She had very little choice at the moment. Marry a man who, if what she was told was true, was as vile as he was cruel, or marry the man standing behind her. A man who, she was quite certain, would be kind. A man who she believed would never hurt her. If she did not marry Brogan before her uncle returned, she would be married to Courtemanche. Her life, she was certain, would end at the altar.

The decision was simple enough to make in her mind. But in her heart?

"I fear goin' against me uncle," she admitted.

The night grew darker, the air cooler, but that was not why she shivered.

"I do no' ken the ways of yer clan, lass. But Gertie and Tilda tell me that ye are to inherit all that yer father left ye, aye?"

Was that why he had offered? To get his hands on what she might inherit? Angry, nay furious, she spun around to face him once again. But before she could scream her displeasure with him, he spoke.

"If ye are the rightful heir, then, does that no' make ye chief of yer clan?" he asked. "Can *ye* no' decide yer own future? Why must ye listen to yer uncle? Or does yer clan no' allow women to lead and rule?"

His questions stunned her anger away. Aye, 'twas true. She was, by default, the chief of her clan. However, she had never taken up the position. Instead, she had willingly handed those responsibilities off to her uncle. She had been too grief-stricken to lead. And if she were honest with herself, she'd been too drunk to care. But according to her father's will, she must be married and with child before she reached the age of five and twenty. But she could act as chief, at least for now.

"What are ye sayin'?" she asked, still uncertain as to where he was heading.

"If ye are the rightful heir, then *ye* are the rightful chief. If yer clan has no rules against a woman bein' chief, then ye should *be* chief. And make the decision regardin' who ye marry, without worryin' ye'd be goin' against yer uncle." Gently, he placed his hands on her shoulders. "Ye do no' have to marry *me,* Mairghread. Ye can marry whomever *ye* wish. I be just askin' that ye no' marry Courtemanche."

He made sense, which was something that did not happen much of late. He spoke nothing but the truth. She was the rightful heir, and the rightful chief. For too long, she had listened to her uncle, allowing him to lead, to make decisions concerning *her* future. She'd done so happily, for it allowed her to be alone with her misery, her grief, and her wine.

"Though I will tell ye true, I will be sorely disappointed if ye decide to marry another," he said with a warm, thoughtful smile.

There was not a doubt in her mind that he spoke truthfully and from his heart. It made her decision all the easier.

"I will marry ye, Brogan Mackintosh," she told him. But before she could add the conditions to her agreement, two distinct voices spoke up from the shadows behind Brogan.

"Thank the Lord!"

'Twas Gertie and Tilda.

Chapter Three

Much to Gertie and Tilda's relief and happiness, the banns were posted first thing the morning after Mairghread accepted Brogan's proposal.

For two weeks, they fluttered around the Mactavish keep, planning and preparing for the wedding, with as much determination, seriousness and fervor as a Scotsman preparing for war against the English.

To Mairghread's relief and delight, they left her alone almost the moment they returned from Mackintosh lands. She cared not for wedding plans. Did not give a whit about what she would wear, or what foods would be served at the wedding feast. Nay, she only cared about getting back to her room where she could drink copious amounts of wine and try to forget she had ever agreed to marry Brogan Mackintosh.

Guilt assaulted her.

She was marrying again.

At the funerals of her husband, James, and son, Connell, she had made them each a promise. To James, she declared never to marry again for he was the one true-love of her life. To Connell, her sweet babe who was only three weeks old when he was murdered, she had promised never to hold another bairn in her arms until she could be reunited with them in heaven.

What must they think of her now?

Did they think her a liar? A betrayer? A fool?

Och, how they must hate her! Hate her for breaking the solemn vows made that day.

More likely than not, however, they already hated her, if what her uncle said about her was true. If what he hinted at about the night her husband and babe were murdered was true.

Aye, if he spoke the truth — and she had few reasons to believe he did not — then, aye, the two people she loved most in the world, already hated her with unwavering vehemence.

Leaving Gertie and Tilda to their work, she hid in her room for days, as she attempted to drink away her fears, her worries, and her guilt.

She drank away all the pain, all the burning questions of what really happened that night. Or at least she made a gallant attempt.

Nay, no matter how much wine or whisky she consumed, the questions were always there, at the back of her mind. *Does Uncle speak the truth? If so, how could I have done such a thing?*

The night before her wedding, Gertie came to see her.

"Och!" she declared the moment she stepped into Mairghread's room. Clothes were strewn about the room. Trenchers of uneaten food were scattered here and there along with empty flagons and cups. The scent of stale food, sweat, vomit and urine filled the small space and assaulted Gertie's senses. She immediately went to the windows and pulled open the furs to let fresh air in.

Tears welled in the auld woman's blue eyes when she found Mairghread, huddled in a dark corner, holding a half-empty flagon.

"M'lady," she cried as she went to her and sat on the floor in front of her. Her bones creaked and protested the action, but she thought nothing of it. Her lady needed her. "M'lady," she said again as she placed a warm hand on Mairghread's cheek.

Mairghread pushed her hand away and mumbled drunkenly. "Go away."

Gertie forced a smile. "Nay, m'lady, I will no'. Ye need me."

"I do no' need any one," Mairghread protested weakly. Her words were slurred, her nose red from crying.

"'Tis an auld dance we do, aye?" Gertie said. "Ye get into yer cups, declare ye need no' a soul in this world, and I argue ye do, and in the end, I win. What say we try a new dance, aye, and just skip the protestin' and arguin'."

Mairghread pushed her hands away again, though without much force. She was too far into her cups to do much damage. "I do no' want to dance, ye foolish auld biddy!"

Years ago, those words would have hurt. But Gertie had been playing this game with her lady for far too long. She had to believe that somewhere, under the drunken stupor, a little bit of who Mairghread *used* to be, still existed. 'Twas the only hope she had to cling to. Without that little thread of hope, there was no purpose, no reason to go on.

"Wheest, now," Gertie said, her tone soothing and filled with tenderness. She took the flagon away and set it on the floor. "The morrow is a big day, fer ye. Ye need to be sober fer it."

Slowly, Mairghread opened her eyes to look at Gertie. "The morrow?" she asked.

"Aye, Brogan arrives on the morrow. And the day after, ye shall marry him," she replied.

Mairghread moaned, closed her eyes, and hung her head. "Nay, I can no' do it."

Gertie quirked a brow. With a heavy sigh, she pushed herself to her feet. "Aye, ye can, and ye will," she said. "I shall go and fetch Tilda now. We'll get ye to bed and on the morrow, ye shall feel much better."

Even in her state of profound inebriation, Mairghread knew 'twas a lie. She'd never feel better.

BROGAN SAT ATOP HIS MOUNT AND LOOKED OUT AT THE MACTAVISH lands and keep. 'Twas as beautiful a place as ever he'd seen, ranking it *almost* as beautiful as the keep he grew up in. He and his men stood atop a large hill and looked down at the sight before them. Overhead, large white clouds cast some of the land in shadow, whilst the sun shone brightly on others.

Made of dark gray stone, the structure stood three stories tall. Not as big as his father's keep, nor was it as imposing, but it was still quite remarkable. Brilliant green grass spread almost as far as the eye could see. 'Twas dotted with numerous cottages, too many to count. Little streams of smoke billowed from their chimneys. All manner of wild flowers grew amongst the tall grass that bent and swayed in the breeze. Not far away was a small loch that sparkled like glass against the sun.

The keep itself sat high and proud on jagged cliffs. Surrounding it were low built structures, one unmistakably the stables, along with other buildings of varying sizes.

But just beyond the keep, was the ocean. Large, foamy waves crashed against the craggy shores. The air smelled of grass, horses, and sea. For some reason, he found it calming and peaceful.

What concerned him however, was the outer wall that enclosed the keep. So low it was, he knew he could climb over it with no effort at all. His horse would have been able to jump it without protest or worry as to its safety. 'Twas no wonder the keep had been attacked with such ease three years ago. There were no defenses against it.

There were no guard towers either. Even the expensive and coveted Mactavish horses were allowed to roam free and unhindered.

It was all just as it had been the last time he was here, a year ago. Nothing had changed. Brogan was left to wonder why the keep hadn't been attacked more often.

"Where be the guards?" That particular question came from Comnall Mackintosh. A young man with dark hair and blue eyes, eager to experience a new adventure in his life. He'd eagerly volunteered to join Brogan and a handful of other men to come to the Mactavish keep.

"That be a verra good question," Brogan replied. His jaw ticked. *How could her uncle allow the keep to be so exposed after what happened to Mairghread's husband and son?* Could the man truly be that inept? It would be months before he'd be able to ask Aymer Mactavish in person. At the moment, he wished it would be years before the meeting.

"Let's pray they be well trained men," Henry Mackintosh added from Brogan's left. Henry was three years older than Brogan, and he very much resembled Ian, for his mother and Ian's had been sisters. He had the same blonde hair, blue eyes, and handsome features. Though he never lived the kind of debauched life Ian had before he'd met and fallen in love with Rose. Nay, Henry was much like himself; an honorable man.

Brogan was ashamed to admit the truth. "Ye can pray all ye want, Henry, but 'twill do ye no good. The McLaren men are better trained than the Mactavish men."

Henry shuddered at the thought. He'd only joined the Mackintosh and McLaren clan a few months ago. The comparison of McLaren to Mactavish was disheartening. Ian had been working with the McLaren men for over a year. While they had heart, and were filled with determination, those things together did not necessarily make for good warriors.

"Do ye think they be trainable?" Comnall asked with a raised brow.

Brogan shrugged his shoulders. "That might be where Henry could put his prayers to better use."

ONLY ONE PERSON STOPPED TO SPEAK TO BROGAN AND HIS MEN AS they made their way through the opening in the wall. Brogan estimated him to be around fifty, his light brown hair just beginning to turn gray at his temples. He recognized him from the night he'd proposed to Mairghread. "Ye be the Mackintosh?" the man asked as he stepped in front of Brogan's horse, forcing him to stop abruptly. Brogan didn't appreciate the man's actions nor his tone of voice.

The man's face held a most serious expression. His tone left no doubt Brogan was not much welcomed here.

"Aye, I am. Who be ye?" he asked as he dismounted. His men followed suit.

Thus far, no one approached to take their horses to the stables. He took a quick glance around the courtyard. There were other people milling about, pretending *not* to be interested in the new arrivals, but thus far, they were leaving them alone. 'Twas odd, but then, so were most of the Mactavishes he had met.

"I be Reginald Mactavish, the steward of this keep," he said with a cold tone. Grim lines formed around his mouth.

Though they had not been officially introduced, either the last time he was here or two weeks ago back at his brother's home, he behaved almost as if they were auld enemies. His cold attitude made little sense, for Brogan could think of nothing he had done to earn it. If his instinct was correct, his demeanor was born out of the fact that Brogan was here to marry Mairghread. That had to have brought forth a good deal of uncertainty for her people. They did not know him.

Realizing no one was coming to take their horses, Brogan asked, "Where be the stables? We would like to tend to our horses."

That simple statement seemed to change the man's attitude, albeit slightly. "This way," he said as he turned around and led them in a westerly direction, to the rear of the keep.

The stable was in better condition than some keeps Brogan had seen over the years. Two tall, wide doors stood open, to allow fresh air inside. Before they could enter, an aulder man, with shockingly white hair and a slight hunch in his back, hurried out to meet them. His eyes grew wide when he looked up at Brogan, then to his men.

"This be Seamus Mactavish, our stable master," Reginald said with a nod toward the auld man.

"This be *them*?" Seamus asked, with a good deal of surprise laced into his craggy voice. He kept his fearful eyes glued to Brogan and his men. As if he half expected to be gutted where he stood. Brogan thought his behavior most odd.

"Aye," Reginald said, as if he were ashamed to admit it. "This be *them*."

"What?" Seamus said in a raised voice.

Reginald rolled his eyes before raising his own. "I said, Aye! This be them!"

The auld man nodded his head violently. His white hair flapping in the breeze as he mumbled something about demons.

Henry and Comnall cast curious looks at one another before turning their attention back to the stable master. Henry wasn't sure, but he thought he'd heard the auld man mumble something about demons again before he found the wherewithal to speak once more.

"I be Seamus," he all but shouted. "I be the stable master."

Brogan and his men were a bit startled by the man's loud voice.

"Ye must be the Mackintosh men I heard about," he shouted once more.

Brogan bit the inside of his cheek to keep from laughing. *Heard?* He doubted the man could hear a horde of angry Highlanders if they were right behind him.

"Aye, I be Brogan," he said, raising his voice so that the auld man could hear him.

"What?" Seamus shouted as he turned his head and leaned forward offering him his right ear.

Brogan rolled his eyes. "I said I be Brogan Mackintosh!" he shouted his reply.

The auld man pulled back with a perturbed expression. "Ye need no' shout! I gave ye me good ear!"

Henry and Comnall chuckled.

Brogan found no humor in it.

"Do ye wish to bed down yer own?" Seamus asked with a most eager tone.

Brogan saw no point in trying to answer. He simply nodded his head.

Seamus looked up at Reginald. "That says a lot about a man's character," he said looking quite pleased. "If I have told ye once, I have told ye a hundred times. Any man who takes care of his own mount is a good man. And look at their horses," he said as he inclined his head in the direction of their mounts. "Nary a mark on any of them! Ye can see they do no' beat them and they do no' look worn. Which is *also* another sign of a man's character."

Brogan thought he might lose his hearing if he stayed here much longer, but the man's compliment did warm his heart.

Seamus looked to Brogan once again. He eyed him up and down for

45

a moment. "If ye do no' beat yer horse, can I also assume ye do no' beat yer women?"

From behind him, Brogan heard the unsheathing of eight swords, each of his men fully prepared to defend such an insult. Brogan stayed them with a raised arm.

"Of course we do no' beat our women," he said in a raised voice. "Neither do we beat our children." To which he quickly added, "Or dogs, or anything else fer that matter."

'Twas evident the auld man not only heard Brogan's words, but felt the conviction in his tone. Seamus gave him a smile that showed missing teeth. "Ye will do, lad," he said. "Ye will do."

❧

THE DAY SHE HAD BEEN DREADING FOR TWO WEEKS WAS FINALLY here, with the arrival of Brogan Mackintosh. Tilda and Gertie had come racing into Mairghread's bedchamber to let her know he had arrived along with eight of his men. Dread and worry settled into her heart.

Gertie, having known Mairghread longer than any other living soul, took one look at her lady's frown and shook her head. "Now, do no' be gettin' yerself down. Brogan be a good man. Far better than that Frenchman yer uncle was goin' to marry ye off to."

Tilda agreed, her smile bright and warm. "'Tis true, m'lady. He be below stairs now. He did no' growl at us when he saw us."

It had been a delightful change since last the two auld women had seen him. "He even smiled at us," Gertie added, with her own happy grin and nod.

Mairghread cared not at the moment what Brogan had or hadn't done. "Be gone with the both of ye," she said as she pulled a flagon of wine from the table next to her fireplace.

Gertie stepped forward and took the flagon away. "Now, lassie, I'll no' have ye goin' below stairs to meet yer betrothed in a state of drunkenness." She handed the flagon off to Tilda, who held it against her chest.

Mairghread rolled her eyes, went to the cupboard in the corner of her room. 'Twas where she stored her clothing, shoes, and such. "I am a woman full-grown, Gertie. I would thank ye kindly to quit treatin' me as if I was still a bairn." She pulled the door open and began to rummage inside.

Gertie was rocking back and forth on her heels, something she did without realization, whenever she was up to something.

Mairghread pulled her head out of the cupboard and glared at Gertie. "What did ye do with them?" she asked, referring of course, to the flagons of wine and whisky she kept stored inside next to her shoes.

Raising her chin, Gertie glowered back. "I hid them," she said proudly.

"Why must ye be so bothersome?" Mairghread asked as she slammed the door shut.

"Because I love ye, lass, as if ye were me very own."

Mairghread glared at her. "That used to work on me when I was a child, Gertie. 'Twill no' work now."

Gertie shrugged her shoulders indifferently. "I speak nothin' but the truth. 'Tis because I love ye that I do no' wish ye to make a fool of yerself this day or on the morrow."

"Bah!" Mairghread shouted, drawing her hands into tight fists. "I get tired of hearin' about yer love fer me. Ye only love makin' me life miserable."

Tilda, wanting very much to stop them from coming to blows, stepped in between them. "M'lady, Gertie truly does have only yer best interests in heart. She — like the rest of us — only wants to see ye happy."

Mairghread cast her a near murderous glare that sent her all but running to the door. "Ye need no' worry about me makin' a fool of meself," she told them. "Fer I do no' plan on marryin' Brogan."

THE TWO WOMEN WOULD NOT HAVE BEEN MORE SURPRISED HAD their lady sprouted a tail and wings. "But ye *must* marry him!" Gertie cried.

"The banns have been posted!" Tilda added.

"And the feast has been prepared!" Gertie said.

Mairghread rubbed her forehead with her fingers. "I do no' care about banns or feasts or anythin' else. I will no' marry Brogan, or anyone else fer that matter. Now be gone with the both of ye!"

For a quarter of an hour, the two auld women did everything in their power to change their lady's mind. In the end, Gertie threw her hands into the air and declared she had given up. She also added a few choice words about how disappointed she was. "Yer mum be rollin' in her grave, I swear it!" she declared right before she and Tilda left the room.

In the hallway, a teary-eyed Tilda asked, "What do we do? Do we tell Brogan?"

Gertie shook her head, frustrated with the sudden turn of events. "Nay, we tell Reginald."

Tilda looked much relieved. "Och! She loves *him* even more than she loves her uncle. Mayhap he can talk some sense into her."

Gertie could only pray that Tilda was right.

❧

"NAY," REGINALD DECLARED AS HE SAT AT HIS DESK IN HIS PRIVATE room. "I will do no such thing. If our lady does no' want to marry Brogan, 'tis her decision."

Gertie and Tilda presented a united and determined front as they stood opposite his desk. "But ye must," they said in unison.

Reginald replied with a grunt and a wave of his hand. "Ye two are the most meddlesome women I have ever kent. If ye had left her alone to begin with—"

Gertie was not about to listen to his argument again. As far as Reginald was concerned, everyone needed to leave their lady the bloody hell alone. And he included her uncle amongst those who need to stop interfering with her.

"If we *had* left her alone, think ye that when her uncle returned with the Frenchman, she would have had the good sense to argue agin it?" Gertie asked with a good deal of fury. "Nay, she would no' and ye verra well ken it, Reginald Mactavish."

Tilda agreed wholeheartedly. "What would ye do then? What would any of us do? Ye ken she'll no' go against her uncle."

"Aye, 'twas only through the grace of God she agreed to marry the Mackintosh," Gertie said. "Just think what her life would be like married to the Frenchman. Then compare it to what it could be like with the Mackintosh man."

Reginald appeared to be giving consideration to her words. He sat back in his chair, with his arms spread out against the edge of the desk. He thrummed his fingers onto the wood, his face growing darker and darker. "Ye do no' even ken this Mackintosh man," he said. "How do ye ken she will fare better with him than the Frenchman?"

Gertie gave an inward roll of her eyes before answering. "Ye've met the Frenchman, have ye no'?"

Reginald's curt nod was his only reply.

"And ye have met the Mackintosh, aye?"

He gave another curt, impatient nod.

"Then even ye can see who she must marry."

He let loose with a frustrated breath. "Why must she marry anyone?" he asked gruffly. "Why can ye no' all just leave her be?"

'Twas all Gertie could do to keep from wrapping her gnarled hands around his stubborn neck. "Ye ken *why!*" she said. "If she does no' marry and have a child by the next anniversary of her birth, her uncle will inherit everythin'. Think ye he a better choice to lead us than the Mackintosh?"

Even Reginald had to admit the truth of her statement. Deflated, his shoulders slumped and he hung his head low. "What I would no' give to ask Donald Mactavish what the bloody hell he was thinkin' when he created that insane will of his!" 'Twas not the first time he'd question such, since the man's death some four years ago.

Gertie humphed her agreement. Though in truth, she could not read nor write to save her soul from the devil, she would however, if she could have one wish in this world, 'twould be she was able to read and see with her own eyes just what Donald Mactavish actually wrote in his will. Thus far, no one save for Aymer, had ever seen it. Gertie trusted Aymer as much as she trusted the Frenchman: not at all.

"Heed me words, Reginald. If we do no' get her married to Brogan Mackintosh, her uncle will return with that bloody Frenchman and he will force her to marry him that verra day."

Reginald didn't like the idea of *that* particular union any more than Gertie or Tilda did, loathe as he was to admit it. He had been wracking his brain for months, trying to come up with a viable solution. The only thing he had come up with was taking his sweet lady and leaving. But Mairghread would never have agreed to such a plan.

He had met Brogan Mackintosh not more than an hour before. And as much as it irked him, he had to admit he did like the Mackintosh fellow far more than the Frenchman. He thought back to the conversation between Brogan and Seamus. Mayhap the auld man was right in his estimation of Brogan and his men.

With a heavy sigh of resignation, he looked at the two women. "Verra well," he said as he pushed himself to his feet. "But I warn ye now, ye will stay out of our lady's personal affairs from now on!"

Though they were smiling and nodding their heads in agreement, he knew better. They'd interfere whenever and wherever they thought 'twas needed.

&.

RELUCTANTLY, REGINALD GAVE A GENTLE RAP AT HIS LADY'S DOOR.

"Go away ye auld biddies!" came his lady's reply from within.

"'Tis me, Reginald, m'lady," he replied, hoping she would turn him away as well.

Instead, the door flung open. "Thank God it be ye and no' those two auld women!" she said, looking quite relieved.

He offered her a slight bow before she pulled him into her chamber and shut the door behind him. "Have ye any whisky on ye?" she asked.

He knew his lady's love of strong drink. Although it saddened him to no end to see her so addicted to it — and against Gertie's wishes — he had tucked a flask into his pouch before he had left his office. He had hoped that a sip or two might soften her heart and aid in changing her mind.

Mairghread was yanking it from his hand before he could even offer it to her. She guzzled down a good deal of it in short order. He watched as she closed her eyes and breathed in deeply. With the back of her hand, she wiped at her lips, looking grateful and relieved.

"Thank ye, Reginald. I ken I can always count on ye," she said before taking a chair in front of the hearth. "What brings ye here this day?" she asked before taking another drink. This time, she sipped more than guzzled.

When he was silent for too long, Mairghread gave a nod to the chair across from her, inviting him to sit. He sat and studied her closely for a long moment. Such a beautiful woman she had grown into. Although he knew he was working from his heart, he still felt very much the betrayer of trust. He'd know his lady since the day she was born. Loved her as much as if she were of his own blood.

"Ye look as if ye come to bear me bad news, Reginald," she said. "What be the matter?"

"Ye ken, m'lady, that I think of ye as the daughter I never had."

She smiled warmly at him. "Aye, I do. And ye have been much like a father to me, since me own died."

'Twas true. He had gladly stepped in to roll almost the moment after Donald's unexpected death. "And ye ken I would ne'er give ye poor advice."

Those beautiful green eyes flickered with understanding. Her smile faded almost instantly. "If ye have come to tell me I *must* marry Brogan Mackintosh—"

He stopped her with a raised hand. "Nay, m'lady. I would no' tell ye that ye must marry him."

Much received, she took another sip.

"But I would tell ye that ye *should*."

"What is the bloody difference?" she asked. Pursing her lips together, she waited impatiently for his response.

"The difference is that ye have a *choice*. Ye can marry him or no', 'tis up to ye."

Her eyes filled with skepticism. "And I be choosin' no' to marry him."

"As is yer right," he said agreeably. "However, I fear that if ye do no' marry him, yer uncle will force ye to marry Courtemanche."

There was a time, long ago, when Mairghread would have been able to hide her true feelings. But now? Either because of the heartache or too much strong drink, she no longer possessed that ability. Lord, how he hated playing on her fears. But if it would keep her safe, and out of the hands of Claude Courtemanche, he would do it.

"M'lady, this be no' a simple time. Were it up to me, ye'd no' ever marry again, unless it was yer wish to do so."

He allowed her one more long pull from his flask before he took it away. "M'lady, I love ye as if ye were me verra own daughter. Me wife and I were never blessed with children of our own, as ye well ken. But if ye were me daughter, I would tell ye to choose verra wisely. And I would tell ye that Courtemanche is *no'* the wise choice. Ye and I both ken ye do no' like goin' against yer uncle, and I fear that if ye do no' marry Brogan Mackintosh, ye will be forced into a union with the Frenchman."

When her shoulders slumped and her face fell, he knew he had gotten through to her. He felt no better for it. He leaned closer, resting his elbows on his knees. "M'lady, I have met Brogan Mackintosh and his men."

"And what do ye think of them?" she asked, her voice naught but a trembling whisper.

He rolled his tongue across his teeth. "As much as I hate to admit it, I believe they be men of good character." He chuckled at remembering the interaction between them and Seamus. "And Seamus thinks verra highly of them."

Mairghread gave a half-hearted laugh. "Let me guess, he measured their worth on the condition of their mounts?"

"Aye, m'lady, he did."

She stood and went to stare out of her window. It faced the ocean. Betimes, when a stormed brewed or the breeze was strong enough, 'twould bring the salty spray right into her room. There were times, many times, she wished she had a great ship upon which to sail away.

"I've never kent Seamus to be wrong before, m'lady," Reginald offered hopefully.

There was no way for her to argue otherwise.

Reginald went to stand next to her at the window. "What are ye truly fearful of?"

She'd have to be far more drunk in order to answer that question. Instead of being honest with herself or him, she said, "I will marry Brogan on the morrow."

Chapter Four

Though Rose had just discovered she was once again with child, she refused to miss this most momentous occasion. Much to Ian's vexation, they had arrived only a few short hours before the ceremony was set to begin. Of course, Ian was usually vexed when it came to his lovely wife. She had that effect on him, and Brogan doubted she would ever change. He also doubted Ian would want her to.

Deep down, Brogan was glad they were here. Were it not for Rose, he would never have met the lovely Mairghread. Although he had fought gallantly against the idea of marriage, once he set eyes upon her, his determination never to marry again began to wane. In less than twenty-four hours, he found himself agreeing to the idea.

As for the rest of his family, none would be able to attend. Undoubtedly, his father and step-mother were only just now receiving word of his upcoming marriage. They lived on the opposite side of the country. And the last he had heard from his father, the Camerons were threatening war again.

Frederick and Aggie were safely ensconced at the Carruthers holding that her blood father had gifted her. Just last week, she had given birth to a son. Her second, Frederick's first by blood. Their other children, Ailrig and little Ada, were thriving and healthy. Ailrig, under the good care of his parents, was, according to Frederick, growing like a weed and at only two and ten, was only a few inches shorter than he. *He has the making of a fine warrior,* Frederick had declared in his last letter. *And wee Ada? Och! I fear she will be the death of me when she is aulder, fer she is as beautiful as her mum.*

Also in attendance were Alec and Leona Bowie, who Rose had championed on their behalf for an invitation. Leona and Rose were cousins, the best of friends, and quite happy to both be with child at the same time. 'Twas all they could talk about that morn.

However, Brogan knew the main reason Rose had championed so vociferously was so that Alec could potentially broker a deal with the Mactavish clan to purchase his barley. Because he had only just arrived himself, he left Alec in the good care of Reginald. The steward would have a much better idea on how much, if any, barley they could purchase. Though in truth, it still amazed him that the Bowies were now living lives as farmers instead of murderous thieves. Oh, how the world sometimes worked and turned in peculiar ways.

Brogan now stood at the altar, with his brother at his side. His stomach was tied in knots, and no matter how many times he wiped his palms upon his trews, sweat continued to form in them. Rarely, if ever, was he *this* bloody nervous. He certainly had not been this nervous when he had married Anna. Nay, he'd been younger and more arrogant then, and madly in love. He'd gone to that wedding like a proud, puffing peacock. But today? Today was different for a whole host of reasons.

Older than Brogan by only a few years, the priest was short but thin and had light brown hair and hazel eyes. Brogan had only met him moments ago. Now, he stood on the dais, cleared his throat, and gave a quick nod to someone at the back of the kirk. Moments later, the doors opened wide, allowing the sunshine to spill through. A heartbeat later, Mairghread appeared on the arm of Reginald.

MAIRGHREAD WAS NOTHING SHORT OF A BREATHTAKING VISION OF

beauty. When Brogan first caught sight of her, standing at the entrance to the tiny kirk, she stole his breath away. He heard Ian chuckle when he gasped. Standing taller, he watched as she slowly made her way down the aisle.

The pale green, silk gown clung to every curve. Her auburn hair hung loosely over her shoulders and down her back. Tiny pale blue and yellow flowers dotted her hair, making her appear like a fey creature or a goddess.

But when she drew nearer, on the arm of Reginald, Brogan caught a glimpse of resignation in her emerald green eyes. Resignation and a profound sadness. Then she cast her eyes to the floor, as if she could not bear to look at him.

For a brief moment, he thought of stopping the ceremony and taking her to a private spot so that he might inquire as to why she looked so pensive and distraught. Was it, by chance, simply a woman being nervous on her wedding day? Something niggled at the back of his mind that it was far more serious than that.

She had refused to meet with him after his arrival yesterday. Refused even further to sup with him last night. Nay, that look... that sorrowful glint her in eye was more than just nerves.

When Reginald placed her trembling hand in his, her skin felt cold and clammy. She managed to smile up at him, but there was no warmth in it, no tender regard. 'Twas a forced, indifferent smile. He did not like it one bit.

Before he could stop the proceedings from going further, to take her away and inquire as to her true feelings on this union, the priest began the proceedings.

He only half-listened as the priest blessed the union, so focused he was on the woman who would soon be his wife. She, however, looked only at the priest.

"Please face one another," the priest directed.

Even after they turned to face one another, Mairghread chose to look down at her feet. Was she *refusing* to look at him, or was she afraid? The question burned on the tip of his tongue.

"Do ye, Brogan Mackintosh, promise to have this woman as yer wife, fer all the rest of yer days? To protect her, cherish her, and keep yerself only unto her?" the priest asked.

"Aye, I do so promise," Brogan answered. His tone was nothing but warm and sincere.

"Do ye, Mairghread Mactavish, promise to have this man as yer husband, fer all the rest of yer days? To honor and obey him, cherish him, and keep yerself only unto him?"

Brogan could barely hear her soft reply.

The priest was satisfied with her answer, but Brogan was not. Far from it. He wanted her to *look* at him when she said the words. He wanted to know, in his heart, that this marriage was what she wanted.

Tamping down the growing dread, he decided that after the cere- mony, he would take her aside and ask her, whilst they were alone. Aye, there was always a bit of uncertainty at times like these, when a marriage is made not out of some great fondness or love for one another.

Nay, they were no' a love match. There was no great romantic story they could pass on to their children. This marriage was born out of her need to *not* be forced to marry Claude Courtemanche. Then it hit him, like a large stone thrown at his head. He was simply a means to an end. Nothing more.

But Brogan *wanted* to be more than that. He *needed* more. He needed for her to at least *look* at him when she gave that promise. If not now, then at some time in the very near future. He did not know what he might do if she could never think of him as more than the man she had to marry to save herself from a fate worse than death.

&

ONE BRIEF GLIMPSE INTO BROGAN'S EYES, AND SHE WANTED TO scream and run from the kirk. Aye, Mairghread saw only kind adora- tion in his green eyes. An adoration she felt she neither deserved nor wanted.

Had Reginald not been holding onto her, she might very well have collapsed. Or ran. She wasn't sure which of those inclinations were strongest. Instead, she took in deep breaths and went to her doom. To the altar where she would have to lie to God, to herself, the people watching, and worst of all, to Brogan.

Mayhap she would have been better off marrying Courtemanche? She would have felt no compunction about lying to a man like him. Nay, 'twould have been a lie that would have rolled offer her tongue with ease.

But to lie to Brogan? Nay, such deceit was not fair, nor just no' right to such a nice man as he.

But lie she did. Right through her teeth. But not to his face. Nay, she could not look him in the eye and say the words the priest demanded. So she kept her gaze on Brogan's boots.

What made the day even more difficult was the fact that Gertie and Tilda had hidden her whisky. They had allowed her only one small glass of wine to help settle her nerves. Damn them! Damn them and Reginald for talking her into this.

Soon, her only thoughts were of hurrying through the ceremony so that she could go to the feast. Not to eat, but to consume vast quantities of wine. 'Twould be the only thing to give her enough strength to get through the rest of this day.

Then the moment came when the priest declared Brogan could now kiss his wife. 'Twas yet another moment among many that she dreaded.

With her eyes closed, she lifted her chin ever so slightly, and waited.

❧

IF SHE THOUGHT HE WOULD KISS HER WITHOUT FIRST LOOKING INTO her eyes, she'd be waiting a very long time. The uncomfortable silence stretched on and on until he could take no more.

"Please, look at me lass," Brogan whispered. 'Twas a plea, not born out of desperation, but of something she could not readily identify.

Reluctantly, she drew her eyes upward and looked into his. He smiled. Warmly, thoughtfully, before pressing his lips to hers.

'Twas a warm, sweet kiss filled with tenderness. A tenderness she had not felt in more than three years. It nearly sent her to her knees.

Guilt piled upon more guilt until her eyes were damp. She refused to shed the tears, lest he think they were tears of joy. Remorse, bitter and harsh, began to rise in the form of bile. Not because the kiss sickened her. Nay, 'twas because of what the kiss signified and how it made her heart skip a beat or two.

Thankfully, the crowd erupted into loud cheers right before Gertie, Tilda, and a handful of other women swarmed her. They were overjoyed for their lady, happy she had made such a fine choice in Brogan. None were reluctant to tell her just that.

Having nearly smothered her with hugs, kind words, and giggles, they ushered her out of the kirk and into the keep, leaving Brogan standing alone at the altar with his brother and his men.

SHE SEEMED IN MUCH BETTER SPIRITS ONCE THE FEAST BEGAN. Brogan and Mairghread sat side-by-side on the dais that took up one entire wall of the gathering room. Reginald sat to her left. To Brogan's right sat Ian and Rose and next to them, Leona and Alec Bowie.

The rest of the room was filled near to bursting with Mactavish clanspeople.

Brogan and Mairghread barely had a chance to say a word to one another, for they were constantly being interrupted by well-wishers.

Overall, the mood of the people assembled was cheerful as they joyously partook of fine food and drink. In the corner, a group of men -- two playing lutes, one a flute, and another a drum — played one lively tune after another while the guests ate.

Flowers were placed on every conceivable space. They even hung from the chandeliers and the massive beams overhead. Bouquets of them lined each table. Even the backs of the chairs on the dais had been draped with sweet-scented blooms.

Mairghread's spirits seemed to lift as she ate and drank the seemingly endlessly flowing sweet wine. He drank only cider, watching the feast and revelry with clear, sober eyes. After a time, his new bride actually smiled at him and even agreed to a dance or two. Not only with him, but she also agreed to dance with Henry and Comnall, as well as Ian. Brogan was intelligent enough not to allow jealousy rear its ugly head when she danced with his men. And he knew Ian was too much in love with his own wife to do anything untoward.

Much relieved to see that sorrowful look of regret removed from his bride, the worries he'd had at the altar earlier faded away. He could honestly say, that he was the happiest he had been in a very long while. 'Twas with great anticipation that he looked forward to leaving the grand hall and taking his bride above stairs. His fingers all but itched with the anticipation of divesting her of her green gown and finding the paradise that surely lay under it, and within her.

After their third dance, they returned to their table where Mairghread picked up a pitcher of wine and poured herself another cup. "Here," she said, pouring wine into an empty mug and offering it to Brogan. "More wine fer me new husband!"

He chuckled, accepted the mug, and placed it on the table without taking so much as a sip. Mairghread was too busy drinking her own to notice. Then Reginald drew her attention away. Brogan didn't mind, for her mood had changed for the better since the ceremony.

Ian leaned in to speak to him. "Does she no' ken?" he asked. There was no need for Brogan to ask what his brother was referring to.

"Nay," he said. "But there will be plenty of time on the morrow to tell her." Aye, on the morrow they would discuss why he never imbibed strong drink.

He chanced a glance at Rose. She bore an odd expression on her face as she watched Mairghread take to the dance floor once again. Concluding she was tired from the long journey as well as from being with child again, he decided against asking her how she fared.

࿔

AS THE HOURS WORE ON, MAIRGHREAD BECAME MORE INEBRIATED. So much so that even his men noticed her slurred words and glassy eyes, and they had been drinking just as much as she. Brogan supposed she was not used to consuming so much wine. She'd simply gotten carried away, along with everyone else around her.

When she swayed in her chair, holding on to the table for balance, he decided mayhap 'twas time to retire. Though 'twas still light out, the sun just beginning to set.

"Mairghread," he said through smiling lips. "I think it be time to retire."

She threw her head back and laughed heartily. "Och! The night still be young, like we!" she said as she spread her arms wide and looked up at the ceiling.

Her declaration made him chuckle. Aye, she was a free spirit, deep down. He was going to enjoy that about her. He'd not quash it, not tell her to behave like a proper lady. "Aye, we be young, lass."

Grabbing a mug, she gulped down more wine, and slammed the empty mug on the table. "More wine!" she declared with a giggle. "More wine fer all!" she called out as she jumped to her feet. Unfortunately, she'd drunk too much wine and had stood so quickly that it made her dizzy.

Brogan caught her around the waist before she could fall to the floor. She let out an 'oomph' when he swooped her up into his arms. Ian jumped to his feet as well, looking quite concerned for his new sister-by-law. "Is she well?" he asked.

Before Brogan could respond, Mairghread looked up into Brogan's eyes. "Och!" she said with a smile. "Me champion."

When she rested her head against his chest and sighed, Brogan could not resist smiling. A fast moment later, he felt her go limp in his arms.

He gave a roll of his eyes and a shake of his head. The passionate wedding night he had imagined was no longer possible. His bride had passed out in his arms.

❦

BROGAN HAD CARRIED HIS WIFE ABOVE STAIRS AND TOOK HER TO her — now their — bedchamber. Her head lolled from side to side, a sure sign she was indeed passed out. With great care, he laid her upon the bed. As he was deciding how to remove the pretty gown, Gertie and Tilda appeared at the door.

"Is all well, m'laird?" Gertie asked with a voice laced with concern.

Brogan looked up and gave her a warm smile. "'Tis naught to be concerned with," he said. "She will no' be the first bride to drink too much at her weddin' feast. She'll be right as rain on the morrow."

The two women were much relieved. "Would ye like us to help ye?" Tilda asked, with an inclination toward her lady.

He had divested more than one woman of her clothing in his lifetime. But usually, that was during a passionate moment. He accepted their help gratefully. In short order, they had Mairghread down to her chemise and under the covers.

The women had been unusually quiet during the process, which Brogan found exceedingly odd. Thinking they were worried only for their lady's well-being and safety, Brogan said, "Do no' fash yerselves. Yer lady's virtue and well-being is safe. I shall let her sleep this night."

He received no thanks of relief from either woman. They left without uttering so much as good eve.

Chapter Five

It had not been the wedding night Brogan had been envisioning for the last two weeks. Though his groin ached with desire for his new bride, he wanted her to be awake and fully alert when they finally consummated their marriage.

There were times when being an honorable man was painful. Especially when he slept next to her, breathing in her scent — a blend of flowers he could not name — and listening to her soft breaths. The night was made even more painful when twice he woke to find her round derriere pressed against his loins, and once with her head in the crook of his arm.

A man could only take so much temptation.

Dawn came and went and still she slept. He remembered well those days when he himself had drunk far too much. Mornings were usually a blend of regret and upset stomach. Believing she would wake feeling the same way he used to, he decided it best to leave her be. There would be time for loving later. Hopefully as soon as the evening meal was over.

Reluctantly, he left the bed, making sure to pull the fur around her shoulders. He pulled dark blue trews and an even darker blue tunic from his trunk. After he dressed, he added wood to the fire, took one longing look at his sleeping bride, and left the chamber.

Because he had anticipated a much different wedding night, he had given his men this day to do with as they please. There was no sense in destroying their hopes now, just because he was not now basking in the afterglow of a night of loving his new bride.

The gathering room had already been put back to rights from the feast of last eve, the floors swept and new rushes laid. Flowers still hung from the beams, but other than that, there was no sign a feast had even occurred.

As he stood in the middle of the large space, he heard voices fast approaching. When he turned, Ian, Rose, Alec and Leona were coming down the stairs.

"Och!" Rose declared as she bounced her babe on her hip. "We did no' think to see ye before we left!"

Ian gave him an affectionate slap to his back. "Ye look as though ye have no' slept," he said with a wink and a grin. "I wonder why that be?"

The last thing Brogan wanted to do was explain his wedding night to his brother.

He patted the top of John's head. "Ye take good care of yer mum and da, aye, laddie?" he said, affectively ignoring Ian's jest.

Tears welled in Rose's eyes. "Ye will no' believe this, but ye shall be missed," she told Brogan.

He quirked a brow, tempted he was to say something sarcastic. Instead, he said, "I will miss all of ye as well."

"Mayhap ye could come home fer Christmas Tide," Rose suggested with a good deal of hope.

They discussed the possibility for a time before Alec declared 'twas time to leave. "We wish ye and Mairghread all the best," he said warmly. "May ye and she be as happy as Leona and me."

Brogan thanked them and led them out of the gathering room, down the stairs, and into the courtyard where their horses and the men who had accompanied them were waiting.

Rose handed John off to Ian and turned back to look at Brogan. "I mean what I said, Brogan. Ye will be missed. But I be verra happy ye have married. Ye will be good fer her," she said before wrapping her arms around his waist in an affectionate embrace.

Before he could ask what she meant by *ye will be good fer her,* Ian said, "Come, Rose. There be the promise of rain in the air. I do no' wish to be caught up in it."

Rose swiped a tear from her cheek with the tips of her fingers and said, "Please, send word if ye need anythin', anythin' at all."

While Leona held the bairn, Ian helped his wife to mount first, then handed the babe up to her. He went back to Brogan, hugged him, and said, "Ye will do well here. Send word if ye need anythin', anythin' at all."

Brogan bit his cheek to keep from laughing, for Ian had just said what Rose had. "Thank ye, me brother. And should ye need me, do no' hesitate to ask."

Ian gave a quick nod before climbing up behind Rose. He wrapped his plaid around her and their babe and gave a quick kiss to the top of her head.

"We shall see ye come October," Alec said as he stepped forward with an extended arm. "Reginald has agreed to purchase barley from us."

That was news to Brogan, but then, he had been too busy with all the activities of yesterday to even begin thinking about barley, or agreements. "'Tis good to ken," Brogan said as he wrapped his hand around Alec's forearm. "Ye take care of Leona and send word when she has the babe, aye?"

Leona gave Brogan a warm embrace. "We wish ye all the best," she said before turning away.

Brogan watched as Leona and Alec mounted. He stood in the courtyard for a long while as he watched his family and friends leave through the non-existent wall, where a gate should have stood.

There would be no time to spend missing them for there was far too much work to be done here.

HE'D BEEN TOO LATE FOR THE MORNING MEAL. WITH A GROWLING

stomach he went in search of the kitchen in hopes of begging for something to break his fast.

As in most keeps, the kitchens were set apart from the rest of the keep. These were only slightly different in that a long covered walkway connected the kitchen to the main building. He thought back to Mrs. McCurdy, the woman who had served as Mackintosh cook when he was growing up. If you missed a meal for any reason other than death or severed limb, you would have to wait to fill your belly until the next meal was served. He hoped the Mactavish cook was not thusly inclined or nearly as frightening.

He stepped into the large space and nearly leapt with joy at the smells coming from within. 'Twas alive with busy servants undoubtedly preparing the nooning meal. A young lass of mayhap four and ten was the first to notice him. Her eyes grew wide as she bobbed a curtsey. "M'laird," she said with a quavering voice. One by one the rest of the people stopped what they were doing to look at him.

"Good morn," he said with a slight bow.

In the center of the room, at a long table, stood mayhap the skinniest, tallest man Brogan had ever seen. Mayhap no more than forty years of age, his light brown hair was cut close to his scalp. With a clean-shaven face, a dimple in his chin, and a large, hawkish nose that sat between dark brown eyes, he was, to say the least, a most peculiar looking man. "M'laird," he said as he put down the large knife he was using to slice meat.

"Good morn," Brogan said once again. "I ken I be late for the mornin' meal," he began as he continued to look about the room for someone who might possibly be the keep's cook. "But I thought, mayhap, I could get a bit of bread and cheese to break me fast."

"Of course," the skinny man said. "I shall send Sarah out with a tray, if ye'd like to eat in the gatherin' room. Or up to yer chambers mayhap?"

Brogan offered him a sincere smile. "If it be no' too much trouble," he said. "Unless the cook here is like the one where I grew up." He chuckled at memories of Mrs. McCurdy. "If ye were late fer any meal, she would chase ye out of her kitchens with a broom. 'Tis how I learned to run fast and never be late to sup."

The hard lines of the man's face softened. "Sounds like me auld grandminny," he said as he wiped his hands on a drying cloth hanging from his belt.

Brogan stepped forward. "I be Brogan Mackintosh," he said.

"We ken who ye be," the man said. "Everyone here kens who ye be," he said.

"Aye," Brogan said. "I hope to learn everyone's names in time. Mayhap, ye could introduce me to the cook and rest of the staff."

The man tried valiantly not to laugh at Brogan. But the rest of the staff could not resist a chuckle or giggle. He turned around and glared at each of them. "Ye're lookin' at him," he said. "I be Lowrens Mactavish, the cook."

'Twas not as if Brogan had never met a male cook before. Still, he was a bit surprised by the presence of one here. "'Tis me pleasure to meet ye, Lowrens," Brogan said. "And I shall do me best never to be late fer a meal again."

Lowrens gave a slight nod and went back to his food preparations. "The gatherin' room or yer chamber, m'laird?"

"The gatherin' room will be fine," Brogan said. "And I be no' yer laird. Brogan be fine."

The entire room came to an abrupt halt. "We could no' do that, m'laird," Lowrens said with wide eyes.

"I am neither laird nor chief," Brogan replied.

Lowrens gave a quick glance over his shoulder, as if to warn his people it mattered not what Brogan said. They would all show him the respect he deserved simply by being Mairghread's husband. Turning back to Brogan, he said, "We shall have a tray brought to ye anon."

Brogan thanked him and left the kitchens to wait in the empty gathering room.

WITH HIS STOMACH FULL, HE WENT IN SEARCH OF HIS MEN. According to the scullery maids, they had been given quarters in the armory.

The armory sat on the northeastern side of the keep. 'Twas a short, squat building made of wood, which looked to have been erected within the last year or two. The edge of the thatched roof met him near the center of his chest. He wondered how on earth a man was able to stand upright in it, for it looked to have been built for children and not grown men.

It took several moments before he found the entrance, in the back of the building. He had to take a few steps down in order to reach the low door. Whoever had designed the building apparently didn't give one thought to an easy exit.

One quick look around the empty space told him if he were forced to live in such a cramped space, he'd go mad. It was dark and smelled of dampness. Sections had been carved into the walls and covered with thin mattresses. Eight spaces in all and not a one appeared big enough for his men.

What stunned him most, however, was the fact there was not a weapon to be found anywhere within. Not so much as a dirk or an arrow or a bow.

If he hadn't seen their rolled up pallets and other belongings stacked neatly against the far wall, he would have believed someone was playing a prank. Sadly, they weren't. Undoubtedly, he would hear his men's complaints at the noonin' meal. That was, if they didn't seek him out sooner.

First there was no outer wall to offer any protection from invading forces. Now, he was discovering the so-called armory was not fit enough to house more than a dozen small men. And it was completely void of any weapons.

Even the Macintosh and McLaren clan his brother now ruled had better supplies and sleeping quarters than this place.

Determined to find out why the Mactavishes felt no need for even the simplest forms of protection, he went in search of Reginald.

REGINALD MACTAVISH'S OFFICE WAS NOTHING MORE THAN AN alcove located in the rear of the keep at the end of a long, dark corridor. The space was so small, it didn't warrant a door and was barely wide enough to hold the small table and chair within. Brogan imagined the poor man had to either crawl under or over the table in order to get to his seat.

Reginald stood when he saw Brogan. "Good morn to ye, laird," he said with a slight inclination of his head. There was no warmth or regard in either his tone or his eyes.

"Good morn to ye," Brogan returned the greeting.

Brogan glanced around the tiny confines of the alcove. "Be this truly your office?"

"Aye, 'tis in fact me office," Reginald said dryly.

Though 'twas entirely possible the man had chosen this space for the solitude it offered, he had to wonder how the man could do his job effectively. "I mean no offense, but be there a reason why ye are so far removed from the rest of the keep?" Brogan asked.

"I go where I am told," he replied.

There was something off about his tone, as if there was more he wished to say but dared not.

"I wonder if ye would take a walk with me," Brogan said. "There be much I wish to learn about the day-to-day runnin' of the keep."

Reginald pushed his shoulders back, finding insult where none was meant. "I have been runnin' this keep fer nigh on ten years now. I suppose ye will be wantin' to make many changes now, and I be one of them, aye?"

Crossing his arms over his chest, Brogan leaned in. "I never said, nor did I insinuate such. I merely want to do what I can to help me wife. She *is* chief of this clan and 'tis me duty to help her wherever I can."

Thunderstruck, Reginald was momentarily at a loss for words. With raised brows and yawning mouth, he stammered for a moment before he was finally able to speak. "Our lady? Chief of the clan?"

"If what I am told is true, then aye, she is the rightful chief of this clan. Unless me information is incorrect." Until this moment, there hadn't been a doubt in his mind that Mairghread was the rightful heir and chief. But mayhap Reginald knew something he didn't.

Reginald was quiet for a long moment before his shoulders

slumped ever so slightly. "Aye, ye be right, laird. She be the rightful heir and chief."

"But?" Brogan asked.

"She has been grievin' for more than three years, ye ken. Her uncle stepped in—" he paused, no doubt trying to choose his words carefully. "Aymer Mactavish stepped in after that awful night and he has been actin' as chief ever since."

Brogan studied him closely for a moment. "Do ye no' think she has been grievin' long enough? Mayhap it be time she takes over?"

"Ye have no' yet met her uncle, have ye, laird?" Reginald asked with a good deal of caution.

He had to admit that he hadn't. "I am no' a man to make assumptions," Brogan said. "But need I worry that Aymer will no' take the change well?"

"I will no' speak ill of our lady or her uncle."

Brogan had to admire the man's loyalty. However, he was smart enough to know that sometimes, loyalty could be misplaced. "I am no' askin' ye to," he replied. "Yer loyalty to yer lady is admirable. I only wish to help her and the clan."

"And if the Mactavish disagrees?" he asked with a raised brow.

"If ye be referring to Mairghread as the Mactavish, then her opinion is of great importance. But if ye be referrin' to Aymer as the Mactavish, I would recommend ye stop givin' him a title he has no right to." Though he had yet to meet Aymer Mactavish, what he did know of the man, he didn't like. "I am no' as interested in Aymer's opinions as much as I am yers."

Puzzled, Reginald cocked his head to one side. "Me opinions?" he asked.

Brogan offered him a warm smile. "Any chief worth his salt will tell ye that a good steward is just as important as a good chief. I ken it be yer good work that keeps the clan runnin'."

Pleased with Brogan's compliment, Reginald sat a bit taller and smiled. "I do me best, laird."

"Please, do no' call me *laird*. I be yer lady's husband. I have no title."

"So ye'll be takin' the Mactavish name?" Reginald asked with a devious smile.

"Nay," Brogan returned his smile. "Just as I would no' insist she take mine."

'Twas apparent he liked his answer as much as his previous compliment. His lips curved into a warm smile. "Then let us walk together. Step back please."

Brogan took a few steps away. Reginald shoved one corner of the table forward, stepped around it, before shoving it back into place. Brogan chuckled.

"I wondered how ye got behind it," he admitted.

Reginald gave him a shrug of indifference as he led him down the corridor.

"Would ye no' do better to have an office closer to the center of the keep?" Brogan asked as he gave a glance back toward the alcove.

"At one time, it was," Reginald told him. "But the Mactavish—" he stopped and corrected himself. "Aymer took me office as his own and moved me to the alcove."

"And there was no other, better place to move ye?" Brogan asked.

Reginald remained quiet. Undoubtedly, he did not trust Brogan enough to speak his mind freely. An intelligent man is oft the most quiet, or so Brogan believed.

"If we were able to procure ye a bigger office, one in closer proximity to the rest of the keep, would ye be offended?" Brogan asked as he clasped his hands behind his back.

"I am but a lowly servant, m'laird. I go where I am told."

Brogan was growing frustrated with how the man spoke in circles. "Reginald," he began, choosing his words carefully. "I will never ask ye to speak ill of anyone. But when I ask fer yer opinion, I expect ye to give me an honest one. I will accept nothing short of complete honesty from ye."

Reginald said nothing as they made their way down the corridor.

"And ye are far from a lowly servant. Ye be the steward here. Ye ken this keep better than anyone, I would imagine."

"I take me duties quite seriously, m'laird. Still, I be yer servant, nothin' more."

Brogan came to an abrupt halt and pinned the man in place with a hard glare. "If ye call me laird one more time, I shall reduce ye to cleanin' chamberpots for the next year."

Reginald raised one bushy brow, but continued to remain mute on the matter.

"I imagine, that if we work together, and are honest with one another, we could potentially be strong allies. Mayhap even friends."

His other brow went up. "Friends?"

"Me father is chief of Clan Mackintosh. He considers his steward one of his closest friends. Loves him like a brother. So aye, Reginald, me hope is that we can someday be friends."

They stepped out of the keep and into the large, open courtyard. A breeze blew in from the west. It leant a crispness, a cleanliness to the air.

Their boots scraped lightly over the cobblestones whilst Reginald explained the workings of the keep. A group of women were huddled together, talking as they watched children playing nearby. Brogan heard the faint echo of a smithy banging a hammer against his anvil floating in from origins unknown.

"We have three and forty people who live within the keep. Save for our lady and her uncle, and now ye, they all be servants. The cook, the scullery maids, and the like."

To Brogan's way of thinking, it seemed like an awfully lot of people to take care of Mairghread and her uncle. But he kept his opinion on the matter to himself.

"Ye've met our stable master, Seamus. He lives in the tack room there, but sups within the keep. He has two younger lads who help him do those things he can no longer do."

Brogan listened intently as Reginald continued to give him the rundown of daily life here. "We have nearly three hundred clanspeople. We have farmers, weavers, and even a few whisky makers. All in all, we do well."

Reginald led him to the rear of the keep. At seeing the armory, Brogan asked, "Pray tell, why the armory seems built for children? And why be there no weapons?"

"Ye would have to ask the — Aymer," was Reginald's reply.

"He be no' here," Brogan reminded him. "Ye have me word that whatever ye tell me will remain in strictest confidence."

Even with Brogan's oath to keep whatever was said betwixt them, betwixt them, Reginald was still reluctant to answer. "Accordin' to Aymer, 'twas built as a disguise of sorts. Any potential raiders would no' look twice at such a building."

Though that might seem a good idea in theory, it lacked any practicality. "And the lack of weapons?"

"They were moved to a safer location, by Aymer's order."

Safer location? A lot of good weapons would do if no one could get to them.

❦

"WHAT OTHER SURPRISES DO YE HAVE IN STORE FER ME?" BROGAN asked as they passed by the granary.

Reginald shrugged a shoulder. "Many, mayhap," he said.

As they passed by a corral filled with horses, Brogan asked, "Ye do breed the finest horseflesh, aye?"

"That we do," Reginald said proudly as they stopped to admire the animals. One came forward to nuzzle against Reginald's chest. He patted the horse and spoke to it affectionately.

"Tell me," Brogan said as he leaned against the top rail. "Why is there no outer wall here?"

Reginald's fond smile toward the horse faded almost instantly.

"Let me take a guess and say 'twas Aymer's good plan?" He felt he already knew the answer.

Reginald let loose a heavy breath of frustration. "Aye, 'twas Aymer's good plan."

Brogan shook his head, afraid to learn the why of it. "What, pray tell, was the reason fer removin' the wall? Especially after what happened the night Mairghread's husband and child were killed."

Reginald pushed away from the corral and began walking toward where the wall had once stood. "He removed it *before* the raid. Six months before."

"Good, lord!" Brogan exclaimed. "And he did no' see fit to replace it after?"

"Let me explain it to ye," Reginald said as he clasped his hands behind his back. "A month before Mairghread married James, her father died. During that time, some stones came loose in a section of the wall. Aye, 'twas an old wall. Decades old. But instead of repairin' it, as we have done in years past, he ordered the entire wall be taken down and rebuilt."

Brogan looked around but could find no signs that any building was taking place. "That makes no' a bit of sense," he replied.

From Reginald's grim expression, he agreed.

"And has he said when he plans to rebuild that wall?" Brogan asked.

"Nay, he has no'. And we be under strict orders no' to ask."

Brogan mulled the situation over in his mind. He was not the chief of this clan. His wife was. Ultimately, the decision to rebuild the wall should be hers. But after all the wine she had drunk the night before, he seriously doubted she'd be in any condition today to make such a decision. "As husband to yer chief," he began, choosing his words carefully. "I believe she would agree with me that a wall is verra important to the safety of this clan."

"Ye can say that, can ye? After only a day of bein' married?" Reginald asked, dubiously.

"Aye, I can."

They reached what was left of the outer wall and climbed over it. They were several yards away from the cliff, overlooking the ocean. Gentle waves rolled against the rocky shoreline, splashing over boulders and jagged rocks that were as old as time.

"What happened to the stones from the original wall?" Brogan asked.

"Yer lookin' at it," Reginald replied.

Confused, Brogan quirked one brow. He studied Reginald for a long moment. The man was staring longingly at the sea. Then it hit Brogan profoundly. "Ye jest," he replied, his voice low and breathy.

"Nay, I do no' jest."

Brogan turned and walked to the edge of the cliff. Once glance over the edge was all it took to prove his assumption.

On the jagged rocks below, he could see countless stones. Stones that had once made up the wall that encompassed the holding. Many had broken into smaller pieces. Others, over time, had been washed into the sea.

"The bloody bastard had them all tossed into the sea."

BROGAN HAD TO TAMP DOWN HIS BURNING RAGE. HOW COULD ANY man leave his clan so exposed? How could a man remove the one thing that kept invaders at bay? He decided then and there, that when it came to the safety of this clan, he was not going to wait to discuss the matter with his wife or her uncle.

"Reginald, my man, we are goin' to rebuild that wall," he said as he stomped away from the edge.

Reginald was in hot pursuit. "Without Aymer's permission or order?"

Brogan stopped abruptly. "Aymer is no' the chief of this clan. Me wife is. And it will be to the benefit of all, if everyone starts believin' it. I do no' give a rat's arse what Aymer wants. We will begin this verra day to make this clan and this keep safe again."

Reginald was beyond pleased. "I have a feelin' most will be agreeable to Mairghread takin' her rightful place," he said as he stepped in beside Brogan.

"Most?" Brogan inquired gruffly.

"Some are loyal to Aymer, though I do no' ken rightly why."

"Fear, mayhap?" Brogan offered.

Reginald thought on it for a long moment. "Aye, many are fearful of Aymer," he admitted.

Brogan came to a stop, placed his hands on his hips and faced Reginald. "Ye have me permission to always speak yer mind, whether it be on Aymer, me wife, or the runnin' of this keep."

He wasn't sure what to make of Reginald's blank expression. It would, he imagined, take time before the man would be able to trust him. 'Twas best, he reckoned, to lead first by example.

"Come, Reginald," Brogan said, resuming his quick pace.

"Where?"

"To make plans fer our new wall and guard towers."

Reginald smiled, showing almost straight white teeth. "I should like ye to meet someone first," he told him. "Then we shall make our plans."

❦

MOMENTS LATER, THEY WERE APPROACHING THE BLACKSMITH'S barn. 'Twas a tall, wide structure, with two large doors pulled open to let fresh air in and the heat out. The previous clanging had stopped and now an eerie silence fell over the place.

"Iarainn!" Reginald called out from the entrance.

Moments later, a very pretty woman, with dark brown hair plated around her scalp, appeared from the shadows. She wore a heavy apron over tunic and trews, a combination Brogan found odd, for a woman.

With an amused grin, Reginald introduced them to one another. "Iarainn, this be our new laird, Brogan Mackintosh," he said. "Brogan, I would like ye to meet our smithy, Iarainn Mactavish."

Astounded, 'twas all Brogan could do to keep his chin from hitting the ground. Very few things surprised him anymore, but this? "'Tis a pleasure to meet ye," he finally managed to say.

"We met last eve," Iarainn told him. "At yer weddin' feast."

Brogan searched his mind for the memory.

"Of course, I was no' wearin' me apron or trews," she said with a smile.

Of course she wouldn't have been, he mused. "I fear I met many people last eve," he told her. "But 'tis a pleasure to meet ye again." He offered her a slight bow at his waist.

An awkward silence filled the air. Reginald had his hands clasped behind his back as he rocked back and forth on his heels. His amused grin was beginning to irritate Brogan.

"How long have ye been smithy here?" Brogan asked.

"Three years now," Iarainn replied. "Learned at me da's knee, I did. I was his only child. Much to me mum's vexation, he taught me all he knew."

Brogan detected more than just a trace of pride in her voice. He could see it twinkling in her dark blue eyes. "Let me guess," he said, returning her smile. "Yer mum would have preferred ye took up sewin' or weavin'?"

Iarainn quirked one delicate brow. "Nay, she wanted me to be a fine horsewoman, like she was. Trained some of the best war horses in all the land, she did."

Would the surprises within this clan never cease? A female smith? A woman who trained war horses?

Reginald decided then to laugh at Brogan's befuddlement. "We be no' like most clans," he said.

That was quite apparent. Brogan looked down at the project she was currently working on. It appeared to be the beginning of a large cooking pot. "Besides cookin' pots, do ye also make the weapons here?"

Her reply was nothing but a shrug of indifference. Reginald leaned in closer to her. "He can be trusted, Iarainn."

With a dubious brow, she studied Brogan for a long while. "Be ye certain?" she asked Reginald, though she didn't take her eyes off Brogan.

"He has just ordered the rebuildin' of the wall," Reginald told her.

Brogan took note of his relieved tone and glint in the man's eyes.

"Why be ye wantin' to do that?" she asked Brogan directly.

He felt quite certain this was a test of his character. "A keep without a wall or guard towers? Ye might as well just invite yer enemies in. 'Tis folly to believe none will attack when they've already done so in the past."

Apparently pleased with his answer, she raised her voice. "I make mighty fine cookin' pots, m'laird. As well as eatin' knives and such. Mayhap ye would like to give yer new bride a gift? I have a few special pieces in back."

Though her behavior was odd, his curiosity was too piqued now to turn away. Silently, he followed her and Reginald to the back of the building. She took a quick left turn and led them into a very small room. The floor was covered with rushes, but otherwise, it appeared empty.

Iarainn waited until both men were inside before closing the door behind them. Going to the far wall, she crouched low, and began to pull on one of the wide wooden boards that made up the wall.

"Right before the attack, Aymer had ordered the armaments removed from the armory," Reginald explained. "He had a few of those men loyal to him, take them to a *place of safekeepin'*."

Iarainn grunted her disproval. "An eejit if ever there be one," she said with a good deal of disgust. "Whoever heard of keepin' weapons in a 'safe place' away from one's keep?"

Brogan stood in profound confusion and amazement. He'd been wondering the very same thing.

With the board now removed, Iarainn set it against the wall and stood. Purposefully, she blocked Brogan's view of what lay behind the space. "I be no' one to go against my laird's orders. But fer the good of our people, I felt compelled to do just that."

Brogan crossed his arms over his chest. "If ye be referrin' to Aymer, he is no' yer laird. Mairghread is."

Relief washed over her, causing her shoulders to relax. "I be right glad to hear another voice what I have believed fer three long years now."

"The safety of this clan, as well as me wife, is my main concern, Iarainn," Brogan told her.

"And when Aymer returns?" she asked with a raised brow.

"With Mairghread as chief, it matters no' what Aymer wants or believes," he told her.

She cast another glance at Reginald before turning back to Brogan. "Be she willin' now, to take on the role?"

Reginald replied before Brogan had a chance. "She will be willin', now that she has a husband who will support her."

"If word gets out to Aymer, 'twould mean me neck in a hangman's noose," she told him.

"If word gets out about what?" Brogan asked, drawing her attention back to himself.

Warily, she looked to Reginald once more. He gave a quick nod of his head and a moment later, she stepped aside. "Of that."

BROGAN EYED EACH OF THEM SUSPICIOUSLY FOR A SHORT MOMENT before curiosity got the best of him. Crouching low, and with his hand cautiously on the hilt of his dirk, he peered inside. It took a moment for his eyes to adjust. But when they did?

"Jesu!" he exclaimed.

Dozens upon dozens of finely crafted swords lay within. Carefully placed on soft blankets, they took up most of the space. On the wall hung finely made bows. Next to them hung quivers filled with arrows.

"Were these the weapons taken away fer safekeeping?" he asked.

"Nay," Iarainn replied. "Only Aymer and his men ken what happened to those."

Brogan studied the weapons for a long moment before giving a shake of his head and pulling himself back up.

"I have to be verra careful in the makin' of these," Iarainn explained. "Fer if Aymer found out, I have no doubt he would take them. Then order me hanged."

"Hanged?" Brogan asked incredulously. "Certainly ye jest?"

Iarainn and Reginald exchanged glances with one another. "After the removal of the wall and weapons, we put nothin' past the man," Iarainn said. While Reginald might not be willing to speak ill of his lady or her uncle, Iarainn was not thusly inclined.

"We must be careful, m'laird, fer Aymer has spies everywhere," she told him as she replaced the wooden plank.

"I can assure ye, that yer secret is safe with me," Brogan told her.

Chapter Six

Brogan sent word to Mairghread that he hoped she was feeling better and he looked forward to seeing her at the evening meal. Then he and Reginald went in search of his men. Together, they would scout out the best place from which to quarry the stone for a new wall.

Although he would have preferred something much closer to the actual keep, in the end, they had to settle for a spot a mile away. "With enough wagons and strong backs, we could begin buildin' on the morrow," Reginald declared with far more hope than Brogan in truth felt.

This was not the first wall Brogan had ever built. He knew it would take months of backbreaking work, mayhap more than a year. But it was necessary. He could not think of a keep in all of Scotia that did not have at the minimum a wall made of wood.

In addition to finding a place to quarry, plans were also set in motion to guard the keep. "We need to erect towers," Brogan told Reginald and the men. "We can harvest the necessary lumber from the forest." He nodded toward a deep, dense forest that lay not far from the keep.

"What about patrolling the borders?" Henry asked.

Brogan looked to Reginald for advice.

"Aye, we do patrol the borders," he replied. "But only at night."

The more Brogan learned, the angrier he became. No wall, no towers, and men who only patrolled at night. 'Twas appalling.

To Henry and Comnall he said, "I will leave the two of ye in charge of patrolling the borders. I am certain Reginald can help ye to choose good men to help. When we get back to the keep, we will send word that we want all able-bodied men to assemble in the yard first thing tomorrow morning."

"How often do yer men train?" Henry asked Reginald.

Ashamedly, he replied, "We do no'."

Brogan made a decision, then and there, not to ask any further questions as it pertained to the safety of the keep. The answers made his head throb. "I believe, fer now, it be more important to begin first with the wall. Once we have that started, we will begin trainin' the Mactavish men."

BROGAN AND HIS MEN BATHED IN THE LOCH BEFORE RETURNING TO the keep. Brogan needed the cold water to help cool his burning temper, more than he needed to be clean.

"Have ye ever kent a man to order the tearin' down of a wall?" Comnall asked to no one in particular.

"Or one whose borders be patrolled at only night?" Henry offered.

Their questions were answered with resounding 'nay's' from the rest of the men.

Nay, Brogan had never known such a man. If his suspicions were correct, the last thing Aymer Mactavish wanted was for his clan to be safe. 'Twas the only plausible explanation. No man could be so foolish, could he?

Thankfully, it would be months before he would meet the man in person to find out for himself. Taking in a lungful of air, he plunged under the cold water. He counted to thirty before coming back up for air.

It dawned on him then, that in a few short months Aymer would be returning with Claude Courtemanche. *That* was not a meeting he was going to enjoy. Courtemanche was as cruel as the day was long. 'Twas a meeting he would not relish, but he would stand firm and resolute in any decisions he might make before their return.

"I be starved," Henry said as he began making his way out of the loch. "Do ye suppose this evenin's meal will be as good as the feast we had last night?"

Brogan smiled. He was not as interested in the meal as much as he was looking forward to spending time with his new bride. *Tonight,* he told himself, *would not be wasted on excessive consumption of wine. Tonight, we shall finally consummate this marriage.*

Thinking of Mairghread put a smile on his face and a near skip in his step. In truth, he was looking forward to the consummation. But he was also looking forward to getting to know her better and telling her about the plans for the new wall, and how the people — most of them anyway — were looking forward to her taking over as chief.

By the time they returned to the keep, the evening meal had already begun. Brogan raced up the stairs and to the chamber he shared with Mairghread. The room was empty. He donned a clean tunic, ran his fingers through his still damp hair, and bounded down the stairs. He was quite eager to see his new bride, to have a quick meal, and return to their rooms. Tonight, he promised himself, would be a night of exploration. An exploration of body as well as mind.

The gathering room was crowded, filled with almost as many people as the night before. The same men who had played at the wedding feast were once again in the corner playing.

He heard her laugher before he saw her. 'Twas mayhap one of the sweetest sounds. Lilting and alive, and filled with so much happiness.

Then he saw her, at the table on the dais. Her hair was plaited elegantly around her head. A veil made of a soft, wispy material hung down her back from plait. What he could see of her burgundy gown made his desire for her surge.

As he eagerly approached the dais, he saw her pour herself a glass of wine. *No' this night,* he told himself.

The sweet laughter and bright smile faded rapidly when she saw him step onto the dais. So quick was the change, he paused on the stairs for a brief moment. Mayhap she was embarrassed over the events of last eve.

Before taking his seat next to her, he took her hand in his, bowed over it and placed a sweet kiss on the soft skin. "Good eve, me lady wife," he said with an affectionate smile.

A light blush crept up her neck, to the roots of her hair. "Good eve," she said.

But there was no warmth in her tone, nor could he find any in her eyes. Instead, all he saw was the same sorrowful resignation as yesterday, when she stood at the altar.

"How fare ye this night?" he asked as he took his seat.

"I am well," she replied without looking at him. She sipped on her wine as she looked out at the people below. They were alone on the dais this night, for his brother and friends had left that morn.

A maid offered him wine, which he politely refused. "I would like cider, please," he told her.

The young woman looked perplexed. "Aye m'laird, as ye wish."

As soon as she left, Brogan turned his attention back to Mairghread. "What did ye do this day?" he asked, hoping to break the silence and the coolness between them.

She took another drink of wine before answering. "No' much."

Why did he get the sense she was angry with him? "Mairghread, are ye well?"

Another drink emptied her cup. "I am well, as I said before."

"Then why do I get the sense ye're upset with me?" he asked as he took a good portion of meat from the platter in front of him.

"Why did I find myself undressed in my bed this morn?" she asked. Aye, her tone was as cold as ice on the loch in winter time.

Brogan resisted the urge to laugh. "If ye mean to ask me did I take advantage of yer state of inebriation last eve, the answer is *nay.* Gertie and Tilda helped me get ye into bed."

His answer did not seem to appease her. "And after?"

He chewed and swallowed the savory meat, set his eating knife down, and leaned in to whisper into her ear. "Lass, when it comes to lovin', I would prefer each of us be sober."

Mairghread's eyes grew wide as her skin burned, almost as deep as the color of her dress. He took a good deal of satisfaction knowing 'twas he who made her blush so deeply.

The maid returned with his cider, poured a mug of it, and dipped a curtsey. Without thinking, he took a drink. One taste and he was carefully spitting it back into his mug. He looked around for the maid, found her in the corner, and called her forward. He'd gone through the same thing the night before, but with a different serving maid. "Lass, could I please have some soft cider?"

He'd seen the confused look in her eyes before. Seen it countless times in bar wenches and serving maids. "M'laird?" she said, looking confused. "Do ye mean the kind we give the bairns?"

Brogan smiled warmly at her. "Aye, I mean the kind ye give the bairns."

She bobbed another curtsy before leaving to fetch the soft cider.

"Why soft cider?" Mairghread asked as she drank more of her wine. "Did ye have too much whisky last eve?"

He tore off a hunk of bread and reached for the bowl of butter. "Nay," he replied. "I touched no' a drop of hard drink last eve."

She looked aghast. "What do ye mean ye touched no hard drink last eve?"

"Why is that so hard to believe?" he asked.

"'Twas our weddin' feast. Did ye no' wish to celebrate the momentous occasion?" Was that disdain he was detecting in her voice?

Brogan chuckled softly at her inquiry. "I did celebrate. Quite happily as a matter of fact."

She gave him and 'oh, I see' look. But of course, she didn't really understand.

"I never partake of strong drink," he told her as he cut off a hunk of venison.

"Never?" she asked suspiciously.

He gave a slow shake of his head. "Never."

She was quiet for a long moment. Finally, she drank down the rest of her wine and immediately set out to pour another cup. "I've married a bloody monk," she said under her breath.

Brogan leaned in once again to whisper in her ear. "Nay, lass I am no' a monk. And if ye come to our marital bed sober this night, I shall prove it to ye."

Anger burned behind her bright eyes. Intentionally, she drank down the entire cup of wine before slamming it down onto the table. She began to pour another cup, when Brogan halted her by placing his hand on hers. He was about to tell her he thought she'd had enough wine last night to last a grown man a week, but Henry appeared before them.

"Brogan," he said. Out of breath and looking flustered. "We need ye in the courtyard."

"What be the matter?" Brogan asked, still keeping his wife from pouring more wine.

"There be a bit of a problem betwixt Comnall and a Mactavish man."

Brogan rolled his eyes. "Let me guess," he began. "There be a lass involved."

"Aye, there be."

He turned to face Mairghread. "Please, lass," he whispered. "Do no' over drink this night. There is much I wish to discuss with ye." He dared not add, *and much I wish to do with ye.*

§

THE COURTYARD WAS FILLED WITH MEN AND WOMEN OF VARYING ages. They were surrounding Comnall and a young Mactavish man Brogan did not know. The two were face to face, toe to toe, staring one another down. Though Comnall was a good three inches taller, wider in the shoulders, and more muscled, the angry young man glowering at him did not cower.

"Ye will stay away from me sister," the young man growled.

Comnall smirked. "Yer sister be auld enough to make up her own mind."

Brogan groaned inwardly. "Comnall, stand down," he ordered as he approached.

Comnall continued to smirk at the younger man, shrugged his shoulders once before taking a step back.

Just what he whispered under his breath before stepping away, Brogan couldn't hear. But the young man did. In a flash, he lunged at Comnall, wrapping one arm around his neck, and pulled him to the ground.

A cheer broke out among the Mactavishes. "Get him, Neyll!" someone from the crowd called out.

Brogan stood over the two men for a brief moment. He'd never seen Comnall taken down so quickly before. Especially not by someone who was shorter and seemingly less strong. Neyll had one arm wrapped around Comnall's neck, with his free hand pressed on top of his head. His wiry legs were wrapped around Comnall's torso, summarily keeping the bigger, strong Mackintosh man exactly where he wanted him. Comnall's eyes were beginning to bulge, his face purple — either from sheer rage or lack of air.

"That is enough!" Brogan barked out. "Let him go!"

"No' until he apologizes," Neyll ground out.

Brogan let out a quick, frustrated breath. "Well, he can no' apologize if he be dead, now can he?"

The young man thought on it for a brief moment before finally giving up and letting loose. Comnall rolled onto his hands and knees, and took in great, deep breaths.

Brogan extended his arm to Neyll. The lad looked at it as though it were covered in cow dung. Declining his offer, he got to his feet and stared murderously at Comnall.

"What did he say?" Brogan asked.

Neyll raked a hand through his dark blonde hair. "He said he did no' want anythin' to do with a Mactavish whore. He called me sister a whore!"

Brogan watched as Comnall struggled to his feet. "Be that true?"

"*He* was the one who started it!" Comnall thundered. "I was merely introducin' meself to Briggid, when *he* came out of nowhere, tellin' me he did no' want a Mackintosh anywhere near his sister."

Brogan sighed inwardly. "Comnall, mind yer tongue and yer tone."

Duly chastised, Comnall pursed his lips together and continued to glare at Neyll.

"Briggid is far too young and innocent fer the likes of *him*," Neyll said through gritted teeth. "Ye make yer man apologize, m'laird, or I will."

Comnall spat on the ground. "No' bloody likely!"

Before they could come to blows once again, Brogan stepped in between them. He pressed a hand on each of their chests. "That is enough!"

Neyll looked mad enough to take on one hundred men. Comnall looked as though he was planning the young man's death.

"Comnall, did ye in fact call he sister a whore?"

When Comnall looked at his feet instead of directly in his eye, Brogan had his answer. Turning to Neyll, he said, "I will apologize on behalf of Comnall, because apparently, he does no' have the honor nor the ballocks to do it himself."

Comnall began to protest, but Brogan halted him with a stern glare of reproach. "On the morrow, and until further notice, ye will no' be patrolling the borders at night. Ye will be working in the quarry with me and the others."

"The bloody quarry?" Comnall asked incredulously.

"Aye, the bloody quarry. Unless ye'd like to pack yer things and go back to Ian and explain to him why ye've been sent back."

Comnall's face burned deep red. 'Twas quite apparent he wished not to be sent back to Ian.

"As fer ye," Brogan said as he turned his focus back to the younger man. "Neyll, is it?"

He replied with a curt nod.

"Ye seem to ken how to take care of yerself. I have never seen anyone take Comnall down the way ye did."

"I have four older brothers," Neyll replied. "I had to learn to take care of meself at a young age."

Brogan was beginning to like the lad. "What are yer duties here?" he asked.

"I work in the stables," he replied. "I also raise cattle with me da."

While noble pursuits, Brogan thought the young man might prove more useful elsewhere. "Would ye object to patrollin' the borders?" he asked. "Ye certainly ken how to take care of yerself."

"I can at that, m'laird," Neyll said. Although he did not look nearly as murderous as he had a few moments ago, Brogan knew he was still quite upset. "And I can assure ye, Comnall will not be a bother to ye or yers again." He turned to look at Comnall. "Is that right? Can I give this young man that promise?"

Looking sheepishly and duly chastised, Comnall replied with only a quick nod and a murmured 'aye'.

"Good," Brogan said. "'Tis settled then. But fer future reference, when issues such as these arise, please seek me out so that I can offer ye good counsel and mete out punishments where necessary." 'Twas a message meant for all of the Mactavish people and one he hoped they would have the good sense to heed.

ALTHOUGH HE HAD BEEN GONE LESS THAN A HALF AN HOUR, WHEN he returned to the gathering room, he discovered his wife was nearly as drunk as she had been the night before. He returned to his seat and now cold meal. Mairghread did not even acknowledge his return. She sat, staring out across the room as she drank.

Worry began to settle deep into his gut. Was she so disgusted with the thought of sharing her bed with him, that she could not do it without being drunk? Was she regretting her decision to marry him?

He looked down at his trencher, his appetite now gone. There were many things he wanted to discuss with his new bride. But from her expression and demeanor, now mayhap, was not the best time. Chancing a quick glance, he could see the flush in her cheeks and glassy eyes, a sure sign she was well on her way to being sotted drunk.

"On the morrow, I should like to discuss a few things with ye," he said as he took a drink of cider.

"Such as?" she asked.

He took note of the slight slur in her speech and it angered him. It had been a long, worrisome day. What with learning what he had regarding Aymer and the lack of walls, weapons and other common defenses, and then the brawl between Comnall and Neyll, his patience was as thin as a spider's web. And now, with his wife well into her cups, he doubted he could have any sort of adult conversation with her pertaining to anything of import. "On the morrow, when ye are sober, would be best."

She threw her head back and laughed. 'Twas not the same, sweet laughter he had heard earlier. Nay, 'twas filled with something dark and quite ugly. Malice blended with disgust. "If ye think I will be sober on the morrow, ye are sadly mistaken."

He felt his skin burn hot with rage and had to take in a deep breath to keep it in check. "Do ye need the aid of strong drink in order to bed me?" He regretted the question the moment he heard himself ask it.

Mairghread leaned over, ever so slightly. "Aye, I do."

'Twas not only *what* she said, but *how* she had said it that sent him over the edge. He slammed his mug down so hard, it shook the entire table. Mairghread's eyes grew wide with a blend of fear and astonishment as he grabbed the cup of wine from her hand and slammed it down next to his.

In one fell swoop, he picked her up and slung her over his shoulder, rump up. He stormed through the now stunned-silent guests and headed for the stairs.

"PUT ME DOWN!" SHE CRIED OUT AS SHE KICKED HER FEET.

Brogan said not a word as he thundered down the corridor to their chamber. "Ye bloody son of a whore!" Mairghread screamed as she hit his back with her fists.

He kicked open their bedchamber door. It banged against the wall with such force he thought he might have broken it. Inside, he crossed the floor in a few quick strides and tossed her onto the bed.

She landed on her back with an oomph.

Towering over her, he stood with his hands on his hips and glowered. "Why did ye agree to marry me?" he demanded. "If the thought of beddin' me drives ye to drink?"

Before she could answer, Gertie and Tilda were in the room. "M'laird!" Gertie cried out. "Please, do no' harm her!"

Brogan spun on his heels and glared at the two women. "I have never, in my life, harmed a woman! Out! Now!" His voice echoed off the walls. Hesitantly, each woman tried to look around the wall of muscle blocking their way.

"Out!" Pointing to the door, he ordered them once again to leave. "I said *out*."

From the bed, Mairghread called out, "If ye find me dead on the morrow, ye ken 'twas him!"

Never in his life had he been tempted to hit a woman. Nay, he did not wish to hit her so much as to throw her over his knee and...

He was done. If he did not leave now, he might very well do or say something he would regret for the rest of his life.

Raking a hand through his hair, he took one last look at Mairghread. Aye, she was drunk and frightened and God only knew what else, for he certainly didn't. Neither, at the moment, did he care.

"Tend to yer lady," he grumbled at Gertie and Tilda before he stormed out of the room.

※

THE COOL NIGHT AIR DID NOTHING TO TAMP DOWN THE FLAMING hot anger coursing through his veins. He had stomped out of the keep, down the stairs, and into the courtyard. Henry had tried to stop him, to inquire as to what was wrong, but one savage glare from Brogan made him back away.

Now he found himself crossing the old wall and heading toward the cliffs.

He stood there, just at the edge, staring out at the moonlit sea, wishing for all the world he was anywhere but here.

Why did she agree to marry me? He wondered. *If the thought of joinin' with me is so deplorable she must drink to do it?*

None of it made a damn bit of sense. She was not the sweet, pretty woman he remembered from their first meeting. And what about that night, back at his brother's keep, when he'd first proposed?

What had happened in these past two weeks to change her?

Was it remorse? Had she changed her mind? Was she so filled with regret at her decision?

If that be it, why did she no' come to me?

Was it fear of *him* that kept her from speaking to him? Was she afraid of what he might say or do if she came to him?

He hated losing his temper with her. Hell, he hated losing his temper, period. *But a man can only take so much.*

"If she is in fact afraid of ye, how ye just behaved toward her did neither of ye any good," he said shamefully. Looking heavenward, he prayed. "God, help me to help Mairghread see that I be no' a monster. That I be a good man. A man she can trust." He puffed out his cheeks and let the air out slowly. "And please, help me control this Mackintosh temper."

BROGAN STOOD AT THE CLIFF'S EDGE FOR AN HOUR. THE WIND HAD picked up, bringing with it the salty sea spray. Prayer had helped calm his fury, helped ease his worries away. With the firm belief that God had put Mairghread in his life for a reason, he finally let go of his anger and dread.

Holding his head high, he went back into the keep. A few maids were still about, cleaning up the last of the evening meal. They stopped at once, looking up at him as if he was a great beast sent from the bowels of hell to wreak havoc on them and the lady they all loved so dearly.

If his father, John Mackintosh, had taught him anything, it was to own up to one's mistakes. He paused at the stairs and offered them his most sincere smile and apologies. "I be terribly sorry fer losin' me temper earlier," he told them. "I did no' mean to shame yer lady, myself, or ye."

Three sets of stupefied eyes stared back at him. The maids each bobbed a curtsy before he left them to do their work and headed up the stairs.

Their bedchamber was quiet and still, save for the soft crackle of the low burning fire in the hearth. He could just make out Mairghread's sleeping form in the bed. Quietly, he made his way across the room and sat down on the edge of the bed.

"Mairghread," he whispered her name. She moved not at all, so sound asleep was she.

"I came to apologize fer losin' me temper, lass. 'Tis no' like me to behave so poorly. Especially toward a woman."

She did not so much as stir at the sound of his voice. Or the gentle nudge he gave her shoulder. Undoubtedly, she was in a deep sleep from all the wine she had consumed earlier.

On the morrow, he told himself. *On the morrow, we shall have it all out and begin anew.*

MAIRGHREAD FEIGNED SLEEP, SO AS TO AVOID ANY KIND OF communication with Brogan. She was not nearly as drunk as she wanted to be. *Let him think what he wants,* she told herself when he gently nudged her shoulder. *I care no'.*

Finally, mercifully, he sighed once, covered her with the fur then left the room. She lay as still as fawn in springtime long after he left, afraid he would come back. She did not want to see him, let alone speak to him.

I do no' care what he thinks of me.

But she did care. Cared far more than she wanted to admit to herself. Guilty tears built behind her closed eyes.

Although he'd been here but two days, he'd apparently earned the admiration of nearly everyone within the keep. Even Reginald seemed to admire him.

Nay, she was not nearly as drunk as she wished to be. Chancing a peek from under the covers, she made sure the room was empty before slipping from the bed. In the dark, she made her way to the cupboard and withdrew a bottle of whisky. After years of consuming the amber liquid, it no longer burned going down. It calmed her, made her feel warm and safe.

In nothing but a light chemise, she stood alone in the dark and drank. Something she had done innumerable times before. Barefooted, she padded to the window and pulled the fur open. Stars dotted the indigo sky above and a cool breeze flittered in through the open window.

Nearly every night these past three plus years, she stood at this window and thought of her husband and son. God, how she missed them. Not even the whisky could dull that ache in her heart, no matter how many times she tried.

"I be sorry James," she whispered into the night. "I should never have married him. I broke me oath to ye and to our babe."

If she were ever sober enough to be honest with herself, she might admit that was what truly ate at her soul. She had survived and they hadn't. She was moving on with her life.

Why did I live? Why did God take them from me?

Just as every other night she'd asked those questions, she found no answer whispered back from the stillness nor from the bottle.

Chapter Seven

Brogan's hope at starting anew with his wife the following day was delayed. He had slept in an unoccupied room down the hall from hers. A fitful, restless night.

'Twas just before dawn before sleep finally claimed him. Not long after, he heard someone enter the room. Instinctively, he reached for the dirk he kept under his pillow and held his breath.

"Did ye ferget about the wall?"

'Twas Reginald standing at the foot of the bed.

Shite. Grumbling — though relieved 'twas no' anyone here to do him any harm — he sat up in the bed. "Be it that time already?" he groused.

"Aye," Reginald said with a nod and amused smile. "It be that time."

Brogan swung his legs over the edge of the bed, raked a hand through his hair, and took in a deep breath. The last thing he wanted to do was go work in a quarry all day. There were things he needed to discuss with Mairghread, things he needed to say. Most likely, she would sleep half the day.

"Verra well," he said as he got to his feet. "I will meet ye below stairs in a few moments."

Reginald gave a quick nod before quitting the room.

❧

IT HAD BEEN A BACK-BREAKING DAY. MOST OF IT, BROGAN HAD spent in the quarry, with an axe, chipping away at earth and stone. At first, it felt good to strike hardened steel against stone to help get rid of some of his anger.

He, along with a group of five men, worked at chiseling away the needed stones. Another group was in charge of hauling them via wagon and rope, to a section of land less than a hundred yards away. There, another group of men would work at carving the stones to the appropriate size to be used for the much needed wall.

He reckoned in a few days' time they could begin taking the stones to the keep. For now, 'twas all about gathering and chipping. Gathering and chipping.

'Twas much harder work here than what he had done back at his brother's keep. Aye, they had a good deal of men to help the process, but the earth here was harder and far less forgiving than his brother's lands.

His company also was different. Comnall was still in a foul mood because Brogan had sided with the Mactavish lad the night before, which made any hope at a congenial conversation futile. After a while, Brogan had had enough of Comnall's insolent behavior and sent him out of the pit to work above.

The man who took Comnall's place, though in a far better mood and spirit, was not the talkative kind. Mayhap his silence was born out of the fact that he didn't know Brogan at all.

At noon time a group of women had come bearing a meal, for which all the men were mightily grateful. Brogan climbed out of the pit, took a trencher from one of the women, and went to sit away from the group.

The men ate as they rested in the warm afternoon sunshine. 'Twas a bright, beautiful day, one Brogan felt he should be enjoying more than he was. But envy — an emotion he rarely struggled with — began to cloud his heart.

Most of the women who had brought the nooning meal were wives of the men working here. On blankets spread out on the cool grass, they ate and laughed together, these couples. Many of those men stole kisses from their wives. Even the older men.

They were at ease with one another. Comfortable in their marriages, with their spouses, and their lives. Would he ever have ease and comfort with his own wife? And why the bloody hell had she gotten drunk again last eve?

He envied them, these people. He envied the simple life they lived. He wanted what they had. Mayhap, in time, Mairghread would look upon him with the same sweet smile as these women looked upon their husbands. But as thing stood now, that day was a long way off.

❧

BROGAN AND THE MEN HAD WORKED FROM DAWN TO DUSK. BY THE end of the day, there was nary a man not covered in sweat and grime, and aye, even a bit of blood.

Tired from the long, arduous day, they rode back to the keep in the backs of wagons. The Mactavish men, friends one and all, ignored Brogan and his men for the most part. Besides, he was too tired to make small talk. And his mind was on only one person; his new bride.

Some of the men joined them at the loch to bathe, while others went home to their wives. Undoubtedly, a hot bath and hearty meal were waiting for them there.

What, he wondered, was waiting for him at the keep? Undoubtedly, Mairghread was still sorely angry with him for how he had treated her the night before. He could not rightly blame her. He had behaved poorly. Aye, he knew she had intentionally badgered him into losing his temper. But what had been her purpose? Was she intentionally trying to make him look like a beast? Like a low-born man without an ounce of pride or honor in his body?

Diving into the cold loch did nothing to ease his worries.

Why? He asked himself the same question a hundred times today. Why did she provoke him? Why did she look at him with such profound disgust and sorrow?

He had more questions than answers. And the only one who could give him those answers was his wife.

§⚶

BROGAN WAS ONCE AGAIN LATE TO THE EVENING MEAL. Mairghread was already at the table on the dais. From his vantage point at the bottom of the stairs, she looked regal and elegant in a dark green gown made of soft silk. His fingers all but itched with desire. Desire to whisk her above stairs, to their chamber, where he would first apologize for his behavior from the previous night. Then he would slowly divest her of the aforementioned dress and spend the rest of the night *showing* her that she could trust him, with her body and her heart. One look at her and his anger subsided, replaced with a need so acute and intense, 'twas nearly frightening.

But he refused to play the fool this night. Nay, he would be every bit the gentleman she needed. He would apologize, take his time to explain his reasons for his poor behavior, then he would bloody well demand an explanation for hers. And he would not give up until he had it.

Standing on the stairs, he quietly watched his new bride as she downed one glass of wine before immediately pouring another.

Something began to niggle at the back of his mind. His imagination was taking him to a place he did not wish to visit. A dark, ugly place, filled with memories of the time in his own life when he was nothing but a drunken, empty shell of a man.

He glanced about at the people assembled to sup. Not a one paid Mairghread any mind or notice. They were all too busy eating and chatting amongst themselves.

The serving maid, the same young lass from the night before, stood cautiously in the corner of the dais, far away from Mairghread. But her eyes were glued to the woman. Worried eyes.

Mairghread gulped down the freshly poured wine. As soon as that cup was empty, she poured herself another. The maid immediately grabbed another flagon from the sideboard to replace the empty.

'Twas all done with such ease to signify this was habit.

He thought back to the wedding feast. He had assumed she had simply been enjoying the festivities and, as many a bride had done before, had drunk too much.

And last night. She had been drinking long before he had arrived to sup with her. He knew that now, beyond a shadow of a doubt.

He scanned the room for Gertie and Tilda and found them. They sat at a table just in front of the dais. Each of them was watching their lady with as much worry as the serving maid. 'Twas as if they were waiting for something to happen.

He knew this dance. Knew it backwards and forwards. 'Twas as familiar to him as the back of his hand. He could have danced it in his sleep.

Nay, he warned his mind. *Do no' make any assumptions just yet.*

Before he would act upon his suspicions, he would gain the facts. Assumptions did no one any good.

While his mind and heart knew that to be true, his stomach tightened into knots of warning.

"GOOD EVE TO YE, MAIRGHREAD," BROGAN SAID AS HE TOOK HIS seat next to her. "Ye look verra bonny this night." She was beyond simply bonny, she was damned beautiful.

Cold and distant, she responded to his compliment with a shrug of indifference.

Scooting closer to her on the bench they shared, he said, "I would like to apologize for how I behaved last eve."

Mairghread snorted derisively. "Do ye mean when ye tossed me over yer shoulder like a savage in front of everyone? Or when ye scared the bloody hell out of me when ye threw me onto me bed?

In truth, he could not rightly blame her for being upset. Still, he was offering an apology, and olive branch of sorts. "For all of it," he replied.

She drank down her wine and poured another. "I do no' ken how men treat women in yer own clan, but here, we respect our women, our wives," she said.

The maid appeared at his side. "Would ye like wine, m'laird?" she asked, holding a pitcher over his mug.

"Nay, lass, but thank ye. I would like cider." Before she could ask which kind he said, "Aye, the kind ye give the bairns. I never partake in strong drink."

She cast an odd glance at her mistress before stepping away from the table.

Mairghread sighed. "Pray tell, why do ye never partake in strong drink? Are ye no' man enough to handle it?"

Brogan had too much experience at *being* a drunkard and dealing with drunken people, to allow the insult to injure his pride. He smiled and began piling food onto his trencher. "I fear I can no'," he admitted. "It turns me into someone I neither like nor admire."

He had hoped his honesty would soften her demeanor. Instead, it had the opposite effect.

"Lord!" she exclaimed under her breath. "Yer honor is sickening."

With those four little words, he knew without a doubt that his wife was a drunk.

ϡ

BROGAN SAT IN STUNNED MUTENESS. HE DID NOT LIKE THE realization he'd just come to. He had, in fact, married a drunkard. Feeling very much a fool for allowing himself to be deceived by the woman's beauty, and the two auld women sitting but ten steps away from him, he placed his eating knife on the table. Taking in deep, steadying breaths, he decided he would not allow her to provoke him again.

"Ye can insult me all ye wish, lass," he said, hiding his anger behind a warm smile and soft voice. "But 'twill no' have the effect ye want."

"How would ye ken what I want?" she seethed.

Cocking his head to one side, he said, "Ye're right. I would no' ken what ye want, because ye hide yerself inside the flagon."

If looks could have killed, he would have been a dead man. "How dare ye?" she asked through gritted teeth.

"Am I wrong?" he asked. "I can assure ye that I would like nothing more at the moment, than to be wrong."

She gulped down the rest of her wine and set the cup down with a clang. "Ye are a sanctimonious bastard, Brogan Mackintosh."

He had been called much worse in his lifetime and told her as much.

Before she could respond, Gertie and Tilda were standing behind her. "M'lady," Gertie said in a soothing voice. "Ye look tired. Mayhap ye should let us get ye to bed."

"Go. Away." Mairghread's words were clipped and filled with anger.

"M'lady, me thinks mayhap ye have had enough to drink this night."

"I would have to agree," Brogan said.

"I will drink as much bloody wine or whisky or ale as I desire," Mairghread told them spitefully. To prove it, she called for the serving maid to bring whisky.

"Mairghread, lass, I wish ye would no' do this," Brogan pleaded with her. He was trying to remain as calm as possible, which was not easy at the moment.

"To the devil with ye, Brogan Mackintosh," she said. The maid appeared and did her lady's bidding, pouring her a cup of whisky. When the young maid tried to step away with the flagon, Mairghread said, "Leave it."

The girl did as she was told, though with a good deal of reluctance. The rest of the room had grown quiet. Brogan could feel all eyes in the room upon them.

"Gertie. Tilda. Ye may take yer seats and finish yer meal," Brogan told them reassuringly. "Yer lady and I wish to finish eating."

The two older women were hesitant to leave their lady.

Gertie placed a comforting hand on Mairghread's shoulder. Mairghread shrugged it away, focusing on the cup of whisky in her hands.

With a good deal of reluctance, the women returned to their seats.

Brogan didn't feel much like eating. Although his stomach was in knots, he managed only a few bites before he pushed his trencher away. Mairghread continued to drink and ignore his presence. The conversation they needed to have was going to have to wait.

Silently, he observed his bride as she sat like a sulking child, drinking one cup of whisky after another. By the fourth, she couldn't get the cup to her lips without spilling it.

Whisky mixed with wine — or anything else for that matter — was never a good combination. From experience, he knew she was not going to feel well come the morrow. And if she kept drinking as she was, it might be days before she fully recovered.

"Do ye drink every day?" he asked, choosing to speak in a soft, non-accusatory tone.

She swayed ever so slightly as she turned to face him. "Aye, I do." The vehemence from earlier was gone. Now, Brogan detected sadness, mayhap even a tinge of regret.

"May I ask *why* ye drink?"

She closed her eyes and leaned back in her chair without answering. She was quiet, her breathing slow yet steady. Brogan began to wonder if she hadn't fallen asleep.

"I drink fer many reasons," she finally answered. "None of which I wish to share."

He could only hope that she would someday share those reasons with him. If anyone understood what could make a body to drink from sun up to sun down, 'twas he. Now, however, was probably not the best time to share his own past with her.

There had been no formal declaration calling the meal to an end, but people were leaving just the same. Just how long his new bride had been drinking like this, he could only guess. He concluded it probably started not long after she lost her husband and babe.

Servants came and began clearing tables. Quietly, he assumed, so as not to disturb Mairghread. He wondered how many nights had been like this one? When Mairghread drank until she fell asleep and people tip-toed around her. He doubted 'twas respect that bade them behave this way. More likely than not 'twas out of fear. He'd been the victim of her razor sharp tongue more than once these past two days. These people had probably been living with it for years.

Just as he was about to offer to help her above stairs, she sat forward in her chair and poured yet another cup of whisky. She looked out at those who remained behind. "Where has everyone gone?" she yelled. "I have no' dismissed anyone!"

Brogan took in a deep breath. "I did it fer ye, Mairghread," he lied. "The hour grows late."

Having heard Mairghread's displeasure, Gertie and Tilda once again came to the dais. "There, there, now lass," Tilda said. "Gertie and I will see ye to yer bed."

Mairghread spun around on the bench and jumped to her feet. She swayed, holding a cup of whisky in one hand, her other reaching out to find something to hold onto. Tilda took her hand in hers to help steady her.

"I wish ye'd all quit treatin' me like a bairn!" she shouted. Her words were slurred, and filled with malice. Her eyes were glassy and unable to focus on anyone or anything. Aye, she was bloody well stinking drunk.

Brogan stood and took the hand Tilda had been holding. "Come, Mairghread, let us help ye above stairs."

She wrenched her hand free of his, fire burning behind her drunken eyes. "Do no' touch me!"

Gertie looked fit to be tied as tears welled behind her auld, blue eyes. "M'lady, please, let us help ye," she said as she reached out to take her hand.

"I said, leave me be ye auld whore!" Mairghread cried out as she drew back her hand, the one with the cup, and swung out with it. She hit Gertie's face with such force it sent her to her knees and the cup shattering to the floor. Blood began to run down her face, from a cut just below her eye.

Tilda bent down to help her friend while Brogan grabbed Mairghread about the waist. Before he could lift her off her feet, she kicked out at Tilda. Her foot struck the woman's shoulder hard enough to send her tumbling to her back.

"Enough!" Brogan yelled as he pulled the kicking and screaming Mairghread away from the women and the table. "Settle down now!"

She fought like the devil to free herself from his tight hold. Kicking, cursing, clawing at his hands. He was undeterred. As fast as he could, he took her above stairs, all the while she screamed like a women possessed by the devil himself.

By the time he was kicking open the bedchamber door —

again for the second time in as many days — Mairghread was lying limp in his hands. Either she had passed out or she was feigning as much. Either way, he wasn't about to take the chance and set her free.

He tossed her onto the bed, out of breath, his forehead covered in sweat. 'Twasn't from exertion, for she was not heavy in the least. Nay, 'twas anger and frustration, nothing more.

She mumbled something incoherent as she tried to roll over, fighting, struggling drunkenly, as if she were swimming in a sea of thick honey.

Brogan knew 'twould do no good to try to talk to her in her current state. He doubted she would remember anything come the morrow. Instead, he stood with his hands on his hips, watching and waiting for what she might do next. He'd not leave her alone, not for a moment.

"Whisky," she mumbled. "I need more ..." her words trailed off as she took in ragged breaths.

Nay, he thought to himself. *Ye need no' whisky or wine or ale.*

Slowly, in a drunken stupor, she rolled onto her belly and tried to climb out of the bed. Brogan took a few steps back, observing, wishing for all the world he was not witnessing any of this.

"They all be fools," she muttered. "I hate them. I hate him."

He would take to heart nothing she said this night, or any other while she was drunk. Brogan knew they were nothing more than words induced from too much strong drink.

It took a good deal of effort before she finally managed to get her head over the edge of the bed. "All of them. I hate all of them." She dropped her head over the edge. "Why can I no' remember?" she continued to mumble, most of which he could not decipher.

From behind him, came the soft yet quavering voice of the same young woman who had served them their evening meal. "M'laird," she whispered. "Gertie and Tilda sent me to help."

She had stepped forward with a bowl of water and washing cloths.

"Nay," Brogan said, holding his hand up. "Ye may leave that on the table, but ye are no' to help yer lady this night."

Aghast, she asked, "But we must. We help her every night she gets like this."

The tick in Brogan's jaw returned with a vengeance. "I said, nay. Ye do no' help her by cleanin' up her messes."

Clearly, she did not understand.

"What is yer name?" he asked.

"Mairi," she replied, looking between her lady and Brogan.

"Mairi, the best thing ye can do fer yer lady right now, is to leave her be. Let her awake on the morrow to see what her actions have wrought."

He could tell from her confused expression she still didn't understand. "Go, tend to Gertie and Tilda," he told her. "They be hurting far worse than yer lady at the moment. Send fer yer healer as well. Gertie might need stitches."

She made no effort to move as she continued to stare with worried eyes at Mairghread.

They had been doing this for so long, it had become the norm. It would be up to Brogan to change it. "Lass, go now. I promise I will tend yer lady. No harm will come to her this night."

Hesitantly, she placed the bowl and cloths on the table. "M'laird, we love our lady verra much. She has no' always been like this."

Brogan had no doubt she spoke the truth. If Mairghread had always been nothing more than a drunk, her people would not hold her in such high regard. "I believe ye, lass. Now go, tend to Gertie and Tilda."

She bobbed a curtsey and left, closing the door softly behind her.

Brogan turned his attention back to Mairghread, who had as yet not moved. Her head still hung over the edge of the bed. He knew 'twas going to be an awfully long night.

His anger began to wane, replaced with a good deal of pity. Working quietly, he set a fire in the hearth. Next, he searched her room from top to bottom for hidden bottles of wine, ale, or whisky. By the time he was finished, he had found five bottles of wine and four of whisky. He'd also found empty bottles under her bed, along with one slipper. He put the slipper in her clothes cupboard and the bottles on the table in the corner.

After that task was done, he pulled up a chair and sat near the corner of the bed, where he could keep an eye on her. Not long after, she began to stir. He could hear her begin to wretch, so he quickly grabbed a chamber pot and placed it on the floor under her head. Most of it did manage to make it into the pot. Other than placing the chamber pot under her face, he offered no other assistance.

He refused to remove it or clean up the mess. *Nay, she must see what her drinking does.*

When the smell became too much, he pulled back the furs from the windows to let fresh air in and returned to his chair.

Och, Mairghread, I pray ye will be able to give up the drink.

Chapter Eight

B rogan slept all the night long in the chair at the foot of her bed. He awoke at dawn, with a stiff neck and an arse that had fallen asleep. Near as he could tell, Mairghread hadn't moved. She still slept with her head dangling halfway off the bed.

Quietly, he stood and stretched and hurried below stairs. He found Mairi in the gathering room, helping to set out the morning meal. "Mairi," he said. "Would ye please go sit with yer lady?"

"Aye, m'laird," she said as she bobbed a curtsy.

"Leave her be, as ye found her," he warned. "But if she wakes, come find me at once."

If she thought it an odd request, she didn't remark on it.

"Where be Gertie and Tilda?" he asked.

"In their quarters," she answered. "Down the hall, and the second door on the right."

He thanked her and headed off to see the auld women.

He gave a gentle rap at the door and heard a muffled voice bid entry. Carefully, he opened the door.

'Twas a small, well-kept room. Gertie and Tilda were in small beds set against the opposite wall. One small table sat between the two beds. To his left, was the hearth with two chairs flanking it.

The women were surprised to see him enter their room. "Och! M'laird!" they cried out almost in unison as they started to scramble from their beds.

"Nay, ladies," he said holding up a hand. "Stay abed please."

They cast curious glances at one another and pulled their blankets up around their chins.

"How be our lady?" Gertie asked, concern filling her eyes and voice.

"Still asleep," he said. "Do ye mind if I sit?" he asked, nodding his head toward one of the chairs.

"Och! Of course ye can!" they replied, again, in unison.

He stifled a chuckle as he pulled up a chair to sit between the two women. He had been wise to call for the healer the night before. Gertie had required a few stitches for the gash under her eye. It looked painfully swollen, blue and purple and red.

"How do ye fare?" he asked each of them.

"We'll be right as rain in no time," Tilda said. "'Tis naught but a bruised shoulder for me and a black eye for Gertie."

To Brogan's way of thinking, it was far worse than bruises. The pain ran far deeper, no matter how hard they might try to deny it.

"How long has she been like this?" he asked them bluntly.

Gertie stammered for an appropriate answer, while Tilda was unusually quiet. "Ladies, I ken Mairghread has a problem with drink. I am neither a fool nor a simpleton."

Suddenly, his mind took him back to the very first time he'd met these two women. Gertie's words resounded loudly now. *She needs a strong man,* she had told him that day. Now, he understood all too well what she meant by it.

"Why did the two of ye seek me out? To marry Mairghread, I mean."

They cast conspiratorial glances at one another before Gertie answered. "I met ye when ye came to buy horses, a year ago. Well, no' met as much as overheard ye discussin' things with Harry, Seamus's apprentice." Her cheeks flamed red with her admission of eavesdropping. "Months later, when Aymer announced he had brokered a deal with the Frenchman, well, we had to do somethin'. Me and Tilda stole away from the keep and went to yers. 'Twas then we first met Rose Mackintosh."

"She be a fine woman, that one," Tilda broke in.

"Aye, a fine woman indeed," Gertie replied with a warm smile.

Brogan rolled his eyes.

"Well, we explained our plight to Lady Mackintosh. 'Twas her idea to speak to ye."

Brogan pondered it for a brief moment. "Did Rose ken of Mairghread's problem with drink?"

Gertie averted her eyes to her hands. "Aye, m'laird, she kent it. Well, mayhap not all of it."

Brogan took in a deep breath through his nostrils and let it out slowly. *But Rose knew enough,* he reckoned quietly. *No wonder she thought Mairghread and I would suit.*

"When did her drinkin' start?"

"The day they buried James and wee Connell," Tilda answered.

"'Twas the saddest time in our lives," Gertie added. "We lost more than James and Connell that day, M'laird."

"We also lost our lady," Tilda said.

❧

BROGAN UNDERSTOOD ALL TOO WELL THE DEPTHS OF THEIR PAIN. They loved Mairghread as much as if she were their very own daughter. When Mairghread hurt, they hurt.

"What exactly happened the night of the raid?" he asked.

The two women grew eerily silent.

"I can no' help Mairghread if I do no' ken the reasons behind her drinkin'."

"Is it no' enough that she lost them?" Gertie asked, tears welling up in her blue eyes.

He knew, from personal experience, that if one did not face the cold hard truth, if ye kept it hidden, deeply buried, it would eat at ye until there was nothing left of yer soul. "Nay, I need the truth of it. What happened that night?"

Gertie wiped away a tear with the back of her hand. "In truth, we do no' rightly ken, m'laird. We were attacked, and to this verra day, we ken no' by who."

Brogan found that a peculiar bit of information. "Ye do no' ken who?"

The two women shook their heads, looking beleaguered and sorrowful.

"How many were there?" he asked.

Gertie shrugged her shoulders. "Some say only five, others say twenty or more. No one kens fer certain."

"And James and Connell were killed as well?" he asked, hoping to encourage them to give him more information.

"Aye, they were killed as well. Attacked, they were, in their bedchamber," Tilda said in a low voice.

"How many others lost their lives?" Brogan asked.

"Two guards," Gertie told him. "And we almost lost Mairghread as well."

That bit of news astonished him. Of course, he and his wife had not necessarily had the time to discuss such things. "What happened? To them and to her?"

"James's throat was cut. And wee Connell," she choked back a sob, unable to get the words out.

"Connell, he was only three weeks old, ye ken, just an innocent babe!" Tilda said. The look of sheer hatred in her eyes at the man or men responsible was quite evident. "They cut his throat too!"

The women wept at the memory of the awful night, of the loss of an innocent babe. "He was such a good babe," Tilda said. "Such a sweet babe."

'Twas no wonder Mairghread drank. 'Twas difficult to imagine losing one's child in such a manner. "And Mairghread?"

The two women looked at one another before Gertie replied. "She was stabbed many, many times. We almost lost her. If we had no' found her when we did, she would have died as well."

"Ye found her?" He directed his question to both women.

"Her uncle and I did," Gertie said. "I heard her screamin'. I do no' think I have ever run so fast in all me days."

He was stunned into muteness for a long while. 'Twas difficult for the women to talk about that night. For some reason, he felt there was more to this story than they were willing to admit. But what, he could not begin to guess. Looking at them, he could see they were tired and worn from the telling.

"Our lady," Tilda began as she wiped away another tear. "She has no memory of that night, or even of the day."

"Aye," Gertie said. "I think 'tis too much fer her to bear, ye ken. She has blocked that night out, to save her mind from madness."

Brogan found no fault in her reasoning. He knew men who had suffered on the field of battle and for years, could not recount a moment of what had happened to them. It was perfectly reasonable to assume Mairghread had done the same.

Now, it all made perfectly good sense. She drank to ease her pain and suffering.

"She was no' always like this," Gertie told him. "She was such a sweet, kind lass. I swear, this I tell ye true."

"Aye, 'tis true. She always put the needs of her clan before her own," Tilda added.

"Her mother, her father, they cherished each of their children, and Mairghread was no different," Gertie said through sniffles. "When Connell was born, ye never saw a woman so blissfully happy."

"Aye, she did no' stop smiling from the time he was born until—" Tilda stopped herself, pressed her fingertips to her lips, and began to cry again.

"I swear, m'laird, if ever I get me hands on the man who did this to her, to us, I will kill him, I will," Gertie said. There was such a resoluteness to her tone that he did not doubt for a moment she spoke the truth.

They sat in silence for a long while. Brogan felt empty and at a loss on what he should do next.

"Do ye think ye can help her?" Tilda asked.

"Help her?"

"Stop her drinkin'," she replied hopefully.

God, if it were only that easy, he mused.

༄

'TWAS LONG AFTER NOON TIME BEFORE MAIRGHREAD WOKE, GROGGY and with such a pain in her head she thought 'twould surely be her death. "Och," she groused as she slowly reached up to rub her temple, afraid just yet of opening her eyes.

For some odd reason, her neck ached, and she felt oddly cold. Something did not quite feel right. Slowly, she opened her eyes, and instantly regretted doing so. Sunshine was streaming in through the open windows, burning her orbs. Quickly, she shut her lids tightly.

It took every ounce of energy she had to roll over. 'Twas then she realized her head had been dangling over the bed. *What on earth?* Though she only thought the question, it seemed to echo loudly in her mind, clanging like the smithy's hammer against an anvil.

She took in slow, deep breaths, hoping to calm her stomach. It roiled and churned. Before she could stop it, she was forced to roll over again, to vomit. It came in great, harsh waves, burning her throat. She retched until she had nothing left.

Sweaty, her dress clung to her skin uncomfortably so, but she didn't have the strength to remove it. She wiped her face on the sleeve and rolled to her back. Lying as still as a mouse, she waited for her stomach to settle.

How much time passed, she couldn't have said. Though she was certain she was alone in her chamber, the silence was deafening, maddening. *Where be Gertie? Tilda?* She wondered. Not a morn had passed that they were not here in her chamber, the moment she awakened. 'Twas as if they had some sort of special power to know when she needed them most.

When she was quite certain she'd not wretch again, she rubbed her lids gently with her fingertips. Groaning slightly, she lifted herself on her elbows and took the chance once again to open her eyes.

Brogan was sitting in a chair at the foot of the bed. "Good morn," he said.

Shame crept up her skin in a dark shade of red. She could feel it, deep in her bones.

"Where," her tongue and throat were as dry as wool. She cleared her throat and tried again. "Where be Gertie?"

"Resting," he replied.

"Resting?" she asked. Worry grabbed at her heart. "What happened? Is she ill?"

For the first time since he married her, he saw genuine concern in her eyes, heard it in her voice. *The auld women had no' lied,* he realized. But was there enough of the auld Mairghread left in her to change? To want to change? "Ye do no' remember last eve?" he asked.

Leaning back against the pillow, she fought hard to find a memory of the night before. But there was nothing. "Nay, I do no'," she said as she opened her eyes and slowly sat up. "Is she ill?" she asked once again. "Has the healer been called?"

He had to admit he was glad to see the genuine concern in her eyes. He did not relish for a moment telling her what he must. "She be no' ill, Mairghread. But, aye, the healer was called, to tend to her wounds."

"Wounds?" she asked, sounding quite worried. "Did she fall?"

Brogan shook his head slowly. "Lass, ye were quite into yer cups last eve. Ye became quite angry when we suggested 'twas time to put down yer whisky and go to bed."

From her confused expression, she hadn't a clear memory of the night before. Nor was she anticipating what he was about to tell her. "Ye hit her with yer cup of whisky. It shattered against her face and she required stitches. She has a black eye, but she will live."

Wide, shocked eyes stared at him from across the bed. "Nay!" she cried out. "I would never hurt Gertie!"

"I ken ye would no' do it if ye were sober, Mairghread," he told her, keeping his tone even. "But aye, ye did hurt her last eve."

Swallowing back tears, she shook her head as she buried it in her hands. "Nay, ye lie! I—"

Brogan stood then, and came to sit beside her on the bed. "Mairghread, I would no' lie about such a thing."

Unable to look at him just yet, she kept her face buried in her palms. "Nay, nay, nay," she murmured.

His memory took him back to the day he had learned he had hurt his nephew. Lord, how guilty he felt when he'd learned the truth. 'Twas the first time in his life that his father had ever laid a hand on him in anger. His was black and blue for a week after. But he had sworn that day, never to touch a drop of anything stronger than soft cider. Thus far, though he had been tempted on more than one occasion to drink, he had kept his promise.

The tactics his father had used on him would not work on Mairghread. He couldn't very well beat the living daylights out of her. But he could talk to her, from his heart.

"Mairghread," he said as he placed a hand on her shoulder.

She shrugged it away. "Nay, please go. I wish to see no one right now."

"Mairghread, ye be no' the first person to have an addiction—"

She lifted her head so quickly, he was surprised her neck did not snap. "Addiction?" she asked, her brow knotted. "Ye think I have an addiction?" The disgust she held for him was plainly evidenced through angry eyes. "I have no addiction! Go! Leave me be!"

With a sigh of resignation, he stood to his full height. "Do ye see these?" he asked as he pointed to the bottles on the table. "These all belong to ye. Five bottles of wine. Four of whisky. All hidden about yer room. Ye can no' deny it any longer, Mairghread. Ye are addicted to the drink."

Fire burned behind her eyes. Fire, hatred and denial. "Leave me!" she shouted as she grabbed a pillow and flung it at him. It landed on the floor at his feet.

"Ye can deny it all ye wish, but the truth remains. Ye are addicted. Ye drink until ye black out. Ye hurt the people around ye. No' just with yer words, but with yer deeds and actions."

"To the devil with ye Brogan Mackintosh!" She was seething with anger. Her face was purple with rage, her chest heaving up and down.

There was only one way to get her to see the truth; let her see it with her own eyes.

﹅

BROGAN RETURNED TO MAIRGHREAD'S BEDCHAMBER AN HOUR LATER. With him, he had Reginald, Gertie, and Tilda. In order for her to understand what her drinking was doing to herself and those around her, he needed to show her. She had to see it with her own eyes.

Neither Gertie nor Tilda wanted to do what he asked of them. The women simply did not wish to bring Mairghread an ounce of pain. They felt she'd already suffered enough with losing her husband and babe. It took a good deal of convincing on his part to get them to see how important this was to Mairghread's potential recovery.

As for Reginald, he would rather die than bring a moment of upset to Mairghread. However, he understood 'twas for her own well-being. Her life depended on it.

They were in Mairghread's bedchamber now, pleading with her to see reason.

"I could no' have done what ye said," Mairghread argued as she sat on the edge of her bed.

Forlorn and sorrowful, Gertie took a step forward. "Lass, I ken ye would ne'er do such a thing on purpose, least while not sober. But aye, we tell ye the truth."

"Ye became quite angry last eve," Tilda added. "We ken 'twas the whisky and no' ye."

Tears crept into Mairghread's eyes. Unable to look at them, she turned away.

"Lass, we want to help ye," Reginald said from his spot by the window.

"Help me?" she asked, wholly confused.

"Aye, help ye stop drinkin'," he said.

"Bah!" she exclaimed as she once again turned away from them. "I do no' need help to stop. I do no' *need* to stop. Ye are all makin' more out of my occasional glass of wine—"

Brogan stepped forward then. "Occasional glass of wine?" he asked cynically. "Ye can no' be serious."

She refused to look at him.

"Mairghread, yer drinkin' is more serious than an occasional glass of wine. Ye are not only hurtin' those people around ye, yer killin' yerself. Be that what ye want? To die a bitter, sad, lonely woman far too young?"

Anger, as good and dear a friend as the whisky, enveloped her. She picked up the candlestick near her bed and flung it at him. "To the devil with ye Brogan Mackintosh! To the devil!"

Chapter Nine

Mairghread did not know how to *not* drink anymore. She didn't think she could continue to breathe without the aid of strong drink. Would her heart even beat anymore without it? She refused to admit such aloud to these people.

The people who loved her most in this world — Gertie, Tilda, and Reginald — surrounded her now, looking at her with pity-filled, sorrowful eyes. Pleading, begging her to set down the strong drink, to walk away from it.

But they didn't understand. Not one of them. How could they? They hadn't lost everything they loved. None of their spouses or babes had been murdered in the dead of night. *They* hadn't killed them as she probably had done because she had lost her mind one night. It hadn't been *their* own hands that held the knife and sliced through throats, only then to turn the knife on themselves in a wave of guilt and regret.

Nay, they could not understand.

"Lass," Gertie said as tears clung to her lashes. "'Tis only because we love ye that we are here. If we did no' care, we would leave ye to rot."

Bile rose in her throat, burning and painful. "Ye do no' understand," she whispered as her heart seized, wishing it could stop beating.

"Then *make* us understand," Gertie replied as she swiped away a tear.

Mairghread shook her head violently. She would rather die than admit to Gertie —or anyone else— why she drank, why she was filled with such self-loathing.

Brogan left his spot by the hearth, made his way between Tilda and Reginald. "Leave us," he said in a low, firm tone.

She found no malice, no fury or disgust in his tone. Neither did she find it in his eyes when she searched them. Unable to name what she *did* see, she took in a deep breath and let it out slowly. She fought back the urge to rail against him, to lash out and scream, to tell him to leave her the bloody hell alone. But she didn't possess the strength anymore.

Without a word, they left her alone with Brogan.

As the door softly clicked closed behind them, Mairghread finally managed the strength to turn away from him. She couldn't look into his eyes anymore. 'Twas like looking into a mirror and she despised her own reflection.

"I ken how ye hurt, Mairghread," Brogan began. "The day I lost me wife, Anna, I picked up the nearest flagon of ale. When that was gone, I turned to whisky. 'Twas the only way to dull the pain in me heart. I did no' stop drinkin' for more than a year after."

Pain blended with anger and it came rushing out, turning her tongue as sharp as a razor. "Ye lost yer wife to a sickness. She was no' murdered!" She spun around so fast it made her dizzy. All she wanted was her whisky. Not *him* with his self-righteousness, the *I feel yer pain* look in his eyes. "Ye can no' ever understand it! *Ye* were given time to say goodbye! Ye were allowed to tell her all that was in yer heart. I did no' have that luxury!"

Unfazed by her outburst, he stood his ground. "So my pain was no' as great as yers?"

"Nay! 'Twas no' as great as mine you ignoble fool!" she spat out. "I never want to hear ye say such again. I want ye gone from me. Gone from me life. I do no' need ye to look at me with pity in yer eyes. I do no' need ye to tell me ye understand fer ye surely never could! I do no' need ye turning Gertie and Tilda and Reginald against me."

He did not so much as bat an eye. "They love ye. They care. They see ye slowly dyin', bit by bit each day. They do no' want to lose ye, Mairghread. No' like this."

"Everything was fine until ye came here!" Her throat was beginning to ache from shouting and crying but she continued her onslaught. "But ye sail in here like ye own the place, like ye own me. Ye'll never own me, Brogan Mackintosh. I'll never be yer wife. I hate ye and the earth on which ye walk. Ye're a fool to think otherwise. Yer an eejit. A coward!" She pulled in a deep breath. "Ye say ye care. Ye say ye want to help. But all ye care about is me land and bein' chief of me clan. And ye can no' have either unless ye get me with child. And that will never happen! I'd rather hang than bed such a pious, foolish, ignorant, ugly man as ye."

BROGAN KNEW HER WORDS WERE BORN OUT OF HER ADDICTION. They weren't the true words of her heart. 'Twas the whisky speaking on her behalf. It didn't want to be set aside and forgotten.

"Ye may hate me all ye wish, lass. Ye may despise me and wish me dead. I do no' care."

"Then why do ye no' leave me?" she demanded.

He took note of her trembling hands, her quivering lip, and the paleness of her skin. "Because I *do* care."

"Bah!" she said, throwing her hands in the air. "Ye do no' even *ken* me!"

"Ye're right. I do no' ken ye fer ye have been drunk since the day we married."

Brogan watched as she swallowed hard. He knew she was searching for more spiteful, hate-filled words to launch like arrows, hoping to wound him.

"Then why do ye remain here?" she asked. "Are ye so desperate to have a wife? Can ye no' even pay fer a whore? Or does that go against yer high moral standards?"

He offered her an indifferent shrug. "I do no' bed women I am no' married to."

She threw her head back and laughed until she was breathless. "I will no' bed ye," she said cooly. "No' now, no' ever. So ye might want to reconsider whores or willin' wenches."

"In truth, I do no' wish to bed ye."

He stated it so calmly, so matter-of-factly, that it caught her off balance. "Ye lie."

He gave a slow shake of his head. "Nay, lass, I do no' lie."

Mairghread snorted derisively. "Then it be the company of men ye prefer?" she asked with a raised brow.

Brogan took in a deep, steadying breath, crossed his arms over his chest, and leaned over, ever so slightly, so that he could look directly into her eyes. "Ye are intentionally tryin' to bait me. Ye are also changin' the subject."

Glowering at him, she said, "I wish ye to leave."

Another slow shake of his head. "Ye are a drunk, Mairghread. A mean-spirited drunk to boot. But hear me and hear me now. I be no' leavin' ye. I will no' give up on ye. I be yer husband. I want also to be yer friend."

She pursed her lips with a look of disbelief.

From the table by her door, he retrieved a flagon of whisky and tossed it to her. She caught it with both hands, and held it to her chest. Confused, she looked at him but said nothing.

"I be told ye can no' go more than three days without drink," he said. "At this point, I doubt that ye can go more than three hours without it." He kept his expression cool and calm, which belied what he truly felt inside. "I be leavin' ye alone with that," he inclined his head toward the flagon in her hands. "Fer ye seem to love *it* more than ye love those people around ye." He stepped toward the door that lead to his room. With one hand on the lever, he said, "While ye drink, I want ye to think about Gertie's black eye and swollen lip. I want ye to think about the scratches ye left on Reginald and Tilda. I want ye to think about all of the people ye have hurt because ye can no' set the drink down." He opened the door, but remained where he stood for a long moment. "Ye have a decision to make, Mairghread. Ye either put the drink down for good, or ye continue to live yer life being mean and ugly and vicious. Ye stop yer drinkin' and start *livin'* yer life to do good in the world, or ye kill yerself slowly. The choice is yers. I will be here to help ye if ye wish, because I do want to be yer friend. But I will no' stand by and watch ye die."

And with that, he left her alone to think on his words.

§◊

MAIRGHREAD STOOD FOR A LONG WHILE, STARING AT THE CLOSED door. Her mind was a jumbled mess of nonsense as it battled with her traitorous heart.

She played his words over and over in her mind. *The choice is yers. I will be here to help ye if ye wish, because I do want to be yer friend.*

My friend? She mused disgustedly. *A friend does not call ye a drunk. A friend does not say such vile things right to yer face!*

Bah! He does no' wish to be me friend. He only wants me land. The title of chief. If he knew the real *me, he would no' be so eager to help.*

My friend. Nay, he is no' me friend. Friends do no' treat ye like he has. Friends are no' judgmental. A friend, a true friend, leaves ye be. A friend —

Then it hit her, like a kick to her stomach.

I have done the same.

Her head swam with the realization. Tears of guilt filled her eyes and streamed down her cheeks. Slowly, she made her way to her bed and sat down.

"I have accused him of the exact same things I have done," she whispered to the cold, chilly air. Her chest felt tight, as if someone were pressing down on it with the weight of a heavy boot. Her stomach roiled and churned as her hands trembled.

One tear fell after another, soaking her chin and neck until she felt weak and tired. She looked at the flagon in her hands. 'Twas filled with the warm, amber liquid that had been her constant companion for more than three years.

Uisge-beatha. Water of Life.

It had been her life force for more than three years. The one and only thing that made her want to get out of bed each day. The one thing she could count on when the nights were cold, bleak and dark. Neither the wine nor the whisky had ever let her down.

She kept the flagon pressed against her chest, clinging to it, fearful of letting it go. After much time had passed, she began to hear a soft, gentle voice in the back of her mind. *Drink me,* it said. *I can help ye more than they can.*

Mayhap they were all right. Mayhap she had lost her mind, or was dangerously close to losing it.

The voice grew louder. *Drink me. I be the only one who can help ye.*

She hugged it tighter, harder, hoping the voice would grow silent. She did not wish to listen to it, at least not for a little while. There were too many other things to think about. Such as her clan, her people. Gertie and Tilda and Reginald.

Either she was sober enough or not drunk enough yet, it mattered not. The truth hung in the air like a dark, heavy cloud. She had hurt them. She had hurt them all more times than her foggy mind could count.

And all for her love — nay, 'twasn't love. 'Twas feral *need.* She'd hurt them all because of her desperate need of the drink.

But the drink had been there for her when no one else was. Or at least she had once believed. Now? Now she was consumed with doubt and guilt.

Taking a deep, steadying breath, she leaned over and set the flagon on the floor under her window. "I can go *more* than three days, without it. I do no' need it all of the time," she said with a good deal of determination. "I will show them, I will show Brogan that he be wrong."

Mairghread sat alone with her thoughts until the candles went out and the hearth grew cold. Twice she got up to move the flagon farther away, so that she wouldn't hear it whispering to her, tempting her to take just one wee drink. Just enough to make her hands quit shaking. Just enough to clear her head.

At some point she fell asleep, curled into a ball in the middle of her bed. Her dreams haunted her all the night through. In one, 'twas as if the flagon had its own beating heart. *Ba-bump, ba-bump, ba-bump* it beat over and over, growing louder and louder. Its voice was deep and soothing. *I be yer friend, Mairghread. A drink or two will no' hurt. Drink me. Ye will feel better. 'Twill ease the ache in yer heart.*

Several times throughout the night, she awoke soaked in sweat, fighting for air. By the time morning dawned, she felt worse than the day before.

Her hands still trembled, her stomach began to hurt. And the voice grew louder and louder.

BROGAN HAD LEFT HER ALONE WITH THE HOPE THAT SHE WOULD think about what he had told her. The decision was now hers and hers alone. He had done all he could to help her see what she had done and what she was continuing to do. Not only to the people around her, but to herself.

There was no enjoyment in the evening meal. He barely ate at all and ignored the attempts his men made at small talk. His mind was above stairs, on Mairghread.

Thus far, he had only caught brief glimpses of the woman that Gertie and Tilda swore still existed. Tiny moments when she was almost kind. Almost sweet.

Aye, she might be bonny to look upon, but that was where her beauty ended. On the outside.

Finally, he could take no more of simply *sitting* and pretending all was right in his world. It felt as though the walls were closing in around him. At times like these, he knew where he must go. Pushing himself away from the table, he left without so much as a backward glance.

The sun was just beginning to set when he stepped out of the keep and into the courtyard. To the east, the sky was still a vivid blue, with just a sprinkling of fluffy white clouds. But to the west, the sun cast everything in vivid shades of orange and red.

He made his way around the keep to the tiny kirk. In his mind, he could hear his father's words. *There be times to act, times to pray, and times ye need to do both.* Brogan had done a lot of praying these past few weeks. But always when he was alone in his room. Visiting the kirk was long overdue.

He stepped inside, for the first time since his wedding day. At this hour of the day, the space was empty but still lit well enough from the sun that he could make his way to the altar. He found a bit of flint and lit one tiny candle before kneeling to pray.

"How could I have been so wrong, Father?" he asked God as he hung his head and clasped his hands together. "Did I let her outer beauty sway me?" Aye, there was no denying that truth. He'd been so caught up in her auburn hair, her green eyes, and the luscious curves of her body, that he had not taken the time to look deeper.

"I ken ye have sent me here for a purpose, Father. I be doin' me best to help the people of this clan. I be doin' me best, as well, to help Mairghread give up the drink. But I fear failin' at either."

How long would it take before her people began to look at him as a leader? As someone they could trust? And how long would it take before Mairghread would look at him with anything but hate-filled eyes?

Four days ago, he had arrived here with a light heart filled with hope for his future. Foolishly, he had believed the Mactavish people would welcome him with open arms and accept him almost immediately. The people were beginning to come around. But his wife?

Day by day, his hopes of having that happy hearth and home, of bairns and a loving wife, were diminishing. Mayhap God did not want him to have those things. Mayhap, he was as cursed as he felt.

"If not *this*, God, then what? What is yer purpose fer me? What is it ye want from me?"

Silence filled the tiny kirk. Oh, what he would not give to speak to his father, John, right now. He would have just the right words to sooth his aching heart.

For a long while, he remained quiet and still, with the fervent hope that God would somehow answer him. The silence yawned and stretched over the kirk.

After some time, he began to think back to the time in his life when he too was so drunk he could not see straight. 'Twas indeed a dark and ugly time. Half of it, he could not remember. The other half he wished he couldn't.

He could remember with vivid clarity that moment in his life that made him want to put the drink down. Aye, his father had been after him for months to stop drinking. But Brogan had obstinately refused to listen. *Leave me the bloody hell alone!* He had shouted more times than he could count. But his father, who was even more stubborn and obstinate than Brogan, had refused to *leave him the bloody hell alone.*

But that had not been his turning point. His father's determination to pull his son out of the abyss of drunkenness had helped *after* he had made the decision. But it hadn't been his deciding factor.

It happened on a bright summer afternoon, when he was supposed to have been watching his seven-year-old nephew. Little Connor had been begging him for weeks to take him fishing. The boy's father — Brogan's older brother, Daniel — had been off in Inverness to buy supplies for their keep. After much begging and pleading from Connor, Brogan finally gave in and agreed.

He'd been half drunk when they left the keep to head to the loch. Never did he leave his room without a flagon or two of whisky. That day was no exception.

They sat on the bank of the loch, with little Connor chattering on about nearly every topic under the sun. Brogan did not even pretend to listen or feign interest. Nay, he was too busy drinking.

Hours passed by, with little Connor talking incessantly, and Brogan drinking. When he woke the next morn, on the bank of that loch, he was surrounded by his father, his mother, and a very angry sister-by-law, Connor's mother, Elsbeth.

His mind was still foggy, the whisky not quite out of his system, he looked up at them through bleary eyes. "What do ye want?" he asked, his tongue feeling thick and dry.

"Yer head on a pike fer a start," Elsbeth said.

He waved a dismissive hand toward her and rolled over to go back to sleep. He cared not he was sleeping on large pebbles, or that the water was lapping at his feet. "Leave me the bloody hell alone," he slurred.

A moment later, Elsbeth kicked him in the arse, then the gut. Blind fury welled up as he rolled over, holding his aching stomach with one hand, his other on the hilt of his dirk. "What the bloody hell was that fer?" he yelled as he stared up at the three people.

"Connor, come here please," John tossed over his shoulder as he continued to stare at Brogan with a murderous glower.

A few moments passed by before Connor came to stand next to his grandfather. He clung to John's leg for dear life, as he looked at Brogan with fearful eyes. One of which was black and blue and nearly swollen shut. There was also a cut along his bottom lip.

"What happened to him?" Brogan asked, looking his father in the eye for the first time in a very long while.

"*Ye* is what happened to him," John ground out through a clenched jaw.

"Me?" Brogan asked, unwilling to believe he had harmed the boy. "Yer daft."

"Leave us, now," John said. 'Twas the coldness in his tone that, if Brogan had been standing, would have sent him to his knees.

Elsbeth and Eleanor quickly lead Connor away, whispering words Brogan could not quite make out.

John waited until they were well away before he laid into his son. It had happened so quickly that Brogan, in his current state, had no time to respond or react. John had grabbed him by the front of his tunic, with big, meaty hands, and hauled him to his feet. "Ye can no' even remember!" he growled at him. "Ye beat that boy until he was black and blue and ye can no' even remember it!"

"Me?" Brogan tried to argue. "I would never hurt him! He is just a boy!"

Furious did not begin to describe John's current mood. His blue eyes turned so dark, they were nearly black. "Ye would no', would ye? Then why did that wee lad come screamin' into the keep last eve, covered in blood, terrified and cryin'? Why would he say *ye* — an uncle he loves and admires — beat him near senseless? Have ye another explanation?" He tried shaking the answer out of Brogan.

He tried searching his mind for some memory. Anything that would explain how the boy was injured. His stomach rolled and lurched when he realized Connor would not have lied about such a thing.

"I have begged ye and begged ye to put the drink down, to step away from it. But ye will no' listen to reason or my good counsel."

Brogan tried stammering out an apology. "I — I do no' ken what happened!"

'Twas then, in that moment, that his father could take no more.

'Twas the first beating his father had ever given him, and he was eight and twenty. Afterward — though the beating had very little to do with his actual decision — he vowed never to touch a drop of strong drink.

Although John was sickened by his son's actions, he did not shun him or turn him away. Instead, he helped. For two weeks, John never left his side, so determined was he to help his son get through what he called *the takeaways*. "Yer body is upset with ye, fer takin' away that one thing it believes it needs as much as air," he explained one afternoon. Brogan was naked, curled into a ball, shaking violently. "Ye have been givin' yer body excessive amounts of drink for a year now. It got used to it. This is what happens when ye take it away."

It was weeks before he felt right again. Even longer before he began to feel more like his old self; the man he was before he lost his wife. 'Twas one of the most difficult things he'd ever gone through. He was not sure yet if his wife could survive something similar. He could only pray that she would soon make the decision to give up the drink. If she didn't, he doubted she would live another year.

EARLIER THAT MORN, BROGAN HAD MOVED HIS THINGS — WHAT FEW there were of them — out of Mairghread's bedchamber. He took the room connected to hers. 'Twas a nicely appointed space, with a big bed that sat near the fireplace. Placed under the two fur-covered windows was a small table and chair he could use as a workspace.

'Twas long after the midnight hour as he lay in bed, wide-awake, staring up at the ceiling. It had been hours since last he'd seen Mairghread. He strained his ears to listen for any sounds coming from her room. But other than a few, occasional muffled sounds, she had remained quiet.

As much as he wanted to go to her, to check to see that she was all right, to see that she had eaten the meals sent to her room, he knew he couldn't. She had to come to him. If there was any hope of her ever giving up the drink, the decision had to be hers and hers alone. No one could make the choice for her.

In addition to his worries for his new bride, he worried over the fortification of the keep. On the morrow, he would rise, dress, and return to the quarry. He would spend the day digging into the earth, looking for stones. Stones that would eventually be used to build a wall. A much-needed wall to keep the inhabitants of the keep as well as the clan safe from invaders.

But he would take no enjoyment or satisfaction in his work. At least, not as he had done when he worked side by side with Ian for more than a year. Back then, he had not possessed a wife to come home to at the end of each day. Still, he had taken great pride in his work, because he was helping his brother.

Now, everything was different. He did have a wife, but not the one he had imagined. Not the kind of wife he would look forward to coming back to at the end of the day. Not a wife who would welcome him home with loving arms. Not a wife like Anna had been.

Anna. Just thinking of her now made his chest feel tight, constricted. Oh, the things they could have done, the life they could have built had she lived. He certainly would not be where he was today, this very moment, had she lived.

She had suffered for weeks with the wasting disease. The healer had warned him that it could take months upon months before she finally succumbed to the dreaded illness. In the end, it hadn't taken that long. Too long for her suffering, but a life cut too short.

"I promised ye, Anna, that I would marry again," he whispered into the darkness. "Now look at me. I am certainly no happier for it." He had married yet another woman who was dying. But her death was coming at her own hands, by her own choices and deeds. 'Twas not like the wasting disease Anna had died from. Nay, this slow, ugly death was being wrought because of drink.

HE WAS AWAKE BEFORE THE SUN. NOT BECAUSE HE WAS EAGER TO begin a new day, working in the quarry. Nay, the walls of Brogan's chamber seemed to grow smaller and tighter the longer the night wore on.

After dressing in the darkness, he quietly stepped to the door that connected his room to Mairghread's. He placed an ear to the door and listened. Not a sound could be heard coming from within.

Suddenly, he was overcome with the need to see that she was all right. Quietly, he opened the door and peered inside.

He found her, curled into a ball in the middle of her bed, fast asleep. Lying next to her on the bed was an empty bottle of wine. A quick glance at the table where he had placed all the bottles the day before told him she had drunk more than one. Two were now missing.

She was a vision of beauty, when she slept. Lying as she was now, still fully dressed, curled up with both hands under her cheek, no one would be able to tell what she was like when she drank.

With a slow shake of his head, he stepped back into his room, quietly closing the door behind him. He sent a silent prayer heavenward for patience.

For the remainder of the day, he worked in the quarry alongside the Mactavish men. Comnall, who was still upset with Neyll as well as Brogan, brooded for the better part of the day. Brogan, having enough problems of his own at the moment, did not truly care about his friend's sour disposition.

At the noonin' meal, Reginald came to him with designs for the new wall.

They stood under the canopy of hundred-year-old oak trees while Reginald explained what he had come up with.

"It is verra much like the auld wall," he said as he pointed to the parchment he had spread on the grass. "But this time, I think we could make it taller and add parapets not only on the four corners, but one higher, here, on the north side."

Brogan liked the idea. From that location and height, they would be able to see for miles in any direction. "'Tis a good plan, Reginald," he told him as he studied the plans closely. "What be this?" he asked, pointing to a spot near the suggested north parapet.

Reginald cleared his throat before answering. "I ken we've no' been attacked in many years, save for that night when we lost James and Conner. But..." his words trailed off.

"But?" Brogan asked, encouraging the man to speak his mind.

"Ye ken I do no' wish to speak against Aymer," Reginald said.

Brogan did his best not to roll his eyes or curse under his breath at the mention of Aymer's name. "Aye, I ken that. Yer loyalty is admirable, Reginald. None would ever say otherwise."

He let out a heavy breath and raked a hand through his brown and graying hair. "I think we should have a secret means of escape. A way out that only certain people are aware of." He cast a furtive glance at their surroundings, as if he were afraid someone might overhear their conversation.

Brogan ran a hand across his stubbled jaw. "Reginald, I believe that is the most intelligent thing I have heard anyone say in a verra long time." A secret passage, that only he and Reginald, and mayhap someday Mairghread, would know about.

Reginald grunted.

"I wish ye to make another set of plans, Reginald. One for the men to work from, and another that only ye and I shall ever lay eyes to."

"Verra well," he said as he rolled the parchment up.

"How exactly do ye plan on hidin' the door to the passage?" Brogan asked as he stood up and stretched his back.

"I saw one once, when I was a little boy. We were visiting me da's uncle, outside of Aberdeen. The hidden gate looked just like the rest of the wall and ye could no' tell it was there."

"Aye, I understand that," Brogan told him. "But how do ye open it?"

"I be gettin' to that part," Reginald groused. "Anyway, we found it by accident. Me cousins and I were playin' ye ken, like lads will do. One of me cousins was attempting to climb up the wall, like a spider. Of course, we told him it could no' be done." He smiled fondly at the memory. When Brogan cleared his throat impatiently, Reginald continued. "Well, he began to slip, and he grabbed one of the sconces to hang on to. At first, he thought he'd pulled it out of its brackets. But then, a part of the wall slid sideways. Just enough room for a grown man to get through, ye ken."

"Ingenious," Brogan said with a raised brow, eager to hear more.

"And?" he asked, growin' more and more impatient. "How did it work? How was it done?"

Reginald shrugged his shoulders. "I do no' ken. I was a lad of six at the time."

Brogan rolled his eyes and cursed inwardly. "So ye do no' ken how it actually worked?"

"Nay," he replied.

Brogan let loose a frustrated breath. Aye, 'twas a good idea, to have a hidden passage, a secret means of escape. But he had no earthly idea how to make it work.

Chapter Ten

lone in her room all the day long, Mairghread kept thinking on Brogan's words. Unable as well to get the vision of Gertie's black eye, the cut on her auld skin just below it, out of her mind.

Gertie.

Gertie was the one person the whole of her life who she could truly count on. When Mairghread was but ten years of age, her mother had died. Gertie had gladly stepped in to assume the role — even though she had taken it the day Mairghread had been born.

It had been Gertie who had given her 'the talk' every mum has with her daughter on the eve of her wedding. It had been Gertie who had seen her through childhood illnesses, had gotten her through the first months of morning sickness. It had been Gertie who held her hand while she had given birth to Conner.

It had been Gertie who nursed her back to health after the attack. Gertie was the one who had given her the bad news, had held her for hours while she wept and cried until she had no more tears left.

Always, always Gertie. No matter what horrible things she had done or said, Gertie never stopped loving her.

"And how do ye repay her?" Mairghread whispered her question into the dark night. She stood at her open window again, caring not that she was letting the rain in. It fell gently against the side of the keep, and softly against her skin. It chilled her, yet she cared not. Nor did she feel she had the energy necessary to move.

Numb. She was numb from head to toe.

How had her life been reduced to this? With so much sadness, regret and grief filling her heart there was no room for anything else.

The whisky was whispering to her again, begging her to take *just one drink. Just. One.*

What would James think of her now? God, how she hoped he could not see her. Would he be ashamed? Would he understand?

Would he hold her and tell her all would be well? Or would he walk away, with his head hung low, ashamed of the day he'd ever met her?

And what of her babe? 'Twas a physical ache to think of him, that sweet, innocent babe. Taken far too soon and in such a horrific manner. Thinking of him made her sick to her stomach, made her fingers tremble.

Last night, she had failed, had succumbed to the whisky's power, its ethereal voice speaking to her, begging her to take just a sip. She had wakened that morn with a heart filled with regret and humiliation.

She had told herself all the day long she could try again, for it was a new day. She could get through just this one day without drinking. Just one day.

And now, 'twas the middle of the night and her hands were beginning to shake with that all too familiar need to put the bottle to her mouth and drink.

Her thoughts turned to her father, someone she had not thought of in years. She was seven and ten when he died. Less than a month before she was to say her vows to James. *"I be so verra proud of ye lass,"* he had told her the day before his death. *"Ye and James will lead this clan well, lass. He be a good man, and ye're a finer woman."*

And just like that, he was dead the very next day. Fell from his horse, his skull cracked open on a rock, just as had happened to her brother Charles, five years prior. Why was her family cursed? To suffer as many deaths and tragedies as they had? Why?

She'd lost everyone she had ever loved. Both her parents and four brothers. Then her husband and babe. The people she loved more than anything in this world were all gone now.

Save for Gertie, Tilda and Reginald.

No matter how hard she tried to choke back the tears, they came. Streaming down her cheeks, blending with the rain. Her shoulders shook as she cried, her stomach tightened. And all the while, the whisky and wine called to her. Both of them now, just as they had done last night, together, in unison. Like ugly, discombobulated voices calling to her from a grave.

Drink me.

Below stairs were three people who had stuck by her through it all. Three people who loved her as if she were their very own child. No matter what she said or did, they did not stop loving her.

And in the room next to her, was a man she barely knew. A man she had wed days ago for no other reason than she did not want to marry the man her uncle had chosen for her. A complete stranger, no matter what the church might have to say about it. A man she barely knew. Brogan had sworn he would do whatever he could to help her give up the wine and whisky. But why? He did not know her, not like Gertie or Tilda or Reginald did.

Slowly, she slid to the floor with her cheek against the cold stone wall. For the past three years, she had felt all alone in this world. Without James, without her babe, she had no true reason to go on living.

Or so she had convinced herself. Or was it the wine or the whisky that had done it?

Those two *things* had been her constant companions, never far from her reach. Always there, no matter the time of day or night. Helping to ease the pain, the grief, the heartache.

People died.

Whisky would always be there for her. Once a bottle was drunk, there was always another to reach for.

But people? People went away. People died. People were murdered. People couldn't come back.

The lack of memory from that awful night tortured her to her very marrow. She remembered none of it that night, nor anything that happened prior. 'Twas all nothing more than a black void. All she could remember was waking up three days later, near death, with Gertie and Tilda hovering over her, with tear-filled eyes.

Everyone thought she drank to forget. To help ease her pain. That might have been the case in the beginning, but later on, when little bits of her memory started to return, the reasons she drank changed.

During her waking hours, when she was sober, she could remember nothing. But late at night, when she was well into her cups, in that place between passing out and falling asleep, little images had begun to appear. Nothing she could cling to. 'Twas like trying to hold the fog in your hands. You could see it, almost taste it, but the moment you pulled your hand into a fist, 'twas gone.

So she drank in hopes of remembering. Of remembering what truly happened in that room down the hall, the one boarded shut, the one no one was allowed to go into. The chamber that she had shared with James. The chamber where he and their babe had been murdered.

Had she truly done it? Sliced both of their throats with her dirk? The dirk James had given to her on their wedding day? The one with the beautifully carved hilt that she now kept hidden in the bottom of her cupboard?

"Though 'tis true I did no' see ye do it, Mairghread," her uncle told her when she was finally well enough to sit up. *"But I did find ye on the floor, cryin' like a banshee that ye had killed them. That ye had lost yer mind and in a fit of blind rage, that ye killed them both."*

He had promised to keep her secret. He had promised not to tell another living soul. But somehow, people had found out. How, she did not know, nor did she truly care. There were times when she heard them whispering behind her back. Long ago, those whispers had hurt just as bad as a fist to her face.

"Could I have done what they say?" she whispered against the cold, stone wall. "Why can I no' remember?" *Why can I no' remember?*

Pulling her knees to her chest, she wept quietly. Occasionally, she would wipe her face against the fabric of her gown. Though she clung to her knees for dear life, she could still feel the tremble in her hands. For a long time, she sat there, worried that if she let go she would come undone entirely.

Twice before, she had tried to give up the drink. Once, two years ago, for reasons she could no longer remember. An entire five days without a drop. But then something happened that sent her over the edge and back into the welcoming bottle.

Then last year, around the anniversary of James and Conner's deaths. Gertie had convinced her it was time to say goodbye and put those ever present bottles down. She'd made it a full seven days. But on the anniversary of their deaths, she could take no more and dived right back in.

Was it even worth trying again? To what end? What was there for her?

All she loved was gone.

All she had left were two auld women and a steward who looked upon her with pity-filled eyes, wanting the old Mairghread back. The Mairghread they were proud of. The girl they had loved and admired. The woman she had grown into that would have made her parents proud.

But that woman no longer existed, at least not as she had once been.

Her thoughts turned once again to her father and how proud he had been of her. *'Ye and James will lead the clan when I be gone. I will never worry over the two of ye. Ye will continue with our legacy, Mairghread and build one of yer own."*

A legacy.

She snorted derisively at the memory. "A legacy," she murmured into the still night. "What legacy? I have no one to leave it to."

When she closed her eyes, she saw her dear father's face, his rich, dark red hair and bright blue eyes. So clear was his image 'twas nearly frightening. He looked so very sad. Not disappointed, just utterly, truly sad. *"There still be time, Mairghread. Do no' let Aymer lead. He never understood what ye and I did."*

The sound of his voice stole her breath away. Her eyes flew open as her breast pounded against her chest. *He never understood what ye and I did.*

Her father's words played over and over again in her mind,

pounding loudly against her skull, drowning out the sound of the whisky's warm voice.

It all began to make sense. Like a rush of cold water from the falls.

"I be the last one," she said aloud. "I be the only one who can continue me father's dreams. I be the only one who can continue the legacy that was his."

Without a doubt, she knew then, what she must do.

ONCE AGAIN, BROGAN LAY IN HIS BED STARING UP AT THE CEILING. Although he was tired to his bones, sleep was elusive. His mind kept bouncing around from one thought to another. Of Mairghread, then Anna, the wall, his new home and its people. He also thought of his father, his stepmother, all of his brothers and sisters. He missed the Mackintosh keep. It seemed a lifetime ago since last he'd been there.

He'd travelled west with Ian to help him rebuild the McLaren keep, their sister-by-law's home. Though he had enjoyed the hard work and felt he had found his purpose in life, something was still missing.

'Twas not until he saw Mairghread for the first time, that he realized what that *something* was; a wife, children, and loving home.

This, this current state of dread and worry, this keep with its odd inhabitants, its lack of walls, none of it was what he had imagined for his future. And he most assuredly had not imagined a violent, mean-spirited wife with the tongue of a harpy and the soul of a banshee.

There had to exist within her something *more.* More than she was allowing him to see. Aye, he'd caught brief glimpses at their first and second meetings. Even earlier that day when she thought Gertie had fallen ill. Enough so that he believed she was truly a kind and gentle woman. Was that nothing more than a facade to ensnare him? To lead him to the altar?

Could he truly have been so naive? So desperate for wife, hearth and home, as she had accused him?

He rolled over and stared at the low burning embers in the hearth and thought on the matter. Nay, he finally concluded, he was neither naive nor desperate. Aye, he might have had his head turned by her auburn hair and emerald eyes. But there was something else about her. Something that called to him. Something he could not name or reason out.

He puffed out his cheeks and let his breath out in a rush of frustration. "God, I must believe ye brought me here for a reason," he whispered to the embers. "Was it to help Mairghread give up the drink? Or was it to watch her die? Am I here only to help her clan, to make it safe once again?"

Part of him wanted to grab her up and toss her into a small room somewhere hidden within the keep. Put her there while the alcohol worked its way out of her system. Until she could once again breathe and function without it.

But he knew 'twould do her no good. The moment he let her out, into the light of day, she would seek out that which she loved more than any living person. She would be drunk in a matter of hours.

Nay, he could not force sobriety on her. Forcing someone into sobriety would be the same as trying to force them into loving someone. 'Twas as impossible a feat as any there was.

Closing his eyes, he strained his ears to listen for an answer. He was met with nothing but the soft crackle of the fire and the gentle rap of rain against the outer walls of the keep.

"What is me reward in all of this? What does my hard work in the quarry even mean? Will I build a wall only to have Aymer order it torn down?" he scoffed at the notion. He knew he'd fight unto his own death before he allowed Aymer to do that. And just why he felt this pull, this need to protect these people? 'Twas certainly not because they all adored him. And it was certainly not to impress his wife. Nay, Mairghread could not care in the least about these people. She was far too gone now, to hope she could change.

Mayhap I should just pack me things, round up me men, and leave here. Go home, back to Mackintosh lands. Have me marriage to Mairghread set aside and forget these past few weeks had ever happened.

He knew he would not do any of those things. 'Twas not just his honor that held him back. He had made a promise to Mairghread and to God, a sennight ago. He could not break the oath he made to either of them. In doing so, he would let his Father down, as well as his blood father. A Mackintosh never went back on his word.

Not even when he was deceived and lied to.

"God, what do ye want from me?"

This time, his question did not go unanswered.

§▲

MAIRGHREAD.

He heard her open the door, felt her presence before he even saw her.

Rolling over, he sat up on one elbow and waited. She stood in the black doorway, the light of his hearth casting her in dark shades of gold. Still wearing the same dress from three days ago. He was unable to determine if she was drunk yet again. Patiently, he waited for her to say or do something.

"Brogan," she whispered his name, her voice trembling with dread and fear. At hearing the faint tremble, his heart begged his legs to get up and go to her, to take her into his arms and sooth away the tears he watched fall down her cheeks. But his mind knew better. She must come to him.

"Mairghread," he said, nearly choking on the name.

He took note that she was clinging to the door with one hand as if she were afraid to take that all-important step forward. The woman was proverbially stuck. But was she here to curse at him again? Or to ask for his help?

For a long while, she stood there, trembling, shaking, uncertain. Brogan too, remained where he was.

"Did ye speak the truth?" she asked him, breaking the long length of silence.

Confused, he asked, "When?"

She swallowed hard, took in a deep breath and finally let go of the door. He watched as she swayed ever so slightly before she spoke. "When ye said ye wished to be me friend. When ye said ye wanted to help me."

"Aye," he replied softly. "I spoke the truth."

She swayed again, for a brief moment before falling to her knees. "Please, then, help me," she cried.

HE WAS OUT OF THE BED AND SCOOPING HER INTO HIS ARMS IN THE span of a few heartbeats. She wept without restraint against his bare chest. "I can no' do it on me own," she cried. "I do no' want to hurt anyone else."

"Wheest, now lass," he whispered soothingly against the top of her head. She reeked of stale wine and vomit, but he could smell no wine or whisky on her breath.

Gently, he sat her on the edge of his bed, but she clung to his shoulders, unable or unwilling to let go. "I do no' want to hurt anyone else," she repeated. "The whisky, the wine, they call to me, beggin' me to drink them. I swear I hear them, Brogan. Please, make them stop!"

Crouching before her, he gently pulled her hair away from her face. Her porcelain skin was blotchy from crying. Her eyes were glassy and red, and filled with so much fear it made his chest feel tight. "Wheest, lass, I am here."

"I tried, I did, Brogan," she told him. The words came out in a rush, so fast he could barely make them out. "I can no' go three days without it. I've no' had a drop since last night, and I swear, I feel as though I want to die." She fell against him, into his arms, once again. He pulled her down to the floor, where they sat by the fire.

The more she cried and begged for his help, the more constricted his chest felt. Her pain, the anguish, 'twas all almost more than one man could bear. But bear it he would.

Gone was the harpy with the sharp tongue. In his arms was a woman in need. A woman who had gone through more in the past few years of her life than many would in an entire lifetime. Her losses were significant and she'd born many of them with aplomb and grace, if what Gertie and Tilda said was true.

But when she lost her husband and babe? The only way to bear the loss was with the aid of strong drink.

"Wheest, now, lass," he whispered against her cheek.

He kept his arms wrapped around her, smoothing away the ache as best he could, with tender caresses and sweet, whispered words. After a long while, the tears began to wane, and she began to hiccup, much like a babe might.

"Mairghread, I need to ken that ye truly, with all that ye are, want to give up the drink," he said. His voice was but a whisper, barely audible over the crackle of the fire.

She pulled away to look him in the eyes. "Aye, I truly do," she said as she wiped her wet cheeks with the backs of her hands. "I do no' wish to hurt anyone ever again."

'Twas a good reason, but it could not be the only one. "And?" he asked, encouraging her to speak freely.

Mairghread's brow furrowed. "Is that no' enough? I have behaved horribly to everyone left who cares about me. I wish no' to hurt them anymore."

"I be glad to hear that," he told her as he caressed her cheeks with the pads of his thumbs. "If I am to help ye, I must ken why it is ye drink and why it is ye wish to stop."

She swallowed hard, searching his eyes for what he could only assume was any hint of dishonesty on his part.

"Do ye drink to help ease the pain of losin' yer husband and son?" he asked.

Mairghread gave a slow shake of her head. "Nay," she said. "That was why I started drinkin', but no' why I continued."

"Do ye drink to ferget?" he asked.

She took in a deep, cleansing breath and let it out slowly. "Nay, Brogan. I drink to remember."

From Brogan's furrowed brow and perplexed expression, he did not quite understand what she meant.

It took several deep breaths before she could explain. "I can no' remember anything of that night, or even the day. No matter how hard I try, 'tis naught but a piece of blackness in my memory. But sometimes, when I be well into me cups, I think I see blurry images. Little pieces that I can no' quite make out. 'Tis like bein' in a foggy dream, where ye see somethin', somethin' ye swear ye could touch if ye could just reach a bit further with yer fingers. But no matter how fast ye run to get to it, it keeps movin' away."

Brogan did not need much time to consider what she was saying. "I think, were I in yer shoes, I would have done the same thing. It must be maddenin', to not be able to remember." He rubbed a palm against his stubbled jaw and was quiet for a time. "Lass, what will it do to ye if ye can never remember that night?"

She had lived without any clear or concise memory for such a long while now. But she had never stopped to ask herself that *what if* question. Tears pooled in her eyes again, but she remained mute, afraid to answer that question either to herself or to him.

Brogan touched the tip of her chin with his index finger. "Lass, if I am to help ye, ye must always be honest with me. Even if ye think yer answer will distress me."

A slight shake of her head expressed her true disbelief in his promise. She was not foolish enough to believe she could speak her mind, freely or openly.

"Lass, I imagine it be difficult fer ye to believe me, fer we are, in a sense, strangers. I promise that I will always be honest with ye, no matter the time or circumstance. I ken no' any other way to be."

She searched the depths of his bright green eyes for any hint of disingenuousness. Bright green, with little flecks of black stared back at her. They reminded her of a glen after the rain, when the grass was at its brightest, the trees and rocks nearly black. For reasons she could not begin to fathom, she felt at peace. A calmness settled in around her. 'Twas something she had not felt in many a year and it frightened her. How was it possible to find that sense of peace and calm that had eluded her for three years in the eyes of a man she barely knew?

"If ye will treat me with the same respect, Mairghread, I ken I can help ye."

Mayhap she had been so deep in the bottle for such a long time that she was willing to listen to anyone who could help her. Or, mayhap, God had truly put Brogan in her life to help her. Either way, she was willing to listen.

Swallowing hard again, to fight back tears and keep the threatening bile down, she said, "I no longer wish to die."

❦

THOSE WERE THE WORDS HE NEEDED TO HEAR. "IF YE TRULY WISH to live, then aye, I can help ye. But ye must be willin' to put up the good fight."

Scrunching her brow, she said, "The good fight? I thought I was supposed to give up fightin' against the world."

Brogan chuckled at her sincerity. "Aye, ye can keep fightin' the world, when ye need to. But now, ye must learn to fight the drink."

"I admit I be afraid, Brogan."

"I ken, lass. I warn ye, 'twill no' be an easy road ahead of ye."

Too weak, tired and ashamed, she could not lie to his face and tell him she was fully prepared for such a fight. The thought frightened her to her marrow.

"I will be with ye every step of the way," he told her. "I will no' leave ye, lass."

Looking into his eyes, she found that sense of peace and comfort once again. And she believed in Brogan's Promise.

❦

BROGAN LEFT HER ALONE IN HIS BEDCHAMBER ONLY LONG ENOUGH to wake Reginald. His room was down the hall from Gertie and Tilda. Brogan decided to allow the auld women to sleep. Chances were good that he would need them more as the days went on.

Bleary eyed, Reginald opened the door to his chamber. As soon as he saw Brogan standing in the dimly lit corridor, his expression changed immediately to concern. "What be the matter?" he asked.

"All is well," Brogan replied. "Mairghread has come to me. She wants to give up the drink."

The man's shoulders sagged with relief as he let out the breath he'd been holding. "What can I do to help?" he asked as he let Brogan into the room.

Brogan explained what he would need. "A small room. One where the rest of the keep can no' hear her."

Reginald lifted one brow. "Why would ye need to keep her away from others?" he asked dubiously.

"'Tis fer her own good," Brogan replied. "The next few days will no' be easy fer her. I want to keep the waggin' tongues from causin' her any undo harm. They will no' understand what is happenin', but it will no' keep them from talkin' about it."

Reginald nodded his approval. "Lord kens there be enough gossips about the place as it is," he said as he ran a hand through his hair. "I would do nothin' to bring our lady any distress."

"I fear the next several days will be nothin' but difficult for Mairghread. I need yer help, Reginald."

"Anythin' at all, Brogan, ye ken that," he said as he pulled a tunic from the end of his bed and began to dress.

Brogan knew the man meant well. However, he was uncertain he understood the seriousness of what was being asked of him. "Have ye ever helped someone give up the drink before?"

Reginald paused in pushing his foot through the leg of his trews. "Nay," he said, sounding offended by the question. "But there is naught I would not do fer our lady."

"I do no' doubt yer sincerity," Brogan told him. "But these next few days will be difficult enough to test even the strongest man's mettle."

Angrily, Reginald continued to dress. Grim lines formed around his mouth and Brogan knew the man was biting his tongue.

"Reginald, I can no' do this alone. I do no' doubt yer love fer Mairghread. But there will be times over these next days where ye might be tempted to give in to her, only to ease her pain and sufferin'. And believe me, she will be in a good deal of pain."

"Good lord!" Reginald exclaimed. "What do ye plan on doin' to her? I'll no' allow ye to hurt her."

Brogan held up his palms and shook his head. "I will no' be doin' anything but takin' the drink from her, Reginald. When a body has drunk as often and as long as Mairghread, the takeaways can be horrific."

"The takeaways?" he asked perplexedly.

"Aye," Brogan said. "'Tis a phrase me father coined, to describe what happens to a person when ye take the drink away. They will cry, shake, lash out, and cry again. The tremors are enough to bring down a stone wall. She might vomit, more than once. She will become a person ye do no' recognize. But I swear to ye, those takeaways will no' last. 'Tis just her body demanding to have what it wants. And what it wants is the strong drink."

"But that be what is killin' her slowly," Reginald replied.

"Aye. But there will be a time or two where she will swear she be dyin'. But I can assure ye, she is no'."

Reginald thought on it for some time. "I will do what I must, in order to help her."

Brogan could only pray the man would be able to hold fast and keep his word.

Chapter Eleven

On the northeastern side of the keep, a room was prepared for Mairghread. 'Twas a small space carved out of the attics on the fourth floor, with low ceilings, arrow slits, and only one small window that faced the ocean.

Reginald procured a small bed and set it up on the wall nearest the door. A brazier was brought in and placed in the center of the room. A few other essentials, such as a chamber pot, a short stool, as well as linens, and the space was complete. Before the rest of the keep had begun to stir to start their day, Brogan took Mairghread to her new, but temporary chamber.

With her hand in his, he led her into the room. Confusion and trepidation flashed behind her eyes.

"Do no' fash yerself," Brogan said with an encouraging smile. "'Tis only temporary."

She ran a hand across the edge of the bed. "What happens here?" she asked with a slight tremor in her voice. "Why are ye lockin' me away?"

Brogan placed gentle hands on her shoulders. "We have ye here fer yer safety. These next few days will be tryin' times, Mairghread. The takeaways will be difficult. Yer body must get used to no' having whisky or other strong drink."

Although he was using his most sincere smile and warmest voice, it did not have the affect he desired. Her fear was as palpable as the rain falling against the keep.

"I shall remain by yer side through it all, lass. I will no' leave ye."

At the moment she didn't know which frightened her more; him never leaving or being completely alone.

"I shall be with ye as well, m'lady," Reginald promised her. "As will Gertie and Tilda. Remember, always, that we are here because of our fondness fer ye. We want only fer ye to get better."

Mairghread smiled amiably as she took his hands in hers. "I thank ye, Reginald."

His eyes began to grow misty. He made an excuse about needing to tend to something below stairs. "But I shall return to ye soon, I promise." Moments later, he quit the room, leaving Mairghread alone with Brogan.

"I fear I do no' ken what to do now," she laughed nervously.

"'Tis naught but a game of patience, now," Brogan replied.

Mairghread began to wander about the room, though in truth, there was nothing much to see. Brogan lit a fire in the brazier then pulled up the stool to sit near it. He remained quiet, she supposed, for her benefit and peace of mind.

She had not taken so much as a small sip of wine for two days. Her hands trembled and her stomach began to roil. Unfastening the bits of leather that kept the fur in place over the window, she tossed it aside to let in much needed fresh air.

From the high vantage point, she could see the ocean waves rolling in, spraying salty sea air as they crashed against the craggy cliffs. The rain had ceased, but the sky was still a dull, ugly gray. A few white seagulls flew overhead. Mairghread watched as they dove into the water to catch a meal.

"When I was a little girl," she began in a soft voice, "we used to fish on the little beach down below." Oh, how her life had changed over the years. She had been a carefree child once. Always ready for an adventure, afraid of nothing, willing to try anything at least once. Much to her mother's dismay, her three older brothers had always encouraged her search for excitement.

"My brother, Walter, drowned in that ocean." Wistful and sorrowful, she stared at the ocean for the longest while. "We never found his body. He was only eight years old when we lost him."

§❧

BROGAN HAD BEEN LISTENING INTENTLY FROM HIS SPOT BY THE brazier. He too, had lost a brother at a young age. He had been nine years old when they lost Harry — all of seven — to the ague. The loss had been nearly unbearable for their father, for he'd already lost their mother.

"We lost our brother, Harry, to the ague," he told her. "There be no' a day that goes by when I do no' think of him. And that was more than twenty years ago." Standing to his full height, he tried to catch a glimpse of the ocean beyond where she stood. "I can no' imagine the pain ye must have suffered at losin' him as ye did."

"I think his death put me mum in her grave, fer she died less than a year later," she told him, never once taking her eyes off the ocean. A deep sense of melancholy fell over her, weighing down her shoulders.

"I lost me mum when I was five," he told her. "I do no' remember much of her. Me da always told me she was a good woman. Quiet," he said with a chuckle. "Which is the exact opposite of his current wife, Elsbeth(?)"

Finally, she tore her eyes away from the window and began to wander around the room again. With her arms wrapped tightly around her stomach, she asked, "How many times has yer da been married?"

"Four," Brogan replied. "Betwixt all of them, he had eleven children. Eight still live."

With her index finger, Mairghread began to trace the outline of the stones in the wall. "And grandchildren?"

Brogan chuckled. "Too many to count," he replied. "But last I heard, there were seventeen."

She turned to face him. "And ye? Do ye have children?"

Why her question pulled at his heart the way it did, he was not entirely certain. "Me wife, Anna, died before she got with child."

"I be terribly sorry, Brogan," she replied with a deep frown.

They were silent for a long while. Mairghread was the first to look away. "Do ye want more children?" she asked, feigning disinterest in his answer.

"Aye, I do," he said.

"And if I am unable to give ye any?"

He answered as honestly as he could. "I want children. Preferably with ye, Mairghread. But if we can no' conceive them together, I am no' against adopting."

She spun around to face him, her face contorted, twisted in confusion. "Ye would do that?"

"Aye," he said. "I would. There be many poor children in this world in need of a good home."

"But they would no' be yers by blood," she pointed out the obvious.

Brogan smiled warmly. "Does blood matter when a child is in need? I would love them just the same."

She twisted her lip for a moment, pondering his answer. "Ye are an odd man, Brogan Mackintosh."

Chuckling, he said, "Aye, so I have been told."

❧

FOR THE NEXT HOUR OR SO, THEY SPOKE OF MANY THINGS. NONE OF them of any importance. Brogan found that when she was talking, she was not thinking about the tremor in her hands or the stomach he knew must be twisting in knots.

"How do ye ken so much about these *takeaways* ye mentioned?" she asked as she plopped down on the edge of the bed.

"Because I have suffered through them."

As her eyes flew open, she exclaimed, "Ye jest!"

His lips curved into a warm smile. "Nay, lass, I do no' jest."

She gave her head a good shake in disbelief. "Ye? The honorable and pious Brogan Mackintosh?"

He doubted she meant it as an insult. "Aye, me. The honorable and pious Brogan Mackintosh," he replied with a wide wave of his hands and a bow.

"Do tell," she challenged as she rested an elbow on her knee, her chin planted against her fisted hand. Settling in as if she were awaiting a bard's tale, she eagerly awaited for more.

"'Tis a simple tale, truly," he began as he retook his seat. "Within an hour of losing me Anna, I picked up the nearest bottle of wine. When that was done and did not give me the calm I desired, I picked up a bottle of whisky. I did no' stop drinking for a year after."

Puzzled, she said, "Ye truly do no' jest."

He gave her a shrug of his shoulders, as if to say she could believe him or not, it didn't matter.

"That is why ye drink the bairn cider," she said as clarity began to dawn.

"Aye, lass, that be why."

Suddenly, she became aware of the totality of her current situation. "Will I never be able to have a glass of wine again?" she asked, appalled at the notion.

"Nay, lass, ye will no'."

His matter-of-fact attitude brought her to her feet. "But I do no' like cider!" she exclaimed.

He bit his cheek to keep from laughing aloud. "Then drink milk," he told her. "Or a tisane."

Mairghread began to pace about the room. "I like milk as much as I like cider," she declared.

Brogan could see she was beginning to fade rapidly into the first stages of the *takeaways*. Unwilling to distress her further, he stayed rooted on the stool and watched.

"Cider! Milk!" she scoffed. As she paced about the room, she twisted the hem of one sleeve betwixt her fingers. "I am no' a bairn," she told him. "I do no' see why I can no' have at least one glass of wine with me meals."

"Because one will always lead to two. Which in turn will lead to another and another, until ye are once again quite drunk. It defeats the purpose of what we be doin' here."

A low growl built deep in her belly. "Why does me skin itch?" she demanded, but did not wait for his answer. "It feels like I have been rollin' around in itch weed."

"I do no' ken why," he told her. "All I ken is that when ye take the drink away, it does odd things to yer body as well as yer mind. 'Tis as if the drink be fightin' ye from within, tellin' yer body ye need it to live."

"How long do these takeaways last?" she asked, growing more exasperated with each passing moment.

Brogan stood up and began to brace himself for the tirade he was certain was building up within her. "Lass, do ye remember that I told ye I would always be honest with ye?"

"Yes!" she exclaimed. Pacing frenetically around the room, she did not stop to answer.

"The takeaways can last as much as a fortnight."

She waved a dismissive hand and continued her tour around the room. "A fortnight?" she said disdainfully. "Bah! I swear ye only tell me things to see my distress!"

He knew there would be many moments like this, where she would be calm one moment, only to scream and rail the next. He chose his words very carefully. "Remember why we be here, Mairghread."

She came to an abrupt halt and glowered at him. Though she remained quiet, he was almost certain she was wishing for his immediate and painful death.

"Do ye think ye could stand to eat a bit?" he asked with a measured tone.

"Nay," she told him. "But I would certainly love a sip of wine right now."

He knew she was both serious and jesting at once, for he caught a glimmer of something playful in her green eyes. "Would ye settle for a bit of broth and bread?"

"Be I a prisoner now, only to be served meals fit for criminals?" she asked.

He let loose the chuckle he had been holding back. "Fer the time bein'. But I have it in good with the gaoler. There be a chance yer sentence can be reduced fer good behavior."

Another roll of her eyes, and she turned away from him. "Ye be a daft man, Brogan Mackintosh."

"So I have been told."

꩜

GERTIE AND TILDA CAME TO SEE HER AS SOON AS REGINALD TOLD them what had happened. They came rushing into the room, all a twitter, and worried sick over their lady. "Why did ye no' come to get us?" Gertie demanded of Brogan. She did not wait for his reply. Instead, she went immediately to Mairghread, who was once again at the window. Wrapping her auld arms around the young woman, she said, "Och, lass! How do ye fare? What do ye need?"

Mairghread smiled and shook her head. "I am well," she said. "As fer no' coming to fetch ye, I told Brogan to allow ye both to rest."

"Rest?" Gertie scoffed at the notion. "I be no' some decrepit auld woman. I work as hard as any of the young ones ye have workin' in this keep!"

Mairghread calmed her by giving her a warm embrace. "Wheest, now, Gertie! Ye'll work yerself into an apoplexy."

Gertie pushed away, appalled with her lady. "Ye be no' too old fer me to pull yer ears, lassie!"

A delightful laugh filled the room. The sound of it warmed Brogan's heart.

"Tilda would no' allow ye to do that," Mairghread replied mischievously. "She has always loved me more than ye did."

Tears pooled in Gertie's blue eyes. They were not tears of sorrow nor insult, but of sheer, unadulterated joy. "Lord, it be good to hear ye jest like this," she said.

Mairghread quirked a brow playfully. "Who says I be jestin'? 'Tis only the truth I speak. Not once in all her years did Tilda ever pull me ears, or paddle me bottom. I say 'tis because she loves me more."

She went to Tilda then, and pulled her into a warm hug. "'Tis true, is it no'?" she whispered.

When Tilda closed her eyes, an errant tear made its way down her cheek. "Aye, lass, it be true. No matter what Gertie says."

Brogan was enjoying this tender moment between the women. His curiosity, however, was piqued. "What, pray tell, could this lovely lass have done to earn a pulled ear or a paddled bottom?"

"Och!" Gertie exclaimed. She clucked her tongue and shook her head in dismay. "She was forever disobedient! Always sneakin' off with her brothers when she was supposed to be learnin' how to be a lady."

"Because me brothers enticed me," Mairghread said. "Catching toads, battling pretend enemies or trying to catch fairies was far more fun than learning to sew or how to sit with me back ramrod straight. Who could blame me?"

❧

WHILE GERTIE AND TILDA STAYED WITH MAIRGHREAD, BROGAN left long enough to acquire broth and bread. Thankfully, the kitchen staff did not make any inquiries as to why he wanted such a simple meal.

When he returned, the women were sitting on the bed, with Mairghread in the middle. She was crying and Gertie and Tilda were doing their best to console her.

"What happened?" he asked, setting the tray on the floor.

Tilda wiped away a tear. "She be missin' her mum, m'laird."

He remained quiet, allowing the women to tend to her. Once her tears settled, he offered up the meager meal. "Ye will need to keep up yer strength."

Without argument, she sat back in the bed and tried to eat. After managing a few bites of bread and broth, she declared she could eat no more.

"I think I would like to rest now," she told them.

Gertie and Tilda fussed over her, tucking her into the bed as they had done when she was younger. She was far too tired to argue and was asleep before they bid Brogan goodbye.

❧

MAIRGHREAD'S MOODS BEGAN TO EBB AND FLOW RAPIDLY AS THE

morning wore on. One minute she was as calm as could be, the next, she would begin the frantic pacing.

"I swear me skin be on fire!" She cursed aloud and loosened the ties on her gown. "Lord, do ye have to keep it so hot in here?" Standing at the window, she fanned her face with her fingers.

"Mayhap, when ye're better, ye could show me where ye used to fish," Brogan suggested.

She let loose a long, heavy breath. "I wish I could jump in the ocean right now," she said.

"I imagine it would be right warm this time of year," Brogan jested.

Mairghread chose to ignore him. "I do no' feel well," she finally admitted. "I feel like I swallowed a bucket of eels."

The image made his own stomach churn. "I could ask the healer for something to help settle it," he offered.

"Bah!" she scoffed. "I will have to assume by your statement that ye have no' yet met our fine healer." Wrapping her arms around her waist, she shivered. "She believes sufferin' is God's punishment for misdeeds and sins."

He thought that a rather odd way of thinking for a healer and told her so.

"She is an auld biddy. Prone to gossip and rumors. I'd rather no' ask her fer anythin'."

Uncertain if she was serious or exaggerating due to her current state of ill health, he remained silent. To keep busy, he put the tray in the hallway. His men would be taking shifts in guarding the door, per the request he made earlier.

"Besides, we would have to walk a mile or so before we could get to a place safe enough to climb down, the walk back again, over rough terrain, just to get to the beach."

"Is that how ye did it as a child?" he asked.

With a shake of her head, she said, "Nay. There be steps, right over there," she said as she pointed out the window. "No' far from here. But when Uncle ordered the removal of the wall, he had the men throw the stones over that ledge. They now block the stairs my great-great-great grandfather had carved into the side of the cliff."

Brogan took note of the sorrow in her tone. *So she was aware of the destruction of the wall.* Mayhap she did not love her uncle as much as she wanted everyone to believe. Mayhap, she only loved him because he was all the family she had left in the world.

"Lord! James was so angry when he found out!" That memory made her shiver. "We had gone to Edinburgh fer a honeymoon of sorts. When we returned three months later, the wall had been torn down. Och! James was fit to be tied."

"I take it James did no' agree with yer uncle on this?" Brogan asked for clarification sake.

"Of course not!" she decried. "James was livid. He and uncle fought for weeks over it. James ordered the wall rebuilt. He had the men rig up a system so they could bring those ancient stones back up."

Brogan knew next to nothing about her first husband. But he was beginning to sound like an intelligent man.

"The process was taking forever," Mairghread said. "James was no' happy. But it made sense to retrieve as many of the stones as they could, instead of quarrying for new."

Brogan humphed and nodded his agreement. *I wish I had been so lucky.* "Has anyone told ye that I have ordered the wall rebuilt?"

She turned to face him, with a most quizzical expression. "Ye have?"

"Aye," he told her. "We began to quarry a few days ago. Reginald helped me locate a spot about a mile from here."

"I have been wantin' to do that for more than three years," she told him with a relieved smile. "I thank ye."

He supposed her gratitude should not mean as much to him as it did, but he found he was grateful for it. "'Twas the right thing to do."

"Still, I am thankful to ye," she replied, her smile fading as was the color of her skin. "Brogan, I do no' feel well," she said as she reached out to keep from keeling over.

In two quick strides, he was there, catching her before she fell. With gentle care, he helped her to the bed. "Take in deep breaths," he encouraged her. "'Twill pass soon."

"I feel awfully cold now," she told him as she began to shake. "Please, pull the fur."

He did as she asked, before pulling a blanket around her shoulders.

The shaking continued to get worse and soon, her teeth were chattering.

"I really do no' feel well," she told him again.

Wrapping his arms around her, he held her close. Soon, she was shaking violently, her teeth chattering, and her skin growing paler. "Wheest, now, lass," he whispered. "Try to take in slow breaths."

He was simply doing what his father had done for him. Offering words of encouragement and whatever comfort he could. But seeing her in such distress made his stomach seize.

When she continued to get worse, he began to worry. For the life of him, he could not remember how long he himself had gone through this particular stage of takeaways.

Not wishing to leave her alone to gather more blankets, he continued to hold her as closely as he could. Rubbing her arms and back through the blanket, he hoped it would help warm her and soothe her at the same time.

"I am goin' to be ill," she said through chattering teeth.

Quickly, he grabbed the chamber pot and held it while she threw up the bread and broth from earlier. When he realized he had not thought to get a pitcher of water and washing cloths, he could have kicked himself.

Once she finished, he removed his tunic and gave it to her. Sweat covered her face and neck. The tremors began to subside, but not enough.

"I hate throwin' up," she told him as she wiped her face on his tunic. "I would rather ye stripped me naked, took me to the courtyard and beat the bloody hell out of me."

He was growing to like her sense of humor and could not hold back his laughter. "I feel much the same way," he said.

BEFORE NIGHTFALL, SHE HAD THROWN UP THREE MORE TIMES, AND was now suffering with dry heaves. One minute she was hot, the next, shivering violently.

Gertie and Tilda had come to see her again after the noonin' and evenin' meals. Brogan watched as their hearts broke before his eyes. They felt helpless and were beginning to wane in their trust of him.

Gertie pulled him aside for a moment, and with much seriousness, asked, "Are ye sure ye can no' give her just a wee sip? To help her no' shake so?"

He knew she meant well, that her question came from her heart. "Gertie, I ken ye have never watched someone go through such a thing. I wish I could take all her sufferin' away. But if we give her so much as a drop of wine, we will have to start all over again."

Gertie glanced at the object of her distress. She was lying with her head in Tilda's lap. "I hate to see her suffer so."

"I ken ye love her. No one will ever be able to say otherwise. I ken I be a stranger to all of ye. I be askin' much of ye to put yer faith in me."

She scrutinized him for a long moment. "I do no' ken why, m'laird, but aye, I do have faith in ye."

"Ye must also have faith in Mairghread," he told her.

Gertie drew in her bottom lip and turned her attention back to Mairghread. "She tried, twice before, to give it up. But she simply could no' do it. But I do no' remember her bein' this ill then."

"Be it possible she did no' give it up entirely?" he asked.

"Aye, that be possible," Gertie admitted honestly. "All I ken was she was no' fallin' down drunk back then."

They both looked at Mairghread. For now, she was resting peacefully, but Brogan knew 'twould be short-lived. If his own experience was anything to measure by, the worst was yet to come.

AND THE WORST DID COME.

'Twas long after the midnight hour. Henry had come to the door with a tray of warm broth and bread. Although Brogan was quite certain she would not be able to keep it down, she did need to try at least to keep up her strength. "How fares she?" he whispered from the dark corridor.

"Resting," Brogan answered. "But fitfully." He took the tray and thanked him. "How did it go in the quarry this day?"

Henry scratched the back of his head and yawned. "One of the Mactavish men broke three fingers. He had been chipping away at a stubborn piece of rock when it finally gave way. Smashed his fingers. The healer be wantin' to cut them off, but his wife refused. So we have to wait and see."

"Good, God! How bad did he smash them?"

"Near as I can tell, 'tweren't too bad. But that healer, she says they must be cut off before gangrene sets in. I never kent a man to get gangrene from a broken finger."

"Neither have I," Brogan replied. "I've seen many a broken finger in me time and never has a healer suggested amputation." To his way of thinking 'twasn't treatment she was suggested, but mutilation.

"Me and Charles will be standin' guard here in the hallway. Just give a shout if ye need anythin'."

He thanked him once again and quietly closed the door.

Mairghread stirred and opened her eyes. "Who be here?" she asked groggily.

"Just Henry. He brought ye more warm broth and bread."

The thought of eating was displeasing to her. She scrunched her face and waved the tray away. "Nay, please. I do no' wish to think of food."

Once again, she was breaking into another sweat. Tossing the covers aside, she asked him to please remove the fur to let in fresh air.

He imagined this cycle of hot and cold would run its course in a few days. Dutifully, he set the tray on the edge of the bed and went to the window. "'Tis a chilly night," he remarked over his shoulder as he drew the fur away. "But at least the rain has stopped. Ye can see the moon this night."

From behind him, he heard the crash of the tray. He spun around to see Mairghread scurrying up the bed, pressing herself against the wall as if she were going to climb up it. "Get them away!" she screamed. "Get them away!"

"Mairghread!" he called out her name as he tried to pull her down from the wall. "Mairghread, what be the matter?"

"Can ye no see them? My God! There be worms in the soup!"

He followed her line of vision, but saw no worms. "I see nothin', lass," he told her. "Come down now, let me help ye."

She shook her head violently as she stared at the foot of the bed. Sheer horror was painted on her face and he saw it, deep in her eyes. "Nay! Get them out! Please!"

"But Mairghread, there be nothin' there, lass," he tried pleading with her, but to no avail.

Screaming with such terror that it made his heart pound in his chest. Believing worms were now climbing up her dress, she started to frantically wipe them away. "Nay! Nay! Nay!" she shouted over and over again. Begging and pleading with him to remove the worms that only she could see. "They be on me! Get them off me!"

Henry and Charles came rushing into the room, wide-eyed and uncertain. Brogan explained what was happening as best and as quickly as he could. Then he did the only thing he could think of. "It be all right, lass," he told her as he began to scoop away the imaginary worms. "See? Henry and I be gettin' rid of them. Ye see, lass?"

Immediately, Henry picked up on what Brogan was trying to do. "Aye, m'lady," he said as he too pretended to scoop up the worms. He offered her his most sincere smile, though he wasn't even certain she saw him. "We will get them all out fer ye in no time."

"Grab a bucket," Brogan told Charles who had been standing by the door, looking lost and perplexed. He actually looked about the room for the bucket. Smacking his hand to his forehead, he rolled his eyes at his own ignorance. "I have the bucket," he told Brogan as he handed him the invisible, nonexistent bucket.

It took them nearly a quarter of an hour to convince her they had in fact gotten every last worm. Charles even went so far as to dump the bucket out the window on three separate occasions. All the while, Mairghread cried and pleaded and pointed out the worms they had missed.

Once she was finally convinced all of the worms had been removed, she slid down the wall into a heap of tears and sobs. Brogan knelt on the bed beside her, holding her close to his chest while she wept. He whispered soothing words against her hair and caressed her back.

"Please, Charles, fetch me warm water and more washing cloths," Brogan directed in low, hushed tones.

The young man looked positively relieved for the chance to leave the room.

Henry remained behind, looking harried and confused. Looking at Brogan, he raised a brow as if to ask *what just happened.* Brogan had no answer.

Try as he might, he could not remember suffering with hallucinations during his bouts of the takeaways. Never in his life did he miss his father as much as he did right now.

With little else to do, Henry began to clean up the tray that had crashed to the floor earlier. All the while, he shook his head, unable to put into words what he was thinking. He set the tray in the hallway and returned to offer Brogan moral support, for there was naught else he could do.

Charles soon returned with water and fresh linens. Henry grabbed the little stool and placed it next to Brogan. Charles set the basin on the stool, dipped a cloth in, and rung it out before handing it off to Brogan.

As carefully as a mum tending a child, Brogan wiped away Mairghread's tears. "Wheest, now, lass," he consoled. "All be well now, aye?"

She sniffed and gave a slight nod, but otherwise remained silent. Trembling in his arms, she clung to him.

"I think it be safe fer ye to leave us now," Brogan told his men.

Neither of them dawdled a moment longer than necessary. Once the door closed behind them, Brogan returned to his ministrations. Rubbing his hands against her back, her arms, he whispered repeatedly that all was well.

Mairghread hiccuped once, then again. "There were no worms, were there?" she asked him, sounding ashamed and humiliated.

"Nay, lass, there were no worms."

&.

THE REMAINDER OF THE NIGHT WAS NO BETTER. BETWEEN BOUTS OF shivering cold and sweating profusely, she suffered with dry heaves. Often confused, there were several times she forgot where she was and worse yet, who Brogan was.

By dawn, she could stand no more and Brogan was exhausted. But he continued to fight for her.

"Please, I beg ye, just give me one drink," she pleaded as she clung to Brogan's tunic with white-knuckles. Dark circles had formed under her eyes, and now her skin held a gray, deathly pallor. She was beginning to remind him of his Anna, in the days before the wasting disease had taken her. Gaunt, pale, gray, with dull, near lifeless eyes.

But there had been no hope for Anna. There was naught to be done by the time the healer made her diagnosis. But Mairghread? There was hope there, no matter if she could not see it at the moment.

Brogan remained firm in his resolve not to allow her to fall back into the abyss of drunkenness again. "Nay lass," he whispered. "Ye ken ye can no' do that."

"Just one," she continued to plead. "Just one tiny little drink. I need it Brogan, as much as I need air!"

Prying her hands from his tunic, he held them tightly betwixt his own. "Ye need to live more than ye need to drink," he told her. "Remember that, Mairghread. This will all be over soon, I promise ye."

"Nay," she argued, choking back tears. "I will die, Brogan, I can feel it!"

"'Tis the alcohol talkin', Mairghread. Ye will no' die," he said with a firm, yet kind voice.

With much force, she pushed away from him and began to pace about the room. "I can no' stand this!" she said as she pulled at her own hair. "I be goin' mad, I tell ye!"

He went to her immediately, and pulled her in closely. She fought against him, pounding her fists against his chest, cursing him to the devil. "I hate ye, Brogan Mackintosh! I hate ye with all that I am."

After a long while, she quit struggling and all but collapsed in his arms. "Do no' let me die, Brogan, please," she said as she wept into his tunic.

"Wheest, now," he replied softly. "I will no' let ye die, I swear it."

"Ye swear it?"

He placed a tender kiss on the top of her head. "Aye, lass, I promise."

&a.

WHEN SHE WAS FINALLY CALM ENOUGH TO LET GO OF, BROGAN tucked her into the bed. Drawing the blankets up around her chin, he stepped away, to the window. Looking out at the ocean, he began to pray.

Lord, I know no' what else to do. I have no trainin' in these matters, only my own personal experience. She seems to be sufferin' far worse than I did when I went off the drink. I can no' remember sufferin' through hallucinations as she has. Please, guide me, help me to do what is right for this woman.

As the hours wore on, he became more and more concerned for her wellbeing. He was also beginning to wish he had taken her from this keep, back to his father's home, where John could have helped him through all this. He could have helped Mairghread.

'Tis always easier to look back at a time than it is to live through it, he mused as he turned to look at his wife. Although the bed was small, it looked to be swallowing her whole at the moment. On her back, with her eyes closed, her breathing was ragged and fast. Once again, she was soaked with sweat, and mumbling incoherently.

Plagued with self-doubt now, he began to pace about the room himself. *Be I doin' this the right way?* He asked himself. *Mayhap we should have weaned her off the drink, slowly, over a few weeks, instead of takin' it all away at once.* He stopped and leaned his back against the cold stone wall and closed his eyes.

Thinking back to his own experience with coming off the drink, he could almost hear his father's voice. "We can do this one of two ways, lad. We can take ye off the drink now, or we can take ye off the drink now." The halfhearted jest was filled with truth. "There be only way way to do this," John had said. "And the best way is the fastest way to get yer life back."

Brogan had suffered with unsteady hands for more than a week. And aye, he had also thrown up more times than he could count. There were also times when he swore his stomach was trying to climb its way out of his body, through his bowels.

There were even a few moments where he had forgotten what day of the week it was. But not once had he hallucinated nor had he forgotten who his father was.

Mayhap the forgetfulness was born out of the fact that he and Mairghread truly did not know one another well at all. It was also possible that her addiction was worse than his had ever thought to be.

His quiet reverie was broken by a soft rap at the door. Crossing the room quickly and quietly, he opened the door a crack to find Reginald. Casting a quick glance to Mairghread, he saw she was sleeping, albeit fitfully. Not wishing to wake her, he stepped into the hallway.

"How does she fare this day?" Reginald asked, concern etched in the hard lines of his face.

"'Twas a rough night," Brogan said. He debated on how much he should tell him. Not because he did not trust him. Nay, he simply did not want to bring any undue stress to him. "She be restin' now," he told him. "Hot one minute, cold the next. I be certain she will be well in just a few more days."

His relief was palpable. "We are all verra worried about her," Reginald said as he rubbed the back of his neck with his palm. "Rumors are already beginnin' to get around, that she is no' well. Some say she has finally lost her mind, while others say ye are holdin' her prisoner her."

"And what have ye said?"

"I told them the next person I found spreadin' rumors about our lady would be drawn and quartered then tossed into the sea."

Brogan could not resist smiling. "I be certain yer lady appreciates your dedication and loyalty. Rumors will run amok until they see her with their own eyes."

Reginald raised one bushy brow. "I will be honest with ye, Brogan. I do no' like this, no' at all."

"Ye can no' stop people from gossipin'," Brogan told him. "They will believe what they wish until proven wrong."

He let out a deep breath. Changing the subject, he said, "We be makin' good progress in the quarry. Mayhap by the end of the day we can start bringin' the new stones in by wagon."

That was in fact good news. With Reginald and Henry leading the charge on the wall, Brogan could take care of his wife without worrying over other matters.

Chapter Twelve

The day ended almost as it had begun, with Mairghread begging and pleading with him to allow her just one drink. As he had done every other time she had asked, he calmly and firmly refused.

He did his best to keep her mind off the drink, but at this stage, 'twas impossible. "Tell me about yer brothers," he suggested on more than one occasion.

"Bah!" she cried, as she paced frantically about the small room. "They all be dead! What more do ye need to ken?" Angry and frustrated, she cursed him to the devil and refused to talk about them.

Twilight was just settling in around them, when her frantic pacing and pleas grew worse. Her anger turned to desperation. In a rush, she came to him and fell on her knees. Grabbing his legs, with tears filling her eyes, she pleaded with him. "Just one, Brogan! Just one drink and I swear I'll no' ask ye fer another ever again!"

"Up with ye now, lass," he said as he tried to pull her to her feet.

She refused, still clinging to his legs, choking on tears, her pride was now gone. "I will do anythin' ye ask. Anythin' at all. Just give me one drink!"

"Mairghread, please, stop this," he told her, his own frustration building. If she could see herself in this moment, he knew her shame would be unbearable.

"Is it me ye want?" she asked, her desperation building. "Ye can have me, Brogan. Right now." Crawling to the bed, she climbed on it, and lay on her back. "See? Ye can have me now. I'll no' gainsay ye, I'll no' complain," she told him, her voice shaking, pleading. She was pulling up her skirts with shaking fingers when he stopped her.

Holding her hands in his, he pulled her up to sit. "Mairghread, please, listen to me." He had to raise his voice in order to get through to her clouded mind. "Ye need to *live*, remember?"

"Nay, I need the drink! Please, I beg of ye, do no' make me suffer like this!" The tears were falling again, coming in great waves, racking her shoulders.

My God, he thought to himself. *Did me father go through this with me?*

Firming up his resolve, he took her face in his hands and forced her to look into his eyes. "Mairghread, ye are better than this, better than the drink. Remember, ye need to live more than ye need to drink."

"Nay!" she argued, her voice growing hoarse.

"Aye, ye do. Say it with me lass, say it a thousand times until ye believe it. *I need to live more than I need to drink.*"

She swallowed hard and shook her head. "Nay, I can no' do it."

"Yes. Ye. Can." He was not going to give up, not on her, not on her recovery. "Say it. *I need to live more than I need to drink.*"

She tried, she truly did, but she stammered numerous times. Brogan, however, refused to give up.

Just as she was finding the strength to say it, a loud knock came at the door. Mairghread went limp in his arms.

"Send them away," Mairghread told him. "I do no' wish anyone to see me like this. Please," she wiped her tears on the sleeve of her dress.

"Verra well, lass," he said as the knocking continued.

His stomach tightened with dread, for he had given orders not to be disturbed unless there was an emergency.

Mairghread climbed to the head of the bed and took in deep breaths. Terror and shame shone in her eyes. Lord above, it was killing him to see her like this. So afraid and ashamed, it nearly made his heart stop beating.

Before he could get to the door, it opened. In walked an auld, squat woman, with white hair and eyes so dark they looked nearly as black as her dress. Wrinkles lined her face, drooping around her eyes and mouth.

Mairghread could not see who it was, for the door blocked her vision. Brogan stepped forward so that the woman could not process further into the room.

"Who are ye?" Brogan asked.

"Hargatha," the woman replied. "I be the healer of this clan." Haughty and arrogant, she said it as though her place as healer equaled that of the king.

Brogan heard Mairghread gulp first, then saw her scurry from her bed to hide in the corner.

"Hargatha," he said with a curt nod. "I be Brogan Mackintosh—"

The auld woman cut off his introduction with a humph. "I ken who ye be. And ye are no' who I came to see. Where be Mairghread?"

"Mairghread is restin'," he told her. Never one to lie, he made an exception to this rule out of respect for his wife. That, and the fact that his gut was tightening with warning.

"Bah!" she humphed indignantly. "Let me pass."

He refused to budge. "Nay, we have everythin' under control, Hargatha. We will call ye should we need ye."

Mairghread's whimpers grew louder. A quick glance told him much. She was terrified, pressed into the corner, eyes wide as she shook her head, silently pleading with him. He cared not if her reaction to the woman was justified or not. His primary duty as her husband was to protect her. Even from hard, cold women like Hargatha.

Apparently, she was unaccustomed to not getting her way. "I be the healer here. I have heard she is near death. Why is it ye block me way? What are ye tryin' to hide?"

"Hargatha, I will remind ye that I be Mairghread's husband. I shall decide what is best fer her. And if ye dare insult me again, I shall have ye banned from the keep. Do ye understand?"

She did not so much as flinch at his threat. "The rumors be true then, aye?" she asked with slitted, spiteful eyes.

Mairghread could take no more. "Get out ye auld biddy!" she screamed from the dark corner. "I do no' want ye here!"

Hargatha tried to get past Brogan. Stepping left, then right, he blocked her each time.

"I said get out!" Mairghread screamed again. Leaving the corner, she came to stand behind Brogan. "Ye are a mean, hateful woman! Ye be no' here to help. Ye only want to say ye saw me with yer own eyes so that ye can continue to spread yer vicious rumors!"

Hargatha peered around Brogan. "Just as I thought!" she said. "Ye do no' need a healer, ye need a priest, for 'tis certain ye be possessed with demons!"

All of his patience evaporated in the blink of an eye. "Stop!" he shouted at Hargatha. "Henry! Comnall!" he shouted over her and into the hallway.

"Ye will leave here at once, Hargatha, or I shall have me men remove ye." His tone was firm, unforgiving, and harsh. "Ye will no' return unless *I* personally summon ye. Do I make meself clear?"

"Bah! She needs those demons purged, I tell ye!"

Mairghread screamed and lunged at the auld woman. Brogan caught her about the waist before she could do any serious harm to Hargatha.

"Demon!" Hargatha shouted. "This be a possession if ever I saw one!"

Marighread continued to kick and scream and curse. Brogan had to spin her around to keep her from hurting the auld woman. "Mairghread, please!" he said, raising his voice.

Comnall appeared first, with Henry fast on his heels.

"Brogan!' Comnall called into the room.

Over the din of the two screaming women, Brogan ordered the men to remove Hargatha. "And do no' let her anywhere near this room again!"

At first, they tried to be gentle with the auld woman, but she was having none of it. "Get yer hands off me! Do ye no' ken who I be?"

Finally, they had to pull her from the room while she shouted repeatedly that Mairghread was possessed by the devil himself and needed an exorcism. Mairghread's replies were just as bad. "Ye be a harpy! A mean-spirited, bloody ugly auld hag and I wish ye dead!"

Brogan struggled with his attempts at calming her. "Mairghread!" he shouted. "Settle the bloody hell down!"

'Twas long after Hargatha was out of the room and the door closed before Mairghread finally settled. "I hate that auld woman!" she declared.

"Are ye quite finished?" Brogan asked, squeezing her tightly about the waist to gain her attention.

She let out a long breath, and finally acquiesced. He counted to ten before putting her down. He was now covered in sweat, out of breath, and quite close to losing his temper. Giving a great shake of his head, he went to the window and pulled back the fur. He took in deep, long breaths of the salty air and prayed.

Lord, please give me patience.

AND PATIENCE HE WAS GOING TO NEED WHEN ONCE AGAIN SHE WAS overcome with another bout of hallucinations. 'Twas late into the night when she became convinced there were snakes climbing in through the window, the arrow slits, and cracks in the walls.

"Me God!" she cried. "Please, get them off me!" Once again, she was on the bed, trying to climb the wall in order to escape them. Brogan had to call for Charles and Peter to come help him with her delusions.

Clawing at her dress, pulling at her hair, she screamed and screamed, begging them to help her. 'Twas one of the most gut-wrenching, disturbing events Brogan had ever witnessed.

This night, it took nearly an hour to calm her down.

On the floor, in the corner, next to the door, he held her as she quivered and wept. "I be so sorry," she told him between sobs. "I be so sorry."

'Twas agonizing for him to see her in such a state of distress. Aye, he knew that in the end, these days would be well worth it. But it did not make the going through them much easier. All he could think to tell her was that all was well and everything would be fine.

"I feel so terrible," she told him. "I do no' ken what comes over me."

Though his own takeaways had not been anywhere near as violent, nor haunted like hers with hallucinations, he had to believe hers was worse because she had been drinking far longer than he had.

"Do ye think she be right?" Mairghread whispered against his chest.

"Who?" he asked as he rubbed her back with his palm.

"Hargatha."

He chuckled. "That ye be possessed? Nay, lass. Ye be no more possessed by the devil than I."

She snuggled in closer to him, wrapping her arms around his waist. "Thank ye, Brogan," she said softly.

All the self-doubts and second-guesses he was having over his decision to keep her here fell away with those three words. Filled with such sincerity, warmth, and genuine gratitude, he knew they weren't the words of a madwoman. They had come from her heart.

MORNING DAWNED BRIGHT AND PRISTINE ON THE FIFTH DAY OF her confinement. 'Twas one of those mornings when a man felt alive and thankful. Mairghread was feeling better as well. Though she was far from completely better, the tremors and shakes had subsided significantly. Last night had been difficult for her, but she was finally able to sleep for more than a half an hour at a time. Though 'twas still fitful sleep, interrupted by nightmares, and the hot and cold streaks.

Brogan sent a silent prayer up to God, thanking him for her remarkable progress.

Reginald arrived, bearing another tray of bread and broth for Mairghread, as well as eggs and ham for Brogan. While she sipped at her broth and picked at her bread, Brogan ate his meal like a newly released prisoner of war.

"Ye do look much better, this day," Reginald told her. They were sitting side by side on the bed while Brogan sat on the stool.

"I do feel a bit better today," she told him with a smile that did not quite reach her eyes.

"Each day ye will find yerself feelin' better and better, aye? And before ye ken it, ye'll be out of here, and takin' over as chief."

With a furrowed brow, she sat the bowl of broth down. "Me? Chief?" she asked. "I do no' ken if that is such a good idea."

"Why not?" Reginald and Brogan each asked incredulously.

"Look at me," she told them, holding her arms out. "I fear I would no' make a good chief. I can barely be a wife, or a chatelaine."

Brogan was kneeling before her in an instant. "Ye be wrong," he said as he took her hands in his. "I ken right now might no' be the best time, but when ye're better? Aye, lass, ye'll make a fine chief."

"I agree," Reginald said. "Ye will make a fine chief."

He knew she didn't believe either of them, but it mattered not. Eventually, with time, when her mind was not so cloudy and weary, she would see.

"But let us first get ye through this tryin' time, aye?" Brogan said, offering her a most encouraging smile.

She nodded and swallowed back tears. "I do no' ken why ye're bein' so nice to me."

"Would ye no' help someone in need?" he asked. "If our situations were reversed, would ye no' help me?"

One tear fell away and trailed down her cheek. "I would try, I think."

"There ye have it then," he said.

From her confused expression, she did not completely understand his meaning. "We be alike, ye and I. We help those in need."

Mairghread shrugged her shoulders. "I suppose," she said.

"'Twill no' be long now, Mairghread," he told her. "Ye will see. Ye'll be right as rain soon enough."

A man never truly knows what the future has in store for him. If anyone had told him a month ago that he would marry a beautiful woman — one who should be chief of her own clan — he would have laughed at them. And had they told him he would spend the good majority of his first days as a married man, locked in a room with her whilst he helped her overcome her addiction to alcohol, he would have considered them well and fully mad.

"Thank ye, Brogan," she said as she gave his hands a gentle squeeze.

To his way of thinking, she did not truly owe him any thanks. All he wanted was for her to get and be better. For them to be able to build a life together. For the first time in many days, he was actually looking forward to their future.

§▲

GERTIE AND TILDA CAME TO SEE HER AFTER THE MORNING MEAL. They brought her a fresh dress, chemise, and woolens, along with her comb.

Brogan stepped into the hallway while they helped Mairghread to wash up and change her clothing. Charles and Comnall were standing guard this morning.

"I think, mayhap, ye could use a dip in the loch and clean clothes as well," Comnall chided him playfully.

Brogan ran a hand across his face and realized it had been days since last he had shaved. "I think ye be right," he replied.

"We will keep an eye out for her," Charles told him.

He mulled it over for a time. She had been improving, especially the past two days. The hallucinations had stopped, and the tremors were tolerable. He asked them to wait while he went to speak with the women.

"Och!" Gertie declared with a wide smile. "We shall watch over her, m'laird, of that ye can be certain."

Tilda patted Mairghread's hand. "Is that no' right, lass? Ye will be fine with us fer a time, aye?"

She smiled warmly at both women. "In truth, I feel verra tired. I would like to rest fer a spell, if ye do no' mind."

They went back and forth for a time, with the women not wanting to leave her, and Mairghread wanting very much to take a nap. Amused at what should be a simple decision, Brogan stood by the door and waited patiently for them to make up their minds.

"Gertie," Tilda said, calling the argument to a halt. "Why do no' ye go below stairs and see if cook can come up with something other than watery broth and warm bread for our lass. I will stay here whilst she rests. Brogan, ye can go take a bath and change."

He turned to Mairghread, afraid that if he didn't agree and leave at once, 'twould be midnight before they made up their minds.

"I shall no' be long, lass," he told her. "If ye need anything, send Charles or Comnall for me at once."

GERTIE LEFT WITH BROGAN. LIKE A TRUE GENTLEMAN, HE OFFERED her his arm as they descended the stairs. Gertie giggled and beamed. "I can no' remember the last time a handsome lad offered me his arm," she told him with a wink.

Brogan had to laugh. "I bet ye drove the lads mad in yer youth," he said.

She quirked a brow. "And who says I be no' drivin' them mad now?" she teased.

Brogan placed a hand over his heart. "Fergive me, fair maiden."

After they reached the landing, Brogan led her to the next set of stairs. "'Tis true, m'laird, I can no' remember e'er feelin' so much hope. Tilda and I, we be verra grateful to ye, fer what ye be doin' fer our lady."

"She be doin' the work, Gertie. I am merely there to hold her hand."

Gertie dismissed that statement immediately. "Nay, ye and I both ken it be far more than hand holdin' ye be doin, m'laird. Ye be givin' Mairghread back her life. That be a priceless gift."

"I am merely helpin' her to do what is right," he replied.

"Whatever ye *think* it be yer doin, just ken we are all verra grateful, m'laird."

He patted the top of her hand. "I think, Gertie, it be time ye called me Brogan. I be no' yer laird, nor yer chief. I am simply Mairghread's husband."

She paused and looked up at him. "Ye are far more than simply her husband. And I would rather cut off me hand before I call ye by yer given name. Ye deserve our most humble respect."

Seeing he would get nowhere with her on that matter, he encouraged her forward. "I shall see ye safely to the kitchen," he said. "Then return to ye after I change me clothes, aye?"

Gertie laughed and rolled her eyes. "M'laird, ye be a kind, kind man. But I have been walking the halls of this keep since I came to live here at the age of three and ten. I shall be fine."

"As ye wish," he said when they reached the second landing.

"Now, off with ye. I will make certain cook offers up something other than bread and broth. Our lady be wastin' away to skin and bones."

That was decidedly truer than either of them wanted to admit. These past days had been a trying time for Mairghread, emotionally as well as physically.

"Ye'll see how bonny she is, once she has put on a wee bit of weight, m'laird," Gertie told him.

As far as he was concerned, she was already a bonny lass.

Hargatha Mactavish did not like being told what she could or could not do. For two days, she seethed angrily over what she considered harsh and undeserved mistreatment by Brogan Mackintosh. Did he not understand *who* she was?

'Twas an insult, to be certain, the way he had his men drag her from Mairghread's room. 'Twas also an insult the way Mairghread behaved, like a deranged savage, cursing and screaming. "Any fool could see I was right!"

"Bah!" her anger simmered. "I be the *healer,* no' some mindless eejit!" She pulled herbs from the jars on the shelf in her kitchen and sat down at her table.

Alone in her cottage, this was the first time since that day when she had a moment to herself. Busy with tending to the usual injuries and ailments, she hadn't had much time to plan on how she would retaliate. But now, with the quiet solitude found only in her cottage, she had time to plan.

"He thinks I be some foolish auld women," she said as she ground herbs in her pestle and mortar. "I ken a possession when I see it. The priest would see it too, if he were no' off at the MacRay clan tendin' their flock."

Grinding the herbs always gave her a sense of strength and power that she could not get anywhere else. "I have the power to give life or take it. To ease someone's pain, or make it worse," she mumbled. "Knowin' how the herbs work is a special power, given to me by God himself." 'Twas something she firmly believed.

"'Tis me duty to do His good work. 'Tis no' an illness she suffers from, but the devil himself."

Taking solace in her fervent belief she was doing what God directed, she took the herbs and placed them carefully inside a small pouch with a smile. "We shall purge those demons from her," she declared. "One way or another."

❧

"DO NO' FASH YERSELF OVER IT," HARGATHA TOLD THE YOUNG MAN guarding Mairghread's room. He had not been one of the two men who had pulled her out of the room the other day. This was to her advantage, of course. Another sign, she was certain, that God was on her side.

He was eying her cautiously. "I have spoken to Brogan. He kens what we need to do." 'Twas the cold hard truth, as far as she was concerned. It mattered not to her that Brogan disagreed. "'Tis just a simple tisane, laddie, to help our lady."

"Mayhap we should wait until Brogan returns," he said, the doubt bouncing around in his eyes.

"Aye, we could wait," she told him, even offering up one of her warmest smiles. "But I would hate to see our lady suffer a moment longer than necessary, aye?" She held out the cup, which had been steeping in warm water for more than a quarter of an hour. "Here, ye can take it to her yerself."

Reluctantly, he took the cup, uncertainty clearly evidenced in his eyes.

"That be a good lad," she told him as she patted his arm. "Just ye give that to our lady now, and make certain she drinks every last bit of it. 'Twill help her gain strength and she will be feelin' much better verra soon."

Without waiting for him to reply, she turned and left.

If this does no' work today, there will be other chances, she promised herself.

⁊᷃

TILDA WAS DOZING ON THE LITTLE STOOL NEXT TO MAIRGHREAD'S bed. The gentle rap at the door forced her awake almost at once. Her lady, however, did not stir. *Poor lass,* she thought. *She has been through far too much for someone so young.*

Pushing herself to her feet, she answered the door and found the young Mackintosh man standing there holding a cup.

"What is it?" she asked him in a whisper so as not to wake Mairghread.

"A woman was just here," he said, holding out the cup for her. "She said 'tis from the cook? Said 'tis fer Lady Mactavish."

"What be it?" she asked as she took the cup from him. One whiff, and she was curling up her nose.

"I do no' ken rightly," he admitted. "But she says Brogan kens and that we are to give it to Lady Mactavish straight away. She says it will help her gain her strength."

Tilda was completely behind anything that would help her lady feel better and gain the strength she needed. "Verra well," she said.

Bowing slightly at the waist, he left her alone to return to his post.

With the cup in hand, she returned to her spot by the bed, and set the cup on the floor. "Lass?" she said in a low voice, "Cook has sent ye somethin' to help ye gain yer strength."

Mairghread grumbled and rolled away.

Tilda wasn't about to relent. "If cook says ye need to drink this fer yer strength, then ye should. Come now, lass. Sit up and drink."

It took a little prodding, but she was eventually able to get Mairghread to sit up in the bed. "What is it?" she asked dubiously. "It smells like death!"

Tilda chuckled as she placed the cup in her hands. "I think it be a case of 'the cure is worse than the disease'."

꙳

BROGAN WAS FISHING THROUGH HIS TRUNK FOR FRESH CLOTHING when a knock came at his door. He opened it to find a young lass, with bright blue eyes and dark blonde hair. "Gertie said ye might be needin' this, m'laird."

"Thank ye kindly, lass," he said as he took the pitcher and linens from her. "What be yer name?"

"I be Gretchen, m'laird. I work in the kitchens," she replied as she bobbed a curtsey.

He thanked her again and shut the door behind him. Pouring the fresh, warm water into the basin, he cleaned up as best he could. What he wanted most was a long hot bath, but there was no time for such luxuries at the moment. Mairghread needed him.

Mairghread. He smiled when he thought of her.

During these past several days, he was beginning to learn more about her. She was not truly the cold-hearted harpy he had first believed her to be. Nay, that was the drink taking over her heart and mind. Sober — albeit for less than a sennight now — he could see she was a witty and kind woman.

The trials she had gone through over the years would have pushed anyone to drink. No longer did he believe she willingly *chose* to become the calloused, sharp-tongued drunk. Nay, her drinking was born out of a deep sense of loss. And 'twas more than one loss she endured over the years. Losing James and Connell had been the thing that sent her over the edge.

He took the time to shave the whiskers from his face and nicked his chin. He cursed under his breath, and placed one of the wet clothes against it. Glancing into the small looking glass he shivered. "Ye look like hell," he muttered.

Dark circles had formed under his eyes and even he could see he had lost weight. This morning had been his first real meal in many days.

Clean, shaven, and with still damp hair, he donned a green tunic and black trews. Turning to grab his dirty clothes from the floor, he saw his bed. Tempted though he was to climb into it and take a good long nap, he knew he could not. Mairghread needed him.

჻

WITH A SKIP IN HIS STEP AS HE LEFT HIS ROOM, BROGAN WAS looking forward to seeing his wife. That realization brought forth a chuckle. Much had changed between them these past days. Aye, it had been a living nightmare those first days. But she was getting better with each hour.

Mayhap on the morrow, we can move her out of that filthy room, he told himself. *Give her a nice long bath and a good rest in her own bed.*

He was feeling thankful for many things this morning. Not only was his wife giving up the drink, but the progress in the quarry was going better than even he had hoped for. With Reginald and Henry taking over his duties, he was able to spend the much-needed time with Mairghread. And now, less than a fortnight after beginning the project, they were actually able to begin putting stones into place. His only worry on that front was that it would take at least a year to complete the wall.

He had just reached the stairs that led to the third floor when he was met by Liam, one of his distant cousins who had volunteered to come here with Brogan weeks ago. There was no physical resemblance between them, for Liam had dark brown hair, and dark brown eyes.

Liam looked terrified as well as stunned. Brogan knew at once that something was wrong. Horribly wrong.

"Brogan!" Liam shouted as soon as he saw him. "'Tis Mairghread!"

჻

THE COMMOTION WAS LOUD ENOUGH TO BE HEARD BEFORE BROGAN

reached the attics on the fourth floor. It sounded as though a rabid cat-o'mountain had been let lose in Mairghread's room.

Tilda was sitting outside the door, blood running down her face from a gash on her forehead. Gertie was on the floor beside her, pressing a cloth against it.

Charles was holding onto the door with both hands, as if he were trying to keep a horde of angry murderers from getting out. His face was bloody as well, from a wound Brogan could not see.

A growl so loud, so animalistic in its intensity, came from Mairghread's room.

"I do no' ken what happened," Charles shouted over his shoulder as Brogan raced down the short corridor. 'Twas clear the man was panic stricken.

Brogan did not wait for further explanation. He told Charles to step away, took a deep breath, and opened the door.

What he saw sent a shiver tracing up and down his spine. Mairghread, in nothing but a blood-covered chemise, was in the corner of the room, tearing her mattress to shreds. The strong stench of vomit, urine and feces hung in the air.

All the while, she was growling. A guttural, unnatural growl, that made his heart seize.

"Mairghread," he whispered her name.

She did not even look at him. She continued to growl and snarl and tear at the mattress, pulling the ticking and straw out with bloodied fingers.

He spoke her name again, this time louder, hoping to bring her out of whatever nightmare she was in.

Dark, blank eyes caught his. She stared for a brief moment before throwing the mattress to the floor and lunging at him. Clawing at his face, she scratched his neck before he had the wherewithal to contain her. It happened so fast. Before he knew it they were crashing to the floor.

She was on top of him, flailing away at him, trying to kill him with her bare hands.

Charles and Liam came rushing into the room. It took the two of them to pull her away before she had a chance to scratch his eyes out. Brogan was on his feet in no time.

Charles had her about the waist, while Liam was doing his best to grab her kicking feet.

"Mairghread!" Brogan yelled, but in her current deranged state, she could not hear him.

Rushing toward Charles, Brogan grabbed her waist and pulled her away. With fisted hands, she pounded at his face, his neck; anywhere she could land a blow, she did.

He knew they must restrain her. "Find rope!" He called out to his men. "Enough to restrain her hands and feet."

Liam raced from the room while Charles came from behind Brogan and tried grabbing her hands. It took several attempts before he was able to grab them, but she fought like a madwoman to free herself from their tight holds.

Brogan's heart was pounding against his chest, so stunned by her current state he knew not what to say or do. So he and Charles struggled to keep her under control.

"I killed them! I killed them!" she began to chant, over and over again. In a sing-song maniacal voice. "I killed them!"

LIAM SOON RETURNED WITH ROPE. "I HAVE IT!" HE DECLARED AS HE rushed into the room, out of breath, covered in sweat.

While Mairghread continued her deranged ranting, Brogan fought hard to think on how they would restrain her. The only option was the bed, but the mattress had been destroyed. Only the ropes that held the mattress in place remained.

"Right the bed," he told Liam as he turned around.

He'd fought easier battles against trained warriors than the one he fought with Mairghread. Holding his breath, he held onto her so tightly he worried he would break her ribs. Still, she fought and struggled and growled and chanted.

Once the bed was righted, he pressed forward. Afraid to let her go for even a brief moment, he fell onto the bed, with her on the bottom.

Working quickly, Charles bound her feet while Liam bound her wrists to the posts of the bed.

Mairghread writhed in agony, fighting against the ropes, screaming and cursing in frenzied panic.

Brogan climbed off, out of breath, soaked with sweat, and overwrought with worry. "What the bloody hell happened?" he demanded.

"I killed them! I killed them!" Mairghread continued to chant, lifting her torso off the mattress, fighting against her restraints.

"I do no' ken what happened," Liam said. "She was fine one moment and then like this the next!" He raked a hand through his hair. "We heard a crash, then Tilda screamed. When we came in ... she was banging the chamber pot over Tilda's head!"

Overcome with worry, he crouched beside the bed. "Mairghread," he said her name in a loud voice, hoping by some act of God's grace, she would begin to calm herself. 'Twas as if she could not hear him. Gently, he took her face in his hands, forcing it still, begging her to look into his eyes. "Mairghread!" He called to her again. "What is wrong?"

"I killed them! I killed them!"

He let lose a frustrated breath. "Who did ye kill?"

"Them!"

"Them who, lass?" he asked, lowering his tone significantly.

"Me husband and son," she cried out. "I killed them!"

DUMBSTRUCK, HE WAS NOT CERTAIN HE SHOULD BELIEVE WHAT SHE was saying. She was far too out of touch with reality, panting, wailing, fighting against the ropes.

Nay, he thought. *It can no' be.*

Gertie stepped into the room, twisting her hands together. "Good, Lord," she gasped when she saw Mairghread.

The raving continued.

"What happened?" Brogan asked her as he sank to the floor.

"I do no' ken," Gertie told him over Mairghread's loud rambling.

"I killed them! Everyone kens it! I killed them!"

Gertie rushed to her side. "Nay, lass, nay," she said through her tears.

Brogan studied Gertie closely for a moment. "Does she speak the truth?" he asked Gertie as he struggled to his feet.

Gertie refused to answer. Instead, she brushed hair away from Mairghread's face. "Wheest now, lass, wheest."

His heart sank with dread. He knew Gertie would take her own life before she ever said a word against Mairghread. Even if it was the truth.

His anger rose to terrifying heights. Lies. So many lies. They'd lied to him about her drinking in order to get him to marry her. What else had they lied about? Could she truly have done what she was now confessing to?

He looked about the room as he tamed his ragged breaths. Bile began to rise in the back of his throat.

The chamber pot lay in pieces, scattered around the room. The linens were torn, thrown haphazardly here and there. Feces and vomit were smeared on the wall. Straw and ticking, her dress, had been tossed as well. Even the little stool had been shattered.

And in the middle of it, lay his wife. Tossing her head from side to side, seeing but not seeing, hearing but not hearing. Stuck in some dark, ugly place where he was uncertain she would ever leave.

He could take no more.

"Charles," his voice caught on the knot that had formed in his throat. "Find someone to stitch ye and Tilda. Liam, do no' leave this room until I return. And allow no one entry."

"Do ye want the healer?" he asked as Brogan made his way around the mess toward the door.

"Nay" he replied with a slow, disgusted shake of his head. "No one is to enter."

Quickly, he quit the room and went in search of the one person who could give him answers.

Chapter Thirteen

Brogan was off his mount before the animal had stopped. He thundered across the ground, his lips pursed together, and murderous rage in his eyes. Solely focused on one man in particular, he found him standing not far from a group of stones, talking to two men.

Reginald looked up to see Brogan stomping toward him. Without warning, he grabbed Reginald by the collar of his tunic and began dragging him away.

"M'laird!" he shouted. "What the bloody hell is the matter?"

Brogan did not stop until they were a good distance from the quarry. He pulled him into a small copse of trees before he let him loose, tossing him against a thick tree.

"What be wrong?" Reginald asked, dumbstruck and confused.

Brogan was seething with fury. A fury he only felt on the battlefield. "I want answers," he said through gritted teeth. "And I swear to ye, Reginald, if ye once tell me ye will no' speak ill about yer lady or her uncle, I will kill ye."

"I do no' understand," he said as he righted himself. "What the bloody hell has happened?"

Brogan began to pace before him. "Mairghread," he began, stopped, and started again. "Mairghread. Somethin' has happened to her and I do no' ken what. I left for a few moments, and upon my return, she was ..." he searched for the right words to describe what had happen. "She was in such a frenzy!" he exclaimed. "She attacked Tilda, and Liam. They both require stitches. We had to *restrain* her, Reginald. We had to tie her to the bloody bed!"

The blood drained from Reginald's face. "I must go to her—"

He did not get two steps away before Brogan threw him back against the tree. "Nay, ye will no' leave here until I get some bloody answers!"

Reginald's mouth fell open. "I do no' ken what happened! I have been here since I broke my fast."

Brogan shook his head. "Nay, that is not the answer I seek."

"Then what? What is it ye want from me? And why are ye so bloody furious?"

"I be bloody furious because me wife is locked away in a room, tied to a bed, having lost her bloody mind! I be furious because she is screamin' at the top of her lungs that *she* killed her husband and son!"

"And ye believed her?" he asked incredulously.

"I do no' ken *what* to believe anymore," Brogan told him.

Reginald closed his eyes and took in a lungful of air. He expelled it slowly as he shook his head. "Nay, Brogan, she did no' kill her husband and son."

"Then why in the name of God is she saying she did?"

"Because her uncle told her so."

BROGAN KNEW HE SHOULD HAVE BEEN MORE SURPRISED BY Reginald's answer. "Why in the hell would he tell her such a thing?"

"For the life of me, Brogan, I do no' ken," Reginald replied.

Brogan ran a hand through his hair as he tried to make some sense out of the afternoon's events. First Mairghread all but loses her mind for unknown reasons, now this.

"Tell me what ye ken of that night," he told him. "And do no' leave out a thing."

Reginald shook his head. "I was no' here. I was in Edinburgh."

"But ye have heard of what happened," Brogan said, eying him closely.

He was met with silence and a disheartened look.

"Tell me what ye do ken," Brogan told him. "Leave nothin' out."

'Twas painful for Reginald to speak of that night, but he did it anyway. "From what I be told, Gertie heard Mairghread screamin'. No one knew at that time that we were under attack. Gertie went racin' into Mairghread's room." A distant, forlorn expression came to his face. "All I ken is what Gertie told me, fer Aymer refused to speak of it."

"And what did Gertie tell ye?"

Reginald's jaw tightened, anger flashing in his eyes. "When she came into the room, Mairghread was still screamin'. Aymer was on the floor next to her. Blood was everywhere."

"And?" Brogan asked, encouraging him to continue.

"Aymer told Gertie that when he came into the room, he found James and Connell already dead." He had to clear his throat before he could go on. "He told her he found Mairghread standin' over the bairn with the knife in her hand. When she saw Aymer, she began to stab herself, all the while screamin' she had done it. She had killed them."

Brogan felt his legs grow week. *Nay,* he told himself. He was unable to stretch his imagination that far, to believe her capable of such a thing. Yet, this afternoon? She had lost her mind, had gone mad, had attacked Tilda, Charles, and even himself.

Could her problems be more severe than an addiction to drink? His mind took him back to that attic room, the destruction, the anger blended with insanity.

"I," he could not find the words.

"Brogan, on my dead wife's grave, I swear to ye, that I do no' believe she did it."

He raised a dubious brow as he stared at Reginald. Was his love for Mairghread so strong that he could not believe for a moment she was capable?

"Then what do ye think happened?" He finally asked.

"I think Aymer killed them."

૱

BROGAN WOULDN'T KNOW AYMER MACTAVISH IF HE CAME UP AND kicked him in his arse. He'd never met the man.

But if what he had learned thus far *about* the man was any indication as to his character, then aye, he could believe him capable of murder. Still, there did linger a twinge of doubt, only because of what Mairghread had done less than an hour before. His fury erupted.

"For the sake of Christ, why did ye no' tell Mairghread that?" Brogan ground out as he pushed him against the tree again. "Why did ye let her think she was responsible? For all these years, it ate at her soul, turnin' her into a drunk!"

"What would ye have done?" he asked, his face turning purple with rage. "Were ye in me position? With no one to turn to? With the girl ye love like yer verra own, so overwrought with grief that she could barely remember who ye were at first?"

"Ye could have told her later!" Brogan seethed.

"I tried, but she would no' listen," Reginald barked back. "All I could do was watch over her. Try to keep her safe. Try to keep Aymer away from her, from hurtin' her any further."

"Why did ye no' tell *me?*" he asked, shoving him harder against the tree.

"Because I did no' ken ye! I had to wait, until I knew ye better. And then ye started to help her, and she was doin' so well. I did what I thought was best fer her!"

Disgusted, he let loose his tight hold on Reginald's tunic and set him free.

"When ye started buildin' the wall, when ye increased the patrols, I thought *mayhap, just mayhap* I could confide in ye. But then Mairghread gave up the drink. All I could think about this past sennight, was gettin' her better and buildin' that bloody wall."

Brogan's anger began to wane when he saw Reginald's sincere distress. What would he have done were their roles reversed?

"Ye say that what we speak of is betwixt only us," Reginald said after a long length of silence. "I ask that what I am about to say remain betwixt us as well. If Mairghread knew my suspicions, I do no' ken how she would take it."

"Ye have me word," Brogan said firmly.

"Aymer Mactavish is no' a man to be trusted," he began.

Brogan grunted.

"He has always called the night James and Connell were killed 'an attack on the keep'. Two guards were killed that night, along with James and Connell. But no one saw a bloody thing!" He raked a hand through his hair, disgusted for a wide variety of reasons. "No one saw any *attackers*. Naught was taken that night. The coffers were no' raided, no horses' stolen. Nothing but four dead people, and almost a fifth if ye count what happened to Mairghread. She nearly died that night as well, ye ken." He took in a deep breath before going on. "No' only do I believe Aymer killed James and Connell, I think he also had a hand in some of the deaths of her family."

"What do ye mean some of the deaths?"

Reginald sighed angrily. "Wee Walter, drowned in the ocean, his body never found. 'Twas Aymer who came to Donald, Mairghread's father, and told him he saw the boy floatin' out to sea, but could not get to him."

Brogan's brow furrowed as he listened intently. Mairghread had told him about that death, but these were things she had not mentioned. Was it still too difficult for her to speak about, even after all these years?

"And Charles. Aymer found *him* dead, his skull crushed upon a large rock, his body broken and twisted. Presumably from his mount spookin' and throwin' him."

Brogan's curiosity was more than just piqued.

"And Callam? Fell off the cliff's edge when he was only two and ten. Apparently, he took a walk after dark and fell. And Gavin? He died the exact same way, and in almost the exact same spot as Charles." He let his words sink in for a time. "I think that be far too many coincidences, do no' ye?"

Aye, Brogan had to agree there were too many instances to be coincidence. He thought then of the will that Gertie and Tilda had only eluded to. "Tell me about Donald's will."

Reginald grunted derisively. "Only Aymer has seen it. And according to him, Mairghread be chief of the clan. But the only way she holds that title is if she be married and has a livin' heir before her fifth and twentieth birthday."

Brogan found that information peculiar to say the least. "And then?" he dared ask.

"It all falls to Aymer."

It all began to fall into place then. He could see it with perfect clarity. Aymer had killed as many people as Reginald suspected, including James and Connell. All so that he could inherit the Mactavish lands, keeps, and holdings.

The bloody bastard.

❦

HIS FURY RETURNED WITH THE REALIZATION THAT HIS WIFE WAS IN grave danger. Looking at Reginald, he said, "I want ye to go to every village within fifty miles of here — one hundred if ye must -- and hire every able-bodied man ye can."

Reginald stared in amazement.. "Why?"

"We need to finish this bloody wall before Aymer returns. We have what, three months before he gets back from France?"

"If we're lucky," Reginald replied.

Brogan stomped across the grass to where his mount was grazing. "Leave at once. Take at least five men with ye. I do no' care what it costs, but ye find men. Able-bodied men. Bring them back here." He mounted his horse, and turned to look at Reginald. "Pull the men off the quarry and have them start felling trees. 'Twill be faster to build a wall of wood than stone right now. We will work all day and all night, but we will get it done."

"Where are ye goin'?" Reginald asked.

"First to Iariann," he replied gruffly.

Reginald felt just as anxious about Aymer's return as Brogan did. "And what of Mairghread?"

Brogan pulled rein, and went back to Reginald. "I can no' believe she just suddenly went mad," he told him. "There had to be somethin' that happened. And I be goin' to find out what the bloody hell that was."

&.

B‌ROGAN RODE STRAIGHT TO THE SMITHY'S BARN. I‌ARAINN WAS working on another cooking pot, which today, infuriated him to no end. *Cooking pots!*

"M'laird," she called out as he approached. When she saw the fury on his face, she carefully sat her tools aside and looked at him with an expression of true confusion.

"Beginning immediately, ye are to start forgin' weapons," he told her. "Broadswords, knives, dirks, arrows. Ye will no' forge another cookin' pot or anythin' else, do ye understand?"

With furrowed brow, she wiped her hands on her heavy leather apron. "May I ask why?"

He could not very well tell her the truth without clear and convincing evidence. "I have a suspicion that we might come under attack in the comin' months."

"Do ye ken by whom?" she asked.

Resting his fingertips on his hips, his anger burning almost as bright as the fire in her forge. "Does it matter?"

Twisting her lips to one side, she thought on it for a brief moment. "I suppose no'," she replied. "But what am I to tell people when they see me makin' weapons? Word will undoubtedly get back to Aymer."

His nostrils flared as his eyes turned to slits. "Aymer be no' the chief of this clan. Mairghread is."

"She is well, then?" she asked.

Genuine concern filled her eyes, softening his anger just a bit. "She will be soon enough. But it matters no'. What does matter is that we are defenseless. With no walls, no towers, and no bloody weapons, if we are attacked, there be no way we can win."

"I have been sayin' *that* fer more than three years," she replied solemnly.

"Then ye be with me on this?"

"Aye, m'laird, I am. But what do I say if anyone asks?"

Frustrated with the hold Aymer had on this clan, he let out a heavy breath. "Ye can tell them to mind their own bloody business! And if they have any questions, they can come see me. Ye are workin' under Mairghread's orders."

"Ye ken word will get to Aymer," she said.

Waggling his brows and grinning, he said, "I hope the bloody hell it does!"

They spoke for a little while longer. With her orders clear, he took his mount back to the stables and asked one of the stable boys to tend to it. The lad did as asked without question.

As he thundered back to the keep, he made a solemn vow to himself. "I will no' rest until I find out what happened to Mairghread."

HE HAD HIS ANSWERS IN LESS THAN AN HOUR. THEY WERE ABLE TO piece together the events that led up to Mairghread's mad frenzy.

He stood now in the kitchens, speaking with Lowrens, who looked fit to be tied. "I did no' ken what she was goin' to do, m'laird, I swear it! I only gave her the hot water and cup she asked for. 'Tis Hargatha. Sometimes it is best no' to ask her too many questions." Rubbing the top of his head, he looked positively sickened by the part he unwittingly played. "Had I kent I would ne'er have given it to her."

Brogan had seen Mairghread moments ago. Though she was no longer fighting as strongly as before, she was still behaving like a woman possessed. Her eyes were glassy and dark, her pupils so large and black one could barely tell she had emerald green eyes.

"I do no' ken what she gave her," Brogan said. "I have no idea how to help Mairghread. But none of this be yer fault, Lowrens."

"I should have kent somethin' was wrong when she thanked me fer the cup and water," he said between gritted teeth.

A young lass of no more than four and ten stepped forward. "M'laird," she said, her voice a bit shaky. "I do no' mean to eavesdrop, but mayhap I can help."

Brogan lifted a curious brow. "How?"

"Well, me mum, she be a midwife, ye ken. But she be also right smart when it comes to herbs and such. Mayhap *she* can help ye."

Brogan needed all of one heartbeat to think on it. "Aye, please!" he told her. "Fetch her straight away, lass."

She glanced at Lowrens as if asking permission to leave. He rolled his eyes and waved his hands. "What be ye waitin' fer?" he snapped. "Go fetch Martha!"

The girl didn't even bob a curtsey as she all but fled from the kitchens.

"Martha be a fine woman," Lowrens said. "I ken the womenfolk like her. Our lady used to help her with the birthin's."

Brogan was relieved to hear it.

"I imagine she'll be spittin' mad when she finds out what Hargatha has done," he added.

Brogan doubted anyone's anger over Hargatha's actions would match his own.

Gertie entered the kitchens then. She took one look at Brogan and averted her eyes.

"Gertie," Brogan called to her. "Come here."

Like a child being led to a bath, she drug her feet as she stepped forward. Brogan offered her his arm. She gave him a peculiar look before accepting.

In silence, he led her out of the kitchens and back to the keep. When they were inside and he was certain they were away from ears that could overhear, he stopped. "How be Tilda?"

"She has a nasty cut on the top of her head, and one on over her brow," she replied. "Seamus stitched her and Charles up."

"Why did ye no' seek out Hargatha, the healer?"

"Bah!" she exclaimed. "I do no' trust that woman!"

Brogan nodded his understanding. "Did ye ken that Hargatha had given Mairghread a tisane?" he asked.

Her eyes grew wide with horror. "Nay! I would no' have let her near Mairghread, m'laird."

"Do no' fash yerself," he told her. "I have only just figured it out myself. She tricked Liam into taking a tisane into Mairghread. She gave him the impression that 'twas on my order, which I can assure ye, it was no'."

Gertie's eyes grew wider. "That mean, nasty, foul woman!" she cursed.

Brogan agreed with her assessment of the healer's character. "The other day, Hargatha told me I needed to call a priest. She said she was certain Mairghread was possessed."

He watched as her countenance changed, from anger to horror. "Dear, God!" she exclaimed, as if a something had just occurred to her. "Nay," she said, as if speaking to herself. "Nay, it can no' be."

"What, Gertie?" Brogan asked, growing more curious by the moment.

She shook her head and stammered. "When me brother was ill, with the wastin' disease, she said the verra same thing!"

"I do no' understand," he said with a raised brow. "Who said what?"

Gertie swallowed and fought back tears. "When Andrew was ill, och, he was just a lad. Only two and ten years old. He came down with the wastin' disease. Hargatha said 'twas because he was possessed. The day he died," she could no longer hold back the tears. "He did just what Mairghread did! We had to tie him to the bed! 'Twas as if he *was* possessed by the devil."

Brogan's head began to spin. Was it a poison that Hargatha had given her and not just something to make her go mad?

Brogan regained his composure long enough to give Gertie an order. "Gertie, please, go find one of me men. I do no' care which one. But find them and send one to me!"

"Where be ye goin'?" she called after him.

"To Mairghread's room."

⚜

BROGAN RACED UP THE STAIRS AS FAST AS HIS LEGS WOULD ALLOW. He was afraid to ask if this day could get any worse, for he didn't doubt that it would. When he reached Mairghread's room, he was covered in sweat and out of breath. Liam was still at his post, but now, he stood inside the room, between the bed and the door. He looked up when he saw Brogan and his shoulder's relaxed.

"How fares she?" Brogan asked breathlessly as he entered the room in a rush.

"God's teeth, Brogan!" Liam exclaimed. "I have never seen anythin' like this in me life."

Mairghread's pupils were still large and black. Her body glistened with sweat as she thrashed about the bed, though 'twas no' nearly as bad as earlier. Her wrists and ankles were bleeding from where she fought against the ropes. But thankfully, she was no longer screaming at the top of her lungs.

Dread, trepidation and heartache were nearly his undoing. *Nay,* he told himself, *ye will be no good to her if ye fall apart now.*

"How be Tilda and Charles?" Liam asked in a low, hushed tone.

"Seamus, the stable master, stitched them up," he told him over his shoulder.

"Do ye ken what happened yet?" he asked.

Brogan let his breath out in a whoosh and raked a hand through his hair. "'Twas Hargatha, the healer," he said. He gave him a quick rundown of what he knew thus far. The woman had convinced Liam 'twas by Brogan's order to give Mairghread the tisane. "What we do no' ken was *what* was in it."

Liam began looking about the room, for what, Brogan didn't know. He was too focused on his wife. Kneeling beside her, he brushed his hand across her forehead. She smelled of sweat, urine, and things he wished not to think of. He felt as though his heart being cleaved in 'twain. "Wheest, lass," he whispered to her. "I be here."

For a moment, but only a moment, she stilled at the sound of his voice and turned to look at him. For the tiniest moment of time, he would have sworn she both heard and saw him. But just like that, she was gone again. Mumbling incoherently, tossing her head from side to side. Her breathing was harsh, as if she had just ran all the way from Edinburgh.

Liam came to stand beside him again. "Brogan," he said. "I think I ken what she was given."

Brogan looked over his shoulder, puzzled. Liam was holding the broken cup in his hand. He held it out. "Smell this."

Brogan sniffed. 'Twas a foul, noxious odor, but he had no clue as to what it was.

Liam took it away and shook his head. "Me brother studied with monks in Italy for a time. He be a healer, ye ken, fer the MacFindley clan, up near Aberdeen way."

Brogan remembered him speaking of that once.

"I think this be Devil's Herb."

§

LIAM HAD NO SOONER UTTERED THE WORDS, THAN A VERY BONNY woman came rushing into the room. She had dark brown hair, twisted into a braid. Her pale blue eyes held a seriousness that Brogan rarely saw in someone so young. Behind her was the maid Brogan had met earlier in the kitchens. "Ye be Martha?" he asked, just to be certain. They looked more like sisters than mother and daughter.

"Aye, m'laird," she replied as she took the cup from Liam. Doing as they had done, she took a sniff, then another. "Aye, it be Devil's Herb," she said. "Mixed with a bit of Monkshood."

Liam's eyes grew wide with horror. "God's bones, that could have killed her!" he exclaimed.

All Brogan heard was *could have*. He shot to his feet. "Will she live?" he asked hopefully.

Martha pursed her lips as she went to the opposite side of the bed. She looked into Mairghread's eyes, then placed her ear against her chest and listened. "I will do me best, m'laird," she told him.

"Evelyn," she said, looking up to her daughter with an outstretched hand. "Give me me bag."

Reaching across the bed, Evelyn handed her the worn, brown leather bag, then took a step back. "Fetch me a pitcher of cold water, and a pot of boiling," Martha directed as she began fishing through her bag. "I also need two bowls, fresh linens, and sheets."

Evelyn nodded and left the room to do her mother's bidding.

Martha looked up at Brogan. "Evelyn tells me ye did no' ken what Hargatha was givin' her?"

"I ordered Hargatha to keep away from Mairghread. I was no' here when she came back. I would never have allowed her to give her anything."

Martha studied him closely for a moment. "Ye've ordered the rebuildin' of the wall?"

"Aye," he replied, though he did not see the importance of that fact.

She snorted derisively. "And ye also want her," she gave a nod to Mairghread, "to take over as chief?"

Brogan stood to his full height and crossed his arms over his chest. "Aye, I do."

Martha nodded once, and went back to her bag. "And what do ye plan on doin' to Hargatha?"

Skirting the truth slightly, he replied, "I do no' ken yet."

She humphed once, before turning her attention back to the bag. Carefully, she began removing pouches and jars, and setting them up on the floor at her knees. "If ye be a good and just man, ye'd hang that foul woman."

Dumbfounded, Brogan stared at the woman. "Ye think she should be hanged?" he asked.

"Aye, I do," she replied bluntly. "She does more harm than she ever did good. She walks around like she be the chatelaine of the keep most days. Amputatin' fingers and limbs where there be no reason to. Tellin' people they would no' be ill if they were no' sinnin' all the time. Or worse yet, convincin' them they be possessed." She shook her head with a good deal of disgust. "And now this," she said as she looked at Mairghread. "'Twill be a miracle if she lives through the night."

He felt his chest tighten, as if a hand had reached inside his chest and held onto his heart with the grip of death. Holding his breath, his mind begged him to scream and rail.

Liam stepped forward. "I thought Devil's Herb usually killed within moments," he said.

"If given *enough,* aye, it can. I do no' ken what she mixed with it." Martha explained. "I believe I detect a bit of Monkshood too. What I do no' ken is how much she gave her. The poor woman could lie here for days, dying a slow, painful death."

Refusing to believe she would die, Brogan shook his head. *We can no' have come this far only to lose her now.*

"If that witch had a heart at all, she would tell me how much and what herbs were in that tisane. But I doubt she will. If I only knew, I would be better able to help her."

Clenching his jaw, he drew his hands into fists. "Hargatha will tell us," he ground out. "Or she will hang before the sun sets this day."

&

"I DO NO' CARE IF YE HAVE TO DRAG HER HERE, KICKIN' AND screamin'!" Brogan was barking his order to five of his men. Standing on the third floor landing, his face dark with fury, his hands fair shook with it. "Ye find the healer, Hargatha, and ye bring her to me!"

Not one man asked for a reason behind his order. As soon as they left, he headed back to Mairghread's room. Evelyn had returned with the items her mother had requested earlier. While Martha mixed what she hoped was the right antidote for whatever had been given to her, Evelyn and Liam were straightening up the room.

The smell of bodily fluids was growing worse and he did not know how much longer he could stand it. "Would it be safe to move her?" he asked Martha. "To a room across the way?"

"Ye might wait a bit, m'laird. I do no' ken if the madness will kick in again."

Brogan rubbed the back of his neck with his hand, his heart heavy with worry. "Do ye," he stopped, swallowed once, and began again. "If ye can find the proper antidote, will she..." his words trailed off. He couldn't bear to ask the question.

"Will she recover her mind?" Martha asked the question for him. "I believe so, m'laird. But again, it depends on what Hargatha has given her."

Hargatha. Just thinking of her name left a foul taste in his mouth. How on earth ... much older and wiser now, he knew there were people on this earth who possessed no line they would not cross to get what they wanted. But this auld woman, who was supposed to be a healer? Nay, that was something he doubted he would ever be able to understand.

"Liam. Evelyn," he said. "Let us go and set up the room across the hall."

Each of them nodded and followed him out of the room. Just across the tiny hall, which was really nothing more than a landing, was another small room. Almost identical to the one in which Mairghread now lay. Arrow slits and one small window, cold stone floors and walls, and that was it.

"I do no' ken where Reginald got the bed Mairghread now lies in," he said, speaking to no one in particular. A numbness began to settle into his bones. Weary, tired to the point of exhaustion, he stood in the tiny space, uncertain of what he should do next.

"I ken where to get another," Evelyn offered.

He nodded, but made no attempt to move. Liam placed a hand on Brogan's shoulder. "Brogan, let Evelyn and me prepare this room, aye? Ye can go sit with yer wife."

His wife. Aye, Mairghread was his wife and she needed him, even if she had no earthly idea if he was in the room or in Edinburgh. Up until this afternoon, he had no issue with simply sitting with her, getting her through those difficult times. 'Twas something he rather enjoyed, save for when she suffered with hallucinations. Being there for her had given him a purpose. But now, he had the need to move, to be *out* of those cramped quarters.

"'Tis all right, Brogan," Liam said. "We shall take care of it fer ye. Now, go. Be with Mairghread."

THREE HOURS PASSED BEFORE BROGAN RECEIVED WORD THEY HAD

found Hargatha. During that time, Martha had given Mairghread a simple tisane. One that would help settle her stomach and ease the sweating. One of the Mactavish men had come to the fourth floor with word that his men were approaching. Brogan told the young man to have them wait with her in the gathering room.

"Evelyn and Liam can stay with her," Martha said told him. "I want to speak to Hargatha myself."

Brogan believed that might be best, for he certainly had no knowledge of herbs or healing. "I think that be a verra good idea."

Together, he and Martha left the room. On the way below stairs, Martha said, "I could kill Hargatha with me bare hands."

Brogan quirked a brow. "Because of what she did to Mairghread?"

"Because of how many people she has hurt over the years," she replied. "But I promise, I'll no' strangle her until *after* we learn what was in that tisane."

"I thank ye, and I be certain Mairghread will as well," he said.

His men were practically dragging Hargatha into the gathering room by the time they entered. There was no doubt the woman was angry, for she was letting anyone within earshot know of her displeasure. "Do ye no' ken who I be?" she shouted at the two men who were holding her by her arms. "Ye will hang fer this as soon as Aymer returns."

"If anyone hangs, 'twill be *ye*," Brogan shouted from across the room. "And 'twill be much sooner than Aymer's expected return!"

"And who will order it done?" she shouted back. "Ye?" she harrumphed indignantly. "The Mactavish people will no' hang me."

Brogan stood just inches away from her and leaned down so that he could look into her eyes. "The Mactavish people might no', but me men would be more than happy to do it."

He was met with stone cold silence.

"What did ye give Mairghread?" His words were clipped, firm.

She shrugged her shoulders and feigned ignorance.

Brogan was not a violent man, but this woman was pushing him to his limits. He grabbed her arms and began to shake her. "Ye listen to me, auld woman! If Mairghread dies, I will hold ye personally responsible. Ye tell me *now* what ye gave her, or I swear to ye, we will take ye from this room now, and hang ye from the tallest tower of this keep!"

"You would no' dare," she spat back at him.

Brogan began pulling her toward the stairs. "Henry!" he shouted over his shoulder. "Bring me a rope!"

Hargatha Mactavish chose the wrong day and the wrong man to test.

❧

B̲Y THE TIME THEY REACHED THE THIRD FLOOR, WITH B̲ROGAN pulling her along behind him, she began to see the error of her ways. His men were all right behind him, along with Martha, quietly offering their unwavering support. When he pulled open the door that led to the fourth floor, she began to wail. "Ye would kill a helpless auld woman?" she asked.

"Ye might be auld, but ye are far from helpless," he seethed. A dull ache had begun to form at the base of his skull. So incensed was he that aye, he was ready to hang this woman. Not because she refused to cooperate, but because of what she had done to Mairghread.

As he pulled her through the door, she began to stammer. "Wait! 'Twas no' but a tisane!"

Brogan halted abruptly. "I ken it was a bloody tisane!" His voice boomed and echoed through the narrow stairway.

"If ye kill me, Martha can no' make an antidote!" She was trying to bargain her neck out of the hangman's noose.

"The bloody hell I can no'!" Martha shouted from behind her.

Hargatha growled as Brogan began to pull her up the stairs once again. "Verra well!" she cried. "'Twas naught but Devil's herb!"

Martha heard her and pushed her way through the crowd of men. "And what else?" she demanded to know.

Hargatha turned her head enough to glower at her. "And Monkshood ye interferin' whore!"

If Martha was bothered by the insult, she did not show it. "And what else?"

The auld woman grew silent until Brogan yanked on her arm. "And a bit of lobelia!"

"And naught else?" Martha asked, her glower hot enough to set a grown man's skin afire.

"And naught else!" Hargatha replied with a snort of derision.

Martha studied her closely for a moment. Apparently satisfied she had told the truth, she said, "I ken what to do now. Ye can go ahead and hang her."

Hargatha let loose with a slew of curses Brogan had never heard from a woman's mouth before. Martha ignored the woman's tirade and pushed her way past her to return to Mairghread.

"I told ye what ye wanted!" Hargatha cried. "Ye can no' hang me now!"

Brogan pretended to give her argument some thought. "Aye, I can no' hang ye now," he said before handing her off to Henry. "Henry, find a room to lock her in. Keep her under guard at all times. James, Peter, ye start constructing the gallows. She hangs on the morrow."

Chapter Fourteen

After Martha gave Mairghread the antidote, she began to calm almost immediately. "She will likely sleep for a few days," she told Brogan. "I will no' say she is out of the woods yet, but I think we can move her to the room next door."

Brogan was thankful for the news on many levels. He could not wait to get out of the filthy, malodorous room. But more than anything, he was thankful that Mairghread had finally stopped thrashing and moaning.

Before they moved her into the new room, Evelyn brought a basin and clothes in. Together, she and Martha cleaned Mairghread up as best they could. They bandaged her wrists and ankles, from which she had torn the flesh fighting against the restraints.

They also put her into a clean night rail and warm woolens. "What she needs is a bath, but we will have to wait fer that," Martha told him.

Once she was clean and freshly dressed, Brogan scooped her up into his arms. *God's teeth!* He exclaimed silently. *She has lost so much weight.* As light as a feather she felt in his arms.

With much care and gentleness, he took her across the hall to her new quarters. Liam and Evelyn had done a good job and making the space as inviting as possible. A new bed, larger than the old one, sat against one wall. Fresh linens, pillows, and sheets covered the mattress, along with blankets and a fur. A chair and table were placed next to the bed, and a brazier crackled softly in the corner.

As tenderly as a mum puts her babe in a cradle, Brogan placed Mairghread in the center of the bed. He pulled the covers up around her shoulders, making sure she would be warm and comfortable.

"Why do ye no' get some rest," Martha suggested. "I will stay with her. We will send word if there be any change."

"Nay," he replied. "I will stay with her."

"But laird, ye look like ye have no' slept in days," she argued.

"'Tis true, I have no'," he replied. "But I bade Mairghread a promise that I would no' leave her side. Look what happened to her when I left to change me bloody tunic."

Unable to argue any sense into him, Martha sighed. "Verra well. I will return soon to check on her. But I suggest ye at least *try* to rest, m'laird. Ye'll be no use to her if ye succumb to exhaustion or lack of food."

A grunt was his only reply.

After she left, he took the seat next to Mairghread's bed. "Lass, I be so verra sorry," he whispered. "Please fergive me."

By his order, Henry took up the post as Brogan's second in command. With Reginald's absence, 'twas up to Henry to see to the felling of trees. There were many rumblings and much grumbling when he told the Mactavish men of the change in plans.

"Trees?" And older man named Stuart asked as he scratched the back of his neck. Though he was a short man, he was broad in the shoulders and had arms that looked like they could fell a tree without the need of axe.

"Aye, trees," Henry said as he stood before the group of men. "We have just been made aware of the possibility of an attack in the verra near future."

A gasp, as well as a few curses, broke out over the crowd. These men, of varying ages and sizes, stood dumbfounded in the afternoon sunlight.

"An attack?" came a loud voice from the crowd.

"Aye, an attack," Henry answered solemnly.

"But we have no enemies," someone else spoke up.

Henry thought it a most naive statement, but kept that thought to himself. Earlier that day, when he had visited Brogan in Mairghread's new chamber, Brogan had given him a quick summary of what he knew. 'Twas decided that they would not mention Aymer or what he may or may not have done. If anyone was loyal to him, they might forge an alliance against Brogan and his men. So 'twas decided not to mention any names.

"Who wishes to attack and for what purpose?" someone else asked.

More murmurs fell over the crowd.

Where Brogan was honest to a fault, Henry was not thusly inclined. Where Brogan was usually blunt and to the point, Henry had a more *creative* streak. A way with words that made him a very good storyteller. Now, he knew he had few choices. He could not tell the entire truth of the matter, for there were likely many in this crowd who were loyal to the bastard Aymer. So he decided he would stretch the truth just a bit.

"Right now, in the lowlands, there be a band of murderin', lyin', cheatin' thieves, who have banded together. Their numbers grow by fifty each day."

The murmurs were silenced almost immediately.

Since he had their attention, he decided to continue. "These men do no' band together under any clan name. Nay, they all be sons of whores if ever I saw or heard of one. Their forces stand at nearly five hundred."

Wide, horrified eyes stared back at him. The words 'five hundred' were whispered repeatedly amongst them.

"What do they want from us?" someone asked in a low voice. "Our women?"

Someone chuckled, and replied, "They can have mine! She grouses like a fish-wife!"

Nervous laughter could be heard among them.

"Worse than wantin' yer women and yer lands," Henry said as he stood a bit taller. "The bloody bastards want yer horses!"

One communal appalled gasp was let out, quickly followed by loud curses. "'Twill be over me dead body they take me horses!" one man cried out. His friends cheered him.

"Well, if we do no' get this wall built before they make their way here, ye *will* be dead and yer horses will be theirs!" Henry told them.

Never had he seen a group of men come together so quickly before. Axes and tools that had been set down earlier, were picked up with the same enthusiasm as a warrior picking up his broadsword.

"They can have me woman," the man who had jested before said. "But they'll no' get me horses!"

So Henry had stretched the truth more than was probably necessary. But even Brogan would have to admit 'twas better to have these men motivated by common ground and working *for* him instead of against him.

FOR TWO SOLID DAYS AND NIGHTS, MAIRGHREAD SLEPT. BETIMES, 'twas a fitful, restless sleep. Brogan did not know if 'twas a good or bad thing. Martha had assured him 'twas all perfectly normal, considering all she had gone through the past days.

Brogan had lost all track of time as he kept his bedside vigil. One day had turned to another, and he had yet to leave her side. Meals were eaten in the same chair in which he slept, holding on to her hand.

For the most part, 'twas a silent vigil, save for when she would be jarred by some dream or memory, he was never certain. When those restless moments came, he would hold her hand tightly and whisper words of encouragement in her ear. Although he was quite certain she could not hear him, he spoke them anyway.

'Twas much like the last few days of Anna's life. She'd fallen into a deep sleep from which she would never awake. He never left her side either. But instead of whispering words of encouragement, he spoke from his heart to Anna.

He did not know Mairghread well enough yet, to know what was in his heart. Theirs had been a strained and unusual relationship in the beginning.

The beginning, he mused. *We were married three days before I realized she was a drunkard.* As he sat next to her bed, in the predawn hours, he shook his head in bemusement. Three days of her biting, harsh insults. Three days of not knowing how she had changed so dramatically from their first meeting.

But now he knew the truth, or at least a goodly portion of it. She drank to remember, she drank to forget. Knowing what he knew now, he could not blame her for grabbing the nearest bottle and never looking back. She believed she killed her husband and son.

And 'twas her uncle who put that idea into her head. The bastard begat his lie with one tiny seed, then cultivated it, watching it grow and grow into what now lay on the bed before him. Disgust roiled in his gut.

An attack by outside forces? Nay, he did not believe it. An attack where naught was stolen? An attack where no one saw a thing, save for one man -- Aymer Mactavish. And the bloody bastard placed the blame on an innocent lass who was so distraught, she could not have seen the truth if it had been bludgeoning her with a club.

Looking upon her now, she slept peacefully, on her side, with the covers drawn tightly around her. Those dark auburn tresses had been one of the first things he had noticed about her. Long and thick. Now, they were dirty, stringy and matted against her head and face.

He believed she would not want anyone to see her in such disarray. Or so he imagined she would be like most women in that regard.

Though they had spent several days alone together, locked away in a tiny room, he still knew very little about her. Aye, he knew the dark ugly secrets. Knew about her losses, her heartaches and now the dark truth about her uncle. A truth she was not even aware of.

But he wanted to know *more.* More and different things. What was her favorite food? Her favorite color? Did she have a favorite flower? What were her thoughts on Scotland's current king?

Time, he supposed, was what they needed. Time out of this blasted room. Time where she was not fighting an addiction or now, the tisane that had made her lose her mind, albeit temporarily.

Mayhap, when she was better, they might take a trip somewhere. Mayhap they could go back to his father's keep. Certainly they would learn much about each other on such a long and arduous trip.

But nay, that was not possible, at least not right now. There were too many things that needed to be done before he would feel safe leaving the keep for more than an hour. Thankfully, he had his men working for him day and night now to erect a wooden wall. He imagined he'd not rest well until it was complete. Nay, he'd not rest well until Aymer Mactavish was brought to justice.

DAYBREAK HAD COME WITH A FIRE-RED SKY AGAINST A BRIGHT BLUE backdrop. The sun warmed the earth and air. Filtering in on the gentle breeze were the sounds of sheep bleating, cattle lowing, along with the occasional whinny and snicker of horses.

Birds twittering and flapping at the small window woke Brogan from a not-too-deep sleep. Mairghread was still sleeping peacefully. He stood, stretched his arms out wide, and went to look outside.

The sea was calm this morn, the air crisp and clean smelling. As he had done for many days now, Brogan looked out to the ocean and sky and prayed. He prayed for Mairghread's swift and full recovery. He prayed they would be able to build the wall before Aymer's return. And he prayed for some semblance of peace to fall over his heart, as well as this place he now called home.

The sound of his name being spoken broke through his quiet reverie. He spun to see Mairghread, sitting up on one elbow. She looked confused, worn, and tired, but he cared not. He was overjoyed at seeing her awake and hearing her speak his name.

He rushed to her side, shoved the chair aside, and knelt beside her. "Och! Lass, 'tis good to see ye awake!"

"I be awfully thirsty," she told him, her voice sounding tired and scratchy.

With trembling hands, he poured her a cup of water and helped her to drink. "No' too much at once," he warned with a thoughtful smile.

She tried to listen, tried taking small sips, but her thirst was too large to deny. Brogan had to pry the cup from her hands before she made herself sick. "I promise, this be no' the last cup of water in the keep," he told her playfully.

She let out a slight moan, and fell back against the bed. "Ye look as bad as I feel," she said. Closing her eyes, she took in a deep, cleansing breath.

Brogan chuckled softly, glad for the moment she could not see her own self.

"What happened?" she asked. "Why do I feel like I have been trampled by a horse?"

Brogan set the cup down and took her hand in his. "Do ye remember naught of the past sennight?" He held his breath, worried that her memory had somehow been affected by Hargatha's concoction.

She was quiet and still for a long while. "I remember comin' to ye, askin' fer yer help," she said in a low voice. "I remember bein' quite afraid for what seems like a long while."

Mayhap 'twas a blessing she could not remember what Hargatha had done to her. "Do ye remember anythin' else?" he asked.

Deep crimson flushed her neck and face. She took in a deep breath and let it out slowly. "I remember makin' a fool out of myself," she replied, with a slight tremor to her voice. "Snakes and worms that were no' really there."

"Do no' fash yerself over it," he told her. "All that be behind us now."

Slowly, she opened her eyes and looked up at him. "Why be I in a different room now?"

Lord above, he did not wish to recount to her what had happened three days ago. But he had made a promise to always be honest with her. "I broke me word, to ye," he began. "Ye were doin' well enough that I thought 'twas safe to leave ye with Tilda. I left long enough to wash up and change." He had to clear the knot that was trying to lodge itself in his throat. He explained what had happened in his absence, of Hargatha's wicked tisane. He could not bring himself to tell her all the ugly truth of it. "Ye became verra upset. 'Twas as if the tisane made ye—" he searched for words other than mad, delusional, or insane. "Verra upset and angry. Martha had to give ye a potion to counteract what was in Hargatha's tisane. Ye have been asleep for almost three days."

He eyes grew wide with horror. "Three days?" she exclaimed, as she struggled to sit up.

"I be so verra sorry, lass, for lettin' ye down. Fer breakin' me word to ye."

❧

ABLE TO THINK CLEARLY FOR THE FIRST TIME IN A VERY LONG while, Mairghread looked into Brogan's green eyes. The guilt she saw in their depths, nearly brought tears to her own. "Ye did no' break yer word to me Brogan," she told him. "Ye fought fer me when I could no' fight fer meself."

"But I promised I'd no leave ye," he countered.

"Ye left to wash up and change yer clothes, Brogan. 'Tis no' as if ye went hiein' off to Edinburgh," she said with a soft chuckle. "Nay, Brogan, ye kept yer word."

As far as she was concerned, he had done everything he had said he would. "Ye can no' take the blame fer somethin' ye did no' do. Did ye ask Hargatha to give me the foul tisane?"

"Nay!" he exclaimed with a furrowed brow.

"Then ye have naught to fash yerself over," she told him. "Pray tell me though, where is Hargatha?"

As much as he did want to hang the auld woman, he did not feel 'twas his place to do so. "We have her locked away, in a room on the first floor of the keep," he told her.

"With the other servants?" she asked.

"Nay, lass, she has her own chamber. But she is not allowed to leave, nor is anyone allowed to visit."

Happy with his answer, she lay back against the pillows again. When she thought on her atrocious behavior the past fortnight, she felt ashamed. How could she have treated these people so poorly? 'Twas beyond poor, 'twas unforgivable. Suddenly, the need for a glass of wine began to grow strong. But 'twas not the same gut-aching, visceral need she'd been feeling for three years. Still, 'twas enough to make her feel ashamed.

"Mairghread?" Brogan spoke in a low, soft tone. "Be ye well?"

Unable to look at him for her shame was so great, she simply nodded her head.

The sound of the door opening made her open her eyes.

'Twas Martha. "Och! Ye be awake," she said with a smile.

"She woke a few moments ago," Brogan told her as he got to his feet. "I have told her what happened," he said as he approached her. Mairghread saw him whisper something in Martha's ear. Martha nodded, then came to sit beside her.

"How fare ye?" she asked with a warm, sincere smile.

"Like I have been trampled by horses," she replied. "Verra angry horses."

Martha giggled softly. "I imagine so. Now, let me take a look at ye."

She took the time looking into each eye, then pressed her ear to Mairghread's chest. Once she was done with that, she lifted her hands to look at her wrists. That was the first time Mairghread noticed the bandages.

With furrowed brows, she asked, "What happened to me wrists?" The sudden thought that she might have tried to harm herself was overwhelming.

"The tisane Hargatha gave ye made ye verra upset. We had to restrain ye, Mairghread," Brogan answered.

Relief washed over her, thankful that she hadn't tried to cut her own wrists, as she had often thought of doing in the past. *Upset.* She must have been mightily upset if they had to restrain her.

"Ye're healin' nicely," Martha told her. "The salve I applied worked verra well."

Mairghread whispered her thanks. Although she was relieved, she was still worried. Would this nightmare never end?

Martha next looked at the wounds on her ankles. Shame continued to build. She hated not being able to remember. Those blank moments in time, hours or days, were more than worrisome.

"I think 'twill be safe fer ye to bathe now, and even move into yer real chamber," Martha said as she patted her hand.

That should have been good news. She should have rejoiced in it. Instead, more worry began to settle in. *What if I can no' stay sober outside this room?*

"I must leave ye now," Martha said. "Joan Mactavish's pains started this morn. I can help ye to bathe, but heaven only knows how long this bairn will take."

Brogan stepped forward. "I will help her."

The thought of Brogan helping her bathe made her skin burn with humiliation. They were not yet husband and wife in the truest sense of the word. Bone tired and weary, however, she did not have the strength to argue. Besides, she could smell herself. A bath was much needed and wanted.

§

BEFORE MARTHA LEFT, BROGAN ASKED HER TO SEND EVELYN UP with soap, drying clothes and such. He'd also taken a moment to speak to Liam, but what about, she couldn't hear.

They were each silent while they waited for Evelyn. 'Twas the kind of awkward silence where one would be tempted to speak, if only to break it. From his spot by the window, Brogan finally broke the silence. "'Tis a verra nice day."

She wanted to remark that 'twas usually nice this time of year, but decided against it. There were other far more important things to discuss than the weather. Unfortunately, she did not yet feel brave enough.

Brogan finally turned away from the window. "I must tell you that we have made some recent changes to buildin' the wall."

The wall? Her mind was blank for a moment until she remembered. "'Tis good that we are finally rebuildin' it," she said. And she was sincerely grateful that he was seeing to the construction.

"Much happened in the past few days," he said as he took the chair and sat next to her.

She could see he was fighting with something, but what that something was, she didn't think she wanted to know.

"I have decided that a stone wall will take far too long to build," he began. "So I have the men fellin' trees. We shall build a wall from wood first."

"Because it be much faster?" she asked sleepily.

"Aye, 'twill be much faster."

Her bones were beginning to ache, leaving her feeling tired. The last thing she wanted however, was to sleep away another day. "'Tis good, then," she replied with a yawn. "If ye're lookin' fer me approval, ye have it."

"Do ye want to ken why?"

She shook her head and yawned once more. "Nay. Whatever yer reasons, I be certain they are sound." She did, however, wonder why he looked and sounded so utterly serious at the moment. Or mayhap, 'twas only her cloudy mind and aching muscles that made her think such.

"I am feelin' tired again," she told him. "Will this ever pass?"

He chuckled and said, "Aye, it will."

Her eyelids felt heavy, but she refused to keep them closed. What she needed was a good scrubbing in a hot tub, and maybe something to eat. Something more than broth and bread. She was just about to tell him so when the flutter of something caught her attention. Her eyes flew open, wide with sincere horror. *Good lord, I be hallucinatin' again!* She screamed silently as her fingers began to tremble.

Two little birds, storm petrals they are called, had flown in through the open window. Reaching out, she clung tightly to Brogan's hand. Seeing her distress, he followed her line of vision.

"Och!" Brogan said as he stood up. "Shoo!" he said as he began to wave his hands in the air. The little black and white birds fluttered around in the room, chittering angrily.

"Ye see them too?" she asked with a good measure of surprise.

He turned to look at her, with his arms still in the air. "What?"

"Ye see them too?" she repeated the question with wide eyes and a profound tremor in her voice.

It dawned on him then to what she referred. The worms and snakes she had hallucinated over days ago. She was terrified she was hallucinating once again.

He threw his head back and laughed. Och! The sound of his

laughter booming through the room must have terrified the petrals, for they flew back out the same way they'd come in.

But to Mairghread? His laughter was infectious, and she soon found herself joining in.

❧

'TWAS THE FIRST GOOD, HEARTY LAUGH SHE HAD HAD IN YEARS. SHE laughed until her stomach ached and tears streamed down her face. She felt light and happy as well as much relieved. Relieved that she was not hallucinating again. Relieved that Brogan laughed easily.

Evelyn walked into the room then with a bundle of blankets, towels, washing clothes and soap in her arms. She look perplexed when she saw them laughing so heartily. Her expression made them begin laughing all over again.

Carefully, she set the items on the foot of Mairghread's bed, bobbed a curtsy and all but fled the room.

"I think ye scared her," Mairghread declared once she got her laughter under control.

"Me?" he asked, feigning injury.

"Aye, ye," she said. "Look at ye. A big, braw Highlander, with all that ginger hair, standin' in the middle of a small room, laughin' like a mad man."

She was teasing, of course, and he knew it. "Ye think me braw?" he teased, waggling his brows.

She knew she was blushing like a young maid, so she turned away, so that he couldn't see her. And she refused to answer his question.

Thankfully, he did not push for one.

"Come, let us get ye to the loch."

"The loch?" she asked, aghast at the notion.

Brogan cleared his throat once before answering. "Aye, lass, the loch. I fear 'twould take ten tubs of hot water to get ye clean. We shall start in the loch, to get most of the last ten days off of ye. Then, ye shall soak in a hot bath until yer skin wrinkles if ye'd like. But the loch, first, aye?"

The promise of a hot bath was too alluring, therefore she did not argue. "Verra well," she said as she threw back the covers. Brogan was beside her in an instant, helping her to her feet. With one arm around her waist, the other holding her hand, he waited until she was steady enough to stand on her own.

"If I look half as bad as I feel, I fear I shall frighten the children, mayhap even small animals."

He chuckled again as he grabbed one of the thick, heavy blankets and wrapped it around her shoulders. "I have ordered the courtyard cleared, and no one is allowed near the loch," he told her.

She didn't know if she should be insulted or grateful. Therefore she erred on the side of caution, assuming 'twas nothing but kindness that made him do such a thing. "I thank ye."

He scooped up the linens, handed her the soap to hold, then carefully guided her out of the room. "I be glad we' be walkin' *down* all these flights of stairs. I fear me legs would no' be strong enough to walk *up* them."

"If ye get too tired, I shall carry ye," he said as he gave her a gentle hug around her waist.

There was no doubt in her mind that he would do just that.

≈

'TWAS SLOW GOING, BUT THEY FINALLY MADE THEIR WAY OUT OF THE keep, across the yard, and down to the loch. By the time they reached it, she felt as though she'd just run all the way from Inverness. Her bones ached; her muscles were tired from too many days of nonuse.

The loch was located near a small copse of trees. Several large boulders, some as tall as two men, lined its western banks. On the other, tall grass grew and swayed in the breeze.

Brogan placed the drying and washing cloths on the bank. "Do ye need help?" he asked, his tone thoughtful and warm.

She felt the blush come to her cheeks and couldn't find the wherewithal to answer.

For whatever reason, he blushed right along with her. "Mayhap, I will just help ye into the water," he said as he took her hand in his.

All she could do was nod. 'Twas not as if they weren't married. And she certainly was not some innocent, virginal maid. But somehow, the thought of him seeing her unclothed, did not feel right.

"And ye can leave yer night rail on, lass," he suggested. "Take it off when ye get in."

Why she felt such a sense of relief at the suggestion, she did not rightly know. But relieved and glad she was. Using her toes, she removed her slippers and left them on the bank.

He held her hand and led her into the loch. "It be no' too bad," he told her with a grin as he put one foot in, then another.

"God's teeth!" she cried as soon as her feet touched the water. "This water be cold!"

She immediately began to shiver. "Ye lied," she said, biting back a curse.

He kept leading her into the water. "Would ye have gotten in if I told ye it was cold?" he asked with a grin and a quirked brow.

She refused to answer.

Soon, she was up to her waist in frigid water. "Why be ye no' shiverin'?" she asked curtly.

He chuckled. "I be a warrior. I be used to such conditions."

&

THE TRUTH WAS, HE HAD BEEN ENJOYING THEIR NEWLY FOUND camaraderie a little too much. Although she was filthy, with her hair matted to her scalp, and smelled as bad as anything he'd ever smelled before, he found himself strongly attracted to her. 'Twas her wit. He knew that immediately. The fact that he also knew what she looked like when she was clean and dressed, did not help matters much. The frigid water was exactly what he needed to cool his burgeoning desire.

"I shall turn away," he said. "If ye'd like to toss yer night rail to the bank." He winked once, before turning his back to her.

"Hold this," she said. He turned halfway around to see she was handing him the jar of soap. He took it and waited.

He could hear her struggling to remove the night dress. Playfully, he said, "Do ye need help?"

She grunted once before replying. "Can ye do it with yer eyes closed?"

He had to bite his tongue to keep from blurting out *I can do many things with me eyes closed, but I prefer them open when a lass be near me and naked.* Clearing his throat, he said, "Aye, I think so."

"Fine," she muttered.

He turned to see that one arm was stuck in a wet sleeve. "With yer eyes *closed,*" she reminded him.

He took a step closer, reached out, and handed the soap back to her. A moment later, he tugged the arm out of her sleeve.

"Yer eyes are open," she told him through chattering teeth.

"I be just helpin' ye get yer arms out," he said. "I will close them, ye have me word."

Once her arms were dislodged from the sleeves, he kept his word and closed his eyes. Ever so carefully, he tried to find the hem of her dress. His head accidentally brushed against her breasts when he leaned down. "Sorry," he murmured. She was silent.

Fishing around in the water, with his eyes closed, he finally found the fabric. 'Twas swirling in the cold water. He grabbed a bit of it with both hands, then stood up. But upon doing so, he pulled her forward. She landed against his chest with an oomph.

"So sorry," he said again, with eyes closed and a grin he was trying to keep from turning into a devious smile.

"Never mind," she said as she batted his hands away. "I can do it meself." Handing back the jar of soap, she twirled her fingers, a silent message for him to once again turn around.

With a shrug of his shoulders, he turned. He had to, elst she see his smile.

Long moments and several grunts later, he heard her move toward the bank. Then the plop of the wet night dressing landing in the grass.

He could envision her now, naked, with little goosebumps erupting over her creamy skin. Oh, how he longed to reach out and touch her, make her his very own. But 'twas too soon for that.

"The soap please?" she said as she tapped his shoulder.

He swallowed once and handed it to her over his shoulder.

'Twas then he realized he was still completely dressed. His trews were clinging tightly to his thighs. Deciding that since he was here, he might as well wash, he removed his tunic and tossed it onto the bank.

"May I borrow some of yer soap?" he asked, extending his arm behind him, so that he could keep his word.

§◆

MAIRGHREAD'S FRUSTRATION WAS GROWING BY LEAPS AND BOUNDS. "I need a washing cloth," she whispered.

At hearing the distress in her voice, he spun around. She had ducked down, the water almost to her neck, still holding on to the jar of soap. Brogan took one look at her, nodded his ginger-haired head, and went to the bank. Moments later he was taking the jar from her hands and applying some of it to the cloth for her. "Are ye well?" he asked as he handed the wet cloth to her.

Swallowing back the tears that threatened, she nodded once. He studied her closely for a moment before turning back around.

Taking in deep breaths, she began to scrub her arms, then torso. When she felt something crusty and nasty on her legs, she did not even want to imagine what it might be. Once she was done, she took in a deep breath and dunked her head under the water. When she came up, she saw tiny pieces of what looked like vomit start to float on the water.

Good lord, what happened to me? She pondered the question for a long moment and didn't like any of the answers.

"May I have more soap?" she whispered once again to Brogan's back.

He handed the jar back to her, extending his arm behind his back. She was thankful he couldn't see her on the edge of losing her composure.

Dipping her fingers into the jar, she scooped out a goodly amount. When she applied it to her hair, she could feel how dirty it was. More bits washed out and floated behind the others. She scrubbed and scrubbed until her scalp hurt. Never in her life had she been so filthy.

Dunking under the water again, she rinsed the soap out. Coming back up, she breathed in a good lungful of air. Wiping water from her eyes, she looked at the man, still standing with his back to her.

Not once had he mentioned how disheveled or dirty she was. Weeks ago, she had scoffed at his honor. Had teased him, called him a monk, and worse. Still, he remained by her side, refusing to let her continue on the path of drunkenness. Even then, when they were alone in the attic room, when she had cursed him to the devil countless times, he never once yelled or cursed back. And not once did he throw his hands in the air and leave.

Very close to breaking down again, she took in a deep breath. "I be done," she told him with a shaky voice.

He gave a quick nod before turning around. If he saw her distress, he was kind enough not to mention it. "I will get the blanket fer ye," he said as she climbed out of the loch.

Standing on the bank, he unfurled the blanket and held it up for her. "I will keep me eyes closed," he told her.

Too cold to speak, let alone argue for a better plan — which she did not have— she gave a quick nod. Once his eyes were closed, she made her way out of the loch. Her arms and legs felt as heavy as lead. As quickly as she could, she rushed forward and landed against his chest with a very un-ladylike grunt. Spinning around at the same time, he wrapped her into the warm blanket.

Brogan helped her into her slippers, picked up the soap and other items, and put one arm around her waist. "We'll have ye in a nice hot bath verra soon," he promised her.

It caught her by surprise when she sighed contentedly against his chest. A prickling sensation began to build behind her eye. *Ye just be tired,* she told herself. *And he be warm. There be naught else to it.*

WHEN THEY ENTERED HER BEDCHAMBER, EACH OF THEM WAS A BIT surprised by the number of people within. Tilda, Gertie, Martha and her daughter, as well as two housemaids took up most of the free space in her room.

"Och!" Gertie cried as she rushed to greet her. "'Tis God's truth I am glad to see ye!"

Tilda was wrapping her own arms around Mairghread before she had a chance to respond. The room burst to life with women all chattering, smiling, and hugging their lady. Brogan did the only thing he could; he stepped off to the side and watched.

Mairghread's teeth chattered together, but no one paid it any mind. They — Gertie and Tilda to be most specific — were simply too happy to see her. She offered them the warmest smile she could muster, and listened as they asked what seemed like a hundred questions as once.

After a short while, she looked at the bath sitting in front of her fire. Then she looked at Brogan.

He saw the pleading look in her eyes and came to help her at once. "Ladies," he said, raising his voice so he could be heard over the din. They all turned to look at him. "Mairghread has just come from bathin' in the loch and is quite cold. Leave us now, so that she can get into the bath ye brought her *before* the water chills."

The room erupted once again, in a chorus of *ochs* and *ayes* and *I be sorrys*. Still, no one made any attempt to leave. Instead, Tilda and Gertie led her toward the bath whilst they tried to divest her of her blanket.

"Stop!" Mairghread cried out. Immediately, she felt ashamed for raising her voice. "Please," she said, changing her tone to something warmer and more sincere. "Please, I do appreciate yer wantin' to help me, but I would like a little bit of time to meself."

They repeated their chorus from moments ago as Brogan began to usher them out of the room. Before they would allow him to shut the door, he had to promise Gertie and Tilda he would call them first if Mairghread needed anything.

When he turned around, Mairghread was already in the tub, leaning back with a sigh. He chuckled softly at the sight. Seeing that soaps and cloths had been set on the chair by the tub, he felt a little unnecessary at the moment.

"Be ye hungry?" he asked from the spot by the door.

"Aye," she replied as she placed her arms on the edge of the tub. "Could I have somethin' more than bread and broth?"

Another knot formed in his throat when she pulled herself up and grabbed a washing cloth and jar of soap. Scooping a bit out, she began to smear it over her arms and shoulders. 'Twas one of the most seductive things he had ever witnessed and she hadn't any idea it was so.

When he was silent for too long, she turned her head to look at him over her shoulder. "Brogan?"

He was torn from his wondering thoughts filled with desire. "Aye?" he replied over the growing knot.

"Are ye well?"

He nodded once, cleared his throat and mind. "I shall get ye somethin' to eat."

He thought he might have to jump in the loch again.

ALONE FOR THE FIRST TIME IN A LONG WHILE, MAIRGHREAD thought she might covet the silence. After washing her body and hair again, she sank back into the tub. The water did wonders to soothe her aching muscles and tired bones. Twice, she fell asleep, only to be jolted awake when her chin touched the water.

Worried she was so tired she might drown in her own bath, she begrudgingly brought herself to stand. Grabbing one of the drying clothes, she pulled it around herself and stepped out of the tub.

A fresh, warm nigh rail had been laid out on the bed for her, along with thick woolens. Hurriedly, she dried off her body and toweled her hair before pulling on the night rail. Chilled again, she grabbed the woolens along with a brightly colored woven blanket and sat on the stool by the fire. Try as she might, she found she could not lift her feet to put the woolens on. Instead, she pulled the blanket around her tightly and let the fire in the hearth warm her face.

One question piled on top of another, which brought forth a pounding sensation behind her eyes. Everyone was being gracious and kind to her, even after her horrible mistreatment of them. And she knew it had been horrible mistreatment.

Why? She repeated that same question over and over again in her mind. *Why be they all so kind when ye were nothin' but cruel and mean to them?* For the life of her, she could not find the answer.

And what of Brogan? Nearly complete strangers, they were. Still, he treated her with nothing but kindness and a gentleness she had not felt since James.

James. When her thoughts turned to him, they also turned to Connell.

A sickening sensation began to build deep in her stomach. Lord above, how she missed them.

Nay! She chastised herself. *Ye can no' let yer heart take ye back. When ye do, ye drink. And when ye drink, ye are as cruel and mean-spirited as Hargatha!*

But what was she to do? Not a day went by that she did not think of them at least a few dozen times. They were the most important people in her life.

Then she had gone mad and killed them.

Oh, no one had ever said it outright. Only hints here and there. *Yer uncle found ye bloody, stabbin' yerself with the knife.* She shuddered and choked back the bile forming in her throat. *But did that truly mean they died at her hand? Was that the* only *explanation that made sense?*

And what of the two guards who had died that night? Certainly, she could not have killed them. She hadn't left the main keep since giving birth to Connell. Was it merely coincidence that the two young guards had died the same night James and Connell had?

Whenever she tried to remember, or tried to make sense of it, her head would throb mercilessly, and inevitably, her stomach would churn. Why hadn't sobriety brought clarity to that night? Was it too soon to expect it?

Tears pooled in her eyes, slid from her lids and down her cheeks. *If Brogan knew, if he knew what I had done, would he continue to show me such kindness?* 'Twas highly unlikely.

Eventually, she would have to confess her sins to him. Nay, no' eventually. It must be done sooner rather than later. They had not yet consummated their marriage. There was still time for him to ask for an annulment. Could they part ways as friends if he knew the truth? What then? What if he became so enraged he left her?

Fear traced along her spine. She should have thought of all these things *before* she had agreed to marry him. And most definitely before she decided to climb out of the darkness the bottles gave her.

Confusion begat fear which begat dread. In her heart, she knew she had to tell him the truth. Now, today, as soon as he returned from the kitchen.

❧

WHEN BROGAN RETURNED, SHE WAS OUT OF THE TUB AND SITTING by the fire. She had donned the fresh night rail someone had laid out for her. Her damp hair clung to the clean blanket she had wrapped around her shoulders.

Lost in her own thoughts, she did not move when he set the tray on the edge of the bed. He noticed her fingertips were white, for she was clinging tightly to the blanket. 'Twas also then he noticed the tears dripping off her chin.

"Mairghread?" he said, kneeling down beside her. "Mairghread."

When she finally turned to look at him, she gulped back more tears. "Why?"

"Why what, lass?"

"Why are ye so kind to me when I have been so cruel to ye?"

She broke down completely then, as he pulled her into his arms. Sitting on the floor, with his back against the bed, he held her while she wept. With his palms, he smoothed her hair, and whispered, "Lass, please do no' cry."

"But why? I was so verra mean to ye, Brogan. I would no' have blamed ye if ye had packed yer bags and left after the third day of bein' married to me! But ye stayed and ye helped me and I do no' ken why."

He let out a short sigh as he tried to find the right words of comfort. "In truth, lass, I do no' rightly ken meself. I supposed it had to do with when we met at Ian's. Ye intrigued me. And I could no' verra well let ye be married off to Courtemanche."

"I ken why ye married me," she said against his tunic. "What I do no' ken is why ye stayed."

"I stayed because ye needed me. If I did no' help ye, who would?"

She sniffled, wiped her tears on his shirt, and looked up at him. "So ye stayed out of a sense of honor and duty?"

"Partly," he answered. "But during those first few days, when ye started to sober up and open up to me, I found I rather liked ye."

She groaned once, dropped her face against his chest and began to cry again. He could not imagine why. "Wheest, now, lass," he whispered against the top of her head.

"Nay," she said as she pulled away. "I must tell ye somethin', Brogan. Something ugly and horrible. All I ask is that ye listen to me, let me say it all first. Then ye can rail and cry foul and leave."

He had a suspicion about what she was going to tell him. "Verra well," he said as he brushed the tears from her cheeks with his thumbs. "But I be certain that nothin' ye tell me could make me rail at ye, or cry foul and leave."

His reassurance did not help. Fighting the tears, the bile rising in her throat, she stammered and fought for the words. But they would no' come. "I be naught but a coward, Brogan. I want to tell ye, but me cowardice be gettin' in the way. I want to be honest with ye, as ye have been with me."

Offering her a warm smile, he said, "I believe I already ken what it is ye want to tell me."

Her brow furrowed as she shook her head. "Nay, there be no way ye could ken. Fer if ye did, ye would have left me the moment ye learned of it."

Taking in a deep breath through his nostrils, he let it out slowly. "Be ye wantin' to tell me ye believe ye killed yer husband and son?"

𝕸

EYES WIDE IN HORRIFICATION, SHE COULD NOT SPEAK FOR THE longest while. "Ye ken?" she stammered.

"Aye, lass, I ken the truth of it."

Closing her eyes, she took in deep, steadying breaths as her stomach roiled with self-loathing. "Yet ye stayed," she said, unable to understand how he was able to do just that. Why had he not hied off the moment he learned the truth?

"Aye, I stayed."

She tried to crawl away, but he would not allow her to. "Lass, I do no' believe fer a minute ye did what yer uncle has suggested."

Shame and fear would not allow her to look at him. "Then ye must no' ken all of it."

"Do ye?" he asked.

"I ken enough."

With gentle fingertips on her chin, he coaxed her into looking at him. Why did he not look upon her with shame?

"Ye have told me that ye do no' remember anything of that day, aye?" he asked.

"'Tis true, I do no', no matter how hard I try."

With the pads of his thumbs, he wiped her tears away. "Did ye love him? James? And yer son?"

Her mouth fell open and her eyes grew wide. "Of course I did!"

"Yet ye are convinced ye killed them," he said. "Why would ye think such a thing?"

"Because Uncle told me—"

Brogan cut her off. "Aye, yer uncle told ye he found ye covered in blood, stabbin' yerself, claimin' ye had killed them."

Nodding her head, the words were lodged in her throat.

"There is a verra good possibility yer uncle," he paused, wanting to find something other than, *yer uncle was a lyin', thievin' bastard.* "I believe yer uncle might have been mistaken in what he says he saw."

His declaration made not a bit of sense to her. How could anyone mistake such a thing?

"I also ken no one has ever tried to find out what truly happened that night. Two other men were also murdered. Everyone says the keep was under attack, but I have found no evidence to support those statements."

The murdered guards had never made any sense to her either.

"If the keep were truly under attack, more lives would have been lost, aye? Something would have been taken, the coffers raided, the horses stolen. But none of those things happened."

She had been too grief-stricken in the beginning to ask any of those questions. When Brogan laid it all out before her, she began to see things a bit more clearly. A horrifying thought sprung up in her mind. 'Twas enough to make her ill. "Be ye thinkin' the attack came from within?"

Brogan chose his next words with great care. "I be thinkin' I have suspicions. I be thinkin' I know no' enough to say what truly happened that night, Mairghread. But, with yer permission, I would like to try."

"Of course!" she exclaimed. "I need to ken the truth, Brogan, no matter how vile and ugly it might be."

Chapter Fifteen

With Mairghread on the mend, Brogan sent for Gertie and Tilda. Although she was feeling better, he still did not want her to be alone just yet.

Seeing she was in their good care, he went to the stables to saddle a horse.

"Good day to ye, m'laird!" Seamus shouted the moment Brogan walked in. He was less than five steps away but shouted as if he were calling to him from across a wide valley. It made his ears ring.

"I heard our lady is doin' much better," Seamus shouted. "All due to yer good care."

If he were forced to stay here and shout — for it was far from speaking when you had to raise your voice for the old man — he would not just lose his hearing. There was a strong possibility he would lose his mind.

"She is, Seamus," he replied in a loud voice. "I need me horse."

"Yer horse?" he asked, turning his 'good ear' to him.

"Aye, me horse."

Seamus gave a quick nod, then turned to shout over his shoulder. "Davey! Bring the laird's mount!"

Brogan rubbed his ear with his index finger and prayed fervently that whoever Davey was, he would hurry.

Seamus turned back to him and smiled. 'Twas a big, warm, toothy smile. "'Tis glad I was to hear our lady was better," he shouted.

Hear? Brogan choked back a laugh.

"It also made me glad to learn ye are rebuildin' the wall. I heard about those murderers and horse thieves from the lowlands," he shook his head and whistled. "I will fight any man who tries to steal them!"

Brogan had no earthly idea what the man was referring to. In addition to being deaf, was he also addlepated?

"Ye have me full support, laird," he said. "It be about time someone took it up to defend this keep and its people." He scratched his jaw and went on. "Though I do no' ken how we can defend ourselves against seven thousand thieves."

"Seven thousand thieves?" Brogan asked in stupefied amazement.

"Aye," he replied. "Did ye ever imagine ye'd see the day the king would allow seven thousand horse thieves and murderers to roam this land?" He whistled in disbelief. "But Henry assures us that if we get this wall built, we should be able to hold our own fer a time. Says he to me, 'Seamus, 'twill be a cold day in hell before I or Brogan Mackintosh allow this clan to fall to murderers and horse thieves.'"

Henry. It all began to make sense now. Henry and his penchant for story telling. While he was not necessarily pleased with his method of lying outright, he could not deny the results.

RETRIEVING HIS HORSE, HE LED THE ANIMAL OUT OF THE STABLES and into the yard, eager to get to the forest to see what progress had been made on the felling of trees.

He needn't look far.

There, less than twenty feet beyond the old stone wall, he could see the makings of a fine wood wall. Fifteen, thick, straight round logs had already been set into the ground. Each were at least twenty-five feet tall and four to five feet in diameter.

"Jesus," he whispered with a shake of disbelief.

He vowed then and there never to doubt or even question Henry's methods.

Pulling his horse along by the reins, he soon reached the wall. There were at least one hundred men on either side. Shouting orders in the midst of the chaos was Henry. "Okay lads! Let's put our backs into it!" he shouted over the din. He spit into his hands, rubbed them together, and began to help the men roll the next log into position.

Brogan watched, nearly mesmerized by what he saw happening. Once the log was in position, a team of horses was brought around and hitched to heavy thick ropes tied to the middle of the beam. Ten men, some digging with ropes tied to steel picks embedded into the wood, others using smaller logs, all worked in unison to lift the end of the beam. The man leading the team of horses whistled and shouted commands at the animals. They heaved forward, their massive feet digging into the earth, muscles rippling, nostrils flared.

And in a matter of moments, the very end log was teetering over the edge of the hole. Another team of horses was brought in, placed ahead of the first. Longer, thicker ropes were attached to their harnesses. Another round of shouts, curses and whistles, and before Brogan knew it, the gigantic log was in the hole, swaying precariously from side to side. But 'twas in!

He gave out his own cheer of approval, waved his fist into the air and raced forward, pulling his mount behind him.

"Henry!" he shouted over the voices of the men as he rushed forward.

Henry looked up, smiled, and said something to the men beside him.

"Good day to ye, Brogan!" Henry said as he approached.

"Good day?" Brogan said. "I would call it a miraculous day!"

They embraced briefly, pounding each other's backs, before turning to look at the progress. "How on earth did ye manage it?"

Henry shrugged his shoulders and feigned ignorance.

Brogan's laughter could be heard over all the shouting and horses. "No worries, Henry. I have just come from Seamus and he has told me about the seven-thousand murderers and thieves who are on their way here."

"Now, Brogan, I told them five hundred, no' seven-thousand!" Henry began to explain.

Brogan slapped his back and continued to smile. "Fer once, Henry, I care no' how ye managed it. I be only glad that ye did!"

Henry managed a broad smile then. "'Twas a bit amazin', to tell the truth," he said, rubbing his jaw. "Some were no' upset about the threat of thieves takin' their wives. But when I said 'twas their horses they wanted?"

They laughed together for a moment.

"Any word from Reginald?" Brogan asked.

"Nay, I have no' heard from him. I would reckon it should be soon, though."

Brogan hoped and prayed he would return with as many good men as he could find. 'Twould be entirely possible to have the wood wall erected before Aymer's return.

❧

AFTER LETTING THE MACTAVISH MEN, AS WELL AS HIS OWN, KNOW how pleased he was with their progress, Brogan returned to Mairghread's bedchamber. Her color was beginning to improve, but she still looked gaunt and tired.

Gertie and Tilda were with her, sitting near the fire as they worked on some needlework and chatted. Mairghread sat with a blanket across her lap and looked into the fire.

"Good day to ye, ladies," he said when he came in.

If he didn't know better, he'd say Mairghread was relieved to see him. Something akin to relief flashed behind her eyes.

"Good day to ye, laird!" Gertie and Tilda said as they jumped to their feet. "We did no' expect ye back so soon," Gertie said.

"Nay, 'tis fer certain we did no'," Tilda added with a shake of her head.

"If ye have more things to attend to, m'laird, we surely do no' mind sittin' with our lady," Gertie said with a most hopeful tone.

Mairghread bore the expression of a woman pleading to be saved from the gallows. Biting his cheek, he said, "That will no' be necessary.

Mayhap on the morrow?"

While the two auld women look positively forlorn, Mairghread looked like he had just saved her from the gallows.

He ushered the women out of the room and took up the seat across from Mairghread.

"I love them, I truly do," she said.

"But only in small doses?" he asked.

She puffed out her cheeks and let the air out in a rush. "Aye, in small doses."

He filled her in on the progress Henry was making on the wall. She was glad to hear it. But when he recounted the story of the thousands of murderous horse thieves, she was not as amused as he. "Why would he say such a thing?"

"There are some here who are still quite loyal to Aymer," he said without thinking.

"And what is wrong with that?" she asked. "He stepped in to lead them when I could no'."

Unwilling yet, to share his suspicions with her, for he had no sound proof or evidence, he said, "Ye must admit yer uncle has a strange way of doin' things, aye?"

On that, she could not argue. "Aye, but I do no' understand why ye worry over their fealty to him."

Treading the waters very carefully, he said, "Lass, it is important that we build a wall as soon as possible. If the men did no' have a good, sound reason presented to them, they might still be tryin' to make up their minds. Their loyalty to *ye* is me primary concern. I want them to see that ye are quite capable of leadin' them as their chief."

Her expression said, *'no' this again'*.

"Mairghread, ye are the rightful heir," he told her.

"I ken that," she replied drolly. "But I am in no condition to be the chief right now."

Brogan nodded his agreement. "Ye are right. But soon, much sooner than ye realize, ye will be hale and hearty again. I be merely tryin' to help ye while ye recuperate."

He could see she was mulling something over in her mind.

"Lass, I be yer husband. I want ye to succeed as chief, but only if that is what *ye* want."

She glanced at him before turning her attention back to the low burning embers. "And if that be no' what I want?"

A very large part of him wanted to shout *Why the bloody hell would ye no' want to?* Instead, he chose a more tactful approach. "'Tis a verra important decision ye have before ye lass. I would no' wish ye to make it too soon. But whatever it is ye decide to do, I will support ye in it."

With an exceedingly doubtful tone, she asked, "And if I made me uncle chief?"

He prayed silently that she was only baiting him. "Then that would be a decision we would all have to live with."

&

SHE HAD NO TRUE INTENTION OF MAKING HER UNCLE THE CHIEF OF this clan. Her father would roll over in his grave. Still, she needed to know, beyond any doubt, that Brogan would support whatever decision she made. Just why his approval was so important to her, she couldn't say at the moment. Neither did she possess the energy to reason it out.

"And if I want *ye* to be chief?" she asked with a quirked brow.

"Me?" he asked, more than just a bit surprised. "Lass, I have no desire to be chief of any clan."

In her heart, she somehow knew he was speaking the truth. She didn't think the man could lie if he had a dirk against his neck.

"Besides, I have no' right to it. The chiefdom belongs to ye."

Oh, she bloody well knew that, but it didn't mean she had to like it.

James. James was chief of this clan. She had made him chief on their wedding day. In truth, she never wanted the position. She would have been quite happy being a midwife, having a dozen children of her own, and being the rock that James could lean on. Had he lived, he would have been a great leader and chief.

"James gladly took the role," she told him pointedly. 'Twas not meant as a challenge nor insult. She was simply stating a fact.

"I ken," Brogan replied. "From what everyone tells me, James was a good man."

Not even the tiniest hint of jealously did she find in his eyes. He was a peculiar man.

"But if I asked ye to take over, would ye?"

She watched as he took in a deep breath and let it out slowly. "*If* and *only* if that is what ye truly wanted, then aye, I would. However, I truly believe that ye would make a fine chief."

Just why she was growing frustrated, she didn't know. Mayhap she was still suffering the after-effects of her many days in the attic or from Hargatha's evil concoction. "Are ye *always* so amiable?" she all but spat the question at him.

He had the audacity to chuckle. "Nay, lass, I am no' always so amiable."

She couldn't yet imagine him being anything but. And charming. And kind and generous. While those were all fine traits for a man to possess, they were beginning to get on her nerves. Embarrassed for thinking ill of him, she felt her face grow warm.

"Have ye eaten anythin'?" he asked, looking for the tray he'd brought to her earlier.

"A bit," she told him. Though in truth, the moment the stew hit her tongue, she felt like vomiting. So she stuck to bread and that blasted cider he was so fond of.

"I admit to bein' a bit hungry," he told her as he got to his feet. "Would ye like to go below stairs to sup? Or would ye prefer stayin' here?"

"Here, if ye would no' mind," she told him. She was as yet unready to face her clan.

Evelyn, along with Mairi and another young maid named Jenean, came bearing heavy trays not long after Brogan made the request. Cook apparently thought they were preparing for war, if the three trays were any indication.

Venison, roast duck, roast chicken, dark breads, bannocks, vegetables, cheeses and fruits were piled high on those trays. "Cook never wants to displease, aye?" Brogan chuckled as he sat the small table in front of the fire.

The three girls lingered at the door, each looking rather nervous.

Mairghread smiled at them warmly. "I thank ye, lasses," she told them.

Brogan also offered up his thanks.

When they did not make any attempt to leave, Brogan asked, "Be there somethin' else?"

The girls each cast curious glances at once another, before Mairi burned red, and whispered, "We did no' ken what to bring to drink, m'laird."

Mairghread burned crimson from head to toe. Aye, she had been cruel to these young women on more than one occasion.

"The bairn cider will be fine," Brogan told them.

Mairi leaned in again. "But what of our lady?"

Mairghread's humiliation intensified and she didn't know if she wanted to break down into tears or flee.

"The same fer yer lady," Brogan replied kindly.

Each bobbed a curtsy before leaving the room. Brogan went to the larger table where the food had been set. "What would ye like?" he asked her over his shoulder.

"I be no' hungry," she replied.

He knew better. Taking a little of each food offered, he placed the trencher in front of her. "Eat," he said before going back to fix his own.

He sat and began to eat rather enthusiastically. "Eat."

Lifting her head, she looked at him with murderous rage in her eyes that equaled her tone. "I said I be no' hungry."

"Ye will have to deal with people askin' questions like the maids just did. 'Twill happen repeatedly over the next few weeks, until everyone becomes accustomed to ye no' drinking the hard drink."

She pushed the trencher away and leaned back in her chair.

"I ken it be humiliatin'," he said as he took a bite of venison.

She cast another angry look his way, but he would not be deterred. "Eat."

"How did ye do it?" she asked with a good deal of exasperation.

"Do what?"

She growled at him. "How did ye live *after* ye gave it up? How did ye learn to go about a simple, everyday existence without wantin' a drop of fine whisky?"

He tore off a hunk of bread to dip into the juice of the venison. "Well, first, I apologized to those people I hurt when I drank."

She quirked a pretty brow. "Ye hurt people?" she asked, unable to believe him capable of such a thing.

"Aye, I did," he replied before popping the bread into his mouth.

Mairghread shook her head and drummed her fingers on the table. "Who?"

"More people than I could count," he admitted. "Ye think *ye* were a mean drunk?" he asked with a raised brow. "Lass, ye were an angel by comparison."

With her curiosity piqued, she leaned forward in her chair. "Impossible," she said. "Ye do no' have a mean bone in yer body."

Chuckling softly, he took another bite of bread while he studied her closely. "Ye want the details?" he asked.

"I do," she said.

"Eat, and I shall tell ye."

"I am no' a child," she told him.

"Oh lass, that was one of the first things I noticed about ye," he said, offering her what could only be described as a devious smile. "Think of it as a bargain. I will tell ye the awful things I did when I was a drunkard as long as ye eat."

"How do I ken ye will tell me true?" she said with a challenging tone.

"Ye can ask Henry, Comnall, or any of the other men who came here with me."

She mulled it over for a short moment. Apparently satisfied with his answer, she pulled the trencher back toward her.

Brogan ate in silence until she had taken a few bites of chicken.

Over the next hour, he told her several stories about his days of drunken debauchery. But the one that brought tears to her eyes, was the one involving his young nephew. "I seriously hurt an innocent seven-year-old boy. I could have killed him. 'Twas only through God's divine intervention that I did no'."

Retelling that story left him feeling heavy in heart, his appetite gone. "There be nothin' I could ever do to make it up to him."

Swiping away tears, she swallowed hard. "And that be when ye decided to give up the drink?" she asked.

"Aye," he said. "Well, 'twas more me da's decision than me own in the beginnin'."

Confused, she asked him for further explanation.

"Well, me da, he be a good man. He loves his children without condition. However, when I hurt me nephew, Conner, well, even a patient man has his limits. He beat the bloody hell out of me on the bank of the river that day. I do no' exaggerate when I say I was bloody and black and blue for over a week."

She did not find the humor in it that he did.

"I knew then that no' only had I let everyone down and hurt a little boy, I had angered my father to the point of him beatin' me. So aye, I decided then and there to give up the drink."

She was quiet for a long while, fidgeting with her eating knife. "Ye said that ye also apologized to everyone ye hurt."

"Aye, I did. The hardest person to apologize to was Conner. The adults in me life, they understood well enough, that a drunkard makes poor decisions. Now, they did no' let me off easily, mind ye. But 'twas a hell of a lot easier to explain me actions and apologize to them, than it was to explain to the boy."

"Did ye ask their forgiveness?"

He nodded. "Aye, I did. Nearly everyone fergave me."

"But no' Conner?"

He chuckled softly. "Nay, Conner fergave me quite easily. 'Tis his mum who never has."

"Even after all this time?"

"Aye lass, even after all this time. But I have learned that askin' fer someone's fergiveness is far easier than givin' it. God will judge me some day, of that I have no doubt. I try to live my life now with honor and dignity. Though I was only a drunkard for a year, I did more damage to people in that time than most drunkards do. I have a lot to make up fer."

It dawned on her then, *why* he had been so patient with her these past many days. He had been a drunkard of the worst kind. He had gone through much of what she had during the *takeaway* days. Guilt, she reckoned, still plagued him.

"Were ye honorable *before* ye took up the bottle?" she asked.

"I thought I was. But I did no' quite understand what honor was until after."

That made not a lick of sense to her and she told him so.

"Honor can mean different things to different people. For me, it means bein' a good man. Someone ye can count on in time of want or need. 'Tis why it be so important to me, to be as honest as I can in all situations. I try to do what is right and just. I also try to see things from the other person's point of view."

The more she learned about this man, the more she grew to like him. "Be that why ye helped me? Yer sense of honor?"

"Partly. Lass, I could no' have deserted ye in yer time of need. I made vows and promises to ye on our weddin' day."

"I made promises too," she said. It made her chest tighten to think of those vows. "But I have yet to keep any of them."

Brogan smiled warmly at her. "Ye have done the best ye could under the circumstances. Besides, we've been married a sennight now. We have many years ahead of us, aye?"

She knew he was right but it did very little to quash the guilt quietly building in her stomach. There was one vow she did not think she would ever be able to fulfill. How could she be a wife, a true wife, to this man, when she was still very much devoted to James?

Chapter Sixteen

With each passing day, Mairghread grew stronger. At least in the physical sense. After a week, the dark circles under her eyes were gone; she had gained a bit of weight, but not enough to suit Brogan, and even her hair seemed more lustrous.

However, there was something not quite right about *her*. 'Twas Gertie and Tilda who came to Brogan and pointed it out to him.

'Twas after the morning meal and he was headed out of doors to help with the felling of trees in the forest. The two women practically cornered him before he could leave.

"Good mornin', ladies," he greeted them.

"Laird, we need to speak with ye, and it be verra important," Gertie told him.

"Aye, laird, verra important," Tilda said.

They had lost two days already to torrential rains. He was in a hurry, because they needed to get the wall built as soon as possible.

"Can it no' wait? I am needed in the forest and Mairghread awaits ye above stairs."

"That be what we want to speak to ye about, m'laird. Mairghread," Gertie told him as she blocked the doorway.

He loosed a sigh of frustration. "Verra well."

"She has no' been herself of late," Gertie told him.

"Aye," said Tilda. "She be verra sad."

"Sad?" he asked. He hadn't witnessed her being sad. On the contrary, they had been enjoying one another's company for the past sennight. "I have no' seen her sad," he told them. "A bit tired, mayhap, but no' sad."

"Pardon me, m'laird, but ye do no' ken her like we do," Gertie told him. "We be tellin' ye, she is no' herself."

"Aye, and she be sad," Tilda added.

They were beginning to talk in circles. "Pray tell me, what makes ye think she be sad?"

Gertie stood a bit taller. "She be sad all the day long, until *ye* get back from workin' on the wall. 'Tis only when she sees *ye* that we see her smile."

Oh, he knew it should not have given him the sense of pride that it did, but he could have puffed out his chest and walked around like a peacock in rut for the rest of the day. "And this is bad how?"

Gertie and Tilda cast each other knowing glances. "She was like this with James," Gertie told him.

"Aye," said Tilda. "She was always much happier in his company. But 'twas nowhere near as bad as it is now."

Gertie nodded her agreement. "She sits in her room all the day long. She does no' laugh with us, like she used to in the auld days. She will no' eat, she will no' sew—"

"She be right good with her stitches," Tilda added.

"Aye, she is," Gertie agreed. "Or she used to be."

"Aye, she used to be. She was also good at midwifery, remember Gertie?"

Gertie smiled a bright beaming smile at that memory. "Aye, she was verra good at that."

Brogan saw their concern was genuine. He hadn't known about her not eating or doing anything that might seem 'normal', until now. Whenever he asked how her day was, she would always reply with a smile and say, "Twas good.'

"She sleeps much of the day," Gertie told him.

This was news to him. Of course, he'd been sleeping in the chamber next to her, not with her.

"We do no' want to say it be yer fault, laird," Gertie told him.

"But it is," said Tilda.

"How is it *my* fault?" he asked, wholly surprised by the accusation.

"Well, now, m'laird, do no' get yer trews in a bunch!" Gertie told him. "'Tis a right good thing ye have done fer her."

"Aye, a right good thing!" Tilda said.

"But," Gertie started then stopped.

"But?" he asked with a raised brow.

"She needs a purpose other than ye in her life."

He shook his head in confusion. "A purpose?"

"Aye, a purpose," Tilda said. "A reason fer her to leave her room."

"What exactly are ye askin' of me?" He crossed his arms over his chest, fully prepared for some insane plan or idea they might have.

"We want yer permission to give her a purpose."

He couldn't see any harm in that.

"But we need *ye* to encourage her, m'laird. Mayhap, she should no' be so dependent on ye?" Gertie told him cautiously.

He let loose another frustrated breath. "Aye, ladies, ye have me permission to give me wife a purpose. And aye, upon my return this night, I will talk with her and encourage her to leave her chamber."

They cried their thanks at the same time.

"Now may I please go?" he asked, nodding toward the exit they were blocking.

They stepped aside to let him pass.

He heard Tilda say, "I told ye he would see the sense in it."

"Aye, but I did no' think 'twould be that easy."

ALL MORNING LONG, BROGAN FELT A GOOD DEAL OF PRIDE IN knowing that his new bride pined for him when he was absent. But the more he thought on it, the more concerned he became.

Mayhap 'twas not such a good thing after all. Mairghread needed to be able to stand on her own two feet. She needed to be independent and capable of making her own decisions.

By the end of the day, his pride had turned to worry. What was holding her back from leaving her chamber? Was it fear? Embarrassment? Something else?

He took his frustration and worry out on five good-sized trees. By the end of the day, they had seven more trees felled and ready to be debarked. Although they were making good progress, he still worried 'twas not enough.

If Aymer had somehow learned Mairghread had married another and that a new wall was being built in his absence, he could very well hie himself back at any moment.

And where the bloody hell was Reginald? He'd left a sennight ago and no one had heard a word from him. Brogan prayed he and the men who went with him were well and successful in their mission.

Torn he was between wanting to help his wife and needing to build this wall. His frustration began to build. Mayhap what he needed was a hot bath and some time in the kirk, alone with his thoughts and God.

As soon as the workday was done, Brogan and many of the other men hopped into the loch to wash away the grime. 'Twas becoming habit for him as well as necessity. But this eve, he did not linger or dally long. He wanted to get back to Mairghread.

Just as had happened each of the five days since moving back into her room, the moment he walked in, she got to her feet and smiled. 'Twas only because of Gertie and Tilda's mention earlier that morn, that he paid closer attention to her smile. 'Twas more a smile of relief than an *I be glad ye're back* smile. He also noticed she was in a night rail and robe. No sewing basket sat near her chair.

"How was yer day?" he asked again, as he had been doing for days.

"'Twas good," she replied, as she had done for five days.

Gertie and Tilda each gave him a look that said, *We told ye so.*

"I thank ye, ladies, fer takin' such good care of Mairghread," he told them as he escorted them to the door.

"'Twas our pleasure, m'laird," they said, mouthing their typical reply.

Closing the door behind them, he would have typically gone to sit by the fire with his wife. But not this night. Instead, he asked, "Do ye have a favorite dress?"

A bit taken aback, she blinked, and said, "I suppose I do."

Brogan went to her clothes cupboard and opened the door. "Which one?" he asked as he stepped aside. "The burgundy?"

Still looking confused, she stepped forward and peered inside. "Nay, the green. Why do ye ask?"

"I think we should dine below stairs this night," he said.

Pulling her shoulders back ever so slightly, she said, "I would prefer to dine here, with ye."

"Mairghread, I think it be time ye get out of this chamber, at least for a little while."

Turning her back to him, she went to stand near the hearth. Brogan knew she was fighting an inner battle. He could only guess about what it was.

"I can no' help ye if ye do no' confide in me," he told her as he went to stand near her. "Why is it ye do no' wish to leave yer chamber?"

She replied with a simple shrug.

"Lass," he said as he turned her around to face him. "We have been through much together, aye? Please, tell me."

Her eyes grew damp as she struggled to tell him. "If I leave this room, I will be tempted."

Giving her a warm smile, he said, "So ye plan on stayin' in here all the rest of yer days?"

"Och! I do no' ken how ye do it!" she said with much exasperation.

"Do what?"

"Ye can sit at every meal and no' be tempted to drink! Ye can walk this earth never bein' tempted to take a wee nip."

He could not help but laugh. "Ye think me never tempted?" he asked. "Lass, I be tempted every day."

"Ye are?" she asked disbelievingly.

"Aye, lass, every day. And ye will be as well."

Looking rather deflated, she said, "Och! I do no' ken if I can fight it."

"Of course ye can," he told her.

"But how?"

He smiled once again. "Do ye remember what I told ye abovestairs? Ye need to live more than ye need to drink. That is what I tell meself each time I be tempted to take just a taste." Aye, he had been tempted too many times to count. Especially these past weeks. "I ken I can no' drink, Mairghread, fer if I do, I will become the man I was before. And I despise that bastard."

A light laugh passed through her lips. "Ye're daft."

"So ye keep remindin' me," he teased.

EVENTUALLY, HE WAS ABLE TO CONVINCE HER TO DRESS AND GO belowstairs with him. "I admit to ye, I am fearful," she told him after he returned from his chamber where he had donned fresh clothing.

He didn't necessarily hear her, for he was completely taken aback by how beautiful she looked. Her hair was braided and fell down her back. The gown, a dark green silk, clung to her quite nicely. If he were a lesser man, he would divest her of that dress, take her to the bed, and love her until neither of them could walk.

"I ken I need to ask their fergiveness," she told him as she put her feet into matching slippers. "But I fear I am no' quite brave enough to do that."

Forcing his thoughts to heel for honor's sake, he smiled and offered his arm. "Do no' fash yerself over it."

They were quiet as they left the room and went belowstairs. The gathering room was alive with chatter and music. Henry, Comnall, and the rest of his men stood as soon as they saw them approaching.

The entire room went quiet and stood when they entered. He was beginning to recognize a few faces of the men he worked with. The rest, however, were still strangers to him. Many surprised faces followed them as he led Mairghread to the dais.

Once they were seated, the rest of the room sat as well. An odd, eerie hush had fallen over the place. 'Twas as if they were collectively holding their breath to see what might happen. It had been a fortnight since any of them had seen their lady.

Mairghread leaned in and whispered. "They all be starin' at me."

"'Tis because ye be right beautiful this night," he told her.

She was unconvinced.

Thankfully, the serving maids started filing through the door with platters of food. He hadn't had time to let them know they would be dining here this night. Blessedly, the moment Mairi saw them at the dais, she came to them straight away.

Though she was rather nervous, the maid set a platter on their table. "I will get ye trenchers and eatin' knives, m'lady."

Mairghread whispered her thanks but kept her gaze firmly planted on the table.

Brogan reached under the table and took her hand in his and gave it a gentle squeeze. "After we eat, would ye like to walk with me? Ye can see the progress we be makin' on yer new wall."

"That would be nice," she told him. He detected a slight tremor in her voice.

"Mayhap on the morrow, we could ride together? Ye could show me how beautiful this land of yers is."

Slowly, her shoulders began to relax. "I have no' ridden just to be ridin' in a verra long while."

He was doing everything he could think of to keep her mind off the curious eyes that were staring at her. 'Twas a rather uncomfortable feeling knowing all eyes were upon you.

Mairi and another serving maid were back at their table. Mairi placed trenchers, eating knives and mugs in front of them.

"Mairi," Mairghread said her name in a soft tone. "I would like the same cider this night that me husband is so fond of."

The poor girl tried to hide her astonishment, but not before Mairghread had seen it. Smiling up at the young girl, she said, "And 'twill be the same each night from this point forward."

Mairi returned her smile and gave her an approving nod. "Aye, m'lady."

"And Mairi?"

"Yes, m'lady?"

Mairghread took in a deep breath to steady her nerves. "I want to apologize to ye for how I have treated ye these past few years."

"Och, m'lady!" she said with wide eyes. "There be no need—"

Mairghread stopped her with a raised hand. "Aye, lass, there is. I have treated ye, among others, verra poorly. I behaved deplorably and there be no excuse fer me behavior."

Tears filled Mairi's eyes. "I remember ye from when I was younger, before yer troubles started, m'lady. Always a kind lady ye were. To all of us. Ye never cared if we was poor as dirt or rich as kings, ye treated us all with great kindness. I ken ye could no' help what happened later, fer yer heart was broken."

Damn it if Mairghread's eyes did not grow wet at hearing this young woman's kind words. "Thank ye, Mairi."

BROGAN WATCHED IN FASCINATION AS HIS WIFE APOLOGIZED AND the lass accepted it so graciously. Aye, these people not only adored and respected his wife, they loved her. 'Twas not just those who were close to her, like Reginald, Gertie and Tilda. Nay, she was surrounded by people who cared about her. Suddenly, he was beset with an overwhelming sense of gratitude and his shoulders felt lighter. With these kind and good people surrounding her, there was no limit to what she could accomplish.

He looked out at the people who had filled the gathering room once again. Some of the faces he recognized, but others, he did not.

"Mairghread," he said to her as he began offering her choices of meats. "Who be these people we dine with each night?"

"No mutton, please," she said as he held up a piece. "Mayhap some roast duck."

He placed the meat on her trencher.

"These people are what me da used to call *the lonelies.*"

Brogan raised a brow that asked her to explain.

"The black death hit us in 1351," she told him. "We did no' suffer near as bad as many clans did. But still, we had significant losses.

Entire families were left dead, while others lost spouses, or parents, and children. When Da realized many of these people — some of which were the sole survivors — were all alone in this world, he invited them to sup with us. He could no' stand the thought of a body eatin' each of their meals alone, ye ken. So he started the tradition. Anyone who be *lonely,* without kin or friends to sup with, could sup here. One night or many, he cared not. And so it remains to this day."

"Ye feed this many each night?" he asked, mentally adding up the cost of such a thing.

"Aye, we do."

"But how do ye afford it?"

Mairghread smiled, showing nearly perfect white teeth. "'Tis no' as expensive as ye might think. Much of this food ye see here? Those people," she nodded toward their guests, "provided most of it. The venison? 'Twas probably Ryan McKindle over there — the one with the black hair and blue eyes" — she pointed him out. "And his son, Michael, who hunted it. Ryan lost his wife, Michael's mum, three sons and a daughter to the Black Death. They sup with us a few nights a week and bring game. Usually venison."

Brogan was amazed at learning this.

"The fish was probably caught by George there, and Seamus. They go fishin' a few times a week and share their bounty with us."

Brogan looked at the crowd but did not find Seamus. "Where be Seamus?" he asked.

Mairghread laughed. "Probably abed by now, he rarely sups with us. But auld George be here. He lost his wife, two sons, and three grand-children."

Brogan had lost only his Anna. He could not imagine losing children and grandchildren as well.

"I think I would have liked yer da," he said.

Marighread smiled. "I think he would have liked ye as well."

As he had promised, Brogan took her to look at the progress being made on the wall. The sun was just beginning to set, casting their world in shades of crimson and purple. "'Tis beautiful!" Mairghread exclaimed.

In the past, he might have disagreed about a wall's beauty, but he could not argue with her this night. 'Twas a damn sight better than what was there before, which was nothing at all.

"The men have been working verra hard," he told her.

"So I can see," she said with a smile.

Though it was far from done, it did make him feel better about their future safety as a clan. But if they could complete it before Aymer's return, 'twould indeed be a miracle.

"How many men have ye workin' on it?" she asked as she brushed her fingers across one of the logs.

"At present? Eighty men, working in two ten-hour shifts."

She furrowed her brow at that number. "But our clan numbers at least three hundred, the last I knew."

"Aye, but many have other duties that also must be seen to. There be the farming, the cattle and the horses."

"How long do ye think before it is completed? And what of towers?"

Brogan was pleased that she was thinking clearly and every bit like a chief. "At our current pace? Mayhap six months."

'Twas evident the answer did not sit well with her. "We can no' pull men in from the fields," she said. "But the cattle and horses can take care of themselves, aye?"

"To a certain extent, they can. I think mostly the men be watchin' over them, to make certain they be no' stolen."

She nodded in understanding. "Gertie and Tilda were talkin' earlier, though I admit, I thought mayhap they were exaggeratin'. But they spoke of horse thieves and reivers comin' up from the south."

Brogan was forced to bite his tongue to keep from laughing and sharing the truth with her.

"Mayhap, we should go to the nearby villages and see if we can no' hire men?"

Aye, she was thinking like a chief, all right. Smiling warmly, he said, "I have already sent Reginald to do just that."

Pleased with his response, she returned his smile. "Ye would make a fine chief, Brogan Mackintosh."

"As would ye," he replied.

&.

AFTER TOURING THE WALL AND ENJOYING THE EVENING AIR, Mairghread expressed the need for sleep by yawning several times.

"Mayhap we should get ye to bed?" he suggested as he turned them back toward the keep.

His suggestion was met with silence.

"Gertie and Tilda came to me this morn," he told her. "They be concerned over ye. They tell me ye be no' sleepin' well at night."

She mumbled something about them being traitors and *was nothing sacred anymore?*

Brogan laughed heartily. "Lass, we be all concerned fer ye."

He caught her rolling her eyes out of the corner of his own.

"Be there a reason ye find sleep difficult?" he asked.

She took in a deep breath before answering. "It be many things," she said.

"Such as?"

Another roll of her eyes. Clearly, she did not want to discuss it with him. But he felt 'twas important to her full recovery that she learn to discuss things with him. Even the unpleasant ones.

"I have no' gone to sleep without the aid of drink in three long years."

That made sense. He, too, had suffered for weeks after, being unable to sleep well. He was about to offer her some encouragement, to tell her that this too, would pass, when she went on to say more.

"And I have bad dreams."

"What kind of bad dreams?" Was she perchance beginning to regain some of her memories through dreams?

"Dreams that make no' a lick of sense," she told him.

They arrived at the main stairs leading up into the keep. "Dreams with lions tryin' to eat me feet. Dreams of men in masks comin' into me room and just standin' there, lookin' at me without sayin' a word. Dreams where I be drowning'."

Peculiar, aye, but did they truly mean anything? He opened the large, heavy door and guided her through, placing his hand on the small of her back.

"Like I said, dreams that make no' a lick of sense."

"Aye, they be odd," he agreed.

"Gertie and Tilda be convinced there be a hidden meanin' in them," she laughed, though not heartily.

"Some people do believe such," he told her. "Me step-mum, she believes that dreams are messages from long dead relatives, tryin' to warn us of either impending doom, or a comin' blessin'. Me da, of course, thinks she be daft."

"Whatever they may or may no' mean," she said as they made their way to the stairs, "they be keepin' me up at night."

As they ascended the stairs, Brogan said, "Mairghread, ye can come to me, day or night, ye ken that, aye?"

She cast him a furtive glance. "There be no sense in both of us bein' up all night."

He paused briefly on the stairs. "Mairghread, I be yer husband. I be here to help ye. I care no' the time of day or night. 'Tis me duty to help ye through these times, just as I ken ye would do the same fer me, would ye no'?"

AYE, SHE VERY WELL WOULD HELP HIM, SHOULD EVER HE NEED IT. Though, in truth, she doubted he would ever truly need her help with anything. Of all the men she had known in her life, he was the one who seemed to have a grasp on every situation. "Aye, I would," she told him.

He smiled then, a warm, kind smile she found she was growing to like. But that lead to immense feelings of guilt. How could she like this man, admire him, think him a good friend, and keep her promise to James?

They continued on and were soon entering her bedchamber.

Someone had already seen to lighting candles and a fire. The room was bathed in warm shades of gold.

Brogan crossed to the door that led to his chamber, paused, and turned to face her. "If ye need me, I be right next door."

She nodded her head and thanked him for his kindness. A moment later, he was closing his door behind him. For a long while, she stared blankly at the closed door, wondering how her life had come to be changed so drastically in such a short time.

Of course, three years ago, it *had* changed, in what seemed like the blink of an eye now. One moment, she was a happily married woman, with a brand new bairn and looking forward to having at least a dozen more. The next moment, she was waking up, suffering from her own knife wounds, and being told it was all gone. Her husband, her babe, her entire future. Just. Like. That.

She had shed many tears since that awful day. Even more of late. Tears of frustration, anger, bitterness, and anguish.

This night, she shed them for new reasons. A sense of longing, of missing James and her babe. What would Connell have been like? Would he have been a serious child or precocious? He would have inherited everything one day. He would have married, made her a grandminny ...

Wiping away the quiet tears, she cursed. The tears made her feel weak, as if she was not strong enough to get through just one more day without them. Slowly, as if her limbs were made of lead, she unlaced her dress, stepped out of it, and into a warm night rail. Grabbing her robe, she slipped her arms into the sleeves, tied the belt around her waist, and went to her window.

Night was falling, the hour growing late. Though she was tired, she knew sleep would not come easily.

For in the room next to hers was a fine man. A good man. A man she now knew she could trust as a friend and ally. But could she ever be a true wife to him? A wife who would or could join with him? Give him his own bairns?

Nay, she did not think she could. Just the thought of it made her feel she was betraying James, as well as Connell. To James, she had sworn never to take another husband. To Connell, never to hold another bairn in her arms.

'Twas not fair to Brogan. None of this was.

The man had married her, not knowing of her addiction or of the promises she made at the graves of her husband and son.

She was not some naive, innocent maid. She had eyes and often caught him staring at her, like a wolf about to devour a rabbit. But always, she pretended she hadn't noticed, hiding her guilt behind a veil of ignorance.

There was not a doubt in her mind that he would remain faithful to her all their days. He would not take a mistress, no matter how strong his physical desires and needs might be. Too honorable, he was, to break the vows he made.

But something odd happened when she thought of him with another woman. Her stomach felt tight and uncomfortable. She recognized it almost immediately. 'Twas jealousy. Sheer, deep jealousy.

Why would I feel jealous? She asked herself as she stared out at the water. *He would certainly be justified in takin' a mistress, especially if ye can no' be a true wife to him.* Confusion began to reign supreme. Aye, he was her husband, but in name only.

Nay, she told herself. *He was more than just a husband in name only. He has shown ye more kindness, more generosity than he could have been expected to. He has treated ye with naught but a gentle hand. More gentle than ye deserved.*

She had known women from her past who would toy with a man's heart and ego. They would let on they were interested, would flirt relentlessly, but they would never go that extra measure of actually marrying him. But if another woman caught his fancy, och! Let the screamin' matches and battles begin!

I do no' want to be such a woman as that, she told herself. *Brogan deserves more of ye. He deserves far more than ye can give him.*

Oh, she knew she should discuss this with him, in a mature and respectable fashion. But the coward that she was of late would not allow her to broach the subject. *If I had just a dram of whisky ...*

"Nay!" she whispered harshly. "That would solve nothin'. 'Twould only create more problems, ye fool."

Nay, sleep was not going to come easy this night and it wouldn't be because of bad dreams.

SLEEP DID NOT COME EASILY FOR BROGAN EITHER. UNABLE TO SHUT his mind off, he tossed and turned for two hours before he finally decided to get out of bed.

Never one to sleep in anything but his skin, the cool night air did very little to cool his growing desire for his wife. The wood floors felt cool against his bare feet as he padded to the window. He drew open the fur and let out a heavy sigh as he looked out at the rocky cliffs and water. 'Twas a clear night, with the moon shining brightly, though he could not see it from his current vantage point. There were a few little clouds, but nothing that promised rain.

He was doing his best to think of something else, anything but his wife. Thus far, he was failing miserably in his attempts.

Mairghread was a fine woman, he concluded. Not the sharp-tongued harpy of weeks ago. Nay, when sober, she was a decent, intelligent woman. And God's teeth, was she beautiful!

What he would not give to feel her skin against his own. To hear her ragged breaths of desire and need. To have his lips pressed against hers, against that soft and tender flesh of her long neck.

"If ye keep this up, ye'll need to *sleep* in the bloody loch!" he cursed himself.

In his heart, he knew they had a long while to go before she felt she could trust him completely. There were many reasons, he supposed, that made her hold back. Undoubtedly they had everything to do with James.

The only blessing in knowing Anna was not going to live was the fact that they had time together to discuss the future. His future without her. There was no doubt in his mind that she meant the words she had given him. *Do no' love a dead woman fer too long. I want ye to give yer heart to someone again. I want ye to live, Brogan. And love and have many children.*

A few months ago, that seemed an impossible request to fulfill.

But as for Mairghread and James? Nay, they had not had the time to say their goodbyes. There was no time for James to tell her words such as the one's his Anna had given him.

Though he had not met the man, he was certain James would have done just that. Given Mairghread permission to move on with her life. To love again. To live again. They had both been too young then to think of such things.

Running a hand through his hair, he shook his head and went to stand by the fire. Raking the coals with the iron just to have something to do with his hands.

What must I do to show her she can trust me? Not just with her sobriety, or her clan, but with her heart as well?

He had no answer other than to continue to do what he had been doing all along. But what if that was not enough?

He grabbed a blanket from the bed and draped it over the chair before sitting down. With his head in his hands, he began to feel even more lost and alone.

When in doubt, pray, he heard his father's voice as clear as if he were sitting in the room with him.

He'd been doing much praying of late. For Mairghread's health, her recovery, her continued sobriety. He had also prayed for the quick building of the wall, for Reginald's safe and quick return.

Brogan knew his prayers were not going unanswered. Aye, to the contrary. God had helped Mairghread decide to give up the bottle. He had also helped Brogan get her through those difficult and trying days. And aye, He had even seen to it that their new wall was being built.

Aye, He had answered every one of his prayers most generously.

He began to wonder if he weren't asking for *too* much.

BROGAN HAD JUST SETTLED HIMSELF BACK INTO BED WHEN HE believed he heard Mairghread crying from the next room. He grabbed his plaid, wrapped it around his waist quickly. With his ear to the door, he strained to listen. Aye, she was crying.

Cautiously, he opened the door and peered inside. He found her in her bed, lying on her back. He knew at once she was having another bad dream.

Sitting on the edge of her bed, he placed a hand on her shoulder. "Mairghread." He spoke her name softly in hopes of not startling her too much. "Mairghread, ye be havin' a bad dream."

She sat up so suddenly that it startled him. With still sleeping eyes, she looked at him for a moment, before falling back into the bed with a sigh. Moments later, her breathing became steady and deep and he knew she had fallen back to sleep.

Pulling the covers up over her shoulders, he patted her side, and went back to bed. This time, he left his door open, just in case she would need him again.

Less than an hour later, he heard her crying again.

He went to her once more, again patting her shoulder and speaking her name. Not long after, she began whimpering once again. Finally, he decided to get dressed and sat in a chair by her bed, where he dozed off and on. He woke at dawn to the sound of birds twittering near her window.

Deciding there was no sense in trying to sleep anymore, he carefully pulled the covers up once again and left her alone. Besides, Gertie and Tilda would be arriving soon.

He paused at her door and took one last look at her. He hoped that someday soon she would be able to sleep soundly, uninterrupted by disturbing dreams.

HE STOPPED BY THE KITCHENS TO GET SOME BANNOCKS AND sausages, which he ate on his way to the forest. He'd just finished the last bite of his bannocks when he arrived at the entrance. At least a dozen men were already there, including Henry. This morn, they were each working to debark the trees they had cut down the afternoon before.

"Good morn!" Henry called out when he saw Brogan heading down the path of logs.

Brogan returned his greeting as he looked out at the logs. "'Tis good progress, aye?" he asked. He wasn't offering them reassurance; he was looking for it.

"I'd feel a damned sight better if Reginald would get back here with reinforcements," Henry grumbled.

Brogan felt much the same way. He looked around at the Mactavish men. They all looked as tired and worn as he was beginning to feel.

"Mayhap, we should give these men a day or two of rest," Brogan began.

Henry sported the look of a man who thought him completely insane. Leaning in and speaking in a hushed and frustrated tone, he said, "Then ye might as well just abandon the keep and give it over to the horse thieves."

Brogan quirked an irritated brow. Was Henry beginning to believe in his own lie? "Give *these* men a few days rest by having them trade places with those who are tending to fields and animals."

"Oh," Henry said, only slightly embarrassed.

"Tending animals is work, but no' the back-breakin' work we have before us."

Suddenly, Henry had come up with an idea on how to motivate the Mactavish people to work even harder. "What we need," he said in a low, conspiratorial tone, "is a raid."

Brogan thought it the most insane thing he'd heard of late and told him so.

"No' a real raid," Henry said as his eyes began to fill up with excitement. "Just the *rumor* of a raid."

Brogan let out a heavy sigh. "No. We will no' terrify these people with further lies."

"But if they think more attacks are imminent," Henry argued, "it might be the thing we need to get more men out of their fields and here, where they be needed."

"No."

Although Henry had finally agreed to let the matter rest, Brogan had a sneaking suspicion that he would bring it up again.

Chapter Seventeen

Mairghread had wakened long after dawn, though she did not feel at all well-rested. Slowly, she made her way out of her bed, tended to her morning ablutions and waited for Gertie and Tilda. Typically, they were there bright and early each morn, to sit with her after Brogan left.

She estimated an hour passed and still there was no sign of them. Worry began to take hold of her heart.

When enough time passed that she believed something had happened to one or both of them, she decided to get dressed and see for herself. She had just pulled open her clothes cupboard when there came a knock at her door.

In a rush, she pulled it open, glad they were finally there.

'Twas Evelyn standing on the other side of the door, holding a tray with her morning meal.

"Where be Gertie and Tilda?" she asked with confusion.

Evelyn blinked her surprise and bobbed a curtsy. "Gertie be no' well," she told her. "Tilda be with her."

"No' well?" Mairghread asked, sounding almost as exasperated as she felt. Gertie was of an age where 'not well' could mean anything from being tired to near death's door. Dread and worry began to take over her good sense.

"Aye, m'lady, no' well. Tilda asked me to sit with ye this day." The poor girl looked frightened, the tray in her hand beginning to rattle from her shaking fingers.

Mairghread took the tray from her and placed it on her table. "I be sorry fer yellin', Evelyn. 'Tis only me worry over Gertie that makes me behave poorly."

Evelyn remained rooted in place, uncertain what she should do or say.

"Come in," Mairghread told her. "And tell me what ails Gertie." She tried to remain patient and to look calm.

"I do no' ken, m'lady. Me mum be the closest thing to a healer we have, but she be busy with her midwifin' duties this morn. We do no' ken when she will be able to tend to Gertie."

With Hargatha still locked away below stairs, the clan was without a healer other than Martha. Of course, Hargatha had never been much of a healer to begin with. More like an instrument of fear and death.

Gertie had always been there for her; now it was Mairghread's turn to be there for Gertie.

MAIRGHREAD DID NOT ASK FOR PERMISSION TO ENTER GERTIE AND Tilda's bedchamber. Like a strong breeze coming in off the bay, she opened the door and all but flew inside.

Gertie was in her bed, with the covers pulled up to her chin. Tilda was sitting beside her, holding her hand.

"Gertie!" she said breathlessly when she saw her lying there, so helpless and sickly looking.

Tilda stood and faced her. "Och! M'lady!"

Gertie coughed, a faint, weak cough.

Mairghread took the chair Tilda had just left. "Gertie, what be the matter?"

Another faint, weak cough. "M'lady? Be that ye come to see me?"

Her voice was naught but a whisper. The kind of tired, barely audible whisper that made one's heart seize.

"I be here," Mairghread told her as she took her hand. It felt cool to the touch, but not clammy. That had to be a good sign, hadn't it?

Gertie smiled, albeit weakly. "A sight fer sore eyes, I says."

"What be wrong with ye? Do ye hurt anywhere?" Mairghread asked as she placed the back of her hand on the auld woman's wrinkled brow. "Ye do no' feel feverish."

She coughed again, a little louder this time. "I just be tired. And a little lightheaded."

Tired and lightheaded? What could that be an indication of?

"And a bit piqued in the stomach," Gertie added. "But I be sure I will be well soon enough."

Mairghread was not as certain as she. *Could these be her last days?* As near as Mairghread knew, Gertie was more than seventy years auld. Her heart constricted, tightened until she wasn't sure it was still beating. *I can no' lose her Lord.*

"Though me stomach be a bit off," Gertie said, before letting out another weak cough, "I think I could use a bit of bread and mayhap some broth?"

Just the thought of bread and broth made Mairghread wrinkle her nose. "If that be what ye want, dear, sweet Gertie, then ye shall have it," she said, patting the back of her hand. Giving her a most warm smile, she got to her feet. "Tilda, will ye stay with her while I see cook?"

"Of course, m'lady," she said.

She smiled once more at the auld woman who had loved her through so many trying times. "I shall no' be long, aye?"

WITHIN AN HOUR OF THE MISTRESS'S COMING TO SEE GERTIE, TILDA suddenly fell ill. Mairghread helped her into her night dress and into her bed. *Lord, I can no' lose them both!*

She had heard of husbands and wives dying within days of one another, as well as mothers dying not long after losing a child. Could it be that Gertie and Tilda were so close to one another that they too might die together? The though sickened her, made her heart feel heavy with sadness.

Tilda's cough seemed a bit worse than Gertie's. And her skin seemed warmer to the touch. 'Twas too early yet to say if they both suffered from the same illness. Only time would tell.

Tilda made the same request for bread and broth. This time when Mairghread returned, she had donned an apron and put a kerchief over her hair. She settled in to tend them like a daughter would her beloved mother. In this case, she had two.

She fluffed pillows, tucked blankets in around them, and tended the fire in their brazier. She spoon-fed them broth and tore off bits of bread, for which they were extremely grateful.

While she tended to them, the women reminisced about days gone by. Their youth, the men they had loved and lost, as well as Mairghread's childhood. Fond, warm memories. The kind of memories one reflects upon in their old age or near their death.

Slowly, bit by bit, her heart was breaking in two.

As she was quietly listening — and praying — a knock came at the door. A moment later, Evelyn walked in. "M'lady," she said as she bobbed a curtsy. She looked as though she had something to tell her, but was dreading it.

"What is it, Evelyn?" Mairghread said as she went to the door.

"I do no' wish to disturb ye, but we have three scullery maids who seem to be ailin'. Cook was wonderin' if ye would have time to see them, bein's how Hargatha is locked away and all."

Three ailing scullery maids? "What ails them?"

Evelyn cleared her throat before answering. "They say they be right tired, m'lady. They each have a bit of a cough and say their stomachs do no' feel well."

"Any fevers?"

"No' near as I can tell," she replied, glancing in at Gertie and Tilda.

'Twas an oddity, to be certain. Mayhap the scullery maids, upon hearing of Gertie and Tilda's illness, decided they would use the same excuse so they, too, could rest. She wouldn't know until she saw them.

"Will ye stay with Gertie and Tilda?" she asked Evelyn.

"There be no need fer that, m'lady," Tilda spoke up. "We will just be restin' here."

"Aye, m'lady. We will just be restin'," Gertie added.

"I will no' be leavin' ye alone," Mairghread argued. "Evelyn will sit with ye until I return."

'Twas not just three scullery maids who had fallen suddenly ill. Within a few hours, there were four men and seven women — all of whom worked inside the keep and most of them in the kitchens – who had come down with the same mysterious illness. Some had awful sounding coughs, while others sneezed. Some complained of severe stomach pains, while others said their stomachs were fine. Some had slight fevers whilst others were cool to the touch. The only thing they each had in common was being so weak they could barely stand.

'Twas an odd illness. Mairghread went from one servant quarters to another, bringin' bread and broth and hot cider, blankets, and what comfort she could.

Before she realized it, the nooning meal had come and gone. She had not eaten anything save for one of the hard eggs Evelyn had brought to her that morn. Her stomach began to growl so she went back to the kitchens.

"How fare our patients?" Lowrens asked when she stepped inside.

"Restin'," she told him.

Wiping his brow, he looked around his kitchen. "I fear I do no' think I can prepare an evenin' meal for all the usual people, with only the help of two maids."

The usual people amounted to nearly forty. People who counted on the evening meals, not only for sustenance, but for companionship as well. She truly did not wish to let them down.

"Mayhap we should let people know that the keep has come down with an illness," she said. "And maybe, instead of our usual feast, we keep it simple this night? Mayhap some baked fish and meat pies."

Lowrens thought it a good idea. "I be certain word has already spread, but to be safe, I'll send one of the lads out."

Mairghread went to the long counter and began to wash her hands in a bucket of warm water. "Good, now tell me, Lowrens, what can I do to help?"

§

IT HAD BEEN A VERY LONG DAY OF BACK-BREAKING WORK. BROGAN'S muscles ached ferociously. When he jumped into the loch to bathe, he got a cramp in his leg. *God's teeth, when did I get so auld?* He cursed as he rubbed the pain from his leg.

Cold, tired — nay, near exhausted from lack of sleep the night before — he all but dragged his weary carcass into the keep. He paid no heed to those already gathered for the evening meal. He was just too bloody tired.

He wanted nothing more than a hot bath, a warm meal, and then to fall into his bed. But if last night was any indication of his future, he knew there wouldn't be much sleep this night either.

As he had been doing every night for the past many, he knocked and entered Mairghread's room first.

'Twas empty and eerily silent. Even the hearth was cold. A clear sign the room had not been occupied in hours.

Mayhap Gertie and Tilda had managed to get her out of her room after all. Feeling pleased at the idea, he went to his chamber, washed up once more, this time with soap, and donned fresh clothing.

As he went below stairs, he thought of seeking out Martha, to see if there was a tisane she could give Mairghread to help her sleep. But he worried over side effects of such things. He did not want her to sleep for two days. Just a few hours.

The gathering room was all abuzz this night. It seemed cheerier, lighter somehow. Usually, the people chatted quietly amongst themselves. But tonight, they laughed heartily.

Mairghread was not at the dais, which he found perplexing.

As he searched the room for some sign of his wife, Auld George came up to him with his arm extended. "M'laird," he said with a broad smile that showed several missing teeth. "I just had to come thank ye."

Taken aback, he grasped the man's forearm and shook it. "Thank me fer what?" he asked curiously.

"Fer givin' us our sweet lady back," he beamed proudly.

The man's answer left him feeling even more confused.

"'Tis been far too long, if ye ask me. But we all ken we owe it to yer good care."

Brogan cleared the embarrassment from his throat. "Speaking of our lady, do ye ken where she might be?"

"In the kitchen, helpin' cook."

THERE SHE WAS, IN THE MIDDLE OF THE KITCHEN, WORKING RIGHT alongside Lowrens. Long, wispy tendrils of hair had come loose from Mairghread's braid and the kerchief she wore, and her forehead glistened. He thought she looked magnificent.

She was taking sweet cakes from a baking dish and placing them onto a big platter. There were several other women — not the usual scullery maids — working just as hard.

"Mairghread?" he asked, sounding just a bit astonished.

A bright, beaming smile met his eyes. "Brogan! How fare ye?"

"Well, but I am at a loss as to why ye be here, workin' in the kitchens?"

"A blessin' she has been, m'laird," Lowrens told him, quite seriously.

Mairghread cast him a glance and smiled. "As have the other women who have come to help."

None of it answered the question.

"But *why* are ye here?" he asked, unable to stop smiling.

"We have several people who have come down with an illness," she told him. "I do no' think it be serious. Here," she said, handing him the platter.

Without thinking, he took the platter. Confused, he stood waiting for further explanation.

Mairghread grabbed a platter of fruits and began to leave the kitchens. All the while, Brogan simply stood, quite perplexed.

She paused at the door and said, "Do no' just stand there, come with me."

"Where?" he asked.

Mairghread rolled her eyes. "To the gatherin' room," she replied, looking at him as if he were a simpleton.

❦

FOR THE REMAINDER OF THE EVENING, BROGAN WORKED ALONGSIDE his wife, serving the "lonelies." At first, he didn't think it proper that their lady and chief should be serving *anyone*. But when he mentioned that to his lovely wife, she told him she thought him stark raving mad and to pick up the bloody pace.

He had made numerous trips from the kitchen to the gathering room. Though 'twas not their typical nightly feast, 'twas enough that everyone was fed well. A hearty stew, roasted vegetables, fruits, breads, and cheeses, along with sweet cakes. He could not remember the last time he'd had so many pitchers of ale in his hand that he hadn't helped to drink.

By the end of the night, he was just exhausted, sweaty, and still hungry. But, he had to admit, he was exceedingly proud of Mairghread. For the first time since he'd met her, she seemed truly *happy*.

When it came time to clear the tables, a few of the older women volunteered to help clean up. "We'll set it back to rights, m'lady," an older woman names Clarice said. "Ye go on now, we'll see to everythin'."

"Verra well," Mairghread said before turning to look at Brogan. "I would like to check on Gertie and Tilda now."

He had learned only bits and pieces of what had led to his wife — and subsequently himself — serving the evening meal. Dutifully, he followed his wife out of the gathering room, down a long corridor, and to the women's chamber. Mairghread knocked lightly at the door. "Gertie? Tilda? 'Tis me, Mairghread. And I have Brogan with me."

He thought he heard the fast shuffling of feet coming from within. Looking to his wife, he raised a curious brow. She gave him a bright smile, winked, and then opened the door.

Candles were lit and a nice fire burned in the brazier. Gertie and Tilda were each in their beds, with blankets drawn to their chins. Tilda looked to be sleeping.

"M'lady?" Gertie whispered in a weak voice. "Be that ye?"

Mairghread rushed to her side, sat on a stool and took her hand. "Aye, it be me."

"A sight fer auld, tired eyes, ye be," Gertie replied. Her voice was naught more than a whisper.

But something did not quite feel right to Brogan. Something he could not quite put his finger to.

"Be there anythin' ye need?" Mairghread asked.

"Nay, m'lady. Evelyn took right good care of us."

Mairghread smiled warmly and patted her hand. "'Tis good to hear."

Gertie either coughed or cleared her throat, Brogan couldn't be certain which. "Pray, tell me lady, how be the others?"

"They be doin' verra well," she replied.

"Evelyn said ye took care of all of us."

"Aye, I did. I also worked in the kitchens this day. Brogan even helped us to serve the evenin' meal."

Gertie's eyes flew open. "Ye what?" she nearly shouted her question.

Her voice did not have the same strained tone as moments before.

"Aye, we did. Many of the kitchen staff have fallen to the same illness as ye and Tilda," Mairghread explained in a comforting tone.

"But," she began to speak, but was at a loss for words.

"Do no' fash yerself over it, Gertie," Mairghread said. "'Twas fun."

Fun? Fun was the last thing he would have called the past three hours. Bloody hard work was a more apt description.

"Now, rest," Mairghread said as she stood. "I will be back in the morn to see ye."

Mairghread paused at the door, next to Brogan. She turned to look back at Gertie. "I love ye, Gertie."

Gertie choked back a sob. "And I, ye, lass."

As they walked down the dimly lit corridor, Mairghread began to hum a tune Brogan did not recognize.

"Ye seem awfully happy this night," he remarked.

"I am," she said with a giggle.

He did not think Gertie was as ill as she had led Mairghread to believe. But he was uncertain how he should broach the subject. The last thing he wanted to do was accuse the auld woman of lying. "How sick do ye think Gertie truly be?"

Mairghread laughed, her smile seemed almost as bright as the sun. "As sick as either one of us," she laughed.

Pausing to look at her, he waited patiently for her to explain.

"At first I did believe they were both ill. But when more and more people began to succumb to the same illness, I began to wonder. They had no real symptoms. No fevers, no throwin' up or anything that would keep a body abed."

He raised a brow. "Why do ye think they pretended to be ill?" Then he remembered his conversation he had the morning before with Gertie and Tilda.

"They have been beggin' me fer days to leave me room. I admit I took comfort hidin' away. I worried I would be tempted to drink again, should I get anywhere near a flagon," she told him.

"They did mention yester morn they thought ye needed a purpose," he told her.

She turned to look down the hallway. "Aye, I ken," she said, almost wistfully. "So they *gave* me a purpose."

"They knew ye'd no' be able to stay in yer own room when they were ill in theirs," he said. "But the others?"

"Oh, they were all in on the ruse," she said. "But I can no' hold it against any of them. They meant only to help."

"A lie from the heart?" he asked a bit disbelievingly.

"Aye, a lie from the heart," she smiled up at him.

He was not certain how he felt about these auld women and their devious plots. He supposed, in the end, it simply did not matter. If it had not been for their meddling ways, he would not now be married to the beautiful woman who was currently smiling up at him.

Suddenly, he was beset with an urge to lean over and kiss her. 'Twas an urge he could not resist. Without thought or permission, he leaned in and kissed her, lips to lips. 'Twas a chaste kiss and one she did not return.

When he pulled back, confused and frightened eyes were staring back at him.

"Brogan—" she stammered. "I --" she was at a loss for words.

"I be sorry," he whispered. "I should have asked ye first." 'Twas the fear in her eyes that nearly made his knees give out. "I frightened ye."

"Nay," she said, placing a hand on his arm. "No' frightened, just surprised."

"Surprised that I would want to kiss ye?" he asked.

"Nay," she said. "I mean, that is to say," she simply could not form the words.

"Mairghread, I will no' kiss ye again, unless ye ask me to."

FOR THE REMAINDER OF THEIR TREK ABOVE STAIRS, NEITHER OF them spoke a word. Brogan felt like a heel and the worst kind of cad. Mairghread was fighting her own inner battle.

She had lied when she told him the kiss hadn't frightened her, for it had. But not for the reasons he thought. Nay, it terrified her to her marrow when she realized how much she liked the kiss. How it made her heart beat faster, her fingers tremble, and her knees quiver. Aye, it terrified her.

Because, after all, she had made a promise to James, to never take another man as husband. To never love another.

When she thought of him, her thoughts always turned to how he and Connell had died. A tear slid from her eye, and made its way down her cheek.

Brogan saw it and paused, a look of guilty horrification on his face. "Mairghread," his voice was but a whisper. "I have made ye cry!"

"Nay, Brogan, ye did no'."

His expression told her he did not believe her.

She could not lie to him again. Not even a lie from her heart. "I was thinkin' about James."

She watched as his guilt intensified, as he struggled to say just the right thing. The problem was, there was no *just the right thing* to say. For he did not know what was in her heart, about the promise she had made him.

"The day we buried them," she choked back a sob. "The day we buried them, I bade them each a promise. I promised James I would never remarry, and I promised Connell I would never hold another bairn in me arms."

❦

BROGAN WANTED TO SCREAM, *THEN WHY THE BLOODY HELL DID YE marry me?* But that would solve nothing. He knew he had two choices. One, he could tell her he understood but that James and Connell would not wish for her to live all the rest of her days without someone to love, without other bairns. Or, he could tell her he understood and stop there.

"I understand," he said with a slight nod, and began to walk toward their chambers again.

Mairghread was silent, more tears falling, her hands trembling.

"Did ye make a similar promise to yer Anna?" she asked as she swiped away a tear.

"Nay," he replied as he opened her chamber door. "I wanted to. I tried, but Anna would no' allow it."

Puzzled, she looked up at him. "She would no' allow ye?"

"Nay, she bade me promise to no' mourn long, and to no' save me heart fer ..."

"Fer?"

"Fer a dead woman. Those were her exact words. *Do no' love a dead woman too long.*

Mairghread covered her lips with the tips of her fingers, but the gasp was already out.

"I mourned her loss fer years," he told her, his tone growing softer, more sorrowful. "I could no' imagine bein' able to keep that promise, fer I loved her with all me heart."

"Then why did ye promise her?" she asked.

He shook his head and rested the tips of his fingers on his hips. "Because I did no' want her to worry. She was dyin'. We knew she was dyin'. I used to think 'twas a cruel thing she asked of me."

"And now?"

He smiled wanly. "Now, I *see* how much she loved me. She wanted me to be happy. The thought of me roamin' this earth alone, with a broken heart? Nay, she could no' abide such a thing. She loved me more than that."

Chapter Eighteen

Mairghread was left with much to think about after Brogan bade her good night. When the door clicked behind him, it sounded much louder than it actually was. Like a bucket of sand bein' dropped from a great height.

For a long while, she simply stared at the closed door.

She loved me more than that. So much so that Anna did not want him living the rest of his life alone.

Finally, she moved away from the door and went to undress. She slipped out of her dress, then her chemise and went to wash up in the basin. She got as far as dipping a cloth into the chilly water.

Were her circumstances different, she and James might have made similar promises to one another. If he had not died so suddenly, would he have asked the same of her? If he hadn't died and she had become ill, like Anna, would she have told James to go on with his life? To be happy?

Aye, in her heart, she knew she would have. The thought of James livin' a lonely life made her shiver.

But what had happened to him was much different. He hadn't been injured or ill. He had been murdered as had her son.

More tears filled her eyes, as she stood naked before the basin.

They had been murdered, and no matter what Brogan might believe, there was a good chance they had been murdered at her own hand.

God, please help me, she prayed silently as she held onto the table that held the basin with trembling hands. "Please, return me memory to me so that I might ken the truth, no matter how horrible or ugly or sordid it might be. If I killed them, I need to ken. Please, God, tell me."

'Twas then she heard Brogan's voice. She spun to face him.

"Ye did no' kill them, Mairghread."

FOR A LONG WHILE, MAIRGHREAD STOOD FROZEN IN PLACE. *YE DID no' kill them,* he had told her. But how could he know for certain.

He grabbed a blanket from her bed and wrapped it around her, keeping her shoulders exposed. She held onto the end of the blanket as she held her breath. "Ye did no' kill them," he repeated.

"But how can ye be so certain?" she cried. "I can no' remember and there were no' witnesses."

He removed a dirk from his boot, and handed it to her, hilt first. "Stab yerself," he said.

"Be ye daft?" she exclaimed.

He rolled his eyes. "With the *hilt* lass, no' the blade. Just pretend to stab yerself. And *remember* where it be ye stabbed."

Careful to avoid the blade, she wrapped her fingers around the hilt of the dirk. Awash in uncertainty, she gave him a look that asked if he was certain. His face bore an odd expression, one she could not decipher.

"Stab yerself."

With the dirk in her right hand, she pretended to plunge the dirk into her stomach.

"Again," he said.

She complied.

"Now, stab yerself in yer back," he directed.

Aye, uncle had told her she stabbed herself repeatedly in her own back. Changing the dirk around in her palm. She lifted her arm over her head and stabbed, just between her neck and shoulder.

"Now lower," he said.

Taking a deep, steadying breath, she stabbed at her middle and lower back.

Brogan took the knife from her and returned it to his boot. Next, he turned her around. "Ye stabbed herself here and here," he said, pointing to those places she had just stabbed at. "But yer scars? They be here, and here, and here," he said, touching each scar with his fingertip.

"Unless yer arms be at least a foot longer, then there be now way on God's earth ye could have stabbed yerself as ye were told."

Marighread spun around to look at him, her brow knotted, her eyes naught but slits. "What?"

"Lass, I do no' lie. Ye just proved it, with yer own hands."

BROGAN HAD COME BACK TO HER ROOM TO APOLOGIZE AGAIN. HE knew he would be unable to sleep unless he told her once more how sorry he was for causing her a moment of pain. He had knocked, not once, but twice. When she did not immediately respond, he opened the door just a crack.

Then he saw her standing naked in front of the basin.

At first, his manhood sprung to life, with an intense, aching need. But then he saw the scars on her back and remembered what she had told him. *Uncle found me with the knife in me hand. He said I was screamin' I had killed them, all the while I kept stabbing meself in me back.*

He hadn't truly believed that story, for a wide variety of reasons. It just did not seem possible that a person would stab themselves in the back. The stomach? Aye, that was always a distinct possibility. But their back?

As soon as he saw those scares *he* knew. He knew beyond a shadow of a doubt that she had not done was she had been told. It was a physical impossibility.

He could have simply told her what he knew in his heart to be true. But he decided instead to prove it to her.

Now, she trembled with wide eyes as it all began to sink in.

"I did no' do it?" she asked at first. "I did no' do it."

"Nay, lass, ye did no'. 'Tis simply impossible."

In dumbfounded confusion, she kept shaking her head.

"Now, I have no' seen the scars on yer stomach," he told her. "Ye'll have to look fer yerself if they be where ye put the hilt moments ago."

"I do no' need to look," she said breathlessly. "The scars on me stomach be here." She pointed to an area that was more to the side of her abdomen than dead center where she had demonstrated.

"*Now* do ye believe me?" he asked.

Tears fell again, as she nodded her head. "Aye, I do!" A moment later, she was in his arms with her head resting on his chest. "I did no' do it!" she cried, relieved beyond measure. "I did no' kill them."

AYE, SHE WAS RELIEVED. BUT WITH LEARNING THE TRUTH CAME more questions. "If I did no' do it, then who did?" she asked.

Brogan was rubbing her back and shoulders, offering more comfort than he could ever possibly know.

"And to what end?" she asked. "And why would me uncle tell me ..." her words trailed off as the sudden realization hit her. 'Twas so startling, and so unbelievable that it made her legs weak.

Brogan was eerily silent. "Have ye learned somethin' about that night that ye are no' tellin' me?" she asked as she pulled away to look into his eyes.

She saw it then, just a flicker of guilt. "Please, tell me."

"I have already told ye what I ken. We have been so busy workin' on the wall that I have no' had time to do a proper investigation."

She knew 'twas a lie he just told her. Brogan was a most honorable man. He had promised always to tell her the truth, no matter the circumstance. Then she thought to Gertie and Tilda and what they had done earlier this day. "Are ye tellin' me a lie from yer heart?" she asked him.

He smiled warmly. "Nay, I told ye all I know, lass."

She didn't believe him for a moment. "But ye have an idea of what happened? A suspicion that ye are no' yet ready to share with me?"

Her question was met with silence.

In that little moment of time, she knew several things. Brogan cared for her a great deal. Oh, she wasn't foolish enough to believe 'twas the same kind of love he had felt for Anna. But he did care. He cared enough not to tell her what he suspected. He was protecting her from something she was now beginning to suspect herself. Her uncle was her primary suspect and undoubtedly, Brogan's as well.

Suddenly, she felt exhausted. 'Twas all too much for a heart and body to bear in one night. For now, she would let the matter alone. But soon, very soon, they were going to have a serious discussion.

"I want to go to bed, Brogan," she told him.

He nodded and began to step away.

"Brogan, please do no' leave."

He paused and raised a brow. His eyes flickering with questions he was not about to ask.

"I do no' think I am ready to give myself to ye, like a true wife. But please, do no' leave me alone this night."

"I can sleep in the chair, lass. I will watch over ye."

She swallowed hard and shook her head. "Ye'll get a crick in yer neck," she told him.

He chuckled. "Aye, I did get one last night."

"What do ye mean?"

He told her of her fitful sleep the night before and how he ended up sleeping in the chair. Humiliated, she felt her face burn.

"Do no' fash over it, lass," he smiled as he gave her shoulders a gentle squeeze.

"Would it be too much to ask that ye sleep in the bed with me?" Even she heard the quiver in her voice.

"Nay, lass. That would no' be too much a thing to ask."

Dawn arrived with thunder and rain. Mairghread woke to

find herself alone. Brogan, true to his word, had slept with her the night before, without so much as a request for a kiss good night.

She *had* slept relatively well. Only twice did she wake. Once to a bad dream. The second time to the sound of Brogan's snoring. 'Twas not nearly as loud as James had been. 'Twas more a soft, gentle sound. She supposed it had wakened her because she was unaccustomed to having anyone in her bed, let alone a man.

As she was getting dressed, Evelyn knocked at the door with her morning meal.

"Good morn, to ye," Mairghread said as she let her in.

"M'lady," she said, bobbing a curtsy.

Light flashed out of doors, a moment later, thunder roared. Both women nearly jumped out of their skins. 'Twas Mairghread who laughed first. "I do no' think anyone will be workin' out of doors this morn," she said.

"I think no', m'lady."

She then thought of Brogan and all the men who were working on the construction of the wall. "Have ye seen me husband?" she asked as she pulled on warm woolens.

"Below stairs, m'lady, in the gatherin' room."

Much relieved to hear it, she pulled on her boots. With Gertie and Tilda 'ill', she would have to eat another meal alone. Not as pleasant a thought as it might have been months ago.

"Evelyn, I think that from now on, I will be havin' all me meals below stairs," she told her.

"I shall let Cook ken, m'lady," Evelyn replied.

Mairghread noticed Evelyn's nervous demeanor. The way her eyes darted around the room, looking at everything and anything but *her*. The way she fidgeted with her dress and kept shifting from one foot to the other.

"Evelyn, be there somethin' the matter?"

"N-nay, m'lady," she replied in a low, soft voice.

Mayhap, her nervousness was born out of the fact that for the past years, no one ever knew what to expect when in her presence. A heavy feeling settled into her stomach. She recognized it at once as profound guilt. "Evelyn, I want to apologize to ye, fer how I have treated ye in the past."

Evelyn's expression changed from nervous to confused as she finally looked her in the eyes.

"Ye ken I was a drunkard," Mairghread began.

"M'lady!" she exclaimed, shocked at Mairghread's admission. "Do no' say such things!"

Mairghread could not resist the smile that came to her lips. "Do no' fash yerself over it, Evelyn. We *all* ken it be nothin' but the cold truth I speak."

Unable to look at her anymore, Evelyn looked down at her feet.

"I will promise ye I will do me best to never behave so horribly to ye, or to anyone else, ever again."

IT HAD BEEN ANOTHER SLEEPLESS NIGHT FOR BROGAN. 'TWASN'T necessarily Mairghread who directly kept him awake half the night. Nay 'twas his lustful thoughts and the fact that she kept snuggling into him for warmth.

Now, under any other circumstance, he would have welcomed that pert derrière of hers against his groin with delightful enthusiasm. But to have her there, so close, and unable to touch her? To explore the magnificence hidden under her night rail and not be allowed to touch or caress? 'Twas more torture than any man could be expected to bear.

To make matters worse, they were unable to work this morn. The rain was as relentless as a Highlander fighting against an invader. It, and the wind, pounded against the walls of the keep, fighting against the furs that covered the windows. Bleak, cold and dreary was the order of the day.

"If this rain keeps up, we will need to be buildin' boats instead of walls, aye?" Henry said as he elbowed Peter in the ribs.

Peter did not appear amused.

Brogan saw no sense in setting at the high table, so he was eating with his men when Mairghread coming down the stairs. Regal as always, she was. Dressed in a beautiful gown of deep blue, with a silver belt that draped *just so* around her tiny waist, and her hair braided around the top of her head. She fair stole his breath away.

In her hands, was the tray Evelyn had taken up to her not long ago. Nervously — though why he should feel thus was beyond his comprehension at the moment — he stood. As did Henry, Comnall, Peter, and the rest of his men. Brogan noticed the way Evelyn smiled at Peter before walking away. He also took note of the look Peter gave to her.

"Good morn, to ye, Brogan," she said with a warm smile. "Lads."

They returned her greeting, but all remained standing.

"I did no' want to eat alone," she told them. "Might I join ye?"

The men all happily agreed. Henry moved over so that she could take his spot across from Brogan. They all fell silent and went back to their meal.

"I fear if this rain keeps up, ye'll need to be buildin' boats instead of walls, aye?" Mairghread said with a twinkle in her eye and a slight laugh.

The men at the table — all but Henry — laughed heartily at her jest. Even Peter, who, moments ago, had shrugged off Henry's exact jest. Brogan, upon seeing Henry was about to speak, gave him a look of warning and said, "Henry, here, was speaking much the same thing."

Mairghread looked up at the ginger-haired man next to her and smiled. Immediately, Henry's countenance softened and he returned her smile.

"I dare say there be no' much fer a man to do on a day like this," Mairghread said as she took a sip of cider. She winced as she swallowed it down.

"But a woman's work does no' wait fer weather, aye?" Henry said, still sporting the same besotted smile.

Mairghread giggled and agreed.

"Brogan, have ye found a room yet, to take as yer private office?" Mairghread asked him.

A private office? The thought had never entered his mind. As far as he was concerned, 'twas she who needed such a space, not he. "I do no' need such," he told her.

She quirked a pretty brow. "Me?" she asked. "'Tis no' me who be puttin' the keep back to rights with the buildin' of our new wall. Where do ye keep the plans? Where do ye meet with the men?"

"Henry has the plans," Brogan replied. "And I meet with me men here, in the gatherin' room, or in the forest."

From her expression, he could see she was not satisfied with his answer. "But Brogan——"

"Lass, mayhap this is somethin' we could discuss later, in private."

Taking the hint, she nodded.

He thought, mayhap, she had acquiesced a little too quickly.

THANKFULLY, THE STORM HAD LET UP WITHIN THE HOUR. BY nooning time, 'twas naught but a light mist with the sunshine occasionally peeking out betwixt dull gray clouds. Mairghread left the men as soon as she had finished eating, so that she could look in on Gertie and Tilda.

They were still abed when she entered their room.

I wonder how long they will play at this ruse? She wondered as she painted a concerned smile on her face. "I see ye be no better this morn," she told them.

Each of them coughed slightly and feigned weakness.

"We be certain we will be better verra soon," Gertie whispered.

"Aye, verra soon, m'lady," Tilda said.

As tempted as she was to let them know she knew what they were up to, she decided against it. If anyone deserved a good rest, 'twas these two women. Pulling up a chair, she sat at the foot of their beds.

"I want to thank each of ye," she began with a smile. "Fer always bein' there for me, no matter the circumstance. Ye've been good to me, even when ye had every right not to be."

Perplexed, they remained silent.

"I want to thank ye as well, fer helpin' me to see that Claude Courtemanche was no' the right husband fer me. I think ye chose well with Brogan," she said with a wink.

"He be a right good man," Gertie said with a smile. She sat up with a groan. "A right good man."

"Aye," Tilda agreed.

On that, she would not argue, for they spoke nothing but the truth. "'Tis true, he has been good to me," she said. Without thinking, she added, "But I fear I have no' been as good to him."

Gertie's brow wrinkled. "What do ye mean?"

Mairghread let out a sigh, wishing for all the world she had kept her thoughts to herself. Changing the subject, she asked them, "What do ye remember the night James and Connell were killed?"

Their eyes widened in horrification. "Och! Lass! Why do ye be wantin' to talk about that night?" Gertie asked, appalled with the notion.

Besides the fact that Brogan had been sleeping right next to her, the night her family had been slaughtered had made her feign sleep for most of last night. "I do no' ken anything about that night," she began. "Uncle has always told me that he got to me room first."

"Aye," Gertie replied cautiously.

Tilda remained unusually mute.

"Uncle told me, that upon entering the room, he found me with the knife in me hand. He said I was screamin' like a mad woman that I had killed them." She took in a deep breath, wishing her hands would stop shaking. "He also says I was stabbin' meself. Did either of ye see such?"

Apparently, her malaise had improved immeasurably, for Gertie tossed the covers off and sat on the edge of the bed. Anger was flashing behind those blue eyes of hers.

"Please, I beg of ye to tell me what *ye* saw," Mairghread said. "For Brogan has proved to me, that I could no' have stabbed meself."

Gertie's forward progression out of the bed halted with those words. Slowly, she sat back down, looking for all the world like a sad, forlorn auld woman.

She explained what had happened the night before, when Brogan told her to stab herself. "The scars be in places I simply could no' reach."

She and Tilda looked at one another. 'Twas no' their usual conspiratorial looks.

"There be much ye are no' tellin' me," Mairghread said. She was growing quite frustrated.

Their silence was near maddening. "Ye believe me uncle has lied." 'Twas a statement, not a question. A cold chill of dread made its way up and down her spine. A body could say much without uttering a single word.

'Twas Gertie who broke the silence first. "Neither of us saw what yer uncle speaks of."

"Nay, m'lady, we did no' see such," Tilda said.

"What *did* ye see?"

Then there it was. That all too familiar conspiratorial glance to one another. Mairghread shot to her feet. "Will ye two stop doin' that?" she exclaimed. "And just tell me what the bloody hell ye saw!"

Aye, she had yelled at them before. But only when she was in a drunken stupor. This was different. She was sober, a woman full grown, and determined to get the answers she sought.

"When we got to the room, ye were lyin' on the floor and yer uncle was kneelin' over ye," Gertie said. Ye were no' screamin' like a mad woman. Ye were covered in blood, near death."

So they had only seen the aftermath?

"The knife was in yer uncle's hand," Tilda told her. "No' yer's."

'TWAS NOT WHAT THEY SAID, BUT THE MANNER IN WHICH THEY didn't say it. More fingers of dread traced up and down her spine.

Nay, she told herself. *It could no' be.*

"We do no' ken what truly happened," Gertie said. "But I never believed fer a minute ye killed them."

"Neither did I m'lady," Tilda said. Her eyes had grown damp, tears threatening to spill at any moment. "Ye loved them too much to do such a thing."

Her thoughts turned to her uncle. Why would he have told her such a horrible thing? Why would he have done his best to convince her that she had killed them? But the most frightening question of all was why she would have believed him.

She had to believe there was a reason, a good, sound, logical reason... nay, even she couldn't force herself to believe there was any good or just cause for him to tell her she had killed her husband and child.

Then, as swiftly and suddenly as a bolt of lightening, everything became clear.

"M'lady, are ye well?" Tilda asked from her bed. She too was rising from her bed.

"Aye," Mairghread said breathlessly. "I am quite well."

Neither of them appeared to believe her, not one bit.

"Ye did no' do what he said ye did," Gertie told her as she climbed out of her bed.

"I know," Mairghread said. Her mind was spinning, dozens of questions springing forth. Why would a man do such a thing? Why was he so insistent that she marry Courtemanche, especially when he probably knew the man would want to take her to France? He had to know what kind of man the frenchman was. There was only one answer and it terrified her to no end.

Slowly, she got to her feet. Though she had not regained any memory from the awful night, she could see everything now, with such blinding clarity. "Gertie, Tilda, I ken ye are no' feelin' well," she began.

"Och! I be as right as rain, m'lady," Gertie protested as she took her hand in hers.

"I am as well," Tilda said.

How she managed to smile, she was uncertain, but she did. "'Tis good to hear. I need to leave ye fer a bit."

"Where be ye goin'?" Gertie asked with a furrowed brow.

"To see Cook."

'Twas a lie and mayhap not one of her heart.

GRAYSON MACTAVISH WAS STANDING GUARD IN FRONT OF THE ROOM where Hargatha had been locked for nearly a fortnight. Mairghread had known him all her life. But she also knew him to be loyal to her uncle. Silently, she cursed her misfortune.

When he saw her approach, his bushy gray brows knitted into a line of confusion and surprise. "M'lady?"

"Grayson," she said with a slight nod. "I have come to see how Hargatha fairs this day."

Though he appeared to be puzzled, he still possessed the where-withal to block her from entering the room. "She fairs well, m'lady."

Thinking quickly, she said, "I also have a question regarding healing."

He pulled his shoulders back. "I have strict orders no' to allow anyone in or out of her room, m'lady."

"Ye would deny me entry?" she asked indignantly.

"I be sorry, but I can no'. The only one allowed inside be Brogan."

Pursing her lips together, she tried to think of what she could say or do to change his mind. "But *I* be the lady of the keep," she reminded him.

"I ken well who ye be, m'lady, but orders is orders."

Knowing she was going to get nowhere with the man, she smiled up at him. "Ye do yer duty well, Grayson Mactavish."

He offered her a slight smile, but otherwise, had no reply.

Although she was frustrated, she pretended to be nothing but graceful and dignified. "I shall return later, then, with Brogan."

She saw something akin to fear flicker behind his brown eyes. But 'twas gone as quickly as it had risen. "Keep up yer good work, Grayson."

Inclining her head to him, she turned and walked away. *If anyone has answers, 'twill be Hargatha,* she thought to herself. 'Twas going to seem like an awfully long day before Brogan returned from his work.

Mayhap, she mused, *I should go to him, make me plea and bring him back.*

MIRACLE OF ALL MIRACLES HAPPENED WHEN GERTIE AND TILDA declared themselves cured. Not long after, all but one of the other 'ill' people were out of their beds, declaring they too, were better and able to return to their duties.

Mairghread refused to admit she'd known about their ploy all along. By rights, their plot had worked, so why let on?

When she told Gertie and Tilda that she wished to walk to see

Brogan, they insisted she not go alone. Wanting to hurry, she agreed, just to avoid the delay and argument they would surely win.

Donning cloaks, the three women left the keep together.

"Glad to see the storm has moved on," Gertie remarked as they walked across the courtyard.

That storm be nothin' compared to what lies ahead when me uncle returns, Mairghread thought to herself.

For whatever reason, she found herself invigorated by her sudden realization that her uncle was nothing more than a cruel man. She suspected he was motivated by greed. Why else would he have told her she had killed James and Connell? Supposing he believed that she would die from a broken heart, or simply hand over the chiefdom and everything that came with it to him, her anger continued to bubble.

Not for a moment did it occur to her that he had anything to do with their deaths. Nay, she believed he simply took the opportunity of a very horrid and ugly situation and tried to turn it to his advantage.

And he had almost succeeded.

Almost.

Had it not been for Gertie and Tilda and their interference, she would still be nothing more than a drunkard dying a slow, painful death. Aye, she knew she owed her sobriety to Brogan, but Gertie and Tilda had been the one's to set everything into motion.

"They be makin' good progress," Tilda said as they passed through the opening in the wall.

Someday soon, there would be a heavy gate, an upper wall for guards, towers, and a better sense of safety. Mairghread prayed they would finish the wall before her uncle returned. Simply because she wanted to be the one who threw him out of it.

Aye, she was going to banish him, and anyone loyal to him, for his cruel misdeeds. To make her believe all these years that she had suddenly gone insane and killed the two people who meant everything to her.

It frightened her to know she had almost believed him.

That question still burned deep. *Why? Why would I believe him?*

Was it mayhap because he was the only living kin she had left? Aye, he had played that to his advantage. Although she knew he and her father rarely saw eye to eye on things, she could not believe Aymer would ever do anything to actually harm her.

Until now.

&.

BROGAN SAW THE THREE WOMEN APPROACHING, WITH DISBELIEVING eyes. Mairghread. His heart felt lighter, happier, just at seeing her here. With a quick strike, he lodged his axe into a log and went to meet them.

"Mairghread," he said as he approached them. "I did no' expect to see the two of ye out of bed for a time," he said, referring to their recent illness. "What brings ye here? Is all well?"

"Aye, all be well," she said as she cast a look of vexation at Gertie and Tilda.

"Good day to ye, m'laird," Gertie and Tilda said in unison. "Our lady wanted to take a walk this day. A bit of fresh air, she says." Gertie winked at him before turning to smile at Mairghread.

He didn't know what to make of either the wink or what she said. Knowing that by asking her to explain would inevitably lead to a pounding in his skull, he decided against it.

"Brogan, I wonder if I might speak to ye," she said before looking first to Gertie then to Tilda. "Alone, if ye please."

Neither woman was offended by her request. Nay, they looked positively gleeful. He was no glutton for punishment so once again, he kept any questions to himself. Extending his arm to his wife, he led her away.

Tilda was grinning from ear to ear. "She be fallin' in love with him," she said.

"Aye," agreed Gertie. "She just does no' ken it yet."

They watched as the couple walked away. "Me thinks he loves her as well," Gertie said.

"Of course he does," Tilda said. "What is there no' to love about the woman?"

"Aye, she be about the most lovely and sweetest woman I ever knew."

❦

ADMITTEDLY, BROGAN WAS GLAD TO SEE HIS WIFE. HE WAS, however, confused as to why she chose today, of all days, for a walk and fresh air. The weather was not exactly being kind to anyone.

Leading her away from the crowd, they now stood in the woods. "I see Tilda and Gertie have made a full recovery," he remarked with a grin.

"Have ye spoken with Hargatha since lockin' her away?" Mairghread asked, getting straight to the reason for her visit.

Taken aback, he cocked his head to one side. "I tried to. Why do ye ask?"

"I want to speak to her, about me injuries from the night of the attack," she said.

He raked a hand through his hair. He thought they had settled the matter last night. "I thought I proved to ye—"

"I ken that I did no' kill them," she told him with a smile. "But I have questions."

"Such as?" he asked with a raise brow.

She clamped her lips together as she thought on his questions. "Hargatha be the most loyal to me uncle. I want to ken what else *she* kens about that night, especially as it pertains to me uncle."

"I do no' think she would be willin' to talk to either one of us," he pointed out. "Ye might have to think of other ways to get the answers ye seek."

"I ken no' who else to ask," she said.

He was quiet for a long moment. "I do no' think those who are loyal to Aymer will speak against him." 'Twould likely be a cold day in hell before any of them did. "How many amongst yer people are loyal to him?"

In truth, she could not begin to guess. "In case ye fergot, I have no' exactly been payin' close attention to things these past few years."

He had no response. At least none he could put to voice at the moment.

"I ken that ye have said I can talk to ye about anything," she said as she wrapped her arms around her waist.

"Ye can," he reassured her.

She studied him for a time as she mulled a few things over in her mind. "I have suspicions about me uncle. I be certain he lied to me about a few things."

Brogan was just as certain but would remain quiet on the matter, at least until he heard what she had to say.

"I think he took the opportunity of the attack that night and used it to his advantage. He lied to me, makin' me believe for all these years that I had killed them. I believe he did it knowin' full well 'twould be somethin' I could never fergive meself for. And I believe he did it to gain control of the clan, our coffers, and our holdings."

The only thing Brogan could argue against was the fact she still believed there had been an attack that night. He, however, was convinced something far more sinister happened. 'Twas treacherous ground on which they now stood. He knew he must be careful in sharing his own suspicions until he had more definitive evidence. "I agree that he be no' above anythin' to get what he wants."

She blew out a sigh of relief. "I thought ye'd think me mad," she said.

"Nay lass, I do no'. I have learned much in the past weeks that lead me to believe much the same thing."

"Such as?" she asked, quirking a pretty brow.

"What man removes an entire wall because of a few loose stones? What man would order all weapons be kept *away* from the keep, in a place of safekeeping no one kens of? And what good and decent man would arrange a marriage between his beautiful niece and a man like Courtemanche?"

"So what do we do?" she asked.

Brogan smiled, and said, "We build the wall before he returns and we make new weapons."

"Ye've talked with Iarainn, then?"

"Aye, I have. She be workin' day and night fer us."

"That be good to hear," she said. "Have ye decided what ye will do with Hargatha?"

Rubbing the back of his neck, he said, "'Tis no' me decision to make, Mairghread, but yers."

Mairghread shivered and looked up at the leaden sky. "I should get Gertie and Tilda back to the keep. It looks like more rain be headin' our way."

'Twas apparent to him she had no desire yet to make a decision on the auld healer. "When I return to the keep, we should mayhap sit down and discuss together, Hargatha's future."

"No matter what we decide, we will be needin' a new healer," she said.

He'd been so busy with the wall as well as Mairghread's recovery that he hadn't given much thought to their need of a healer.

"I am told Liam's brother be a healer," she said. "Mayhap we could ask Liam to reach out to him, to see if he would be interested in comin' to our aid."

Brogan chuckled. "Now, ye might want to reconsider that," he said.

"Why? He can no' possibly be any worse than Hargatha."

Liam's brother, Lachlan, had a habit of finding trouble without looking for it. He was just as handsome as Brogan's own brother, Ian. But as Ian had taken advantage of his good looks where it pertained to women, Lachlan was not thusly inclined. The man was a warrior, through and through. However, several years ago, he laid down his sword and picked up herbs to become a healer. Brogan did not know why the man had made that decision. There were too many rumors of differing opinions to piece together an answer. "Well, he be a right handsome man. The lasses tend to throw themselves at him."

Mairghread raised her brow in disbelief. "Be that as it may, we need a healer. I do no' care if he be the most handsome man to ever grace God's earth, or if he looks like the arse end of a three-legged dog."

He chuckled slightly. "Verra well, I shall speak to Liam."

"Thank ye, Brogan," she said.

The mist began to turn to a light rain, then. "Ye best be gettin' back to the keep."

She bid him good day and hurried off to collect Gertie and Tilda.

He was truly beginning to like his wife.

Chapter Nineteen

W aves crashed violently against the craggy cliffs and shores below the Mactavish keep. Lightning danced across the black as pitch sky while the wind wailed like some tortured soul from the bowels of hell.

Because of the inclement weather, no one came to sup in the keep. People stayed in their cottages, for no meal, no fellowship was worth the trek out of doors.

Brogan braved a trip to the kitchens to wrangle up a simple meal for he and Mairghread. Though the pathway betwixt keep and kitchens was covered, it offered very little protection against the elements. The wind whipped through, splattering water against his trews, soaking through his boots.

Lowrens and the servants were seated at a long table. When he entered, each jumped to their feet. "Sit," he said with an engaging smile. "Enjoy yer meal."

"What can I do fer ye, m'laird?" Lowrens asked as he rose.

"A wee supper fer Mairghread and me," he replied.

"We would have sent ye a tray," Lowrens told him.

"We did no' want anyone to have to brave this foul weather," Brogan said. In truth, Mairghread was more worried than he.

"Verra well," he replied. "I will have ye a tray in no time."

While he waited at Lowrens' worktable, the rest of the servants had returned to their meal. They were speaking in low, hushed tones. Just what was being said, he could not hear. But the man with the light brown hair muttered, it was causing a bit of a commotion. Two chairs down was a man who looked to be about Brogan's age. His full beard was a few shades lighter than the dark brown mop that covered his head. But even through all the hair and whiskers, Brogan could see he was not the least bit impressed. Wiry whiskers danced lightly as he worked his jaw back and forth. Clutching his eating knife, his knuckles were turning white.

'Twas apparent the older man telling his story was oblivious to the rest of the people near him. For had he seen the way the bearded man was behaving, he would have shut his mouth by now.

Before Brogan could intervene, the bearded man slammed his meaty fists on the table. A moment later, he was on his feet, scooting the seating bench back, taking the other occupants with it. Startled, they nearly toppled over backward. Soon, they were scurrying off their seats.

"Yer laird be standin' right there, Phillip Mactavish!" the bearded man exclaimed gruffly. "Mayhap ye'd like to give *him* yer opinions of his wife, yer lady and mistress?"

The man named Phillip looked up with wide eyes and mouth agape. "Sit down, Fergus!" he seethed in a whisper. "Have ye gone daft?"

Fergus slammed his fist against the table once again. "Ye are naught but a cruel gossip, Phillip. Again, I ask ye if ye'd like to share yer opinion of our lady with her husband?"

Brogan stepped forward, curious as well as angry. Though he had not a clue as to *what* had been said, it must have been quite foul.

Phillip looked up from his seat, worry and fear etched on his face. "'Twas naught but a jest," he stammered.

With a raised brow, he waited for a further explanation. "Pray tell me, what was the jest?" he asked, the challenge in his tone evident.

"I," he started, stopped, and tried again. "Please, m'laird, 'tis naught I wish to repeat to ye."

Brogan took another step forward. "'Tis a jest ye have no problem with tellin' everyone here, but naught one ye'd wish to repeat to me?" he asked for clarification sake.

Looking across the table to Fergus, Brogan asked, "Would ye like to repeat it fer him?"

Fergus cast an angry glance at Phillip. "He said he wonders how our lady is able to please ye in bed when her hands be too full of flagons of whisky."

At once, Brogan lifted Phillip out of his seat and threw him against the wall. Pinning him in place with his forearm pressed against his throat, he seethed furiously. "If ever again I hear of ye makin' such disparagin' remarks about me wife, who is also yer lady, I will kill ye. Do. Ye. Understand?"

Phillip fair shook with fear, his eyes bulging in their sockets. Sweat broke out across his red face. Unable to speak, he could only nod his head violently.

Brogan counted to five before releasing him. Bent over, Phillip took in great gobs of air as spit dripped from his lips.

Speaking over his shoulder to Lowrens, Brogan said, "This man is no' allowed to work in the kitchens again. He may find work elsewhere."

Turning, he looked at the stunned faces of the rest of the servants. "Anyone who spreads such vile and disgustin' *jests* about yer lady will be immediately banished from the keep. If such talk continues, ye will be banished from the clan."

Although there should not have been a doubt in anyone's mind he meant what he said, two men, about the same age as Phillip stepped forward. "Ye can no' banish anyone," the shorter of the two men said. "Aymer be our chief. Only he can do such."

The taller man with light brown hair and pock-marked face nodded his agreement.

"Aymer Mactavish be no' the chief here," Brogan said through gritted teeth. "Yer lady, Mairghread, is." He could feel his face growing hot with unmitigated anger.

The shorter man scoffed openly, derisively. Pulling his shoulders back and puffing his chest out like a peacock in rut, he said, "I'll no' put me faith in a drunkard."

Brogan and Fergus lunged at the man at the same time.

Brogan reached him first. The table was in Fergus's way, so he climbed over it.

No one came to the peacock's defense. Not even his tall friend who had stood beside him moments ago.

Pulling back his right arm, Brogan plunged his fist into the man's jaw. He fell backward, tripping over a small stool, and landed flat on his back. A moment later, Brogan had him pinned to the floor, on his back, his tunic clutched in his hands. "In case ye had no' guessed, that was the wrong thing to say," he spoke through clenched teeth.

Purple with rage, his eyes naught but slits, he was as angry at this man as he had been at Hargatha. "If ye can no' give yer fealty to Mairghread, ye can leave."

Shoving the man down harder, he got to his feet. So angry was he, he could hear the blood rushing in his ears.

Fergus, just a few inches taller than Brogan, bent over and hauled the man to his feet. Disgusted, he held on to the man's shirt. "What would ye have me do with this, m'laird?" he asked with a good measure of disgust.

Turning to look at the rest of the people around them, Brogan said, "Anyone who can no' give their fealty to yer lady, Mairghread Mactavish, fer *any* reason, will leave now. Pack yer things and go. We will start with *him*," he said as he inclined his head toward the man Fergus was holding.

He would not give in to any pleas for mercy. Assuming these men were loyal to Aymer, 'twas too dangerous to keep them here. And if they were simply ignorant fools who could not hold their tongues? He cared not.

Wiping his forehead on the sleeve of his tunic, he went to Lowrens. "Thank ye for the meal." Taking the tray from the table, he looked back once. "Fergus, I would like to meet with ye after I sup with me wife. Would ye have time?"

"Aye, m'laird, I would."

Brogan gave him a quick nod and quit the kitchen.

ALL THE WAY BACK TO MAIRGHREAD'S CHAMBER, BROGAN DEBATED on what, if anything, he should tell his wife. He did not want to lie to her and he certainly had no desire to keep anything from her.

He could not blame her people for having a lack of faith in her. They had watched as she nearly drank herself into an early grave. But, damn it! She *was* the lady of their keep. She *was* their chief.

It was going to take a long while before she earned their trust again. A long while, and a very long road. All he could do was show his unyielding support for her. Especially when it came to idiots like those he'd just encountered in the kitchens.

Pushing the door to Mairghread's chamber open with his toe, he went inside and set the tray on the table.

"I hope it be warm," Mairghread said as she rubbed her hands together. "Aside from settin' the keep on fire, I do no' ken what else to do to keep out the chill."

"It *was* warm when I left the kitchens," he said. "But it be a long, wet and windy walk this night."

Shivering, she pulled her gray woolen shawl more tightly around her shoulders and sat next to the fire. Brogan placed a bowl of warm rabbit stew on the table, along with a small loaf of brown, crusty bread. Once he saw she was settled, he got his own stew and bread and sat across from her.

As she was lifting the stew to her lips, a clap of thunder rang out, rattling anything that wasn't bolted to the floor. Mairghread nearly jumped out of her skin. "Lord, will this storm ever cease?"

The wind battled against the furs that covered the window, puffing them out like sails on a ship.

"Ye do no' like storms?" he asked as he tore off a hunk of bread.

"Storms? Nay, storms do no' bother me. But the hellish beast currently tryin' to gain access to our keep? *That,* I do no' like."

Brogan chuckled, dipped his bread into the stew before popping it into his mouth.

"Lowrens makes a right good rabbit stew, aye?" she asked.

"I have yet to eat anything that was no' good," Brogan said.

Remembering the cider, he got up, grabbed the pitcher and two mugs and returned to the table. Mairghread's nose curled up. "Will I ever get used to the cider?" she asked as he handed her a cup. "'Tis the truth I have to choke it down."

She was the first person he'd ever known who did not like cider. "Mayhap on the morrow I can ask Lowrens if there be somethin' else he can offer ye."

"Thank ye," she said as she lifted her mug. "Speaking of the morrow, I doubt ye will get much work done on the wall."

He glanced at the furs fluttering against the howling wind. "I would wager ye be right."

"I pray there will be no more delays," she told him. "I want the wall finished before me uncle returns."

On that, they were like-minded. Before he could offer his own opinion on the matter, she said, "I want to be the one who boots his arse through the gate."

He nearly choked to death on his cider.

Mairghread turned her lips inward to quash her laughter. When he stopped choking, she asked, "Ye behave as though ye've never heard a woman use colorful words before," she said with a sly smile.

Once he got his coughing under control, he said, "Usually, when a woman is cursin' around me, she be cursin' me to the devil."

Raising a brow, she asked, "Does that happen often?"

"Unfortunately, aye, it does. Believe it or no', no' all women find me as charmin' as ye do."

"Think ye I find ye charmin'?" she said, feigning an air of nonchalance.

"Of course ye do," he said. "Why else would ye have married me? It certainly was no' fer me coin or me good looks."

She sat up taller. "What do ye mean? Ye be a right handsome fellow." She sounded quite serious.

"Ye find me handsome *and* charmin'?" he asked playfully, waggling his eyebrows and puffing out his chest.

"Handsome? Aye. Charmin'? That remains to be seen."

AFTER THEY FINISHED THEIR MEAL, MAIRGHREAD CLEARED THE table. Brogan added more wood to the fire and returned to his seat.

Mairghread grabbed a blanket from the end of her bed and sat down, draping it across her lap. "I hope Reginald be somewhere warm and safe this night," she said as she looked into the fire.

"Let us also pray he has found recruitments," Brogan added.

She nodded slightly as she chewed on her bottom lip.

"Mairghread, there be more things we need to discuss."

"Such as?" she asked, her eyes temporarily frozen on the flames that danced in the hearth. The heat, the sound of crackles and pops was making her sleepy.

He took in a deep, cleansing breath and let it out slowly. "I think it be time ye made an announcement to the clan, about ye becomin' chief."

Slowly, she pulled her eyes away from the fire to look at him. "I have no' made a decision yet, Brogan."

"Certainly ye can no' be thinkin' of makin' yer uncle chief," he asked with a good deal of incredulity.

"The only way Aymer Mactavish becomes chief of this clan is over me dead body," she told him.

"Then what decision is it ye need to make?" As far as he knew, there was only one choice, and that was for Mairghread to take the helm. 'Twas her right and duty as heir.

"I want ye to be chief," she told him matter-of-factly.

Aye, wives were betimes confusing and frustrating creatures. "I have no claim to it, Mairghread. Yer da wanted ye to be chief. Why do ye resist it?" Truly, he was baffled. "Few women are ever given the opportunity that sits before ye."

"Ye think I should do this for all of womankind then?" she asked as she drummed her fingers on the table.

"In truth? Aye, I do. But there be other reasons as well."

"Pray, tell me what those reasons be," she said sarcastically as she rested her chin in her palm.

"Because 'tis yer birthright. A right many women are never given. Because this," he extended his arms wide, "all be *yers*."

"That's it?" she asked. "Because it be me birthright?" Shaking her head in disbelief, she let out a long breath. "Birthright alone does no' a good chief make."

"I was no' finished," he told her firmly. After she gave him a nod, he went on. "Ye should be chief because I have witnessed with me own eyes how deeply ye care fer yer people. Ye worry over the servants walkin' in the rain with our meal, so ye send me. Ye worried over and tended to Gertie and Tilda, as well as the others, when ye believed them ill. I am beginnin' to see a strength in ye that I have no' seen in another. It comes from here," he pointed to his heart. "Ye be a right smart woman, Mairghread Mactavish. Ye will make a fine chief."

※

His words, spoken from the heart, warmed her. With all her heart, she knew he meant everything he had said. She also knew, unequivocally, that he was not simply saying them because of what might be in it for him.

"Ye truly would no' mind bein' the husband to a woman who was chief of their clan?" She knew the answer, but wanted to hear it in his own words. "I can no' think of many men who would be willin' to step aside while their wife ruled." In fact, she could bring to mind not a one. Many men, she supposed, might feel their masculinity would be questioned. But not Brogan.

"But I be no' steppin' aside," he reminded her. "I married ye already knowin' ye were or would soon be chief."

She felt her eyes grow damp and cursed herself. She thought of James then. Would he still have married her if she had told him she wanted to lead their clan? If she were completely honest with herself, the answer was no. James was a good, generous man. But if she had not told him before he had even officially proposed that she wanted to lead as chief someday, well, that proposal likely would never have happened.

Self-doubt began to rear its ugly head, roaring in her ear that she would make a miserable leader. Too soft in her heart, too kind, and far too forgiving. And God forbid if they ever had to go into battle! She had no idea how to train men to fight. Isn't that what all chiefs did?

"Brogan, I truly do appreciate your confidence in me," she told him. "But I fear I would no' make a good chief. I know nothin' of warrin' or negotiations in times of peace."

Pushing himself to his feet, he came around to stand behind her. He placed a warm palm on her shoulder. "Ye would no' be doin' it all alone, Mairghread. I would be right beside ye."

'Twas the same thing he had told her when she had made the decision to give up the drink. To her very bones, she could feel the sincerity in his words. It felt as warm and sweet as a lover's embrace.

Before they could discuss the matter further, a light knock came at their door. Who on earth could it be at this hour of night?

She followed Brogan as he went to answer. She was rather perplexed to see Fergus standing on the other side. Water poured off his woolen cowl and cloak, leaving puddles on the floor under his feet. Her stomach lurched for the man had never appeared at her door before. "Fergus?" she asked as she stepped around her husband. "What be the matter?"

Giving her a slight bow at the waist, he said, "Did no' Brogan tell ye?"

She gave Brogan a curious glance. He simply smiled and said, "I met Fergus earlier this night. I asked him to stop by so we might discuss a few things."

"Ye be discussin' kitchen matters at this late hour?" 'Twas odd, to say the least.

"Nay, m'lady wife, no' kitchen matters," Brogan told her. "I would like to discuss the possibility of Fergus workin' with us on the wall. And when that be complete, mayhap he would be interested in helpin' us to train the men in defense." He looked to Fergus for his approval.

"'Tis the truth I do no' like workin' in the kitchens, m'lady," he said.

Mairghread could not rightly blame him. "I remember now," she said. "'Twas by Hargatha's order last year, when ye injured yer arm."

Brogan asked for an explanation.

"Ye see, I am used to workin' with horses," Fergus explained. "I was breakin' one to ride and had a right nasty fall. Broke me arm in two places. Seamus, he set the bones. Afterward, Hargatha told the lai—" he quickly righted his mistake. "She told Aymer I could no' work with the horses anymore and to put me to work in the kitchens."

"And he listened?" Brogan asked, astonished as well as confused.

"Aye, that he did, m'laird," he replied.

Brogan looked to Mairghread for more answers. "Why on earth would Hargatha suggest such a thing?"

"The better question is why me uncle listened."

"THAT MIGHT BE AN ANSWER WE NEVER HAVE," BROGAN TOLD HER. Hargatha wasn't exactly eager to share any information with anyone. She was especially angry with *him,* for it had been by his order she be locked away.

"I be certain Lowrens will no' mind," Mairghread told Fergus. "I hope he does no' have too much trouble replacin' ye."

"I be certain 'twill no' be a problem," Brogan assured her, hoping to stop Fergus from making any mention of what had taken place earlier in the night.

He and Fergus made plans to meet in the gathering room on the morrow. After bidding them good night, Brogan shut the door and turned to look at Mairghread.

"Mayhap, on the morrow we could meet with a few of the men. I think 'twould be good fer ye to start daily meetin's with them."

"Can I no' leave ye in charge of the wall?" she asked, as she tried to suppress a yawn.

"Aye, ye can," he said. "But it might mean more comin' from ye. No' necessarily as chief, but as lady of the keep." He had no desire, especially at this late hour, of trying to convince her to make an official announcement, surmising it would be best for her to step into the role gradually. But not *too* gradually for there was much to be done.

She readily agreed to meeting them as lady instead of chief. "The hour be late," she said. "And I be tired."

He, too, was exhausted. He'd had too many sleepless nights of late.

He heard the hesitation in what she said next. "It be an awfully cold night."

"Aye, 'tis that," Brogan said.

She shuffled her weight from one foot to the next. Brogan,

sensing there was something she wished to say but mayhap did not know where to begin, offered, "Be there somethin' else ye want to discuss?"

"If ye would no' mind," she began. "I mean, well, it be an awfully cold night and the storm still rages."

It took no keen intellect to reason out what she was trying so hard to get at. "Would ye like me to sleep in here again?"

Looking to her feet, she replied in a low, soft tone. "I do no' like bein' alone."

He could not resist the urge to chuckle. "Lass," he said as he took a step closer. "Ye never need be ashamed to ask anythin' of me. We be married, after all."

Her skin turned a deep shade of red, beginning at her neck and flaming upward. He knew she was fighting an inner battle with herself. It would take some time before she was ready to be a wife to him in every sense of the word. He'd not push nor demand anything of her. For now, he was just happy she had given up the drink and was beginning to confide in him.

"I will step into me chamber while ye ready yerself fer bed."

AT SOME TIME BEFORE DAWN, THE STORMS THAT HAD BATTERED against the lands most of yesterday and last night, finally blew away. Morning dawned bright, with birds chirping at their window.

But 'twas not the birds that woke him. 'Twas Mairghread's arm she had flung over his chest and the leg across his, that had done the trick. Still in a deep sleep, her head was nestled against his shoulder.

God's teeth, 'twas a glorious feeling!

But what he would not give to roll over and bury himself deep within her. To feel her naked skin against his own, to bury his face into her beautiful auburn locks. To breathe in her scent, her essence.

Tempted as he was — and he was mightily tempted — he took in a deep breath and carefully rolled away, sitting on the edge of the bed. There would be no more sleeping now, for he was fully awake in all respects.

Quietly, he padded barefoot into his own chamber. After washing up and dressing, he left to begin his day.

He was breaking his fast on bannocks and sausages when Liam and Henry appeared. Bidding him good morn, Henry sat beside him whilst Liam took the seat across.

"'Twill be a muddy mess workin' in the forest this morn, aye?" Henry said as he chewed on a bite of sausage.

Brogan yawned as he nodded his agreement.

"Any word from Reginald?" Liam asked.

Brogan could not remember how many days the man had been gone. "Nay," he replied.

"'Twill no' matter if he brings a thousand men back with him. The progress will be slow if the rain does no' cease."

Liam quirked a brow. "It *has* ceased," he pointed out.

Henry rolled his eyes. "I can *see* that," he said through gritted teeth. "I be no' a simpleton. The rain needs to stay away for a time."

Liam chuckled. "No rain in Scotland?" he asked dubiously.

Brogan's head was beginning to ache. "Lads," he said, bringing their argument to a halt. "Rain or no', we must finish this wall as soon as possible. Preferably *before* Aymer returns."

Pensively, Henry glanced at Liam before turning to look at Brogan. "Wall or no', if we do no' have well-trained warriors in place before his arrival, I hate to think what will happen."

Brogan had been giving a good deal of thought to that as well. "I do no' think he'll be bringing a thousand warriors with him," he said pointedly. "From what I am told, he left with only twenty men."

"But how many will Courtemanche travel with?" Liam asked.

"I have only met the Frenchman twice," Brogan said. "He usually travels with at least one hundred men."

Liam whistled and Henry looked worried. "But do no' worry lads. Most of them are servants. The man travels with his bed, linens, and various furniture. Each night, they must set up his grand and spacious tent, serve him a feast fit fer kings, and prepare him a hot bath."

"Ye jest," Henry said with a good measure of disbelief.

Brogan chuckled. He had witnessed that particular show of insanity a few years ago. "Nay, I do no' jest. The man be a spoiled eejit. He could no' more sleep on the cold, hard ground at night, than Edward of England would stay the bloody hell out of Scotland."

"Then ye believe we do no' have to worry?" Liam asked.

"Oh, we need to worry lads. Fer with men like Courtemanche and Aymer Mactavish, ye never ken *what* they will do. Unlike our weather, they be unpredictable fools." And that was the most dangerous kind of fool.

FERGUS CAME TO JOIN THEM AT THE TABLE. "GOOD MORN, TO YE, m'laird," he said.

"Sit," Brogan told him with a nod toward the space next to Liam. "And call me Brogan."

The man paused briefly before sitting. "I can no' do that."

"Aye, ye can and ye will. I be no' laird nor chief nor bloody noble-man." He detested pretense. "Liam, Henry, this be Fergus. He had been workin' in the kitchens until late last night. I have asked him to come work on the wall with us."

The two men scrutinized Fergus for a moment. "The kitchens?" Henry asked a bit skeptically.

"Aye, the kitchens," Fergus replied gruffly. "Thanks to that auld witch Hargatha. Broke me arm, ye see, a year ago. Breaking a horse to saddle and the bugger throwed me off. Broke me arm in two places."

Each man listened intently to his story.

"I had auld Seamus set the bones, fer Hargatha would have insisted on amputation, ye ken. Right angry, she was. Went to Aymer, she did. Told him I was no' fit fer anythin' but kitchen work now. Said I was a broken man, she did."

"So they set ye to work in the kitchens?" Liam asked, a bit appalled at the idea.

"Aye, they did. But thanks to our lai — Brogan, I can get out of there and work on the wall."

"We will be glad to have yer help," Henry said. "I hope ye do no' mind playin' in the mud, because that's what we'll be doin'."

"I have no aversion to mud," he replied with a smile and a wink. "Played in it all the time as a lad."

Henry grunted and Liam rolled his eyes, while Brogan ate his meal quietly.

"I heard a few men were asked to leave the keep before dawn," Liam said, casting a glance at Henry.

"Aye," Brogan replied.

"Good riddance," Fergus said as he tore off a bite of sausage with his teeth. "A lazy lot, they is, and loyal to Aymer they be."

Henry and Liam looked to Brogan for further explanation.

"Fergus be right," Brogan told them.

"I says we round up all who remain loyal to Aymer, and banish them," Fergus said with a mouthful of food.

"I take it ye do no' care fer the man?" Liam asked.

Brogan already knew the answer to that question.

"I do no' trust the man as far as I can pick him up and throw him," Fergus said. 'Twas evident he cared not who might hear him speaking so despairingly against Aymer. "I was loyal to Gavin, our lady's da, may he rest in peace."

"What of yer lady, Mairghread?" Henry asked. "Be ye loyal to her?"

Fergus glowered at him. "I will allow ye that insult only because ye do no' ken any better. Ye're damned right I be loyal to her." He took a pull of ale before going on. "Never a sweeter, more kind lass ye ever did meet. But that was before her troubles. Before her uncle did what he did."

All three men raised brows, questioning the full meaning behind that last statement. "Before he did what?" Brogan asked.

"Turned her into a drunk, he did. Convinced her she had killed her own husband and bairn, he did. All the while he kent it was raiders that done it."

Brogan was still not convinced there had been any raiders that night, but he kept that opinion to himself. "Why do ye think he did that? Convinced Mairghread she had done it?"

Fergus rested his elbows on the table and leaned over. Lowering his voice, he said, "Because *he* wants to be chief. He kent what a kind-hearted lass she was. He kent 'twould destroy her. And it almost did."

Leaning back, he smiled at Brogan. "Most of us ken 'twas yer doin', Brogan, gettin' our lady to finally give up the drink."

Brogan grunted dismissively. "'Twas Mairghread who did that. I only helped."

"Either way, we all be right grateful to ye. The entire keep is talkin' about it. She has apologized, ye ken, to those she hurt. Takes a right strong woman to do that. I do no' think I ken a man alive who would do what she has, goin' around, apologizin'."

Brogan knew she had been trying to set to rights what she had done while drunk. When he had given up the drink, it had been his father who insisted he apologize to all the people he hurt. He was growing more proud of his wife with each passing day.

Aye, his wife was a remarkable woman.

IN MUD UP TO THEIR KNEES, THE MEN WORKED AS BEST AS THEY could under the conditions. 'Twas filthy, back-breaking work, which was made even worse by the exceedingly wet trees. When a man took an axe to one, water that still clung to branches and leaves would splatter them. By noontime, there was not a dry or clean man to be seen.

There were several mishaps, with axes slipping off the wet bark and men falling down in the mud. Before the end of the day, Seamus had to set the bones on two men who had broken fingers from falling, stitches in the head of another when he got too close to a falling branch.

Aye, they were in desperate need of a healer. Brogan approached Liam about asking his brother Lachlan if he would be interested in coming here to act as healer.

"I will send a messenger to him this afternoon," Liam said. "But I doubt ye'll be able to pull him away from Clan MacFindlay. In his last letter to me, he seemed quite happy."

"Then ask fer a recommendation," Brogan said, a bit more gruffly than he intended. He was beyond exhausted. He hadn't had a good night's sleep in an age. When he was not working, he was doing every-thing he could to foster a better relationship with his wife.

"Aye, Brogan, I will," Liam said as he tried wiping the mud from his hands. 'Twas no use, for his shirt was caked with it.

"Be Fergus doin' a good job?" Brogan asked as he was scraping bark from a large log. Liam was working on a log next to him.

"I think so," Liam replied. "The man be as strong as an ox. Of course, this be his first day workin' with us. We shall see how he fairs after a sennight."

"I hope Reginald returns soon," he said. His axe caught on a stubborn piece where a limb had been removed. Grunting, he did his best to remove it. "Bloody hell," he cursed.

Sweat dripped off the tip of his nose. It took several attempts, but he was finally able to get rid of the knot and resume his scraping. Steam rose from his back, a combination of body heat against a soaked tunic and the sun beating down on him. Frustrated, he removed his tunic and hung it over a pile of logs to dry.

No matter how tired he was, he would not be deterred. There was too much to be done and complaining would solve nothing. Though he was mighty glad to see a wagon come up the path. In the back were several women with the nooning meal.

One of those women happened to be his wife.

᠅

MAIRGHREAD HAD BEEN THE ONE TO PROCURE A WAGON FOR THE women to bring the meal to the men. 'Twas far too muddy and slippery for them to try walking from the keep to the forest, especially when they were carrying baskets of food and flagons of drink. "'Twill do them no good if we drop the food in the mud," she had told the women.

One of them remarked, "Me Charles will no' mind. I swear the man would eat anything I set before him. Covered in mud or no'."

The other women agreed with giggles and nods, for they'd seen the man eat.

With Seamus' help, a team of fine horses was hitched to a wagon. Seamus even went so far as to volunteer to drive.

Mairghread was looking forward to seeing Brogan, a sensation she was doing her best to understand and become accustomed to. When she had first married him, she had been beset with a good deal of guilt. Guilt over believing she had killed her husband and babe. And guilt for thinking Brogan a good man.

But so many things had changed of late. She now knew she hadn't killed them. The moment she realized that, she felt the weight of the world being lifted off her shoulders.

Anger and guilt had been as close a companion to her heart as whisky and wine. None of those things had been far from her grasp. She'd been consumed with those four things for years.

Until Brogan Mackintosh walked into her life.

He had set her on the path to sobriety, had proven her innocence in the murders of her husband and son, and now, he was working from dawn to dusk to protect her keep and its people.

Peace of mind and heart, safety, and sobriety. These were all new feelings that betimes caught her unawares in their intensity. Brogan was an intriguing man, a good and kind man.

Her thoughts slipped away when she saw him, there, in the clearing, using an axe to scrape wood from a log. Sweat glistened on his back, and with the sun beating down, his skin seemed to glow. Muscles rippled in his arms and stomach from each swing of the axe. Leather trews clung to thighs — strong, muscular thighs.

She drew in a breath at the sight of him, her stomach flipping and flopping, and it felt as though her blood was growing warmer, spreading the sensation throughout her body. Even to parts that had lain dormant and frozen for three long years: her heart, and parts further south.

Suddenly, she was beset with guilt. She had made James a promise to never take another man as husband. Of course, at the time he was dead and she thought she had killed him.

There was no time to think on the matter further, for the wagon came to a stop. Brogan was smiling at her as he approached. *God's teeth! Did he have to smile so brightly? Did he have to be so bloody handsome and kind and wonderful?*

"Mairghread," he called to her as he neared the wagon. "'Tis glad I am to see ye."

She was not so certain now, that she was glad to see him. *Temptation in a pair of leather trews.*

§

TAKING THE BASKET FROM HER HAND, BROGAN HELPED HER DOWN from the wagon. "I did no' think to see ye here this day," he remarked as he took her hand in his.

"I-I thought..." what *had* she been thinking? *Food. Aye, that was it. Food.* "I brought ye a meal." 'Twas quite difficult to think with him looking so manly, so well-muscled, so...

"I be famished," he told her as he tried to steer her away from a large puddle. "I fear there no' be a place fer ye to stand without bein' in mud," he said, looking down at her feet.

What he did next nearly set her to swooning. With the basket in one arm, he picked her up with the other. With his arm under her rump, he carried her to the nearest log and set her down.

'Tis no' fair! She screamed inwardly. *Ye made James a promise. It matters no' why ye made it, 'twas still a promise.*

"What have ye brought me to feast on?" he asked as he removed the cloth that covered the basket and peered inside.

Me! Her traitorous heart screamed. *Feast on me!*

Warmth spread from her neck to her scalp; she could feel it. 'Twas the muscles betwixt his neck and shoulders that were her undoing. Corded, so well defined, it should have been against God's laws, as well as man's.

"Mmmm, ye brought bread and honey," Brogan said as he pulled the items from the basket and set them on the log.

She quit listening after he *mmmm'd.* Her heart was pounding against her chest and she felt the blood rushing in her ears. *Good, lord,* she thought. *I do no' ken from where these thoughts be comin',, but they be dangerous.*

Brogan was rambling on about something, she had no earthly idea what, for her eyes were transfixed on the dab of honey in the corner of his mouth. Her thoughts turned darned right wicked, obsessed by the desire to reach out and swipe it away with her fingertip. Her fingers fair itched with a need so profound it was paralyzing.

As she was about to jump to her feet and race away, a great shout broke out amongst the crowd.

"Reginald! Reginald has returned!"

IGNORING BROGAN'S WARNING OF MUD AND MUCK, SHE SLID FROM the log and raced back toward the keep.

"Mairghread!" he called out as he ran to catch up with her. "Wait!"

She did not wish to wait. Waiting meant she would have to look at him, talk to him, whilst her traitorous heart and womanly parts fed her mind with thoughts best left unthought.

Bigger, stronger, and faster than she, Brogan caught up with her. "Mairghread, ye can take the wagon back to the keep."

"But I need to see Reginald," she lied to him.

"'Twill be an hour before he be here," Brogan explained as he brought her to a halt with a tug on her hand.

She felt her stomach tighten. "An hour?"

"Aye," Brogan smiled down at her. "They were just lettin' us know he is close to home."

Feeling every bit a fool, she chastised herself for running away. That is what the old Mairghread would have done. *But ye be a woman full grown now,* she told herself.

"I should have refreshments ready for his return," she said breathlessly. "I imagine they will be hungry."

"Aye, I would imagine so," he agreed. "We will have Seamus take us back in the wagon."

We? *Stop actin' like some love-sick lass,* she chastised herself. "Verra well. We shall take the wagon."

Chapter Twenty

Mairghread and Brogan went to their respective rooms to change out of their muddy clothes. For a moment, Brogan thought he might have to call Henry or Liam in to help get his trews off. They were stuck to his skin.

Too hot and too bloody tired, he decided against more trews. He chose a dark tunic, draped his plaid around his waist and over his shoulder, and put his feet into clean boots. As soon as he was dressed, he went to Mairghread, who seemed rather nervous for some reason. He led her below stairs and into the courtyard.

'Twas more than a relief to see Reginald. 'Twas a downright joyous occasion. Especially when he saw he number of men filing in behind him.

Brogan and Mairghread were waiting with eager anticipation in the courtyard. They watched as he stopped in the tall, wide opening where a gate would someday sit. He nodded approvingly before bringing in the rest of the men.

Mairghread, Gertie, and Tilda raced together to meet him. "Reginald!" they called out.

Brogan watched closely for his response. There was a flicker of devotion in his eyes when he looked at Mairghread. The man was naught but a gruff exterior that hid a soft heart.

He dismounted and handed his reins off to a stable boy. "M'lady," he said with a nod to Mairghread.

"Ye look road weary." She smiled up at him. "Come, I have refreshments inside fer ye."

"We need to settle these men in first, m'lady," he said. "They be just as tired and hungry as I."

Mairghread took a step back and looked at the mud-covered men. All but a handful were on foot.

"Put as many as we can in the armory," she said. "Do we still have a few empty cottages?"

"Aye, we do," he replied.

"Fit as many as ye can in those. The rest, we will make room fer in the keep."

Fergus stepped forward to offer his support, as did a few of the other men. "We'll see them settled, m'lady," Fergus said with a proud smile.

"Thank ye, Fergus," she replied before turning to Reginald. "We have much to discuss, aye?"

"Aye, m'lady, that we do."

THE DISCUSSION LASTED THROUGHOUT THE AFTERNOON. THEY SAT together, Reginald, Mairghread, and Brogan, in the gathering room. Refreshments had been brought and eaten while Reginald explained where he had been and the men he brought with. Forty-seven in all, from all parts of the western Highlands. Some were from the fishing village, some were from nearby clans, clans who had been loyal to Mairghread's father before his death. The rest were people without homes or clans. Where they came from did not matter. 'Twas a blessing to have them here.

"At first, I was havin' poor luck gettin' the men we need," he told them as he drank the cool ale. "'Twas odd, fer no' many of the clans were willin' to spare any men. Were ye aware there be a horde of some ten thousand horse thieves headin' up from the south?"

Brogan had to bite the inside of his cheek to keep from laughing.

"Ten thousand?" Mairghread exclaimed breathlessly. "I had heard 'twas only a few thousand."

"Last I heard, 'twas seven thousand," Gertie added. "And no' just horse thieves, but murderers as well."

Brogan cleared his throat. "Ye ken how rumors go. The more it be told, the larger it gets." Wanting to put them at ease, he added, "More likely than no' 'tis only a handful."

"Either way," Mairghread said. "I want that wall built as soon as possible. We'll bring in the women folk to help if we must."

Brogan wished Henry was here, so he could hear with his own ears the panic his 'story' had caused. Still, he could not complain too much. Fear was a good motivator.

"But I did find a few men willin' to leave hearth and home to come help us. 'Twas no' inexpensive."

Mairghread was afraid to ask how much these men were going to cost them. The answer nearly made her shriek.

"Brogan said to do whatever I must to get the men, m'lady," Reginald told her.

She knew 'twas necessary, but it still didn't mean she had to like it. "It matters no'," she said. "We needed them. I might be able to rest at night now."

Brogan choked on his cider. Mairghread pounded her hand against his back until he got it under control.

Rest at night? She hadn't been the one lying awake at night, filled with desire and unmet need. Nay, she slept like the dead, right next to him. The dreams that had been haunting her had disappeared.

"Sorry," he said as he cleared his throat. "Swallowed wrong."

Reginald and Mairghread cast curious glances his way before returning to the topic at hand.

"Ye've made more progress than I thought ye would," Reginald said. "Mayhap we will have it done by Christmastide."

Mairghread snorted and rolled her eyes. "If I have to get out there and help, this wall will be done long before that."

Confused, Reginald asked her to explain.

Leaning in closer to him, she said, "Recently, Brogan was able to prove to me that I did no' kill James or Connell."

Reginald raised a questioning brow toward Brogan while Mairghread explained about the mock stabbing. "I believe me uncle took advantage of a very ugly situation," she told him. "He saw what the raiders had done and blamed me."

The two men exchanged knowing glances while Mairghread talked. "I believe he did it knowin' full well what me reaction would be. He *knew* 'twould be somethin' I would never get over." For a moment, she had a faraway look in her eyes. Brogan reached under the table and patted her hand.

"He wants to be chief. He wants me lands, me holdings, and everything else he can get his greedy hands on. I want that wall built before he returns."

Brogan shook his head, ever so slightly, silently warning him not to share his own opinions of Aymer with Mairghread. Later, when they had a moment alone, they would be able to discuss it further.

"We will do everythin' within our power, m'lady, to get the wall built fer ye," Reginald said.

Placing her hands on top of the table, she leaned forward slightly. "I thank ye, Reginald, fer all ye have done."

Reginald looked fondly upon Mairghread for a moment before returning to his usual gruff self. "What else has taken place in me absence?"

"Brogan locked Hargatha away in one of the servants rooms. We have her under constant guard."

Surprised, he asked, "And what do ye plan on doin' with her?"

Mairghread cast a glance at Brogan. He shrugged his shoulders. "'Tis up to ye, Mairghread."

Pursing her lips, she thought on it for a long moment. These were the kinds of decisions she did not wish to make. Too soft at heart, or so she had been told on numerous occasions.

"We can no' keep her locked away ferever," she said, looking to the men for advice.

"I think she needs to be hanged," Reginald said. "And fer more reasons than what she did to ye."

While she could appreciate his loyalty, she did not think she could order someone's death. "Banish her," she said.

"That seems reasonable," Brogan said.

Mairghread was relieved to hear him agree. Turning to Reginald, she said, "Be there still that auld cottage to the east of here? Near the border?"

"Aye," he replied curiously.

"She may live there. But she is no' allowed to *heal* anyone. Not in any manner or way."

Brogan grunted. "That does no' sound like much of a banishment to me."

"I ken it does no'," she told him. "But she be an auld woman, with no family or kin to take care of her."

"She should have thought of that long ago," he said.

Mairghread knew he was right, but she could not help herself. "Ye would really set an auld woman out without it keepin' ye up at night?"

There were many things that kept him up at night, but worrying about a mean, black-hearted auld woman wouldn't be one of them. "Aye, I would."

She looked appalled with him.

"I understand ye mean well," he told her. "But again, this be no' me decision to make."

"Verra well," she said. "I will inform her of me decision after we meet with the new men."

MAIRGHREAD INSISTED ON MEETING THE NEW MEN IMMEDIATELY. She wanted to personally thank them for coming to their aid. First, they visited the armory, which was able to house only thirty of the men. Because of the tight quarters, they had come out of doors. Cooking fires had been built, where they were roasting rabbit and birds for their supper.

Each man stood and bowed at the waist when Mairghread approached.

"I be Mairghread Mactavish," she told them. "The lady of this keep and heir to these lands."

She was unable yet, to declare herself chief. Brogan hoped she would be able to do that before long.

"We, me husband Brogan and I, as well as the rest of the clan, be glad ye have come to work with us. I be certain Reginald has told ye 'twill no' be easy work. But each of ye look as though ye be no' afraid of anythin', let alone the buildin' of a wall."

Brogan smiled at the way she was complimenting these men. Knowing her as he was beginning to, he believed it to be true.

They were of varying ages and sizes. A few of them were of an age where Brogan wondered if they would even be able to pick up an axe, for they were so old looking. Mairghread apparently did not notice.

"If ever ye need anythin', please do no' be afraid to ask. Come to Brogan first..." her words trailed off as one of the men caught her attention. Brogan followed her gaze to see she was looking at a younger lad, of mayhap seven and ten. He had a bloody bandage wrapped around his head. "Ye there," she said as she pushed through the crowd. "What happened to ye?"

The lad's face burned crimson. "'Tis naught but a scratch m'lady," he said, unable to look her in the eye.

"That be no' what I asked," she said.

He cleared his throat before answering. "We got caught up in that storm yesterday," he said. "I tripped in the mud and hit me head on a rock. But I be right as rain, m'lady. I can work."

"I am certain ye can," she told him with a warm smile. "But we must have that looked at, aye?" Taking him by the arm, she began to lead him away. "I will be takin' ye to Seamus. He be right good with stitches."

"Stitches, m'lady?" the lad exclaimed. "I do no' think it be as bad as that."

"Och! Do no' fash yerself over it. What is yer name?"

"Daniel, m'lady. Daniel MacCreary."

"Well, be glad ye be seein' Seamus, fer if our auld healer were to get her hands on ye, she'd be wantin' to amputate yer head."

Brogan laughed as his wife walked away toward the stables, forgetting for the moment about her welcome to their new men.

Aye, he was learning just how remarkable a woman she was.

"Yer lady, m'laird," one of the older men said as he stepped forward. He was a short, skinny man who looked as though he had lived a hard life. His thinning gray hair lined a wrinkled face, brown with age and much exposure to the sun. Side by side, they stood staring in awe at Mairghread walking away with the lad named Daniel. "She be a right kind lady, aye?"

"Aye, that she is."

"Daniel, he be a good lad, m'laird. He lost his family a year ago, to the ague."

"His entire family?" Brogan asked.

"Aye, m'laird. Every one of them. They lived in Edinburgh. His da was a shoemaker. Anyway, he's been makin' his way across Scotia for months now, doin' whatever work people will give him. He's a good lad, m'laird."

It pulled at his heart, to hear the young man's story. He knew that if his wife learned of his plight, she would undoubtedly offer him a home here. "What be yer name?" Brogan asked.

"Wallace, m'laird," he answered.

"We be glad to have ye all here," Brogan told him.

"'Tis glad we are to be here, laird."

Brogan gave him a warm slap to his back before going off after his wife.

'TWAS LONG AFTER THE EVENING MEAL WHEN BROGAN AND Mairghread entered her bedchamber. It had been a very long, tiring, hard day, but a good one as well. Reginald had returned with good men and his wife was quite happy.

But all Brogan wanted to do was strip out of his clothes, wash up, and slip into a warm bed. He could have slept on the floor for that matter.

"Ye look done in," Mairghread remarked as she stepped out of her slippers.

Brogan raked a hand through his hair. "'Tis the truth, I am."

He took note of the odd way in which she was staring at him. Mayhap she was trying to muster up the courage to ask him to sleep with her again this night. It warmed his heart that she needed him close. But a man could only take so much torture before he went mad. In Brogan's case, 'twould be madness brought on by lack of loving and lack of sleep.

"Brogan," she said as she heard a knock at the door.

He heard her mumble something that sounded like *bloody hell* as she went to answer it.

'Twas Evelyn and she looked on the verge of tears.

"M'lady, I hate to bother ye at this hour, but mum needs ye."

"What be the matter?"

"Briggitt Mactavish, Red John's wife, be havin' her bairn. But something be wrong and mum had me come fer ye. She needs yer help, m'lady. She worries they both might die."

Without hesitation, Mairghread put her boots on and grabbed her cloak.

"Wait!" Brogan called out after them. "I will come with ye."

"What on earth for?" Mairghread asked as she was on her way out the door.

"'Twill be dark soon," he said as he fell in beside her. "I ken I can no' help with the birthin', but I can help with the father."

"He be beside himself, m'lady," Evelyn said. "Poor Red John, he keeps pacin' back and forth outside their cottage."

Mairghread wasn't about to argue. "'Twill be good to have yer help," she told Brogan as they all but flew down the stairs.

AN HOUR AFTER MIDNIGHT, BRIGGITT AND RED JOHN'S SON was born.

'Twas no wonder Martha had to call for help. The little babe was stuck. And stuck for good reason. 'Twas not only that the boy was breach. He was *big*. The biggest babe any of them had ever seen. They had to pull the babe from his mother, using twine tied around his ankles.

'Twas odd, because mother and father were not big people. Red John was only a few inches taller than Mairghread or his wife. Brogan towered over all of them.

He had stayed out of doors with Red John. 'Twas easy to surmise this was his first bairn, the way he paced and fretted over his wife and unborn babe. Mumbling to himself, pacing, running his hands through his hair. It reminded him of his brother Ian when Rose was having their first. Brogan was tired just watching the man pace.

The moment Red John heard the sound of his babe crying loud and fierce, he nearly fell to his knees.

Once mother and babe were clean and presentable, Red John was led into the little cottage.

Exhausted from the past weeks, cold now that the sun had gone down, Brogan nearly fell asleep standing up as he leaned against the side of the cottage. 'Twas Mairghread's gentle hand on his arm that brought him fully alert.

"We can go home now," she told him.

There was a sadness to her tone. When he took the lit torch from her hand, he could see that sadness running deep behind her green eyes. "Mairghread? Is all well?"

Her smile did not quite reach her eyes. "Mother and babe are well," she told him. "I am just tired."

'TWAS NOT A COMPLETE LIE THAT SHE TOLD HIM. SHE *WAS* TIRED. Bone tired.

But she was also feeling quite sad. For the first time since losing Connell, she'd held another babe. 'Twas only for a brief moment, but 'twas enough to set a deep ache in her heart.

For the tiniest moment, when she held Briggitt's babe in her arms, she felt an overwhelming sense of joy. Sheer, unadulterated joy.

'Twas almost as keen as when she held her own for the first time. He'd been such a sweet babe. Connell had rarely cried, took to the breast right away, and slept for a few hours at a time.

Though he'd only been in her arms for such a short time, he'd brought her more happiness than anything else in her life ever had. Aye, she had lost James that night. But the acute pain of losing her son? That was a loss from which she knew she would never fully recover.

Holding Brigitt's babe made her long for one of her own. *That* was what bothered her most of all. She felt guilty for wanting another child. She did not want to replace Connell. 'Twas a struggle in her heart and one she did not know if she could ever settle.

By the time they entered her bedchamber, her chest felt tight and her stomach was in knots.

"I want a dram of whisky," she told Brogan. "More than a dram. I want a whole bloody bottle."

"Why?" he asked as he set the torch in an empty brace on the wall near the door.

'Twas easy to tell him she was tempted to drink. 'Twas impossible to tell him why. With a heavy sigh, she sat on a chair and began to tug off her boots.

"I can no' help ye if I do no' ken what the problem is," he told her as he shut the door.

"Mayhap I do no' want yer help," she said through gritted teeth. "Can I no' be angry or upset or sad without a reason?"

Now, an intelligent man would have left his wife alone for a little while. Or he would have offered to get her a sweet cake, or a back rub. Brogan, having been married before, albeit for only a short while, knew he should just nod and walk away.

"How can ye be angry or upset or sad without a reason? That makes no sense." He thought it a most reasonable question. Mairghread, however, did not.

Shooting to her feet with her hands on her hips, she looked him directly in the eye. "No' everything in life has to make sense, Brogan!

Sometimes I feel sad, or angry, or upset and I can no' explain the why of it. And even if I could, I would no' want to spend the next two hours tryin' to get ye to understand."

He was simply too tired to argue. With his head hanging low, he went to his chamber and closed the door behind him.

He sat on a chair and pulled off his boots. *Women are so bloody confusin',* he mused. *Sleep with me, but do no' touch. Treat me with respect, but again, do no' touch.* He rested his head in his hands. All he wanted now was a good, deep sleep. *Ye may think me beautiful, ye may compliment me. Ye may help me in all things, as a husband should, still, ye may no' touch.*

Mayhap on the morrow Mairghread would be in better spirits. Mayhap, on the morrow, she would tell him why she was upset, why she was tempted to drink this night. But at the moment, he didn't rightly care. He knew 'twas best to just go to his bed, go to sleep, and start anew on the morrow.

Long moments later, the door to his chamber opened.

Mairghread stood in the doorway. She wore her sleeping gown, a heavy woolen thing. She could have worn a sack and still been just as beautiful. His manhood began to twitch.

"Are ye comin' to bed?"

A wiser man would have told her he was too tired, she was too upset, and mayhap a night apart would do them good. Besides, 'twas no' as if they were lovers. They were man and wife in name only right now. 'Twas one more thing that added to his growing frustration.

"I will be right there."

MAIRGHREAD KNEW SHE HAD BEHAVED FOOLISHLY TOWARD BROGAN. 'Twas not his fault her heart was breaking with sadness and longing and guilt. Nay, she could not blame him.

She went to him, fully intending to apologize. But when she saw him sitting in the chair, with his head in his hands, words escaped her.

Instead of apologizing, she asked if he was ready for bed. Her fingers trembled with wanting to go to him, to wrap her hands around his head and tell him she was sorry. Sorry for being rude, sorry for being such a bother all these past weeks. But most, she wanted to tell him how sorry she was for asking too much of him.

Brogan was a man, after all. He was not made of stone. He had feelings, needs, and desires, just like most people.

She heard the exhaustion in his voice, saw the weariness in his eyes when he said, *I will be right there.*

How many sacrifices could she ask him to make? Aye, he'd been making them since the day he arrived. Now, she was asking him to be a husband to her, to sleep with her so she would not be alone, wouldn't be plagued with bad dreams all the night long.

She knew she owed her restful sleep to him. From the first night he stayed with her, the dreams had all but stopped. She found comfort in knowing he was there. Nay, 'twas more than just comfort. 'Twas a sense of peace and safety.

And look at him now. Dark circles under his eyes, dragging his feet as though they were made of led. He'd been working non-stop on one thing or another since he had arrived. He had helped her get through the awful *takeaways* and on the path to sobriety. He was bringing her clan together, building a much-needed wall, and heaven knew what else he'd been doing of late.

She had been so wrapped up with her guilt, her broken heart, and the past, that she hadn't taken the time to think about *him*. Brogan, as a man.

Until the noonin' meal earlier that day when she was suddenly beset with thoughts of desire and warm sensations she'd thought long dead.

That was when the guilt began again. Guilt for desiring him, guilt for wanting another child, and guilt for not being the kind of wife a man like him deserved.

She had painted a happy smile on her face all day long, when inside, she felt confused and even a bit frightened.

The past.

She had been stuck in it for years.

Brogan was, unbeknownst to him, helping her to gradually climb out of it and into the present. What frightened her most, was the future. A future as his wife in all senses of the word. A future where they worked together, building up this clan, mayhap having children of their own. Someday.

As he walked into her chamber and slid into the bed, she sent a silent prayer up to God.

Please, help me to be the wife he deserves. And please, keep him here long enough for me to be just that.

Chapter Twenty-One

As he'd been doing for days, he woke before dawn. Mairghread was snuggled next to him, her head on his chest, one arm draped over his chest.

Ye made her a promise never to kiss her again until she asked, he warned his heart as well as his manhood. His intent was to close his eyes, just for a few moments, to steady his breathing and push any yearning thoughts aside.

When he woke again, he had no good idea as to how much time had passed. The furs were drawn over the windows.

With her bottom nestled against his groin, 'twas next to impossible to keep his desire in check. She stirred, paused, then gasped. Rolling over, she looked into his eyes.

"I be the worst kind of wife," she told him with tear-filled eyes.

He was wholly confused. Reaching out, he tucked a strand of hair behind her ear. "What do ye mean?"

"I ask ye to be a husband to me, to keep me warm and safe at night. But," she swallowed back tears. "But I am unable to give meself to ye."

His brow furrowed and he was at a loss for words.

She nodded toward his lower half. "James used to wake up like that.

I ken what it means. And I lay here each night, enjoyin' yer arms around me, likin' the way ye feel next to me, and how do I repay ye?"

He chuckled softly and shook his head.

"I do no' ken when I will be able to give all of meself to ye, Brogan, and it scares me."

"Mairghread," he said, hoping to find the right words to set her heart at ease.

"I worry ye will grow weary of me and leave. And 'tis the God's truth I do no' want ye to. I be so confused, Brogan. I want ye, I do and it tears me insides to shreds, fer I *still* feel as though I would be bein' unfaithful to James. And to Connell."

"I understand," he told her. "I felt the same way about Anna. I still think of her every day."

"Ye do?" she asked, wrinkling her brow.

"Aye, I do. I loved her. She was me entire world, ye ken. For a very long, long while, even *after* I put down the bottle, I could no' even think about takin' another wife. Hell, I couldn't even visit a brothel—" he stopped himself when he saw her blush. "I still love Anna. I will always love her."

She stared back at him in confusion. "Mairghread, I will never ask ye to stop lovin' James or Connell. I want ye to talk about them. 'Tis all right to share with me yer memories of them."

"It is?"

"Of course, lass. Ye loved them, aye?" When she nodded her head and swiped away a tear, he smiled warmly. "Then never hide yer love or yer memories."

She breathed a relieved sigh.

"And ken with a certainty that I will never leave ye. I made ye a promise and I mean to keep it. When ye're ready, I will be here."

THERE WAS NO DOUBT IN MAIRGHREAD'S MIND OR HEART THAT Brogan was speaking from *his* heart. He *knew*, for he had gone through a loss similar to her own. He understood how much she had loved, and still loved, James and Connell. And he wasn't asking her to stick them into a private part of her heart only to visit those precious memories when she was alone. He was not asking her to stop loving them.

He wasn't demanding anything of her. Nay, he was giving her every-thing she needed. Time, patience, and understanding.

'Twas gratitude that propelled her toward him, to kiss him sweetly. She had meant to offer him her thanks, to explain how relieved and thankful she was for his understanding. But something happened a heartbeat later, after her lips touched his.

Passion took hold. From the very tips of her toes to the tips of her fingers, and everywhere in between. She couldn't stop and realized moments later, she didn't want to. Especially when Brogan groaned deep in his throat. 'Twasn't annoyance or disgust. Nay, 'twas a groan of desire and passion.

He pulled her closer, holding her tightly, pressing her body against his. Their breaths were jagged, desperate, as they fought to remove any barrier between them, their lips parting only long enough for him to pull her night rail over her head. Before her arms were out of her sleeves, he was kissing her again.

'Twas sheer pleasure to feel his skin against hers. The way the soft hairs of his chest tickled her breasts. His hands caressing her buttocks, her back and shoulders.

Using her tongue, she pried his lips open, though there was very little resistance on his part. Touching, searching, seeking, pleasing.

Passion, pleasure, desire, all burned as hot as a blacksmith's forge. She needed him. Wanted him inside her. Now. Without delay. Telling him thus, he happily complied. Albeit not nearly as quickly as she would have preferred.

He fit snuggly inside her and 'twas a blissful, exciting sensation. 'Twas a slow in and out, in an out, all the while he kissed her lips, her cheeks, her neck. Prisoners of war suffered less torture.

At first, she tried to hurry him along by grinding her hips quickly against his manhood. He refused to go faster.

'Twas difficult for her *not* to compare his loving ways with James's. She had always enjoyed joining with him, and he her. James hadn't necessarily possessed a world of experience, but together, they managed to find their way.

Brogan was so very different. Where James had been just two years older than she, Brogan was a decade older. Where James had been thin and wiry, Brogan was taller, thicker, and nothing but hard muscle.

❧

For weeks, he had been imagining this moment. The moment when he and Mairghread would finally become man and wife in the truest sense of the word. He had years of celibacy and weeks of torment bottled up inside him.

As much as his groin ached with a need to find a long overdue release, he fought and resisted. He took his sweet time, exploring her glorious curves. He found great pleasure in her moans and soft sighs. There was even greater pleasure, and aye, a good deal of pride, in hearing her pleas for more.

Her skin was as soft as silk against his calloused hands. Her breath was warm and hot and jagged from unrestrained passion.

When he sank himself into her, 'twas sheer bliss. Though she pleaded with him to go faster, he refused her desperate entreaties. Determination set in. He was going to enjoy every sweet, blissful moment, even if it killed him.

Taught nipples of her plump breasts scraped against his chest, turning his skin to gooseflesh. Hearing no protest on her part, he exposed the peaks with his tongue.

"Please, Brogan," she said breathlessly as she ground her hips against his.

'Twas a desperate need he had to ensure she found her own pleasure before he found his. Soon, as he increased his rhythmic motions, they found their pleasure together.

❧

Sated, content, covered in sweat, they lay on their backs staring up at the ceiling. Each had blissful smiles that Brogan thought would take a few hours to dissolve. He was wrong. It took only a few heartbeats, for there soon came a knock on their door.

"Wheest!" Mairghread whispered as she sat up. "They will go away."

Brogan had serious doubts, but remained quite still. He was too busy staring at her plump breasts.

They knocked again. "Brogan!" Henry shouted.

Brogan groaned, let out a heavy sigh, and started to sit up.

Mairghread stopped him with a wink. Before he could stop her, she was out of the bed, pulling on her robe and heading toward the door. Not wanting Henry to see him fully naked — though God knew he had numerous times over the years — he pulled the covers up.

Mairghread opened the door a crack. "Yer laird will be stayin abed this day," she told him. "He is no' well."

"No' well?" Henry asked, his brow furrowing with concern. He tried to peek inside, but Mairghread stood on the tips of her toes. Little good it did for the man was as big as her husband.

"Ye will have to get along without him," she told him. "Now be gone with ye and allow yer laird his rest."

He replied with a big, knowing grin when he caught sight of Brogan in the bed. Henry knew *that* look. 'Twas the look of a man who had just been thoroughly, exhaustively loved by his wife.

When he looked back at Mairghread, he cleared his throat and quickly got rid of his grin. "I understand, m'lady. From the looks of him, he might need a day or two to recover."

"That is me thinkin' as well," she said, with a most serious tone.

He bid her good day and left. She shut the door after him and put the bar firmly in place.

"I am unwell?" he asked with a raised brow.

"Ye most definitely are," she said as she unwrapped the robe and let it fall to the floor. "Me recommendation is that ye stay abed the remainder of the day. Mayhap, even the morrow."

"And who will be tendin' to me?" he asked as he gave a long, slow perusal of her body, with hungry, greedy eyes.

"I hope ye will allow me to tend to ye, husband," she said as she walked slowly toward the bed. "Unless ye want Gertie or Tilda."

He threw back his head and laughed. "I want no one but ye, lass."

۶۵

BROGAN WOKE JUST BEFORE DAWN, WITH MAIRGHREAD LYING NAKED and warm beside him. There was no need for him to resist any urges. He woke her with soft, tender kisses, which led to loving her fully and thoroughly.

She fell back to sleep with a contented smile on her face.

Although he would have enjoyed nothing more on God's earth than to stay abed for yet another day, he had to resist that temptation. Quietly, he slipped from the bed, went to his auld chamber, washed up and dressed.

Before he left to begin his day, he pressed a sweet kiss on her cheek, and pulled the covers around her.

In the gathering room, he ate like a prisoner of war. Henry, Liam, and Comnall soon joined him. Each of them bore mischievous grins. The kind of grin that said, *we know what ye have been doing.*

Ignoring them, Brogan wolfed down sausages, bread, and eggs. "We have much work to do this day," he told them.

"Have ye the strength?" Henry asked most seriously.

"Aye, we ken ye were no' well yesterday," Comnall added, doing his best to hide a smile.

Ignoring them, he said, "How many logs were set yester-day?"

"Five," Henry answered.

"It still be right muddy," Liam added. "If we get more sunny days, we'll be able to increase our pace."

Five logs. Even with the added help of extra men, 'twas frustrating. He could only hope Liam's assessment was correct. "Then pray fer sun, lads. Pray fer sun."

Chapter Twenty-Two

August had come and gone, and thankfully so had the rain. September brought with it shorter days, and crisper, clearer weather.

Brogan and Mairghread had settled into a comfortable state of wedded bliss. Once they had finally gotten around to officially consummating their marriage, everything betwixt them changed. And for the better.

With each passing day Mairghread grew stronger and more determined to see her clan grow and prosper. Even more determined, however, to see her uncle get what was coming to him.

In turn, Brogan was more determined than ever to finish the bloody wall. There had been too many delays for his liking. If it wasn't the rain, 'twas a bad case of the ague that swept through the clan. Thankfully, it had taken no lives. However, they did lose at least ten full days of good work.

The clan seemed at peace as well. Mairghread was making good progress in restoring their faith in her. Which she was going to need when she finally made a decision on whether or not to be chief.

Carefully, he had broached the subject with her on several occasions. Each time, she answered that she hadn't made up her mind yet.

Just what she needed to think on baffled him. She *was*, for all intents and purposes, as well as by rules of inheritance, the rightful chief.

All in all, those were the best of days. With good weather, a healthy clan, and much progress being made on the wall.

Brogan received a letter from Alec Bowie the first week of September. Their crops were coming along splendidly, as was his wife Leona. She was due to have their babe in early October. Because of that, he might have to send his cousin Dougall as his emissary. Brogan was fine with that and passed the information on to Reginald.

Reginald was happier than a pig in mud these days. While he had been gone back in August to procure more men, Mairghread — with Gertie and Tilda's help — had moved the man's office out of the alcove and back to where it had once been. With mayhap a little too much giddiness, the women had packed away all of Aymer's belongings and stored them in the alcove.

Aye, things were looking up for him, for Mairghread, and the clan Mactavish.

He should have known it wouldn't last long.

ON A CRISP, COOL DAY AT THE END OF SEPTEMBER A MESSENGER arrived. He was a younger lad, named Archibald. Skinny, with dark hair and bright blue eyes, he was exceedingly loyal to Mairghread.

He came thundering into the courtyard on horseback, covered in dirt and grime from his long and hard journey. He raced to the stables and asked Seamus to tend to the horse. "I have an important message fer our lady," he explained.

With most of the men working away from the keep this day, 'twas Evelyn who met the lad in the gathering room. Quickly, he begged to see Mairghread. Evelyn rushed off to fetch her from the kitchens, leaving him alone in the gathering room.

He paced back and forth. He had been gone from the keep since the day after Mairghread and Brogan had married. Though he had no idea what the missive in his pouch said, he knew 'twas important.

"Archibald?" Mairghread called to him as she entered the gathering room. Evelyn and Mairi had come with her.

She had not seen the boy in an age. He looked anxious as well as road weary.

"M'lady," he said as he bowed at the waist. "I was able to catch up to yer uncle."

Her uncle? Her mind was a complete blank. She had no idea at all what he was speaking about.

"Mairi, Evelyn, please bring Archibald some refreshments," she told them. To Archibald, she pointed to the table. "Sit, and explain what ye mean."

He waited until she was sitting before he took a seat across from here. "I did just as ye bid me too, m'lady."

"As *I* bid ye?" she asked.

"Aye, ye sent me to find yer uncle."

Horrified, she looked at him with wide eyes and mouth agape. "*I* sent ye to find me uncle?"

He was growing just as confused as she. "Do ye no' remember?"

"I fear I do no'," she said with a shake of her head. "When did I do this?"

"The day after ye married the Mackintosh man."

Her heart seized. She could not remember much of that day, for she had been so terribly drunk. An uneasiness blended with dread began to settle in. "Archibald, 'tis the truth that I do no' remember. There is very little of those days that I can recall."

He sat in silence, nervous, fidgeting with the pouch on his belt.

"Much has changed since ye left," she said. Her life had changed so dramatically these past weeks. "I no longer partake of hard drink. Thanks to Brogan, I have been able to give it up and live life with a clearer head and better heart."

He blinked once, then again, stunned to hear his lady speaking so openly about what he thought was a private matter.

"So when I sent ye to find me uncle, what did I tell ye to do exactly?" She was afraid to know what she had said or done.

He stammered, searching for words that would not insult or offend.

"Archibald, ye no longer have to fear me wrath or anger. I be no' the same person now, as I was then. Please, be honest and tell me."

The young man cleared his throat nervously. "It be true, m'lady, ye were a bit into yer cups."

"I was a drunkard, Archibald. I be no afraid to admit it. I was so drunk then that I can no' remember now what happened. But continue," she said as she offered him an encouraging smile.

"Well, ye were right angry that night. Ye had Mairi come to get me. Ye sent me off to try to catch up with yer uncle. To tell him ye were no' goin' to marry the Frenchman."

Mairghread nodded as she listened intently.

"We — me and Drayton — we left that night. I did no' want to go alone, ye ken."

That made perfectly good sense to her.

"We finally caught up with yer uncle before he got as far as London. I gave him yer missive and message."

Good lord! What had she written? Dread, fear, worry all mixed together in the pit of her stomach. "Did ye read the missive?"

Archibald cast her a furtive glance. "Well, no' exactly, m'lady. I *wrote* it fer ye. Yer hands, ye see, were a bit unsteady."

"What did I say?" she asked. Taking in a deep breath, she held it until he answered.

"No' much, m'lady. Ye just had me write that ye were no' going to marry the bloo—" he stopped, and started again. "Ye were no' going to marry the Frenchman and that ye had married another."

She let her breath out slowly. "Anythin' else?"

"Nay, m'lady," he said with a quick shake of his head. "That was all."

Willing her nerves to settle, she asked him the most important question of all. "And what was me uncle's reply?"

"He sure was no' happy, m'lady. He kicked Drayton in the leg and punched me in the stomach." Absentmindedly, he rubbed his stomach at the memory.

"Did he say anything else?"

He cleared his throat as his face burned a deep red. "Naught that I would repeat in front of ye, m'lady. But he did give me this." Reaching into his pouch, he pulled out a rolled parchment and handed it to her.

Her fingers trembled; she recognized at once her uncle's seal. Bile rose in the back of her throat and she found her reaction confusing. This wasn't the same anger she had been feeling toward him ever since she learned she hadn't killed James or Connell and had definitely not stabbed herself.

This, this was an altogether different feeling of absolute *fear*. But why? She had never feared him before. Aye, there were times she thought him a bit daft, and did not always agree with him. But fear him? Nay, not until this moment, when she held the sealed missive in her hand.

"Would ye like me to come back, m'lady, and send yer uncle a response?" Archibald asked in a low whisper.

"Nay," she said. I want ye to eat and rest." She got to her feet, thanked him for his diligent work and started for the stairs. "Wait," she said. "Where be Drayton?"

Archibald rolled his eyes. "In Edinburgh, the bug—" Once again, he stopped himself before saying something that would embarrass his lady. "He said he wanted to stay in Edinburgh a few extra days. I knew how important it was to get that," he nodded toward the parchment in her hands, "back to ye."

"I thank ye, Archibald. Please let me know when Drayton returns."

And with that, she hurried above stairs to the safety of her chamber.

I BE THOROUGHLY DISAPPOINTED IN YE, MAIRGHREAD. I HAVE WORKED long and hard to arrange the marriage betwixt ye and Claude Courtemanche. Now, I learn ye have married another? How could ye have betrayed me in such a manner? I can only assume it be yer addiction to drink that made ye act in such an illogical, rash way. Being a drunkard suits ye.

I will have to take some time to sort this news out and come up with a solution to the quagmire ye have put me in. 'Twill not be easy, but I be certain we can get yer marriage to the Mackintosh set aside and proceed forward with your union to Courtemanche. I must warn ye, he will no' be happy to learn of your betrayal, Mairghread. He will be just as disappointed as I. Me only worry is he will no' be as forgiving as I.

Aymer Mactavish

Mairghread read the letter three times. Now that she was sober, she was better able to read what *wasn't* written. She could hear the anger in his voice as clearly as if he were standing in front of her.

In her mind's eye, she could picture his scowl. Could see his face turning purple with fury as he yelled at her for being a fool.

Why had she not seen him in this light before? Was it simply her imagination running away with her, or was it a truer picture of him?

Brogan. She needed him now, more than ever. She raced below stairs, found Mairi and asked her to send someone for him right away. Steeling her nerves, she went above stairs and waited.

It seemed to her an interminable amount of time passed before Brogan finally came rushing into their chamber. Covered in sweat, wood shavings, and grime, she had never been so happy to see him.

"What be wrong?" he asked with worried eyes and panic in his voice.

She rushed to him, not caring how filthy he might be, and wrapped her arms around him. "I did no' mean to scare ye, but it be important." She couldn't let go, not just yet. "I have received word from Aymer."

As she held him, she felt him grow tense. "Where is he?" he asked through gritted teeth.

"I do no' ken. All I have is a missive."

They sat at the small table whilst she explained to him what had transpired with Archibald earlier.

"Honestly, Brogan, I do no' remember sendin' fer Archibald. I do no' remember any of it."

Sensing her distress, he reached across the small table and took her hand in his. "Ye will no' worry over it, lass."

'Twas a thing easier said than done. Taking in a deep breath, she handed the parchment to him and waited. By the time he finished he was purple with fury. He shot to his feet. "Who in the bloody hell does he think he be?" he yelled. Shaking the parchment, he said, "This be a veiled threat is what it be. Set our marriage aside?" he was furious beyond imagination. "'Twill be over me dead body."

Never before had she seen him so angry. Not even when she was still a drunkard, taunting and ridiculing him. "I be sorry," she whispered.

"Why?" he barked. "Ye have done nothin' wrong, Mairghread. Me anger be no' directed at ye, but at the man who calls himself yer uncle."

Suddenly, she felt cold and weary. Trembling, tears pooled in her eyes. "I will no' allow him to set our marriage aside," she told him.

"He has no basis fer it," Brogan told her. "No basis at all."

She could only pray he was right.

AFTER PUTTING MAIRGHREAD'S WORRIES AT EASE, BROGAN SENT FOR the young man named Archibald. Hopefully, the lad had more information than what he had given Mairghread. Although she had initially been quite frightened by Aymer's missive, she drew strength from Brogan.

Together, they met with Archibald in Reginald's office. The lad seemed even more nervous in Brogan's presence than he had been with just Mairghread. Brogan closed the door behind him and approached the young man.

"Archibald? Have ye eaten since yer arrival?"

"Aye, m'laird," he replied. "Evelyn and Mairi fed me well."

Brogan nodded his approval. "I am told by me wife that ye met with Aymer, just outside of London?"

"Aye, m'laird, we did. Me and Drayton." He went on to tell him what he had told Mairghread earlier. Recounting how Aymer had taken his anger out on the two young men.

Brogan pondered several possibilities for a moment. "Did he say if he was returning to Mactavish keep immediately?"

"Nay, m'laird, he did no'. But I think he still planned on goin' to France."

He thought that bit of news as odd as he did curious. "Did he tell ye that?"

"Nay, m'laird. We heard him yellin' at Dennys MacCurdy. Dennys be married to Beatrice Mactavish, ye ken. Anyways, when me and

Dayton was leavin', we heard him shoutin' that they were still goin' on to France, no matter what—" he stopped and looked at Mairghread. "No matter what our lady had decided to do."

Both Brogan and Mairghread suspected that wasn't exactly how Aymer worded it. But there was no sense in pressing for exact details.

For now, they could breathe a sigh of relief.

"Thank ye, Archibald," Brogan said. "If ye think of anythin' else, anythin' at all, please let us know."

He waited until after the door closed behind Archibald before speaking again. "What do ye think? Think ye yer uncle will go on to France?"

Mairghread raised her hands, palms up. "Who kens what he will do?"

"Ye ken him better than anyone."

"I thought I did, until lately. Now, I am uncertain. I would no' put anything past him, Brogan. I mean, look what he did to me? To the wall? To our weapons," she said with a perplexed shake of her head. "I mean, he used James and Connell's deaths to turn me into a raging drunkard."

Brogan had yet to voice to her what he felt truly happened that night. He was convinced Aymer had killed them. The deaths of the two guards was simply meant to make it look like an attack from outside forces.

"I think it be a good possibility he went on to France. From the sounds of the letter, he was verra angry. I also would no' put it past him to bring Courtemanche with him."

'Twas the very thing Brogan was dreading most. "I fear it as well," he told her. The next question was what to do about it.

"Brogan," Mairghread said, tapping her finger against her cheek. "Think ye Courtemanche will bring fighting men with him?"

"Aye, I do think that be possible," Brogan told her. He was not about to try to coat that horrid idea with sweet words. She was chief, even if she hadn't officially taken the title. "Courtemanche is a dangerous man, Mairghread. If he thinks, even for a moment, that Aymer will get our marriage set aside, then aye, he will bring fighting men with him."

From her fierce and determined expression, she was not about to allow either to happen. "We need more fightin' men," she said. "We also need a wall."

Both of those things were painfully true.

"Unfortunately, I do no' ken how many of our men are capable of fightin'."

Brogan doubted there were even a handful.

"We need to be able to protect our people. James saw the need fer that long ago. He had even begun to work with the men." She took a deep breath. "Who can we reach out to fer help?" she asked as she switched from drumming her cheek to drumming her fingers against the top of Reginald's desk. "The Bowies? Yer brother?"

"Aye, those are possibilities," he said.

Deep in thought, with her lips pursed together, she looked and sounded every bit a clan chief.

"I say we put all our focus on the wall. We bring in every able-bodied man, woman, and child to do it. We will bring all the horses in, fit as many as we can within the walls. Mayhap we should also rethink our deal with Alec Bowie and get more grain. I want us to be prepared for an all-out siege. Increase the patrols and if there be any sign of Aymer and Courtemanche, we will bring everyone inside the walls."

Brogan could not resist the urge to smile. Proud, proud to his very bones, of his wife.

"What?" she asked from her seat behind Reginald's desk.

"What ye just said, was spoken like a true chief and leader."

Usually, when he mentioned her officially taking the roll, she would roll her eyes, pretend to be busy, and change the subject. She did neither of those things.

"I want word sent throughout our lands," she said. "I want everyone here before the evening meal."

Curious, he raised a brow. "Ye plan on tellin' them about Aymer?" he asked.

"Aye, I do."

❧

Brogan had moved his things into Mairghread's chamber long ago. Now, they simply referred to it as *theirs*. Since then, they had been using his auld bedchamber as an office, which they both shared. After putting their plans into writing, they went back to their chamber so they both could change into clean clothes.

After washing up, Mairghread changed into a very pretty gown of indigo silk. Over that, she wore the Mactavish plaid, of black, brown, and green. Styling it just as her father had worn his for all those years.

Brogan went to his trunk and pulled out a brooch, one his father had given him when he reached the age of seven and ten. 'Twas a Mackintosh plaid brooch, made of pewter, with the familiar to him cat-o'mountain in the center of a circle. Etched into that circle was the Mackintosh clan motto: *Touch not a cat without a glove.*

"Mairghread, I wish to give ye somethin'," he said as she was fussing with her plaid. "It be something me da gave to me when I was a young lad."

Stepping forward, he took her hand and placed the brooch into her palm. "It be verra special to me, as ye are."

Her eyes grew wide when she saw the beautiful piece. "Och! Brogan, I can no' accept this. I be certain it means too much to ye."

He smiled, warmly and fondly. "No' nearly as much as ye do, Mairghread."

A heartbeat later, she had her arms wrapped around him, and he her. The kiss, one meant to be heartfelt yet chaste, soon turned quite passionate. She could not help herself, for every time she felt him so close, felt his lips against hers, she was a lost, wanton woman with only one thing on her mind; Brogan and she, naked and in the throes of passion.

'Twas Brogan who broke the kiss, "Lass, ye have people waitin' fer ye out of doors," he reminded her.

"Let them wait," she said as she wrapped her arms around his neck. She noted he did not argue again.

Thankfully, Clan Mactavish was small enough, and its

people not so widespread, that it made gathering them at the keep much easier.

Hundreds of her people — men, women, and children of all ages — were assembled in the courtyard. Brogan led her out of the keep and onto the top of the stairs. From there, she could see not only her people, but the wall, and land beyond.

'Twas a lovely autumn eve, with a crisp, cool breeze and clear skies overhead. In the distance, she could hear the sound of waves lapping against the shoreline. 'Twas a sound as familiar to her as her own voice.

Whispers of curious people flittered along the courtyard. They had no idea why they had been summoned here. More likely than not, they thought it had something to do with the thousands of 'horse thieves' heading their way.

Brogan had finally admitted to her what Henry had done. In truth, she did not care *what* had motivated her people. She was simply glad to have them all working together. It might not be genuine horse thieves they were bracing themselves for, but Aymer Mactavish was a thief nonetheless. Because of his greed, he had taken more than three years of her life away.

At the front of the mass of people were Gertie, Tilda, and Reginald. Mairghread smiled warmly at each of them before raising her hands to quiet the crowd.

"*Ceud Mìle Fàilte*," she began. *A hundred thousand welcomes.* "I ken ye all be verra busy and workin' verra hard of late. To each of ye, I give me thanks." It warmed her heart to see these people assembled here. They'd come willingly and quickly. Aye, many were probably here out of curiosity, but it mattered not. They were here. That was what was important. Hopefully, they would continue to support her after what she was about to tell them.

Never before had she talked to her people like *this*. Assembled below, looking up at her. 'Twas the oddest of sensations. Taking in a deep breath and willing her nerves to settle, she began.

"As many of ye ken, more than three years ago, we lost four verra special people on a dark night in spring. Killed by someone whose identity to this day remains unknown."

A hush fell over the crowd then, as they looked to each other with curious expressions.

"As ye also already ken, no' long after, I fell into drinkin'. Day and night, night and day, I drank, because of my deep and profound loss. Not only did we lose two good and kind men that night, I lost me husband and bairn."

She had to take another deep steadying breath. Glancing once to her left, she felt immediately at ease knowing Brogan was there. Always at her side, always supportive.

"I became a mean-spirited, ugly, black-hearted drunkard. I want to apologize to each and every one of ye fer behavin' as I did."

Some of the women had tears in their eyes, for they could understand how much such a loss could hurt. A few of the men simply nodded in understanding. But all were quite surprised to hear her admission as well as her apology.

"Thanks to me husband, Brogan, and me dear friends, Reginald, Gertie, and Tilda, I was able to climb out of the flagon and come back to the land of the livin'."

Nervous laughter spread throughout the crowd when she smiled at them. 'Twas no' easy for her to talk so openly about what her clan referred to as *her troubles*. But she felt it necessary to do so. "I ken that I have three years of poor behavior to make up fer, but make up fer it I will."

Louder murmurs began to race through the crowd. Though it appeared to her they were speaking of their approval, she couldn't quite be sure. Once again, she looked to Brogan for his silent support. He stood proudly beside her, with his hands clasped behind his back. Stoic and proud.

Understanding that she must first bring forth the matter of Aymer Mactavish before she could go any further, she took in a deep, cleansing breath. "I have, just this day, received word from Aymer Mactavish, who was actin' chief on me behalf when I did no' have the strength to do it meself." She paused, looking out at her people. "Aymer was no' happy to learn of me marriage to Brogan." Though that 'twas an understatement, her people did not need to know all the sordid details of her uncle's letter.

"I have learned many things recently, that make me question Aymer's loyalty to us as a clan, and to me as his only livin' niece."

Concerned murmurs and whispers from the people.

"I was loyal to me uncle fer a long, long while. Unfortunately, he has betrayed that loyalty and me trust. He has betrayed me and ye." She waited for the astonished gasps and rumblings to quiet down before going on again. This was one of the hardest things she had ever had to do.

"Aymer," her voice caught on his name. Regret, sorrow, and anger blended together. "Aymer Mactavish lied to me and I be certain he spread that lie to the rest of ye. He convinced me that *I* killed me husband, James, and me son, Connell, and then tried to kill meself. I now ken, that no' be the truth."

Stunned silence filled the yard below her. "I believed him only because he was me last livin' kin. I believed him because I thought he had only me best interests at heart. But that be no' true." She paused, waiting for what she was telling them, to sink in. "He lied because he does no' want me to be chief. *He* wants that title for himself."

Another round of gasps and murmurs rippled through the crowd.

"I ask ye this: why would a man order the removal of a wall, a wall that stood for more than one hundred years? Why would he order it removed yet never rebuild it? Why would he take all our weapons out of the armory — fer safekeeping' — and no' tell anyone where they were?"

On that, the crowd was in agreement. It had never made any sense to anyone. But because he had been acting chief while Mairghread and James were away, her people felt they must obey his orders.

"No good chief would leave his people as exposed as he has. It has only been through God's divine grace that we have no' been attacked since the removal of that wall. Had the wall been in place the night we were attacked, I believe we would no' have lost those that we did." She was growing angry now, just thinking about how her uncle's foolish decision had affected her and her people. She could see, with brilliant clarity, how Aymer had betrayed each of them.

"We know not when Aymer will return to this keep." she began. The murmurs quieted as they paid rapt attention. "But when he does, we will be ready. We will never again allow a man such as he to make decisions that will cost precious lives. We will never again allow foolishness or arrogance to rule us." The more she spoke, the angrier she felt. She refused, however, to allow that anger to make her look like a vindictive woman. Taking in another steadying breath, she went on. "When Aymer returns, he will be permanently banished from this keep, our holding, and our lands. He will never be allowed to return."

'Twas quite apparent that her people did not know what to make of that announcement. Many looked quite pleased, but were, mayhap, afraid to voice their joy.

"Upon the death of James, I inherited not only the keep and its lands, I also inherited the title of Chief. Because of me grievin' and sorrow and drinkin', I was no' able to act as yer chief."

'Twas as if they were all holding their breaths, waiting to hear what she would say next. Casting a quick glance to Brogan, he looked just as curious and eager as her people.

"I be here this night, to tell ye that I am now ready to be yer chief."

Gasps of surprise broke out across the crowd. A moment later, a loud cheer went up. Brogan stood taller, prouder, although he was stunned to hear her finally proclaim it. But he watched the crowd with a keen eye. He had also placed his men in varying locations, looking for any signs of dissent or people who might remain loyal to Aymer.

"With Brogan Mackintosh at my side, I ken we can make this clan as good and strong as it was when me da ruled," the crowd quieted but only slightly. "I want to lead us into a brighter and better future. I ken I be askin' much of ye, especially after the past three years, when the only thing I thought of was the whisky and the wine."

Her heart was pounding in her chest, her palms sweaty, her voice cracking. She hadn't told Brogan of her final decision. But she knew he would be happy, as well as proud. Standing closer to her now, he slipped his hand into hers, and gave it a gentle squeeze before letting go.

"I give to ye this day, me promise and most solemn vow, that none of ye will have to worry ever again about me drinkin'. Recently," she turned to Brogan and smiled at him. "I have learned that I need to live, more than I need to drink."

He returned her smile with one of his own, as well as a wink.

She had to raise her hands again and call for quiet. Once they settled down, she started again. "I will do me best to be a good, loyal servant to all of ye. Aye, I will be chief, but I believe in me heart that a good chief understands he — or she — is no' above his people. Any decision I will make will always be fer the good of the clan, fer the good of its people."

Another cheer erupted, as people shook their hands in the air and called out her name. Not all, but most.

"I be no' so naive to believe that *all* of ye will follow me without question. I ken that I must prove to ye that I mean the words I speak, lest they are just empty words. I will do me best to make ye proud."

More loud shouts of approval and once again, she had to ask for quiet. "I want only what is best fer us, as a people. I will work just as hard as me father did, and with just as much conviction and honor. I will make him proud and I hope to make ye as proud as well."

There was nothing left for her to say now. She wouldn't have been able to anyway, for her people were roaring their approval.

MAIRGHREAD AND BROGAN WALKED BACK INTO THE KEEP HAND IN hand. Though Mairghread's hands trembled significantly. She was at peace with her decision to make the official announcement, she could only pray and hope her clan would continue to support her.

Once they were behind closed doors, Brogan wrapped his arms around her and lifted her off the floor. "I be so verra proud of ye!" he exclaimed with a beaming smile. He twirled her around twice before kissing her soundly on the mouth.

"Were I a man who just announced he was chief, would ye still be kissin' me?" she asked playfully.

He grunted. "I be no' married to a man, lass."

"But ye *are* married to a chief," she said, painting a most serious expression on her face. "And as chief, I give ye me first order."

He raised a brow, his expression awash in uncertainty. "And what might that be?"

She smiled then. "That ye kiss me again."

"As ye wish, m'lady," he replied with a grin.

'Twas a most wondrous kiss. Soft and sweet, but filled with passion and desire. It stole her very breath away, as most of his kisses tended to do.

Brogan, almost always the more level-headed of the two of them, broke the kiss. "Have I fulfilled yer order to yer pleasure, m'lady?" he asked with a most devilish grin.

"Aye," she said breathlessly. "I have another order fer ye, that can only be done in private."

He chuckled. "Ye be insatiable," he told her.

"'Tis entirely all yer fault," she told him.

"Mine?" he asked, incredulously.

"Aye," she said as she kissed his cheek. "Were ye no' so good at lovin', I would no' be askin' fer yer favors as oft as I do."

How could a man argue with that?

WHEN THEY SAT DOWN TO SUP — AFTER STEALING AWAY TO THEIR chamber — Mairghread felt invigorated. Looking out at the tables of the gathering room she saw many familiar and devoted people. But it seemed to her more were in attendance this night. Many had quit attending the evening meal ages ago, no doubt due to her drinking. She was glad to see their return.

On the morrow, she would select a few members of her clan to act as her counsel. She would begin meeting with her people twice a week, as her father had done. Settling disputes between clansman, offering her help wherever she could, had always been easy for her. She could only pray 'twould be the same now that she was chief.

"Brogan, I would like to put ye in charge of training our people to fight," she told him.

"Do ye think it best we finish the wall first?" he asked as he began offering her food from the platters.

"Be there a way to do both?" she asked, politely declining the pheasant with a shake of her head.

"I suppose, with the extra men we have now," he said. "Mayhap we could start with just a few afternoons a sennight."

She was quiet for a long moment, deep in thought. "We do no' stand much of a chance against any trained warriors Courtemanche might bring with him, do we?" Suddenly, she did not have much of an appetite.

Brogan let out a quick breath. "I think ye have set a good plan in place, Mairghread. If we can gain reinforcements from me brother and the Bowie, and if we get the wall finished in time, then I would say we have a good chance."

She trusted him to be honest with her in all things. 'Twas a promise he'd made long ago. Still, doubts sometimes lingered. "Ye would tell me the truth, would ye no'?"

"Of course I would, Mairghread," he said as he set his eating knife down. "There be too much at stake no' to tell ye the truth."

She could not help but smile at him. He was a good and decent man. "Mayhap it be the doubt in meself I be feelin'."

"Remember that I will always be at yer side. If I feel ye be makin' a mistake on a matter, ye can be assured I will voice me opinion."

She patted his hand and thanked him. "I be verra glad that I married ye," she said. "I do no' ken if I have told ye that before."

He gave her hand a gentle squeeze. "Ye may no' have told me with words lass but ye have shown me. And I be right glad I married ye."

It hit her then, a realization so bright and brilliant, and catching her so unaware, that she gasped. Deep in the pit of her stomach, fluttering out like a thousand butterflies to her fingers and toes. *I love him.*

"What?" he asked as his brow wrinkled in confusion.

She couldn't say the words aloud. Not here, not now. She thought of lying to him, making up some story about how she forgot to do something important. But she could not do that to him. "I will tell ye later," she whispered as she fought back tears.

She couldn't have told a living soul why she cried. Her emotions were a jumbled mess at the moment. Tears of regret, remorse, happiness and joy? How could such a thing be?

"Be ye certain?" he asked, still looking quite concerned.

"Aye, Brogan, I be certain."

They ate the rest of their meal with Mairghread half-listening to anything Brogan said. All she could think of was the promises she had made to James and Connell at their graves. Sorrow crept into her heart, leaving her unable to eat more than a few bites of food. She could barely think a clear thought.

'Twas an inner battle between past and present, one that made her head ache and her tongue fair itch with a need for just a wee dram.

Knowing well now that a wee dram of anything was akin to suicide — albeit a long, ugly and dark death that would be years in the making. She knew what she must do and she needed to do it this night. And without Brogan. Nay, this was something she needed to do alone.

"Brogan," she began, her voice unsteady. "There be somethin' I need to do before we retire fer the night."

"Verra well," he said as he removed himself from the table. Extending his arm, he smiled down at her. "What do we need to do?"

Distractedly, she shook her head. "Nay, 'tis naught fer ye to worry over," she told him. "I will be above stairs shortly." Scooting away from the table, she declined his proffered hand.

Ignoring his questions, she fled the gathering room and keep without looking back.

NOT FAR FROM THE KEEP, NEAR THE FOREST, BEHIND A LOW STONE wall, was the Mactavish cemetery. More than a hundred years old, with countless graves, 'twas a well-kept, serene and peaceful place.

Mairghread brought no flowers with her, just her memories, her sorrow, and a lighted torch. The wind whipped through the tiny glen, wrapping her skirts around her legs, bending the tall grass. Betimes, it sounded as though the trees were moaning, grieving.

'Twas a cool night, growing, it seemed to her, cooler with each beat of her heart.

James and Connell had been buried side by side in a spot at the rear, reserved for clan Chiefs and their families. Not far from them was the eternal resting places of her entire family.

Cautiously, she made her way to her husband and son's graves. One large, stone cross, and a smaller one, marked their places. It had been more than three years since the one and only time she had been here. But someone, more likely than not Gertie and Tilda, had tended to these two places with great love and care. Not a weed grew on either spot, and bless them, they had recently left flowers.

Slowly, she sat down betwixt the two graves, her skirts spilling all around her, and jabbed the torch into the ground between their stones.

"All the way here, I thought of what I would say to ye," she said, choking back tears. "But now it seems I be at a loss fer words."

Taking in deep breaths, she sat for a long while, just listening to the sound of the wind. She had hoped, she supposed, to hear the faint echo of James' voice, or mayhap even Connell's sweet baby sighs. But all she could hear was the beating of her heart, the wind, and the moaning of the trees.

"It has been a long while since last I was here. I should no' have deserted ye as I did, but I see Gertie and Tilda took good care of ye." One lonely tear fell down her cheek. How many had she shed over the years? Enough to fill a loch, she supposed. "I have no' come here to say goodbye to ye. I came, I suppose, just to talk to ye. I could no' do that before, ye see, fer I was simply too drunk, too overcome with grief at losin' ye."

Wiping away the tear, she took in a deep breath and held it until she thought her lungs would burst. 'Twas the only thing she could think to do to keep from breaking down completely. Finally, she let go that breath, as she willed her heart to settle its frantic beating to keep it from breaking completely.

"I loved ye both, ye ken. More than I have ever loved anyone in me life. 'Tis why I took yer deaths so hard. 'Twas why I could no' come visit ye before now. 'Tis the most unimaginable hurt a body can ever go through, losin' ye as we did. 'Tis the truth that I did no' want to live. I could no' imagine goin' on with the rest of me life, while ye be stuck in the cold, dark ground. It did no' seem fair."

That deep pain, the agony, that was what first had her reaching for the flagons. The belief she had ended these lives she held so precious, was what send her tumbling into the abyss.

Focusing now on little Connell's grave, she swiped away more tears.

Oh, how she missed that sweet, sweet babe. The way he smelled, the way he would smile in his sleep, how warm and light her heart felt whenever she held him.

"I will no' give ye excuses fer why I have no' been here. I can only give ye reasons. 'Tis true, ye see, that I turned into an ugly, black-hearted drunkard. For a long while I thought 'twas because I killed ye, even though, deep in me heart I knew I could never have done such a thing. But Aymer, may *he* someday burn in hell fer his sins, he convinced me I had done just that. I can no' reason out why I believed him. Mayhap me guilt was so deep that I could no' save ye from him."

All at once she *knew*. She *knew*, deep in her bones, the horrid, sinister truth. 'Twas just a flash of a memory that assaulted her, just as quick and as fierce as lighting cutting through the sky. Just as powerful and deadly.

Sick to her stomach, her heart so cold she was certain it stopped beating for a moment. But then it beat again, thundering, pounding against her breast, blood coursing through her veins, cold and unmerciful.

"Nay," she whispered as she struggled to her feet. "Nay, nay, nay!"

Her world was spinning out of control, making her feel dizzy and nauseous. More flashes of memory raged on. Gruesome, horrid scenes, tiny moments, blazing, flashing all around her. 'Twas as if she were no longer in her body, but staring down at it from above. Screaming, bleeding, begging for mercy, begging him to stop, unable to believe what she was seeing. The dirk, the long, weighty dirk, slashing through the air, through skin, flesh, and bone. Over and over again.

Struggling to get on her feet, her skirts tangled around them and sent her face first into the soft, cold grass with a grunt and a curse. 'Twas then she realized the lightning was real, spidering out in a sky that had grown dark without her realizing it.

Screaming as loudly as she could, she fought once again to get onto her feet. Her throat began to feel raw, her breaths coming in brutal, harsh bursts.

A heartbeat later, terror seized control of her heart and mind when a pair of strong arms wrapped around her torso and lifted her up.

Chapter Twenty-Three

Brogan had followed his wife from a safe distance. Only because she had been out of sorts throughout the evening meal. He wanted to make certain she was safe. And without knowing where the bloody hell Aymer was, he did not want her wandering too far from the keep.

She hadn't bothered to gather her shawl or cloak before leaving the keep. The night air was growing cooler and there was the promise of rain in the air. Stealthily, he followed behind at a safe distance so as not to disturb her. Believing she only needed some time alone, he did not want to intrude. Time alone, especially over these past few months, was a precious commodity.

Out of the wall and down the path she went. He had no idea where she was going or if she had any purpose. Not once had she glanced over her shoulder or the spaces around her. They would have to have a very serious talk about that when they got back to the keep. 'Twas too dangerous to go walking about, without keeping an eye out for any potential danger, whether it be human or beast.

Then he saw her turn off, to the right, down another well-worn path. For months, he had passed by the cemetery on his way to the forest. But he had never dared to step foot inside consecrated ground for he felt he had no right.

Assuming she was going to visit James and Connell's graves, he stayed outside the stone wall and waited. Before he left his father's home, he had visited Anna's grave every day, no matter the weather. Still, he waited just outside the wall. He would not invade such a personal moment as this.

A long while passed, the sky growing darker, the storm clouds moving in. He wished now he had thought to bring his own cloak, but then, he might have missed seeing where she had gone. He did not grow concerned until he saw the lighting flash in the distance. He would give her a few more moments alone, before he would go inside and insist she come back to the keep.

His blood ran cold when he heard her shrieking the first time. Racing into the cemetery, he scanned the space quickly, looking for any sign of her. Nothing. Then he heard her scream again, louder, more pained that before. He did the only thing he could do; race for where the screams were coming from.

With his heart beating mercilessly in his chest, the blood pulsing in his ears, he tamped down the dread, the worry. There, up ahead, he saw the flicker of her torch, then heard that awful screaming that made his blood run cold.

In a thrice, he was lifting her off the ground, all the while she screamed and fought to be free.

"Let me go!" she cried out, as she clawed at his hands.

"Mairghread, 'tis me!" he exclaimed as he fought to keep his hold on her. "'Tis me, Brogan!"

Relieved, she quit struggling and all but collapsed in his arms. He spun her around, holding her close, his heartbeat not yet settled. "What happened?" he asked. "Are ye hurt?"

Between gut-wrenching sobs, she begged for him to take her away from here. "I want to go home, please, I can no' stay here."

Lifting her into his arms, he carried her out of the graveyard as quickly as he could. All the while, lightning danced in the night sky, the wind howled and groaned.

"I remembered," she told him between sobs. "I remembered that night."

His stomach lurched, taking his breath with him. Part of him had hoped she would remember what had happened. But another part begged the opposite, only to protect her heart.

"I saw him, Brogan! I saw him with the dirk. He was covered in blood! I saw him do it!" Sobbing to the point of hysteria now, she stammered, "I saw him. I remember."

It broke his heart to see her in such distress. He felt her pain as strongly and as real as if it were his own. "I be so sorry, lass," he whispered against the top of her head. "I had me suspicions, ye ken, but I did no' want to put them to voice. I did no' want to give ye any false memories."

"Ye knew?" she asked, started as well as angry. "Ye knew and ye did no' tell me?"

He blew out a breath, struggling up the small incline. "I did no' want to speak ill of yer uncle," he said.

"'Twas no' me uncle," she murmured, growing paler with each passing moment.

"'Twas no' Aymer?" he asked, drawing them to an abrupt halt.

Looking up, into his eyes, anguished and devastated, she wiped her face with her sleeve. "'Twas James."

IF HE HAD NOT BEEN SO CONCERNED WITH GETTING HER INTO THE keep before the storm hit, he would have sat down in the path. What she said made not a lick of sense. Pushing forward, he raced back to the keep. Fergus and Comnall saw him approaching, and came running to see what was the matter.

"She had a fright, is all," Brogan told them.

"Do ye want me to carry her in?" Fergus offered.

"Nay!" she cried out. Taking in deep breaths, she said, "I can walk now, Brogan."

He refused to set her down until she whispered, "I be the chief," she reminded him. "I do no' want anyone to see me like this."

Reluctantly, he set her down, but kept an arm around her waist, as he gave orders to Fergus and Comnall. "Run ahead and ask Cook to send up warm cider, and have someone light a fire in our room. But say naught to anyone."

They nodded and ran off to do his bidding.

Mairghread took a few shaking steps. "I can no' breathe," she told him, clinging to his arm for support. "I do no' think I can go in yet."

"Wheest," he said, giving her a gentle hug. "Take one breath at a time, lass."

His head was still spinning with what she had told him.

"Brogan, I do no' feel well," she murmured, swaying and clinging to him.

That was the last thing she said, before fainting in his arms.

He was half-way up the stairs before she began to stir. "Wheest, Mairghread," he whispered as he kicked open the door to the keep with his booted foot.

Gertie and Tilda were still in the gathering room and jumped to their feet when they saw Brogan carrying Mairghread. "Och! What happened?" they asked as they rushed to follow him up the stairs.

"I be fine," she murmured. "I just fainted 'tis all."

"Do ye hear that? She just fainted 'tis all," Gertie said to Tilda, mockingly.

Tilda shook her head in disbelief as they followed Brogan into the bedchamber.

With great care and shaking hands, Brogan laid her on the bed. Gertie and Tilda stood near her, while he began to undo the laces of her dress.

"What happened?" Gertie demanded as she felt Mairghread's forehead with the back of her hand.

"Be she feverish?" Tilda asked.

"Nay," Gertie answered with a shake of her head. "Do ye hurt anywhere? How be yer stomach?"

"Do ye have an ache of the head? Have ye taken a fall recently?" Tilda asked, looking for all the world a very worried woman.

Mairghread batted their hands away and sat up. "I be fine," she said through gritted teeth. "Stop peckin' at me like a brood of hens!"

The two women stopped. With pursed lips and scrutinizing eyes, they studied her closely for a moment. "Ye have been crying," Gertie said. Glowering at Brogan now, she asked, "What did ye do to make her cry to the point of faintin'?"

He rolled his eyes, "I did naught to make her cry or faint."

'Twas apparent she did not believe him.

"What shall we do?" Tilda asked, wringing her hands together. "We have no healer to send fer."

Mairghread sat up, closed her eyes, and rubbed the bridge of her nose. "I need to think," she said, frustrated and angry. "I need quiet fer a moment."

Brogan stepped around Gertie and Tilda and sat on the edge of the bed. Gently, he rubbed her back with his hand, his own heart and mind in turmoil. "Do ye wish to be alone fer a little while?" he asked.

With her eyes still closed, she took her free hand and searched for his. She breathed a sigh of relief when she felt his fingers intertwine with hers. "Nay, please do no' leave me."

He was glad she needed him and wanted him to stay with her. Long moments passed before a knock came at the door. Tilda answered it. 'Twas Mairi, bearing the warm cider Brogan had requested.

Tilda took it, thanked the young lass, and shut the door after her. Bringing the tray to the bed, she set it down. "'Tis warm cider," she said in a low, hushed tone.

"Thank ye," Mairghread replied. "There was never a time I wanted a flagon of whisky more than right now."

"Lass," Gertie said with concern etched on her face and evidenced in her tone. "Tell us, what be the matter?"

"Mayhap another time," Brogan suggested.

"Nay," Mairghread said. Opening her eyes, she looked at Gertie and Tilda, then Brogan. "They might be able to help."

Brogan was not so certain, but after seeing his wife so distressed, he could deny her nothing. He pulled up two chairs for the women to sit on, while he returned to sit beside Mairghread.

"I remembered," she began, taking Brogan's hand in hers. "I remembered what happened that night."

THERE WAS, OF COURSE, NO NEED TO IDENTIFY WHICH NIGHT Mairghread spoke of. For more than three years, it had simply been referred to as *that night*.

Gertie and Tilda cast worried glances at once another.

"No' all of it, just some of it. Little pieces and bits." There were still many dark spaces of no recollection. But tonight, she had seen enough. Enough to make her question everything she ever believed in. 'Twas enough to make her want desperately to drink again. It hurt. Hurt far more than when she had believed they had died at her hands.

"I saw James that night." As soon as she said his name the tears began to fall. "I watched him slicing through Connell's ..." she couldn't bring herself to say it.

"Nay!" Gertie and Tilda exclaimed together. "That can no' be!"

Swallowing back the bile and tears, Mairghread shook her head. "He was so angry. I had never seen him so angry before. He was no' makin' any sense. I tried to pull him away, all the while I was screamin' and cryin', tryin' to get to Connell. When James looked at me, 'twas as if he could no' see me. He was lookin' *through* me!"

Tears streamed down the faces of the two auld women. Neither of them could believe what she was telling them. "James would no' more kill ye than ye him!" Gertie cried.

"Mayhap, 'twas just a bad dream," Tilda offered.

"I was wide awake," she said before going on to explain what had happened in the cemetery.

"I *remembered*," she told them again. "No' all of it, just little bits and pieces."

Brogan had been quietly listening to her recount her memory of that night. Something gnawed at his gut. "Ye said he was no' makin' any sense. What do ye mean?"

She swallowed again and wiped away more tears. "I do no' ken. 'Twas as if he had been possessed by a demon."

He chest felt tight and his stomach lurched. "Good lord," he whispered. *Possessed by a demon...* He looked at Gertie and Tilda. *Aye,* he thought to himself, *they be thinkin' exactly what I am.*

"How could he have done such a thing?" Mairghread cried. "He was such a good man!"

"Mairghread, did ye see anyone else? Besides James?"

She thought long and hard, then shook her head. "I do no' ken. There were dancin' shadows, and cryin', screamin'... 'twas all so verra strange and utterly terrifyin'," she replied.

His suspicions were growing by leaps and bounds. From her description of James, it led him to believe Hargatha and her *Devil's Brew* had something to do with what happened. He thought back to the afternoon the woman had slipped the brew to Mairghread. The way she fought with a murderous rage, how they had to subdue her and tie her to the bed. The way she looked right through him as if he weren't even there.

"Mairghread, I do no' think James acted alone," he told her. "I think he had help."

She looked up at him, with a peculiar expression. "Help? By whom?"

"Hargatha and that bloody *Devil's Brew* of hers."

Mairghread's confusion did not last long. Once his words sank in, she shot to her feet. "I will kill her!" she ground out. "With me bare hands, I swear to ye, she will die this night!"

Brogan went to her and wrapped his arms around her. "On the morrow—"

Cutting him off, she pulled away, anger blazing in her eyes. "I said *this night,*" she said through gritted teeth. "I will no' wait another day, Brogan. We leave at once."

"It be dark and there be a storm brewin' out of doors," he reminded her.

'Twas nothing in comparison to the storm brewing within. "If it were ye who had just discovered someone had killed me, would ye wait?"

Just the thought of someone harming her was enough to incite him to murder. He could not argue against what she wanted to do. "Nay, I would no' wait," he told her. "However, I would hope someone would have the good sense to at least make me wait until the storm passed."

She mulled it over for a moment. "Verra well," she began. "Have the horses and a handful of men readied. As soon as the storm passes, we will leave. 'Twill take us more than an hour to reach the cottage we banished her to."

"As ye wish," he said with a nod. To Gertie and Tilda, he said, "Stay with yer lady until I return."

"Ye'll no' go without me," Mairghread said, with a fierce glare.

"Nay, lass, I will no' go without ye. I will no' deny ye the satisfaction of lookin' in to the auld woman's eyes while she takes her last breath."

She gave him a curt nod and turned away. "Gertie, Tilda, ye understand what I must do?"

"Aye, m'lady," Gertie said as she got to her feet. "Ye have our support."

"Good," she said as she went to her clothes cupboard. "Now, help me find somethin' to wear. I would no' want to get blood all over me pretty silk."

❦

TWO HOURS LATER, MAIRGHREAD AND BROGAN WERE RACING through the walls of the keep. Behind them were Henry, Comnall, Fergus, Reginald and a handful of other men.

While the men were armed to the teeth, wearing full helms and chainmail, Mairghread was in a dark gray wool dress, covered by her blood red cloak. Around her waist, she wore her father's sword belt and sword. Evelyn and Mairi had to dig it out of storage for her. It had been wrapped in fine linen and stored away in a beautifully carved box in the attics.

Never before had she armed herself with anything other than a *sgian dubh*. And that was usually saved for ceremonial purposes. Tonight, however, was different. She was on her way to avenge the deaths of her husband and son.

They rode in silence, with Reginald taking the lead after they passed the quarry. There was no moon this night, but the Mirrie Dancers were in full swing. Some believed the green and red lights were the ancient gods doing battle. Others thought they were signs from the one true God. Either way, they were thankful for this starry, brilliant night.

The air was damp and cool now, the ground wet from the heavy rains. Mud kicked up from the horses splattering the feet and legs of their riders. 'Twas not the best night to be tearing across the countryside. Five of the riders carried lighted torches that danced and flickered against the wind, lending to the ominousness of the night and their purpose.

As they rode along, Mairghread kept thinking of the two young guards who were killed that awful, horrid night. Had James killed them as well? For what purpose? To what end? Mayhap, he'd simply been induced to madness by Hargatha's *Devil's Brew*.

And why on God's earth would she have given him that concoction? Pulling alongside Brogan, she asked him just that. "He had no' been ill," she told him. "I can no' help but wonder *why*. Why would she have done that to him? She had to have known what would happen."

Brogan had been wondering that very thing. Revenge, mayhap? "Had he done anythin' in the days before that would have upset her?"

Pondering the question for a long moment gave her no results. "Nay, at least naught I can remember."

Who knew with Hargatha? Rarely did she do anything a sensible, logical person might do. Still, he had suspicions that she had not acted alone. But he would not set to voice his thoughts until after they spoke with the auld woman.

The ground grew increasingly rocky and hilly, forcing them to slow their pace. The farther east they rode, the more treacherous it became. Soon, they had to dismount and guide their horses around and through the large boulders and rocky way.

For a moment, and only a brief moment, Mairghread wondered how Hargatha had been able to walk through this angry land. *Too bad she hadn't fallen and broken her neck*, Mairghread mused. *But then, I would no' have the chance to look her in the eye and ask her* why. *Why did she do it?*

֍

IT SEEMED TO MAIRGHREAD THAT THEY HAD LEFT THE KEEP DAYS ago, so long the journey felt. But Reginald and Brogan assured her it had not been as long as that.

Finally, they reached their destination. In silhouette, the ancient looking, decrepit cottage sat against a large, grassy knoll. They stayed a good distance away, securing their horses to low hanging branches. Mairghread could see smoke billowing out of the chimney, which gave her a good measure of relief. It meant the auld biddy was within.

In hushed whispers, they made plans for entry. Reginald would go in first, followed by Henry and the rest of the men. Mairghread would enter last.

Testing the door first, they knew 'twas barred from the inside. With a shrug of their shoulders and the count of one, they busted the door down, using their broad shoulders. The space was dark, save for the fire in the hearth. Hargatha sat up in her bed when she heard the door breaking down and began to screech with fright.

When the rest of the men filed in with their lit torches, she grew even more terrified. "I be a sick auld woman!" she cried. "I have no coin!"

"We're no' here to rob ye, ye auld bat!" Reginald declared rather loudly.

Recognition came to her eyes when Fergus held up his torch. "Reginald?" she asked, her hands still shaking. "What in the bloody hell are ye doin' here? Breakin' down me door in the middle of the—"

She fell instantly quiet when the men parted to allow Mairghread through. Her eyes blazed with hatred she made no attempt to hide. Mairghread would not be deterred.

"Why?" she asked through gritted teeth. "Why did ye give James yer *Devil's Brew?*"

"I do no' ken what ye speak of," Hargatha replied indignantly.

"I be talkin' about the night me husband and son died," she said as she leaned over. Just inches from the auld woman's face. "Me memory has returned. Now tell me why ye gave him the brew!"

"Bah! I did no' give James anythin'! The boy would no' let me get near him, or ye, or yer babe. I do no' ken why, fer I am a good healer."

"Yer were no' a healer," Mairghread told her. Her voice was growing harsher, angrier. "Ye be naught more than a cruel, black-hearted woman."

"Says ye," Hargatha said in a most challenging tone.

Not here to argue on whether or not the auld woman was a good healer, Mairghread's anger was growing far more intense. Leaning in closer, she asked her once again. "Why did ye give it to him?"

"I did no' give it to him!"

The words were barely out of her mouth before Mairghread reached over and grabbed a handful of the auld woman's hair. "Why?" she ground out while Hargatha protested. "Why did ye give it to him? Tell me now, auld woman, or ye will no' live to see the next sunrise!"

In a good deal of pain, Hargatha's words rushed out. "I did no' give it to him! I gave it to Aymer!"

"AYMER?" MAIRGHREAD ASKED. "WHY WOULD YE GIVE IT TO HIM?"

When she did not immediately answer, Mairghread tugged hard on her hair again.

"He was me laird! What was I supposed to do?"

Seething with fury, Mairghread's next words would not leave a doubt in anyone's mind what she thought about Aymer being laird. "He was *no'* yer laird. James was! James was yer laird and chief, no' Aymer. And now, *I* be yer chief." Disgusted with the auld woman, she let go of her hair, pushing her away.

Mairghread turned to find Brogan. "Why would Aymer give James the brew?"

Before he could answer, Hargatha piped up. "'Twas no' fer James, 'twas fer ye!"

Spinning around, appalled and angry. "Me?" she asked, only for clarification's sake.

"Aye, ye," the auld woman said as she rubbed the spot on her head that Mairghread had pulled. "He said ye had no' been yerself since ye had the babe. He said ye had no' suffered with the childbirth, as God meant all women to do. He worried ye were possessed."

"Good lord," Mairghread breathed out, awash in stunned disbelief. Aymer had lied to the auld woman, knowing just what to say to her to get what he wanted.

Turning back to her men, she asked of no one in particular, "How would James have drunk it if it were meant fer me?" It made no sense. No sense at all.

"It does no' have to be drunk as a tisane," Hargatha told them. "It can be put in a stew or a broth."

Fergus let out a gasp, drawing their attention to him. He looked as pale as a linen sheet, his eyes wide with horror. "Good lord," he murmured. "I ken how he did it."

"What do ye mean?" Brogan asked him.

Fergus was deep in thought, startled back to the here and now by Brogan's deep voice. "I, I swear m'lady, had I kent, I would never have done it."

"What do ye mean?" Brogan asked once again, his words clipped and sharp.

Fergus ran a hand through his hair and took in a deep breath. "I had only been working in the kitchens less than a week. Aymer came in and told Lowrens he was worried Mairghread was no' eatin' well enough. Lowrens ladled up a bowl of fish stew."

Another jolt to her memory and she was transported for a time, back to that fateful day. She could remember being abed that afternoon, and only because James insisted she take a nap. Connell was in his cradle, next to their bed. They were speaking in whispers, so as not to wake their precious, sleeping babe. *'Twas a lot of hard work ye did, givin' me a son,'* he had told her. *'Ye need yer rest, so that we may make many more sons.*

With vivid clarity she could remember how light and happy she felt, how much in love they were. James with his wild, unruly, dark brown hair, his bright blue eyes, and his lopsided grin.

Then there was someone at their door, and James was taking a tray.

"Och! They must no' ken ye hate fish stew now," James had said, smiling at her. He was always smiling at her, so warmly and adoringly.

She had lost the taste for fish stew when she was carrying Connell. 'Twas one of the few things she could not keep down and to this very day, she still couldn't eat it without wanting to vomit.

She could see James now, handing her the crusty bread, while he eagerly ate the stew. He took several bites before he put the bowl down. *'It tastes a bit off,'* he had remarked.

Then he kissed her, saying he would be back soon. He wanted to check the progress of the wall.

And that was the last time she had ever seen him or her son alive.

"JAMES ATE A POISON THAT WAS MEANT FOR ME." AN INTENSE ACHE grew, deep in her heart. He had been such a good man. Had he lived, he would have been a great leader. Had he only lived. Had she been able to eat the fish stew, chances were they'd not be standing in a run-down cottage in the middle of the night, trying to extract information from a black-hearted old woman.

Mairghread was having a difficult time coming to grips with that. Dazed, she stood in the old cottage, surrounded by her husband and men. None of the men to whom she looked had the answers she sought.

"Had I eaten the tisane," she murmured, her mind going to very dark and unimaginable places.

"Mairghread, it would change naught," Brogan said as he placed his hands on her shoulders. "Aymer was determined. Had that no' worked, he would have thought of something else. And he did. He could say ye took yer own life, denying the blood on his hands." His jaw ticked with barely contained rage at this faceless man named Aymer Mactavish. He did not think it possible to want to take the life of a man he'd never laid eyes on.

She knew he was right. With sober eyes, she could now see the man was beyond nothing, even the murder of innocent sweet babes, to get what he wanted.

Connell.

Connell's death was owned to only one man and that was Aymer Mactavish. Whether or not he held the weapon that took her son's life, the result was the same. Connell and James were dead by his hands.

Like a battle-hardened warrior, Mairghread straightened her back and shoulders. "He can deny it all he wishes, their deaths are his. And I will seek justice for all he has done. No' just to me, but to this clan."

Brogan believed she was sounding more and more a clan chief. "What do we do with Hargatha?" he asked.

Some might have thought 'twas her tender heart leading her decision. But Brogan saw naught but fierce determination flicker behind her dark green eyes. "We keep her alive until Aymer returns. We may need *her* to prove his guilt."

Overwrought with guilt, Fergus stepped forward. "M'lady, I'd rather fall on me own sword than to bring ye a moment of pain."

"None of this be yer fault, Fergus. Do no' fash yerself over it. That be an order." Offering him her most sincere smile she seemed to put him at ease.

"Keep half the men back to watch her," she told Brogan. "On the morrow, we will build a gaol, just fer Hargatha."

He grinned his approval, growing more proud of his wife with each passing moment. There might have been a time or two when he thought she would be too tender-hearted to lead her people, but she was proving him wrong.

THE EASTERN SKY WAS JUST BEGINNING TO BLAZE ORANGE AND yellow, the western sky still inky with twinkling stars when they rode back home. Though she was bone tired, Mairghread knew sleep would not come easy. Her nerves were on edge with her anger bubbling just below the surface.

Guilt had been her constant companion these past years. Just when she thought she could put it to rest, something new seemed to rear its ugly head, bringing the guilt to the forefront. It seemed to follow her wherever she went.

Thankfully, Brogan was able to help her set that guilt aside. He had been right when he said Aymer would have found some way to bring forth her demise. The evil man had proven that with all his lies and falsehoods. She could not and would not take the blame for any of this.

There was no time for guilt. Instead, she chose to focus on the unmitigated fury coursing through her veins. Someday — and she hoped that day would come sooner rather than later — she would have justice for her husband and babe.

Shaken from her murderous thoughts by a scene before her, she pulled her horse to a stop. She was looking at Douglas and Mavis Mactavish's home. 'Twas a small cottage, with gardens Mairghread had always envied. What confused her was that Douglas and his young sons were emptying the contents of their cottage and piling them into the back of a wagon.

With a gentle tap to her horse's flanks, she rode up the small path. Brogan and the others followed behind her.

"Douglas." When she called his name, he paused only long enough to give her a curt nod. "What be goin' on here?"

He placed the heavy trunk he'd been carrying into the back of the wagon. "We be movin'," he replied curtly.

"To a larger cottage?" she asked, though from his angry glower, she didn't think it so.

He made no attempt to stop his work. "Nay."

Brogan, seeing the blatant disrespect, pulled his own mount around to the rear of the wagon. "I would thank ye kindly to stop loadin' yer wagon long enough to give yer lady the respect she deserves." He pinned the man in place with a hard, cold stare.

Douglas put a basket on top of the trunk. "We be leavin' the clan," he said, giving Brogan his full attention. "We be goin' east, to clan MacCray, to me wife's family."

"Why?" Mairghread asked cooly.

He grew silent, refusing to look at Mairghread.

"I asked ye why," she repeated. This time her voice was much firmer.

With a roll of his eyes, he finally spoke directly to her. "Me wife misses her family."

'Twas a full out lie and Mairghread knew it. Breathing in through her nostrils, she let the air out quickly. "Be that true? Or be it the fact that I have taken me rightful place as chief?"

He hung his head for a brief moment. "M'lady, it be no' just me who has concerns with ye bein' chief."

"If ye had concerns, why did ye no' come to me to discuss them?" she asked.

"Instead of movin' out before the sun be up, like a coward," Brogan asked. He was just as angry with this bit of news as she was.

Douglas's eyes burned bright with anger. "I be no' a coward!" he ground out. "I just can no' trust her to lead us!"

His words felt like a kick to her gut. "Because of me past drinkin'?" she asked him.

"Among other things," he replied harshly.

"Would ye have stayed had I made Brogan chief?" she asked only out of morbid curiosity.

Something flickered across his face, but he refused to answer her.

"How many others?" she asked him through clenched teeth.

"Twenty families, last I heard," he replied, indignantly.

Twenty families? That was too large a number to lose at a time like this. Casting a quick glance to Brogan, she could see he was thinking much the same as she.

"Verra well, Douglas," she said as she tightened her hold on the reins of her horse. "I hope ye will be happy wherever ye be goin'. I also pray ye can live with this decision." With that, she spun her horse around to head back to the keep.

"It might be best this way," Brogan told her. "It saves us from havin' to weed out those who would no' support ye when it counts most."

"Is no' *now* when it counts most? When we need a bloody wall built?" she bit out angrily.

"We will get it built, if we have to light torches to work at a night."

She did not doubt *him* as much as she doubted the people who were staying behind. How long before more of them decided to follow in Douglas's footsteps?

COUNTING WOMEN AND CHILDREN, THEY LOST A GRAND TOTAL OF thirty-three people. Not nearly as many as they had anticipated from Douglas's estimation. Still, 'twas enough to make Mairghread worry.

'Twasn't until they were alone in their chamber that she let loose all her anger and upset. It came out in a slew of bleary-eyed curses. "We can no' afford to lose one man right now," she told him as she stripped angrily out of her dress.

"I still say it be better now than when Aymer shows up," Brogan told her. Undoing his sword belt, he hung the belt around the poster of the bed.

Tugging her boots off, she threw them to the floor. "Aye, I ken that. But it does no' mean I have to *like* it."

"Nay, but it be times like these that will test yer mettle as chief. And I have to say ye have handled yerself well these past hours."

She was not in the mood for compliments. The air in the room was decidedly chilly. She left her woolens on as she slipped into the bed. In no time, Brogan had a nice fire going.

"I can no' but help to wonder if they would have stayed had I made ye chief," she told him. Propped up on one elbow, she watched as he stripped out of his tunic. Muscles rippled in the firelight. The sight of him, standing only in his trews, helped tamp down some of her anger. "No' that I regret me decision," she added. "I am fulfilling me father's final wishes."

A thought suddenly occurred to Brogan. "When did ye decide to step aside and make James chief?"

Breathing out a puff of air, she had to admit the truth. "I told him *before* we were married that I had no plans to become chief, even though that was what me father wanted."

Pulling off his trews, he sat down on the edge of the bed. "So even though ye knew 'twas what yer father wanted, ye told James he could be chief?"

"In truth? I thought me father would live a verra long time. By then, he would see what a good man James was. He would see that James was the better choice."

He stood up long enough to slide in under the blankets. "What changed yer mind this time?"

"Ye did," she answered in a low, soft tone. "'Tis yer belief in me that changed me mind."

"Would not James have supported ye as I have?"

She had to admit the truth. "Nay, he would no' have. He was no' as modern in his way of thinkin' as ye. There was no way he would have followed me as chief of the clan. And he made his opinion known to me when he proposed."

He furrowed his brow. "Then why did ye marry him?"

She smiled warmly at the memory of James. "I loved him. He was a good man. I think ye and he would have gotten along well together."

Ignoring the last part of her statement, he said, "So ye married him despite the fact that he would no' have supported ye as chief."

"I was naught but a starry-eyed lass in love then, Brogan. All I have ever truly desired was to be a wife and mum, and to help me people wherever I could. I have never had any desire to be chief. But ye have shown me that I can be chief as well as wife and mum. With ye beside me, I ken I can conquer any task, any problem set before me."

Chapter Twenty-Four

October had arrived, ferocious and cold, with biting winds and unrelenting rain. The proverbial dust had finally settled after Douglas and the others had left the clan. Aye, they could have used the extra men to make their work easier. But in the end, they were able to finish the wall without them.

At least part of it. There was still the matter of towers and walkways.

On this cold, blustery day in mid November, the entire clan was gathered in the courtyard to watch the final bolt be put into place in the hinge of the massive gate made of wood which was reinforced with heavy steel.

The rain beat down like heavy pebbles falling from the sky, the wind whipped harshly at anything in its path. Mairghread would not be deterred from marking this momentous occasion. Though her cloak was made of heavy wool and lined with dark fur, she was still chilled to the bone. In her gloved hands, she held a wooden mallet. Standing in the back of a cart, she looked out at her people.

"This day has been too long in comin'," she said with a smile. "There is still much work to be done, but at last, we can say we built this bloody wall!" The crowd erupted into a loud cheer. "Each of ye have worked from dawn to past dusk fer months now. I owe each of ye a debt of gratitude that can never be repaid." She turned then to look at Henry, who was just a few steps away, standing with her husband. "Because we owe a great deal to Henry Mackintosh, fer over-seein' the completion of this wall, I think he should put the last bolt in!"

The crowd cheered again as she handed the mallet off to Henry. Placing his hands around her waist, Brogan lifted her out of the cart. In front of God and everyone, he kissed her most soundly. Such an intense look of joy could be seen in his green eyes that she almost felt like weeping. "We did it," he said as he kissed her again.

"Och! I owe this wall to ye, Brogan Mackintosh!" she told him as he wrapped his arm around her waist.

The people filling the yard went deathly quiet, as Henry climbed up the ladder. The gate was set in place, waiting for the final bolt. Someone handed him a large, heavy bolt, which he slid into the slot.

"For Clan Mactavish," he called out to the crowd. "May she live long, may she prosper, and may she be strong!"

And with that, he brought the mallet down, once, twice, and yet again. In place now, he held the mallet over his head, and called out once again. "For Clan Mactavish!"

'Twas a quarter of an hour before the crowd settled down and began filing into the keep. A special feast had been prepared and everyone in the clan was invited. Not just the *lonelies*. Nay, this was a night to be enjoyed by one and all.

Mairghread felt a great sense of pride, not only in how her people had banded together, but also for her husband. Tonight would be a night of celebration, one that had been a long time in coming.

A FEW DAYS AFTER THE GATE WAS PUT IN PLACE, DOUGALL BOWIE arrived with wagons of grain and more than two-dozen Bowie men. Their presence caused quite a stir, what with their reputations as blood-thirsty murderers and thieves. All of it was true, of course. But the Bowies were trying to turn over a new leaf, as farmers, whisky makers, and people of good repute.

Gertie and Tilda shook with fear when the men came stomping into the gathering room. They couldn't help but stomp, for they were such *large* men. Everyone one of them seemed to have been cut from the same piece of cloth. Dark hair, darker eyes, and apparently the inability to smile.

"I have letters fer ye," Dougall said, reaching into a pouch that hung at his waist. "From The Bowie, and yer brother, Ian."

Brogan gladly accepted the letters while Mairghread asked after Leona.

"She be doin' well," Dougall said. "Her bairns came a bit earlier than expected."

"Bairns?" Mairghread asked with a smile.

"Aye," he replied, accepting her offer of ale. "Two wee daughters. She has named them Rose and Lily."

"Those be verra pretty names," she told him.

For the first time, she saw the fierce Highlander smile. "She could have named them George and Walter fer all Alec cared. Ye would have thought him the first man in all the world ever to be a father. In truth we did no' think *he* would survive the birthin'!"

Mairghread giggled as she took her seat, then looked at Brogan. He was standing next to the hearth, reading the letter. She could not help but wonder how he might behave if and when she ever got with child. More likely than not, he would be his usual calm and collected self.

"Ian says that Rose be doin' well. Convinced it be a boy again. Rose is hopin' fer a girl," Brogan said as he read the letter.

His mood seemed to be lifted with the contents of the letter. 'Twas not as if he'd been unhappy of late. But whatever was in the letter seemed to bring him much joy. There was a twinkle in his eye that had not been there since the night they placed the last bolt into the gate.

"They have also finished the second story of the keep and have officially moved in," he smiled.

That was indeed good news, though she was more happy *for* him than anything else. Someday soon, she was going to have to admit to him what was in her heart. Deep down, she hoped such an admission would bring him as much joy as the letter in his hands.

❧

SAMHAIN EVE ARRIVED COLD AND DREARY. THE FIRES IN EVERY hearth in the keep and every cottage on Mactavish land was let to grow cold for the entire day, in order to prepare for the evening's impending activities. As soon as the sun set, massive bonfires would be lit. From there, men would light torches, and run from house to house, where they would light fires in each hearth or brazier. Whilst there, they would be served a quick mug of ale, or in Brogan's case, hot, spiced cider. 'Twas an old tradition, its beginnings unknown.

Mairghread was in the gathering room with Gertie and Tilda, preparing for the evening events. So cold was the air within that they could see their own breaths.

"I tell ye, it be auld Brennis Mactavish that haunts the marsh," Gertie was saying. She and Tilda were in a heated argument over what souls haunted what part of their lands.

"And I tell ye it be Red Vernis, the first chief of this clan that haunts it," said Tilda.

Mairghread had given up trying to intervene. She was cold to her bones and tired. Bone tired. She'd been this way for two weeks. Tired and unable to keep anything down. She'd had suspicions, of course, for she had been with child before. But she'd visited Martha yesterday, just to be certain. Though she didn't consider herself the least bit superstitious, she would not share her happy news with Brogan until the morrow. 'Twas bad luck to speak of such things on Samhain Eve.

Gertie and Tilda continued to argue. Mairghread did her best to ignore them. 'Twas naught more than ghost stories to be told each year at this time. Many of her people still held the belief that barriers between the living and dead would be stretched thin at the midnight hour. If one looked hard enough, or strained their ears, one might be able to see or hear a long dead relative.

Mairghread put no stock in that notion. That isn't to say she did not believe in fairies, fey creatures, or demons, for she truly did. She still burned sage once a month to help keep out evil spirits. She simply didn't believe it possible to talk to the dead and have them respond.

She knew because she had tried every Samhain since she was nine-years-old. That was the year they lost Andrew. And every year since, right up until she lost James and Connell, she had tried to reach her dead brothers and parents. Each year 'twas the same: she would talk and pray and hope, for even a tiny glimpse of all those she held dear. But 'twas all for naught.

So she gave up believing in that.

But she still believed in demons. Aye, those were as real as the earth on which she walked. As real as the air she breathed.

One of the younger guards, a brown-haired lad named Charles, came rushing into the gathering room. He was out of breath and covered with sweat. "M'lady! M'lady!" he called from the door.

"What is it?" she asked as she set the bowl of sweets on the table. Whether it was instinct or that the lad looked as though he'd just seen a ghost, dread settled over her.

"Henry sent me to tell ye," he was fighting for breath. Taking in great, deep lungfuls, he was fighting hard to tell her something either important or God-awful

Her first thought was that something had happened to Brogan. "What?" she asked, rushing forward, holding her breath.

Resting his hands on his knees, he said, "Aymer be less than an hour away."

❦

THEY HAD BEEN PREPARING THEMSELVES FOR THIS EVENTUALITY FOR months. Now that it was here, she didn't know if she should laugh or cry or scream.

"Be he alone?" she asked, swallowing hard. Her fingers trembled, not with fear, but with something akin to murderous rage.

"Nay, m'lady," he replied. "The Frenchman be with him and more than one hundred soldiers."

Undoubtedly they were well-trained soldiers, bought and paid for, without any sense of duty or honor to anyone. Save for the man with the biggest purse.

Taking in a deep breath, she straightened her back and lifted her chin. "Charles, run back to Henry and tell him no' to allow Aymer entry until Brogan gives it. And send Liam and Comnall to me at once." Turning to Gertie and Tilda, she said, "Ye two, get Mairi and Evelyn, send them above stairs at once. Then I want ye to go to yer rooms and stay there."

"The bloody hell I will!" Gertie exclaimed. "I'll no' leave ye alone with that monster, no' while I still have a breath in me body."

"And neither will I, m'lady," Tilda added, bobbing her chin once to show she was quite serious on the matter.

"Verra well, ye come above stairs with me," she agreed. There really was no arguing with them at times. Turning to one of the younger maids, she said, "Send Mairi and Evelyn to me, straightaway."

A moment later, she was rushing above stairs with Gertie and Tilda trying to keep up.

"What is yer plan?" Gertie called out from behind her.

Her plan? Other than imagining her uncle's head on a pike, she wasn't certain. "Unfortunately, I will have to meet with him."

'Twas no surprise to see the wall. Aymer's spies had been keeping him well informed of the goings on inside the keep for months now.

He owed the wall to Brogan. A part of him wanted to thank him, for being so diligent on its construction. 'Twould save him time when he became chief.

The Mackintosh was sadly mistaken to believe walls could keep him from his divine right. God had chosen *him* to lead this clan, not his weak and feckless brother, Gavin. Aye, Gavin had become chief by order of birth. But Aymer knew 'twas God's plan for him to become chief. His proof? God would not have allowed him to come this far only to take it all away. If God did not want him killing his brother, or any of the others, He would have stopped him. The only logical conclusion he could come to was that aye, God wanted him to lead.

So it stood to reason, at least in his mind, that 'twas his divine right.

Brogan Mackintosh was naught but a test. A test to see what he was willing to do to get that which he coveted above all things; the Mactavish seat.

Just as the wall had not surprised him, neither did the fact they would only allow he and Courtemanche to enter and with only two guards. The rest of the men would have to make camp outside the newly built wall. It mattered not to Aymer.

Upon entering the keep, he took note of the two men posted at the bottom of the stairs that led to sleeping chambers above. Tall, fierce looking men he did not recognize and was left to assume they had to be Mackintoshes. While he found all these new protections for Mairghread irksome, he cared not. He was so close to having everything he had worked for his whole life. A few guards, a wall, they were simply bothersome. Like midges in the summertime. Annoying, but easy to do away with. One simply needed to be smarter and stronger than the midges.

The frigid air in the gathering room was also to be expected, for it was, after all, Samhain. He had not yet decided if he would allow this ridiculous custom to continue after he became chief.

"Why is there no fire in the hearth?" Courtemanche asked as he rubbed his hands together. The two men with them seemed just as displeased, but said nothing as they took up posts on either side of the cold hearth. Bloodthirsty mercenaries, they stood quietly as a warning to anyone who might try to do him harm.

"'Tis *Samhain*," he smiled, explaining further the custom and ritual.

Courtemanche grunted his displeasure. "Thankfully, I will not have to suffer through another one of these cold nights. Soon, I shall have your niece to help warm my blood."

Aymer chuckled, playing along. Frankly, he cared not what the man did with his niece. She was naught more than another obstacle in his righteous path.

COURTEMANCHE WAS GROWING IMPATIENT THE LONGER THEY WERE made to wait. "I want to leave this place," he said, his teeth chattering.

Soaked to the bone and freezing cold did not make for a pleasant Claude Courtemanche.

Aymer went to find serving maids, but the halls were empty. Growing more perturbed with his niece's lack of respect, he hid his ire behind a smile and air of entitlement.

"Why can we not light a fire?" Courtemanche whined.

Aymer chuckled inwardly at the weak man's distress. "I told ye, 'tis a custom on this night."

"And where are the serving wenches?" Courtemanche asked. "We have been here for half an hour and no one has offered us so much as a crust of bread."

Aymer was certain he knew the answer, but was not about to put it to voice. 'Twas naught more than a way for Brogan Mackintosh to demonstrate his misguided belief that he was in charge. "They are busy preparing a feast for later this eve."

There was no sense in being perturbed or put off by their horrible mistreatment. Nay, he knew the best course was the one he was currently on. His steel, cool reserve had served him well these many years. He would not allow this blatant show of disrespect to define him, or take him off God's chosen path.

Courtemanche was still complaining moments later, when Mairghread stepped into the room.

⚬

DRAPED OVER HER DARK GREEN WOOL GOWN WAS THE MACTAVISH plaid. Worn just as her father had worn his. The only difference now was that it was affixed to her shoulder with the Mackintosh brooch Brogan had given her. With refined grace and elegance, she all but floated into the room.

Aymer saw her first, and went to her at once. "My niece!" he declared happily. If one didn't know any better, one might think he had a genuine love for her. Mairghread, however, knew the truth.

Hiding a myriad of feelings, she allowed him an embrace. Silently, she swore this would be the last time he would ever put his hands on her.

Brogan was standing in the shadows, at the ready. Though he had not approved of her need to meet the man alone, face to face, he understood the importance. Knowing he was just a few steps away strengthened her resolve.

The Frenchman, having heard Aymer, finally stood. "My friend, you were right," he was speaking to Aymer, but looking at her. His dark eyes slowly raking her over, from head to toe. "She is the most beautiful woman I have ever seen." His smile bordered on a sneer and showed a mouthful of crooked teeth. 'Twas difficult not to retch all over his feet.

"Mairghread, I have brought yer betrothed to ye," Aymer said.

"We shall be married at once!" Courtemanche declared joyfully.

Ignoring his declaration, she took the seat at the head of the now empty trestle table. She had ordered every morsel of food removed from the gathering room. Aymer would take naught one more thing from this keep.

"Married?" She cocked her head to one side. "I fear there has been a mistake."

Mayhap she took a bit too much enjoyment in seeing his sneer fall away. "I can no' marry ye."

His face pinched, he looked at Aymer. "Be this some sort of jest?"

She would not allow her uncle to answer. "Nay, I do no' jest. Ye see, I be already married." Directing that last part right to her uncle, she saw just a flicker of anger in his eyes.

"What goes on here, Aymer?" Courtemanche was beginning to sound like a screeching auld woman. "What game do you play?"

"Settle down, Claude," he told him. His gaze was still pinned on Mairghread. "'Tis naught but a small obstacle to overcome."

"Obstacle?" she asked. "Think ye me marriage to Brogan naught more than an obstacle?"

"I am certain ye were no' in yer right mind when ye agreed to marry him," Aymer said, still smiling as if he held some secret she was not aware of. "If ye do no' voluntarily set it aside, I will petition the king to do it fer ye."

She was growing weary of his smugness. "I will do no' such thing."

Her words were clipped and filled with undeniable resoluteness. "No' fer ye, or fer anyone else."

"We shall see," he murmured.

"In case ye have fergotten," she said as she stood. "*I* am the chief of Clan Mactavish. I answer to no one but me king and ME people. I did no' need yer permission to marry."

"But ye made a promise to Claude."

"Nay, *ye* made the promise to Claude," she reminded him. 'Twas growing more and more difficult not to slap the smug sneer off his face.

"How long have you known she was married?" Claude demanded, stepping between the two people, and staring Aymer down. "Did ye bring me all the way here knowing full well she had already married?"

"Claude, me friend, ye worry far too much." Turning away, with his hands clasped behind his back. "I should have warned ye that me niece is no' necessarily of sound mind. Of course, fer the purposes ye want her for, that does no' matter."

BROGAN COULD NOT BEAR TO LISTEN TO ANOTHER INSULT AGAINST his wife. Stepping out of the shadows of the dark hallway and into the light of the gathering room, he came face to face with Aymer Mactavish for the first time.

Taller than he had envisioned, with light brown hair and brown eyes so dark they looked black. Pale skin like an English nobleman who never stepped outside his keep to do an honest day's work. Not at all what Brogan had expected.

"Aymer, I will only tell ye once. If ye insult me wife again, I shall forget me manners and pummel ye into the ground." A tic had formed in his jaw, his fury toward this man barely contained.

If his presence had surprised Aymer at all, none would have known it. Not so much as an eyebrow did he twitch.

"I take it ye are the Mackintosh lad who convinced me niece to marry him under false pretenses?" Aymer sneered.

Lad? Ignoring the insult, he said, "I be Brogan Mackintosh. And it took very little to convince her, considering her alternative." He nodded his head toward Courtemanche who, at the moment, looked as though he might soil his fancy trews. Absentmindedly, he reached up and touched the bridge of his nose and took a few steps back. Aye, he recognized Brogan. Undoubtedly remembering their first meeting when John broke his nose.

Shrugging with indifference, Aymer turned his back to Brogan, as if he were nothing more than a servant boy.

"As I was saying, Mairghread, ye can either set this false marriage aside, or ye can suffer yer fate at the hands of our illustrious king, David."

"If ye're tryin' to frighten me, Aymer, ye will no' succeed," she seethed, her fists clenching and unclenching. "I am no longer afraid of ye."

"Afraid of *me?*" He feigned being appalled. "After all I have done fer ye?" Tut-tutting as if he were offended. "After all yer dirty little secrets I kept?" He quirked a brow, leaned in and hissed. "Does yer current husband ken what ye did to yer last?"

He might have thought he was whispering, but Brogan heard every word. Without warning — or much forethought — he took him about the shoulders and spun him around. Grabbing his tunic with meaty fists, he spoke through clenched teeth. "What secret? The fact that *ye* gave James the *Devil's Brew?*"

Aymer's mercenaries had swords drawn and pressed on either side of Brogan's neck. A rapid heartbeat later, Henry and Comnall were behind each of them, pressing swords to their backs.

"I would no' do that, were I ye," Henry said, his voice calm, his tone low.

"Put yer wee blades away, laddies," Comnall added. "Elst ye'll find mine in yer gullet."

The two mercenaries looked to Aymer first.

"Put yer weapons down, lads," he laughed. "We want no bloodshed this day." Though he was laughing and smiling, Brogan could see the fear flickering behind his eyes. 'Twas apparent he did not think he would be met with such resistance. Neither had he expected Brogan to defend his wife.

After a long moment, the two mercenaries stepped aside and sheathed their weapons.

"Aye, we ken all about what ye did to James," Brogan ground out.

"Ye'd believe the words of a crazy auld woman?" he asked with a smirk.

"Who said anything about a crazy auld woman?"

'Twas then Brogan saw him flinch. 'Twas barely perceptible, but 'twas there just the same.

"The only one I ken who makes that awful stuff is Hargatha," he said in an attempt to dig himself out. "'Twould only make sense it be her ye speak of."

Brogan felt his blood run cold. Aymer was a cunning, deceitful man who would stop at nothing to get what he wanted. This made him far more dangerous than he had previously worried over. However, he had miscalculated one thing: Brogan Mackintosh.

Mairghread stepped forward, her face drawn with anger. "Aymer, ye and yers are no longer welcome here. I banish ye from me keep, me lands, and the clan. Ye will never step foot on its soil again. If ye do, ye will be killed."

Disgusted, Brogan let go his hold. As much as he wanted to gut both Aymer and his weak French friend, he knew he could not. There were over a hundred soldiers waiting on the other side of the wall. The Mactavish men were not ready yet for such a fight as that. Just how loyal they were to Aymer, or to Courtemanche, he could not know. Killing either or both would be suicide.

"Banished, am I?" he asked as he smoothed out his tunic. "'Tis only yer best interests I have ever had at heart, lass."

"Ye have been warned," she glowered at him. She would not listen to his insults or his pleas. Just being in the man's presence made her stomach churn. "Ye will be escorted out."

Though he behaved as though he was not the least bit insulted, Brogan knew he was. He was also calculating his next move. Brogan was doing the very same.

"As ye wish," he said with a bow. "Come, Claude."

Courtemanche did not argue nor protest. More well-armed men filed into the room, swords drawn and at the ready.

As soon as they were out of the gathering room, Mairghread's knees gave out. Brogan caught her before she could fall to the floor.

"I have never been more angry, nor more frightened," she admitted. Clinging to his arms, she took in deep, steadying breaths.

"I will never allow him to harm ye," he murmured. She trembled in his arms. He would kill Aymer Mactavish with his own hands if he so much as put a toe back on their lands. "He be gone now."

"But I fear he will be back. We have no' heard the last of him."

There was naught to argue over, for he knew she was right.

Chapter Twenty-Five

Though they had celebrated Samhain, 'twas not with the same fervor or zealousness of years past. A cloud hung over Mairghread and Brogan, and its name was Aymer Mactavish. Even their clanspeople were subdued.

Many believed his presence on Samhain Eve was an omen. Mairghread felt much the same way. Brogan did not put much stock into omens. However, he did believe evil existed in this world. Aymer was proof enough of that.

Most mornings — *after* loving her soundly — Brogan would leave her to sleep and would be gone from their chamber before she woke to begin her day. However, they had celebrated late into the night and had slept past dawn.

He woke to the sound of her retching in the chamber pot, behind the dressing screen. Propping himself up on one elbow, he waited quietly until she was finished. She looked quite surprised to find him awake when she came around the screen.

"When were ye plannin' on tellin' me?" he asked, smiling warmly.

"Tell ye what?" she feigned ignorance as she climbed back into the bed.

"That ye're with child." He was not an ignorant man. He had, after all, been married before.

"How did ye ken? I swore Martha to secrecy."

Chuckling, he kissed her forehead. "I am no' a lad who has just begun to shave," he told her. "I have been married before, ye remember."

"I wanted to surprise ye!" she exclaimed, looking disappointed.

Unable to contain his joy any longer, he kissed her until her breaths were ragged. "Ye have made me a verra happy man." He was grinning from ear to ear.

Tears welled in her eyes, her joy not anywhere similar to his own. "What be the matter?"

"'Tis true, I thought I never wanted another bairn of me own. But ye changed me thinkin' in that regard."

He studied her closely for a moment, his grin fading to lines of concern. "But still, ye are no' happy?"

"I was verra happy," she sighed. Wiping her tears on the edge of the sheet, she said, "Until Aymer appeared last eve."

"Do no' let him take away yer joy," he told her.

"I can no' help it. What if he does go to the king?"

Her worry was not without merit. "When David was imprisoned and the false king Edward took the throne, where did the clan's fealty lie?"

She thought it an awfully odd question, but answered it nonetheless. "Da was always loyal to David," she told him. "As was James."

"And Aymer?"

"Aymer is loyal only to himself."

"Then we have naught to worry over," he said, kissing the tip of her nose.

Confusion still lined her face and worry filled her eyes. "Ye make no sense."

"Even if Aymer goes to David with his entreaty, it will all be fer naught. I ken David, and he will see right through his lies and treachery."

Wide-eyed astonishment set in. "*Ye* ken David?"

Unable to contain his smile, he kissed her again. "Aye, I ken David. Me da and he are distant cousins."

When her mouth fell open, he chuckled, and gently closed it, a finger pressed to her chin. "That surprises ye?"

"I-I," she fought for words. "Why did ye no' tell me this before?"

Shrugging once, he said, "I have been a bit busy of late," he teased.

Relief finally settled in, as she let out a breath and sank further into the bed. "What other surprises do ye have in store fer me?"

Waggling his eyebrows devilishly, he said, "I have one more, if ye be feelin' up to it."

Rolling her eyes, she slapped his roaming hand away. "*That* be no' a surprise."

"Used to me now, ye are?" he teased.

"Och! I doubt I will ever grow used to ye," she quipped.

In a flash, he was on top of her, supporting his weight with his elbows. Plying her neck with soft kisses, he said, "Ye have made me verra happy this day, love. Verra happy."

Giggling, she placed her palms on either side of his face. "I can tell how happy ye be."

THE NEWS THAT MAIRGHREAD WAS WITH CHILD SPREAD throughout the keep and their lands. Though she and Brogan were overjoyed and excited, nothing could match what Gertie and Tilda felt. As soon as the happy tears were shed — and there were many — they immediately set to work with preparations.

"But the babe will no' be here until the end of May," Mairghread told them. They had come to the spare room she and Brogan used as a shared study of sorts. While she sat behind the table, going over the books Reginald had brought her earlier, Gertie and Tilda stood, eager and happy, across from her.

"Och! Ye'll blink twice and she will be here!" Gertie exclaimed.

"Or *he*," Tilda argued.

"Either way, there is much to be done," Gertie replied with a roll of her eyes. 'Twas her most fervent belief — or mayhap just wishful thinking — that 'twas a girl Mairghread carried. "We need a cradle, clothes, nappies, and bonnets."

"Do no' ferget the birthin' supplies," Tilda reminded her.

"Och! The birthin' supplies," Gertie exclaimed, patting her chest with her hand.

"And new dresses, fer when she starts to show," Tilda added.

Knowing the fervor with they had planned each of her weddings, Mairghread knew they'd not rest until everything was in place. And knowing them as she did, they had everything ready within the week.

Keeping them occupied with the impending arrival would be a blessing. Then they'd not hover over her, constantly pecking at her to rest or to eat.

"Ye will help me then?" she asked, pretending she thought they wouldn't.

"Of course we will!" they replied in unison, aghast that she thought they would not in her hour of need.

Smiling brightly, she said, "Well, I be verra busy with bein' chief, as ye ken. I will be verra glad fer yer help. Do what ye think is best, but within reasonable cost."

"Ye'll still remain chief?" Gertie asked, more than just a bit appalled.

"Aye, I will," she replied. "Our clan needs me now, more than ever."

"But there be so much to do, lass. And ye need yer rest," Gertie said with a motherly scowl.

"I will rest. But I can no' rest unless I ken the two of ye are makin' the preparations fer me."

Holding her breath, she watched as the two of them looked to one another for either approval or to gear up for more arguing.

"Verra well," Gertie sighed. "We will take care of everythin'. As long as *ye* promise to rest and eat."

Letting out her breath, she smiled warmly at them. "Of course, I will."

As they were leaving, she heard Tilda remark in a hushed whisper, "I did no' believe her fer a moment. Did ye?"

"She'll rest. Brogan will no' allow her to tax herself."

Mairghread bit her lips to keep from laughing out loud. Brogan was a logical thinking man. Calm at all times, he was. Nay, he would not insist she do nothing for the next six months but rest and eat, as if they were fattening up the proverbial cow.

❦

MAIRGHREAD'S ASSESSMENT OF HER HUSBAND COULD NOT HAVE BEEN more wrong.

"Ye *will* rest," he was telling her for the third time in the past few moments. She sat at their desk. He stood across from her, with fierce determination etched in his face.

Rolling her eyes, she was growing more perturbed with his misguided belief that she had somehow grown weaker, just by getting with child. "I be fine, Brogan. I will rest when I feel the need to."

"I said ye will rest."

They were going around in circles at this point. Puffing out her cheeks, she blew out her breath slowly. She had no desire to argue with him, but really, he was giving her no choice.

"Brogan, I will need to rest more as my belly grows bigger. This is no' the first time I have carried a babe."

"'Tis the first time ye've carried *my* babe," he said, his eyes turning to slits as he crossed his arms over his chest.

Biting back a retort, she closed her eyes and counted to ten before opening them again. "All I am doin', is goin' over the books that Reginald has brought to me. 'Tis no' like I be plowin' fields by hand, or movin' stones."

He remained silent, still fierce and quietly unwavering.

"Please, God, tell me ye will no' be like this the entire time?" she asked, vexed.

Quirking his brows, he leaned over the desk. "Aye, I will."

There was no changing the stubborn man's mind. Annoyed, she got to her feet, and she too, leaned over the desk. They were almost nose to nose. "Ye can no' treat me as if I be some fragile piece of glass that will crumble at any moment."

"That is no' what I be doin'," he breathed slowly.

"Then what *are* ye doin'?"

He kissed the tip of her nose, throwing her momentarily off balance. "I be treatin' ye as me wife, who I greatly care fer."

That was not the answer she had been prepared to hear. "Ye care fer me greatly?" she murmured as she looked longingly at his lips.

"Aye, I do."

Without touching or kissing her, he was able to disarm her good senses, with nothing more than the soft timbre of his voice. Warmth and need spread throughout her body, the kind of need that made a body ache with desire.

"I will rest, but only if *ye* join me," she murmured.

There was no need to ask him twice.

***

THEIR JOY LASTED LESS THAN A SENNIGHT WHEN ARCHIBALD Mactavish's body was found hanging in the armory. 'Twas Henry and Comnall who found him.

Not wishing to cause Mairghread any upset, they sent for Brogan and Reginald. The two men were now studying his lifeless body, which still hung from the low rafters. A belt, undoubtedly his own, had been wrapped around his neck, before being tossed over the beam. His body swayed to and fro with bulging eyes, his swollen purple tongue protruding from blue lips.

"We knew there was no hope fer him, so we left him, so ye can see fer yerselves," Henry explained.

Brogan studied the scene before him. The lad's feet were several inches off the floor. There was something off about it all.

"I found this, scratched into the wall," Comnall added, drawing their attention away from Archibald's swaying body. Brogan and Reginald came over for closer inspection.

On the wall had been scratched the words *I be sorry fer me sins, A.*

Anger swelled as Brogan turned once again to look at the body.

"What would make a young lad take his own life?" Comnall asked. "What sins could someone so young have committed?"

Brogan snorted derisively. "His only sin was crossing the path of Aymer Mactavish."

Henry and Comnall were confused. "What do ye mean?" Henry asked.

"Look more closely, lads," Brogan said with a nod toward Archibald's body.

'Twas then that Reginald saw it. "God's teeth!" he exclaimed.

Henry shook his head. "I fear I do no' see it."

"He did no' take his own life," Brogan said through clenched teeth. "The lad was murdered."

❧

"MURDERED?" COMNALL AND HENRY ASKED ALMOST IN UNISON.

"Aye," Brogan replied. 'Twas all he could do not to call for a war party to go in search of Aymer Mactavish. But he had no hard evidence that 'twas he who had killed the boy. Only a deep suspicion.

"I still do no' see how ye arrived at that conclusion," Comnall said, shaking his head in disbelief.

"Look at the belt," Brogan told him. "See how close it be to the beam?"

Comnall and Henry took a closer look.

"Now look at his feet."

They did as directed.

"Now tell me, lads, how did he get his sword belt wrapped around the beam, and himself pulled up so high? Without a chair or stool?"

Awareness burned brightly then. "Bloody hell," Comnall muttered.

"Aye," Reginald finally spoke. "He could no' have gotten that close to the beam without aid of a chair or stool."

The four men stood in silence for along while. Their fury was palpable. Someone had taken this young man's life.

"I doubt Aymer was able to make his way beyond the walls, unnoticed. But this was still done by his order," Reginald put to voice what he was certain everyone else was thinking.

"But why?" Henry asked.

"Because Archibald acted at Mairghread's messenger. She sent him, with a letter, to tell Aymer she had married me, a day after our weddin'."

"So?" Henry asked, uncertain what that had to do with anything.

"If Aymer does in fact go to David to have our marriage set aside, as he has threatened to do, Archibald could have stood as witness on our behalf."

"Bloody hell," Reginald raged. "Drayton!"

"Who be Drayton?" Comnall asked.

"Drayton went with Archibald to give Aymer the news."

Comnall whistled in a low yet surprised tone. "Where be he now?"

"No one kens," Reginald replied. "Archibald told us he left the lad in Edinburgh. He has yet to return. It has been months since anyone has seen him."

Dread filled Brogan's gut. "There may be a chance he is still alive."

"Doubtful, but aye, there is a small chance," Reginald said.

"Find at least seven, nay ten Mactavish men who know this Drayton lad. Have them take five of me own men with them. They will look under every rock, in every valley, tavern, and inn between Edinburgh and here. Hell, send them to Inverness if ye must. But I want that young man found!"

Chapter Twenty-Six

Over the next few months, the pall left in Aymer's wake gradually lifted. Though they had yet to receive any word from the men sent to find Drayton Mactavish. The search party could be in Inverness for all he knew.

Though he had told Mairghread of Archibald's death, for days, he debated on whether or not he should tell her the entire truth. In the end, he decided against it. There was no sense in upsetting her, at least not yet.

Daily, he prayed the men he'd sent in search of the young man, would either return or at the very least, send word of where they were and what they had learned thus far. Of course, with the inclement winter weather, travel was much easier said that done.

They had even managed to celebrate Christmastide with good cheer and light hearts. January came and went, bringing with it long nights, blisteringly cold winds, and biting rain and snow. Still, they'd received no other word or threats from Aymer. That alone served to lift Mairghread's spirits a great deal.

Though she was convinced Aymer had given up and mayhap had even gone back to France with Courtemanche, Brogan held an entirely different belief. He had known men like Courtemanche before. He was naught more than a spoilt child in a man's body. A rapist and murderer to be certain. More a danger to young women and the weak. But if he were ever faced with a real battle of wits or muscle or strength, he would undoubtedly scurry off with his tail betwixt his legs.

But Aymer Mactavish? He was a cold, calculating, and dangerous man. Brogan was quite sure more than greed motivated him. He had looked into the man's eyes and saw something that still made his blood run cold: sheer evil. An evil he was able to contain and hide to the outside world. But if one took a moment to look closer, to see what lay hidden behind those dark eyes, one would see the depths of that evil.

The last thing he wanted to do was to bring upset to his beautiful wife. She had experienced enough of that over the years. Nay, he refused to share his true worries with her. Instead, he did everything within his power to make her feel safe and protected.

At night, he would rest his hand on her belly and speak to their babe. Whether it be a son or daughter, he cared not. All he wanted was for this child to live a full and happy life. And there would be naught he wouldn't do to make sure that was a reality and not just a fanciful dream.

As her belly grew, so did his adoration towards her. Fierce, determined, quick-witted, and uninhibited in their marital bed, was his Mairghread. Aye, he'd begun to think of her as *his*. Months ago, of course. But he had yet to tell her what was in his heart.

There were many times when the words were on the tip of his tongue, begging to be set free. However, he was as yet, uncertain how she felt about him. Oh, he knew she liked him well enough, and even admired him. But love? Nay, of that, he had serious doubts.

Months ago, he had told her to speak freely and openly of James and Connell. So she did. But as time wore on, he found himself growing quite jealous of the man. For James still owned her heart. Brogan might have been in possession of everything else, such as her trust, admiration, loyalty, and even her body. But her heart, he feared, would always belong to James.

THE SECOND CRACK IN THEIR FALSE VENEER OF HOPE — THE FIRST being the murder of Archibald — arrived in late February, in the form of David II's emissary. An aulder man, short of stature, but with a torso resembling a barrel of whisky. His name was Walter MacKinnon and Brogan hated him. Not for anything he had ever done to him personally, for he'd only just met the man.

Nay, he hated him for the havoc he wreaked upon his wife and their clan.

Brogan, Mairghread, and Reginald stood in the gathering room, in front of a blazing fire. Though it did very little to ease the cold ache in Brogan's bones.

Aymer had kept his promise.

In his hands, Brogan held the missive from David. 'Twas addressed to Mairghread and Brogan.

> *Upon hearing evidence from Aymer Mactavish, chief to Clan Mactavish, on our western shores, near Caimhainach, your attendance is nearby demanded to answer to the questions set before your beloved and esteemed King, David II, on or before the second day in May, the year of our lord, thirteen hundred and fifty eight. Ye will answer to the charges of intercession, disloyalty to your king, the honorable and beloved David II, interference in family matters, and the murder of James and Connell Mactavish.*

Mairghread was enraged. "He *still* accuses me of murdering them?" Clenching her hands into fists, she did her best to keep from railing against the emissary.

Barely able to keep his own temper in check, Brogan handed the letter to Reginald before turning to face Walter. "Ye go back to David and tell him we can no' possibly be there by the second day in May. Me wife is with child and I will do naught to endanger her safety or health, or that of our babe."

"The bloody hell he will!" Mairghread protested. "I *will* go before David and tell him the truth."

"Like hell ye will," Brogan argued, his face growing darker and darker with each beat of his heart.

"I will no' argue it, Brogan. I will go. I want this matter with Aymer settled once and for all. I will no' live me life in fear of what the coward will do next."

Reginald intervened on Brogan's behalf. "M'lady, Aymer has already killed more than one member of this clan. We can no' take a risk such as this."

With her brow knitted in confusion, she asked, "What do ye mean he has already killed more than one member of this clan?"

Realizing his mistake, he looked to Brogan for help.

Brogan raked an angry hand through his hair. "This might be a conversation best saved for later," he told her as he glanced at Walter.

Drawing her lips into a hard line, she glowered at Brogan.

"Ye go to David and tell him we *will* be there as he has requested," she spoke to Walter, but did not take her eyes off Brogan.

"'Tis too dangerous, Mairghread. It will take weeks to get to Stirling," he pointed out. The thought of her riding across the country in such harsh weather was enough to make him ill. But knowing Aymer could be lying in wait for an opportunity to bring her harm, was more than he could bear.

"Then we best leave at first light on the morrow."

THERE WAS NO AMOUNT OF ARGUING OR COMMON SENSE TO CHANGE Mairghread's mind. They both knew it. However, it didn't stop Brogan from trying.

They invited Walter to spend the night, which he accepted with much gratitude. He had been given a nice chamber, on the other side of the keep. Brogan did not want anything he needed to tell his wife from being misconstrued by over zealous ears.

After the evening meal, which was eaten mostly in silence, the retired to their chamber where Brogan began explaining his long held suspicions. He began with the easiest death; that of Archibald.

"Why did ye no' come to me sooner with this?" she ground out.

"Ye had just learned ye were with child," he told her. "I wanted no' to bring even a moment of worry."

"Good, lord! I be no' a child, Brogan!" she spat, throwing her hands up in the air. "I be the chief of this clan. I need to ken these things." She was beyond incensed.

"Ye be more than just the chief to me," he replied in a low tone. Clenching and unclenching his jaw, he too, was angry, but for far different reasons. "Ye be me wife."

"Aye, I be yer wife. Yer poor, weak wife who can no' possibly understand the workin's of the world. Nor can she survive a bit of bad news," she quipped sarcastically.

"I do no' think ye weak!" he barked.

"Then why do ye treat me as such?"

"Because I—" like a coward, he stopped before he could utter the words. He did not want them to be said in the heat of anger. "Because ye carry me child. Because I care. Because I want only to protect ye and keep ye safe."

Some of her anger fell away. While she understood his need to protect her, she still thought he was doing far too much of it of late. "Brogan, if ye worry I will take up drinkin' again," she began before he cut her off.

"Of course no'," he said. Feeling quite tired, and weary of arguing, he sat down in the chair by the fire and let out a deep breath. "I do no' worry over that."

"Then what *be* yer worry?"

Her question was met with silence, as he hung his head. To her, he looked like a lost soul. Then clarity dawned. "Ye be worried ye will lose me like ye did Anna?"

Without looking at her, he nodded his head. "Aye, that thought has crossed me mind once or twice of late."

For a brief moment, she was quite tempted to tell him she loved him. But the words, for reasons she could not quite grasp, would not come.

"If I promise ye I will do me best no' to do anything stupid, such as gettin' meself killed, will ye promise to quit worryin'?"

"I fear that would be as likely as me sproutin' wings and takin' flight," he murmured.

With a heavy sigh, she went to sit across from him. "Brogan, what else have ye no' told me?"

Again, more silence.

"If I do no' ken everythin', I can no' and will never be safe. I need to ken whom I can trust."

❧

OVER THE NEXT HOUR, BROGAN PURGED EVERY SECRET OR SUSPICION he'd been holding on to for months. All but one; his growing love for her.

'Twas easier to tell her he suspected 'twas Aymer who sliced Jame's throat than it was to tell her what was in his heart. And easier still, to tell her he and Reginald both agreed that Aymer was responsible deaths of her entire family, save for her mother and Lachlan who had both died from illness.

He felt no better for telling her. He worried she'd be so upset and distraught she would fall ill. He should have known better.

Angrily, she paced about the room, her lips pursed, her eyes naught more than slits. "How could we have been so stupid?" she asked, rhetorically of course.

"'Tis hard for the heart to accept someone we love and care for could be so evil," he told her.

"But Da? Me da was no' an ignorant man," she replied. "Certainly he must have suspected?"

"Like ye did?" he asked.

Never had she suspected Aymer of having anything to do with the deaths of her family. 'Twas not until Hargatha admitted to giving him the *Devil's Brew* that she realized he was an evil, greedy man. But this? This newfound knowledge — even if they were naught more than suspicions — was beyond even her wildest imagination.

"I should have seen it," she murmured angrily as she paced. "I should have seen it." She felt ten kinds a fool. Ignorant, dumb, and brainless.

Brogan stood to his full height, resisting the urge to stretch. "Do no' blame yerself, Mairghread. He be a cold, manipulative man."

"But I should have seen it. It should not have taken an outsider to bring me clarity," she seethed.

He hoped she did not mean it as it sounded. "Is that what ye think of me? An outsider?"

"Ye ken what I mean," she said with a roll of her eyes. "I have known the man all me life and could no' see what ye managed to in just a short while."

"Did ye love yer uncle?" he asked.

"At one time, I suppose I did."

"Sometimes, love can make ye blind to the truth. He be yer uncle. Why would ye suspect him of such things? An uncle is supposed to protect ye, love ye as if ye were his own. I ken, were I standin' in where ye are now, I would never suspect an uncle to do what yers has done. 'Twould be unfathomable."

Though she knew he was right, it did little to lessen her anger or disgust.

"Brogan, I need ye to promise me, here and now, that ye'll never keep such secrets from me again." There was no denying her hurt or anger. He saw it in her eyes and the way in which she looked upon him.

Letting out a sigh of defeat, he agreed. "Please, understand I meant only to protect ye."

"I ken that," she replied. "But sometimes, ye can protect a person too much."

She was right, of course. He went to her then and took her into his arms. "I promise, Mairghread."

He could only pray she believed him.

At dawn, the following morning, Mairghread and Brogan left the keep, heading east, for Stirling Castle. Saying goodbye to Walter, who was going to travel south on other matters, they parted ways at the gate. They took twenty-five men with them, mostly his own well-trained warriors. If Aymer were any good at strategizing attacks, he would split his men into two well-armed groups. 'Twould be easier to defend themselves against smaller numbers.

They still had received no word from the search party sent to look for Drayton. Brogan did not like going to meet the king without witnesses to help plead their cause. They discussed taking Hargatha, but Mairghread was certain she would end up killing the woman if she had to spend more than a few minutes alone with her. 'Twas for the auld woman's own safety they left her behind. Instead, they had her write down a statement of facts that they could present to David. Hopefully, 'twould be enough.

They travelled as fast as they could, considering Mairghread's current condition. He refused to allow her to seat her own horse. Instead, she rode, sitting in front of him, wrapped in furs and blankets.

By mid morning the following day, they were riding through the gates of his brother's keep. There had been no time to send word of their arrival, though he knew Ian would not mind.

They were ushered into the newly and finally completed keep. The gathering room was warm and thanks to Rose, 'twas also appealing and inviting.

Rose was sitting near the hearth, holding her newest bundle of joy when they walked in. Her eyes grew wide with surprise when she saw her brother-by-law and his wife.

"Och!" she cried as she struggled to get to her feet. Her immediate joy at seeing them here was quickly replaced by a look of genuine concern. "Why did ye no' send word?"

Brogan steered his wife to the fire. "I be sorry, Rose," he told her. "But it is a matter of most importance that I speak to Ian straight away."

She paled visibly, clearly shaken by his tone. "Mairghread? What be the matter? Why are ye travelin' in this weather?"

"I would prefer to explain it only once," Brogan interjected on his wife's behalf.

Rose studied him closely for a moment. Brogan stopped her before she could begin with her barrage of questioning. "Be it a boy or a girl?" he asked, nodding to the bundle in her arms.

Her worry evaporated instantly when she looked down at her babe. "Another son," she told him. "We have named him Aiden."

"That be a right good name," Brogan smiled down at the sleeping babe.

"Congratulations are in order fer ye as well, aye?" she asked, turning to look at Mairghread. "Och! Ye look frozen to the bone!" she cried.

Mairghread managed a wan smile. "'Tis the truth, I am."

Not wishing to wake her babe by yelling, she handed the sleeping infant off to Brogan. "I shall see to refreshments fer ye," she said as she grabbed a blanket from the back of the chair she had been sitting in. Quickly, she draped it over Mairghread's lap. "'Tis glad I am to see ye. How do ye fair?" She was, of course, referring to her babe. Worry etched into her brow.

"All be well in that regard," Mairghread said.

Blowing out a breath of relief, Rose patted her shoulder. "I shall return shortly."

No sooner had she left the room than Ian walked in. He wore a coat of fur — which Ian thought looked to be bear — and his head was covered in beaver.

"God's teeth!" he declared as he stomped snow from his boots. "Have ye had yer babe already?" he asked, stunned to see his brother with a babe in his arms.

"Nay, ye eejit!" Brogan remarked with a grin. "This be yer babe."

Shrugging off his coat, he hung it on a peg by the door. "I thought that was a bit fast," he said. "But then, ye be a Mackintosh. Who kens what wench ye—" he stopped as soon as he saw Mairghread sitting by the fire. His face burned crimson. "Why did ye no' tell us ye were comin'? And with yer wife?"

Stepping forward, he gave Brogan's shoulder a gentle squeeze before taking his son from him. "I do no' suppose ye just be visitin'," he whispered.

"Nay, 'tis no' a social call," Brogan answered.

Ian grunted his disproval. "Well, tell me what be the matter."

"If I tell ye before Rose gets back, she will skin me alive."

"Ye be right," Rose called to him as she reentered the room. "We will have somethin' warm fer ye to eat verra soon."

"Thank ye kindly, Rose," he replied.

"Well?" Ian asked. "What trouble have ye gotten yerself into?"

AFTER SETTLING ROSE INTO THE CHAIR AND RETURNING HER SON TO her, Brogan and Mairghread began to explain why they were here. They began with the summons from David.

"Jesu," Ian whispered in disbelief. "Certainly David can no' believe the man."

Brogan shrugged. "Who kens what lies Aymer has told him."

"I put nothin' past the man," Mairghread added. "He is pure evil."

Servants appeared, bearing bowls of rabbit stew, breads, cheeses, and other foods. Brogan brought his wife a bowl of stew and bread. "Eat," he said with a wink.

Too tired to argue, as well as far too hungry, she accepted the bowl and bread graciously.

Once the servants left, Brogan began to relate all that he knew or suspected as it pertained to Aymer. He left nothing out nor did he hold back any pertinent information. Standing beside his wife, with his hand on her shoulder, he told them everything.

Occasionally, Rose would gasp, pressing her fingers to her lips in horror or surprise. Ian kept his own thoughts hidden behind a stoic and calm facade.

Once he finished, he looked to Ian.

"How many men do ye need?" Ian asked.

"How many can ye spare? I worry over only two things," Brogan told him. "That Aymer will try to attack the keep in our absence, or, attack us on our way to Stirling."

Ian nodded thoughtfully before asking, "How many did ye leave at yer keep?"

"We have, mayhap, one hundred men," Brogan answered.

"And no' a one of them trained fer battle," Mairghread offered honestly.

Ian looked to Brogan for agreement on her assessment. "Aye, she be right."

Walking to stand behind his wife, Ian said, "I can send thirty good men to yer keep, on the off chance he does attack in yer absence. I would go with ye meself to Stirling, but I worry about leavin' Rose here alone, with two babes."

Rose lifted a pretty brow and craned her neck to look up at him.

"Yer brother needs ye more than we do," she told him. "We can send word to Alec, askin' fer reinforcements here."

Ian scoffed at the idea. "Alec leave his wife and babes? No' verra likely."

Brogan nodded in agreement. "Nay, from what Dougall told us when he visited in October, Alec Bowie will no' be leavin' Leona or their babes any time soon."

"Either way, he could send help to yer keep," Rose countered. She looked down at the sleeping babe. "Besides, I have John and Aiden to look after me."

In the end, Rose won out. Ian was going to Sterling Castle with his brother.

WITH MAIRGHREAD'S GROWING BELLY, IT TOOK THEM A LITTLE more than three weeks to reach Stirling Castle. Frequent stops were necessary, more for Brogan's peace of mind than her's.

With Ian, his men, and their own, more than fifty riders passed through the gates late one spring morning in late April. Mairghread, weary and with a growing belly, had never been more glad to be off a horse.

Brogan presented the castle guards with the missive from David. They had to wait for over an hour before he, Mairghread, Ian, and five guards were allowed inside. The rest of their group made camp near the outer walls.

One of David's men was sent to escort them to temporary quarters within. He was tall and slender with short-cropped dark hair and intense blue eyes. With him were four of David's guards, one just as menacing in countenance as the other.

"I am Donald," he said by way of introduction. "Follow me."

Brogan and Mairghread and their entourage fell in behind him, while his guards brought up the rear. He did not speak again as he led them down the long, winding corridors. They paid no attention to the opulence, to tapestries or furniture. Mairghread's only concern was getting this over with as soon as possible.

Stopping in front of a door, he said, "This will be yer chamber," he said to Brogan. "The rest of ye will be in the next room."

"When do we meet with David?" Mairghread asked.

"On the morrow," he replied. "He is no' seeing anyone this day."

"And what of Aymer Mactavish?" Brogan asked through gritted teeth. "Where might *he* be?"

Opening the door, the man waited for them to enter. Brogan wasn't going anywhere until he had an answer.

"I believe he is in chambers closer to David's," he replied drolly. "We will be posting two men outside each of your rooms."

Neither Ian or Brogan liked that idea. "You're puttin' us under guard?" Ian asked.

"I am only following orders," Donald replied. "If there is aught ye need, tell one of the men and they will see that ye have it." He didn't wait for more questions. With a slight inclination of his head, he hurried down the corridor.

They glared at the guards for a long moment before Mairghread let loose with a heavy sigh. "I am weary," she said, pushing open the door.

Giving up, Brogan, Ian, and their men followed her inside.

࿂

"YER WIFE LOOKS EXHAUSTED," IAN POINTED OUT. "AND SO DO YE."

Mairghread spotted the bed and went to it immediately and sat on the edge. "So what do we do now?" she asked.

Brogan grunted. "Ye will rest."

"And what will *ye* be doin'?" she asked with a tone of suspicion.

He cast a glance at Ian before answering. "Restin' with ye."

Satisfied with his answer, she said, "Good. I think we all need a bit of rest. Later, we can meet here to discuss our plan of action for the morrow."

"Ye need no' worry over it," he told her.

She glowered at him. "Need I remind ye that *I* was also summoned before the king?"

While he admired his wife's determination, he was still worried over her health and well-being. Dark circles lined her eyes, her skin pale, and her voice sounded weaker than was typical for her.

"We will be across the hall, should ye need us," Ian said with a smile. A moment later, he and the rest of their men were quitting the room.

Alone for the first time in weeks, she breathed a sigh of relief. Slowly, she got to her feet and stretched. "I can no' ever remember bein' this tired," she told him with a yawn. "Will ye rest a bit with me?"

Untying her laces, she stepped out of her dress and laid it across the back of a chair. Standing near the fire, in her white chemise, Brogan swallowed hard. Even heavy with child, she was still magnificent to look upon. Rubbing her hands together, she shivered. "Even with this fire, I still be cold."

He had a feeling it had more to do with her worry over what would happen on the morrow than the chill in the air. He went to her then, and wrapped his arms around her. "Mayhap, we should get ye under the blankets."

"I hope yer recommendation will include *ye* under those blankets with me," she said, leaning her head against his chest.

"I might be able to be persuaded," he said with a chuckle. "I could use some rest as well."

CONTENT AFTER THEIR LOVING, MAIRGHREAD WAS NESTLED IN THE crook of his arm. The embers in the hearth crackled and hissed as rain and wind crashed against the walls of the castle. She was glad for the safety she found lying next to Brogan.

Though she was exhausted, she found she could not sleep. Worry over what would happen on the morrow filled her with dread.

"We have no' discussed what we would do if David sets aside our marriage," she murmured.

"He will no'," Brogan told her with a yawn.

"But what if he does?"

He scratched his stubbled jaw. "David will no' set our marriage aside," he said. "Ye be worried for naught."

Lifting herself up on one elbow, she studied him closely. Although she was grateful for his strength she was beginning to wonder if he wasn't *too* self-assured. "How can ye be so certain?"

"Because, I ken David. He will no' side with Aymer."

Frustrated, she let out a heavy sigh. "Because ye ken him?" Her tone was filled with disbelief. "Just because ye ken a man does no' mean he will do what is right or just."

He let out his own frustrated breath and sat up. "David will favor his allies and friends, Mairghread, as I have told ye in the past. Aymer did no' show him any alliance whilst he was with the English. The Mackintoshes did. That alone works in our favor."

"But—"

He would not allow her protests to continue. "And I might also remind ye, that we have the truth on our side. David will see Aymer's accusations for what they be: naught more than lies told by a greedy and self-servin' man."

As much as she wanted to put all of her faith in him, she had too many doubts and concerns. Slipping from the bed, she wrapped a blanket around her shoulders and went to stand by the fire. "I want to believe ye," she said. "With all me heart I do. But we must think of our babe. If Aymer wins, I will no' go back to France with Courtemanche. I need to ken ye would fight to keep that from happening."

He was insulted that she thought he wouldn't. Angrily, he shot out of the bed, not bothering to cover his body with anything. He grabbed her shoulders and spun her around. "Think ye I would no' fight fer ye? Fer our babe?" he asked incredulously. "All I have done since we married was fight fer ye. I fought fer yer sobriety. I fought to build the wall, to have new weapons forged. I fought foul weather and mountains to bring ye here because that is what ye wanted!"

Tears welled in her eyes for she knew she had wounded him. "I ken ye have done all of that!" she cried. "But this is different. This is the king we speak of. If he sets our marriage aside, what then? Will ye fight him? 'Twould be treason."

"I would fight Satan and demons and dragons to keep ye safe. And aye, I would fight David as well. I do no' ken why ye doubt me."

There was no sound reason for doubting him, she knew it, in her heart. The tears fell without restraint. "I do no' doubt ye, but I be terrified of what will happen on the morrow. 'Twould be stupid no' to be afraid. I do no' ken David as ye say ye do."

"But ye ken *me*," he countered angrily.

"I worry over our babe, Brogan. I can no' stand the thought of losin' another bairn." The tears fell then, unrestrained and unchecked. That had been her biggest worry of late, that Aymer would make an attempt on her babe's life. And now, she worried she would be forced to set aside her marriage to Brogan and go to France with Courtemanche.

"I will no' allow anythin' to happen to ye or to our babe, Mairghread," he said, his tone softening with each tear of hers that fell. He took her hands in his and placed them over his heart. "As long as I still breathe, as long as me heart still beats, I will protect both of ye."

Mayhap 'twas the babe making her addlebrained, or the fact that they were here in Stirling and their entire future resting in the hands of a man she'd never met. No matter the cause, she still worried. "I ken that," she said.

"But still ye worry?" he asked with a raised brow.

"I can no' help it!" she cried.

He smiled then, and placed a tender kiss on her forehead. Pulling her into his arms, he held her tightly. "No matter what happens on the morrow, Mairghread, naught betwixt us will ever change. If we have to steal away to far away lands to be together, we will."

She giggled half-heartedly. "Right now, far away lands does no' sound so bad."

Patting her back gently, he pressed another kiss to the top of her head. "I will do whatever I must to see that we are together for all the rest of our days."

Wiping her tears on her shoulder, she said, "I do no' ken why ye be so kind to me all of the time." There were times she felt quite unworthy of his kindness.

He pushed her away enough so that he could look into her eyes. "Ye do no'?"

"Nay, I do no'," she answered. From the start, he'd been nothing but kind, even when she didn't deserve it.

"Because I love ye."

⁂

THE WORDS HE'D BEEN LONGING TO SAY WERE FINALLY RELEASED. He held his breath whilst he gauged her response. Dumbfounded, she looked up and into his eyes, silent, for what seemed like an eternity.

"How?" she finally muttered. "How can ye love me after all I have put ye through?"

'Twas not the reply he had hoped for. Deflated, he let go of her arms. "If ye be referrin' to what ye went through whilst still addicted to drink, or when ye were goin' through the *take aways,* that be all in the past. I do no' love the woman I married, I love the woman she has become."

She began to weep again, for new reasons. "Brogan, I—"

He held up his hand to stop her. "I ken ye do no' love me, Mairghread. I ken ye still love James. Still, I needed to give ye the words. No' to make ye feel better, but because holdin' them in these many months has been akin to carryin' a boulder on me back. 'Tis enough knowin' ye care about me. I will no' ask ye fer more."

She waited silently, with her shoulders back and her chin up. "Are ye quite finished?"

Furrowing his brow, he nodded.

"I did no' think it would ever be possible to love another man after James. I still love him, 'tis true and I will no' deny it."

Hanging his head, he turned his back to her. He didn't think he was strong enough to look her in the eye while she said what he was quite certain she was going to say; she didn't love him and doubted she ever could.

"There were many things I never thought possible until ye came into me life. I did no' think it possible to *live* again. To enjoy feelin' the sunshine on me face, or to laugh without guilt. Or to look forward to seeing the sunrise in the morn. All those things were lost to me, Brogan."

He heard the quiver in her voice. So he had helped her to live again. What did it matter if she could not *love* again? He knew he should not be upset or hurt, yet he was.

"I swear if ye do no' turn around to look at me, I will stab ye with yer own sword!" she exclaimed breathlessly.

Taking in a deep breath, he turned to face her. Tears streamed from her tired, red-rimmed eyes. He felt guilty for making her cry. "Mairghread, do no' fash yerself. I am a-"

"I love ye, Brogan Mackintosh!" she blurted out. "I have fer a long while but was afraid to tell ye fer fear ye could no' love me back." Rushing forward, she threw herself into his arms.

His heart swelled with adoration and joy. They had both been afraid of the very same thing; unrequited love.

"Wheest, love," he told her as he rubbed his hands up and down her back, hoping to smooth away her distress.

"I do no' ken why I keep cryin'," she admitted woefully.

Chuckling softly, he hugged her tighter. "'Tis all right, love. Ye can cry as much as ye want to."

She loved him and that was all that mattered.

BROGAN HAD AWAKENED LONG BEFORE DAWN WITH MAIRGHREAD nestled in the crook of his arm. He was enjoying the sound of her steady breaths, the way she smelled of lavender soap and all the loving they had done the night before.

With the knowledge that she did in fact love him, he had awakened with a new-found resolve. No matter what happened this day, he was even more determined to keep her safe and out of the clutches of her greedy uncle.

Although his father, John, had been a long time friend and ally of David, who knew what Aymer was up to. David was not above reproach, if the recent murmurings of his friendship with England were any indication. Rumor had it, it was growing more and more difficult to pay the ransom payments to England. A man in his position might be swayed if the bag of gold was big enough.

And Claude Courtemanche, being the son of a wealthy French nobleman, had enough gold to pursue just about anyone.

Silently, Brogan prayed David would be just and fair. Justice and doing what was right had to mean *something*, even to their king.

His quiet musings were disturbed when he saw a shadow enter the bedchamber. Carefully, so as not to disturb his wife or let the intruder know he was aware of his presence, he reached for the dirk he kept under his pillow. The shadow moved quickly, yet silently.

When he stepped in front of the fire, Brogan let out the breath he'd been holding. 'Twas his brother Ian.

Whispering, Ian said, "I have good news fer ye brother."

Brogan slid from the bed, covered his wife, and stepped away so they might talk without waking her.

"What is it?"

"Ye have a visitor."

AFTER THREE WEEKS OF TRAVELLING THROUGH MOUNTAINS, OVER hills, and through glens and valleys — in mostly rotten weather — the day Mairghread had been looking forward to, had finally arrived: They were meeting with King David II.

After a good night's rest, and a hot meal, she now stood in a room so big and grand, she thought she could have fit her entire keep within it. For the occasion, she chose a dark green gown of wool, with matching slippers. Over that, she wore the Mactavish plaid and Mackintosh brooch. After braiding her hair, she donned a gossamer veil with a plain silver circlet. All in all, she felt she was at least presentable to the king. Brogan remarked he thought she looked like a goddess.

'Twas a bleak and dreary morning, but she'd not allow the weather to dampen her spirits. Though her insides were shaking, she drew strength from her husband. He stood on her left, while Ian stood on her right.

Straight ahead was the throne on which their king would sit. 'Twas not made of gold as she had imagined as a child, but was made of hard wood, with an ornately carved back. Standing near it was the object of her consternation and the upheaval of her world; Aymer Mactavish.

Dressed in dark blue trews and an opulent silk tunic — from money he no doubt stole from her coffers. The burgundy overcoat looked to have been made from silk with gold stitching. It might have looked better on a king or nobleman, than Aymer. She found his air of righteousness appalling and immediately looked away. Though she could feel him staring at her, even after she turned away.

They waited for what seemed and eternity, before someone announced David's arrival. He entered from a small door near the hearth. Mairghread held her breath as she clung to Brogan's hand. "Wheest," he whispered. "He be just a man."

Mairghread prayed David hadn't heard him, for he might beg to argue.

The king took his seat as he looked out at the crowd. He was not at all what Mairghread had expected him to be. Light brown hair framed his long, bearded face. She thought his nose rather hawkish, being extraordinarily long, with a little hook at the end of it. He looked bored, as if he'd rather be *anywhere* else but here. She sent a silent prayer upward, asking for strength for herself and a kind ear on David's part.

When he spoke, his deep voice all but echoed off the walls. "Read the charges," he said with a wave of his hand.

An older man, of mayhap fifty, with salt and pepper hair and bowed legs, stepped forward. In his hands he held the parchment listing Aymer's false accusations. He cleared his throat before he began to speak. "The charges against Brogan Mackintosh are as follows: Interference with family matters, marrying one Mairghread Mactavish illegally and without permission from her uncle and guardian, Aymer Mactavish. Thievery of coin and resources belonging to Clan Mactavish. Abuse of Mairghread Mactavish. Abuse of the members of the aforementioned clan, by forcing its people to work from dawn to dusk, in all manner of inclement weather, without proper sustenance or recompense. Disregard of rules set in place by Aymer — the rightful heir and chief of clan Mactavish — during his absence."

The man paused long enough to take a deep breath and glance out at the crowd.

"The charges against Mairghread Mactavish are as follows: Disobedience, excessive consumption of alcoholic beverages which thereby left her unable to make sound decisions. She is also accused of the murder of her first husband, James, and their three week-old son, Connell, on the third day of April, in the year of our lord thirteen hundred fifty-four where she willfully, whilst in a drunken rage, hacked to death her infant son before turning her knife to her husband and slicing his throat."

A collective gasp could be heard all around her, which soon turned to loud murmurs. Knowing she was innocent of these charges helped strengthen her resolve albeit only slightly. Had Brogan not been holding on to her, she might have fallen to her knees.

"Quiet," David ordered in a quiet voice. The room hushed almost instantly. He still looked bored, as his elbow was rested on one arm of his chair, his index finger pressed against his cheek.

Clearing his throat once again, the man continued to read. "Her abuse of alcohol has rendered her incapacitated on countless occasions, rendering her unable to make sound choices. That she did willfully and with disobedience, marry Brogan Mackintosh without her uncle's approval or knowledge."

He rolled the parchment up and went to stand a few steps away from David.

David sat up, looked directly at Brogan and Mairghread and motioned them forward.

Protectively, he led her forward. With one hand on her back and holding her hand, he helped her to curtsey, then he knelt before his king.

"Rise," David said.

'Twas difficult for her to get up and down, what with her large belly, but she managed to do so with grace and aplomb.

"Brogan Mackintosh, what say ye to these charges?"

Without blinking an eye, he replied, "'Tis horse shite, yer grace."

Mairghread felt the blood rush from her face as she gasped at her husband's reply. The crowd laughed and the king chuckled. In wide-eyed astonishment, she looked at her husband. Her expression said she thought him mad for speaking to the king in such a manner.

"Ye be John Mackintosh's son, all right."

Brogan smiled. "Aye, I am. He sends his regards, yer grace. He wanted to be here, but the Cameron's have been raidin' the borders of late."

"Still feudin' with the Camerons?" he asked with a raised brow. "I will deal with that later. Fer now, we have some serious accusations ye need to answer to."

'Twas then he looked at Mairghread. "Ye be the woman I have heard so much about of late?"

Stunned, she managed an awkward nod and stammered, "I be Mairghread Mactavish, wife of Brogan Mackintosh." She took in a deep breath before going on. "And the rightful heir and chief of Clan Mactavish, yer grace."

His bushy eyebrows perked up. "Ye be the chief of Clan Mactavish?"

"Aye, yer grace."

Aymer stepped forward then, with a shake of his head, looking on her with pity-filled eyes. "'Tis just as I told ye, yer grace. She is often given to delusions of grandeur."

Brogan's jaw ticked, his eyes turning to slits. "She speaks the truth and ye well ken it."

Keeping his eyes focused solely on David, Aymer said, "As I have told ye, yer grace, she drinks too much and now believes she be the chief. 'Tis sad, 'tis truly sad." He gave a slow shake of his head for added emphasis.

"I warned ye once no' to speak ill of me wife," Brogan told him. "I will no' remind ye again."

As if he were surprised, Aymer stood taller, and pulled his shoulders back. "Ye mean when ye threatened to kill me with yer bare hands?"

"Nay," Brogan replied cooly. "When I *promised* I would kill ye with me own two hands."

Aymer threw his hands up in feigned frustration and turned back to David. "He admits to threatening me life, yer grace. How is a man to protect his only flesh and blood?"

"Protect her?" Brogan asked through gritted teeth. "Is that what ye call it? Tearin' down the outer wall? Hiding weapons? Givin' her husband a poison that would make him lose his grip on reality? By tryin' to force her into marrying one of the most cruel and sadistic men ever to grace God's earth? Is that how ye protect yer only flesh and blood?"

For the first time since meeting the man, Brogan saw him flinch. 'Twas brief and barely perceptible, but 'twas a flinch all the same. "He is just as mad as me niece, yer grace," Aymer said with a sneer.

"Poison?" David asked as he leaned forward in his chair. "What is this poison ye speak of?"

Aymer scoffed openly. "'Tis naught but a lie, yer grace."

"Like hell it is."

That comment came from Mairghread. All eyes turned to her then. Aymer was furious and Brogan looked quite proud. But her king? He seemed to be amused by her outburst, for he was grinning.

"Tell me, Mairghread, about this poison," David requested, his grin fading as he took on a more serious stance.

"Yer, grace, 'tis naught but a fantasy made up by—"

"I do no' believe I was speakin' to ye, Aymer," David said, glowering at him for a long moment before turning back to Mairghread. "Continue."

Clearing the growing knot from her throat, she stood a bit taller. "Aymer gave me husband, James, a tisane called *Devil's Brew*," she began.

David sat up with a jolt. "*Devil's Brew?*" he asked, looking appalled. "That stuff can kill a man."

"Or make that man behave in an insane manner for hours and hours," she added.

David glanced angrily at Aymer before turning back to Mairghread. "And ye say yer uncle gave that concoction to James?"

"Aye, m'laird, he did. And I have witnesses to prove it." She looked right at Aymer when she spoke.

"A crazy auld woman?" Aymer's tone was challenging.

"Among others," she said before turning back to David. "Me uncle had me all but convinced that it had been *I* who killed me babe and husband and that I was so overcome with guilt that I tried to kill meself. I could no' remember all that happened that day, yer grace, until recently. Now, I ken the truth."

Intrigued and beyond curious, David leaned forward in his chair, hanging on to her every word. "What is the truth?"

"I loved me husband and son, yer grace. More than anything or anyone else in this world. They were me entire life. I did no' kill them and I certainly did no' stab me ownself."

"Then who killed them?"

"James and Aymer."

A COLLECTIVE GASP CAME FROM THE CROWD BEHIND THEM. THE onlookers were just as surprised at her story as David was.

"James and Aymer?" he asked with a good measure of stunned disbelief.

Aymer began to protest her accusations, but David put a stop to it immediately. "One more outburst from ye and ye will find yerself in the dungeon."

Brogan watched as the blood rushed from Aymer's face.

Mairghread took a deep steadying breath and nodded. "Aye, yer grace. Because James was in a fit of rage from unknowingly drinkin' the *Devil's Brew* that was meant for me, he killed our son. Then he turned the knife on me."

"Wait," David said. "Are ye sayin' the brew was meant fer ye?"

"Aye, yer grace, it was."

His bushy brows furrowed. "Then who killed James?"

It seemed everyone in the room was holding their breaths.

"Aymer. Aymer sliced James' throat."

Another stunned gasp and murmurs flittered from the crowd. Drawing strength from Brogan, as well as the fact that David seemed keenly interested in her tale, she went on. "Aymer was about to kill me when Gertie and Tilda came into the room. They be me maids, yer grace. They had heard me scream something fierce and came to see what was the matter." Most of what she had just told him was the truth. Only part of it was conjecture. She could not remember seeing Aymer slice James's throat, but 'twas the only thing that made sense. If Aymer could accuse her unjustly, then she ought to be able to do the same.

Her blood ran cold when she saw the flash of fear and surprise in Aymer's eyes. In that instant, she knew she had not been wrong.

David's lips drew into a thin, hard line as he looked at Aymer. The entire room fell silent. "What say ye, Aymer?"

"'Tis a lie," he stammered angrily. "She killed them, then turned the knife on herself. And now she wishes to blame me so that she might take over as chief."

"But I *am* the chief," she argued. "According to our laws, our traditions, and me father's will. Which, yer grace, Aymer has refused to produce to anyone."

"Where be this will?" he asked, pinning Aymer in place with a hard glare.

"'Twas destroyed," Aymer said indignantly.

David did not look convinced. "How inconvenient for all concerned."

Aymer swallowed hard, his eyes darting from David to Mairghread, and back again. "She is tryin' to place the blame for her own bad behavior on me, yer grace. It still does no' change the fact that she is a drunkard and a bigamist."

IT TOOK EVERY OUNCE OF SELF-CONTROL TO KEEP HIS TEMPER IN check. Clenching his jaw, drawing his hands into fists, Brogan was furious. "How can a widow be a bigamist?" he ground out. From David's confused expression, 'twas the first time he was hearing this accusation as well.

Aymer, feeling as though he once again had the upper hand, gave him a furtive glance before turning back to David. "I be no' speakin' about James. I speak of another."

"That is a lie!" Mairghread exclaimed. For a fleeting moment, she thought mayhap, he was telling the truth. There were many things she had done whilst drunk that she could not recall later. Had she unknowingly married the Frenchman? Dread settled into the pit of her stomach.

Speaking over the growing din, Aymer said, "She was married by proxy, to Claude Courtemanche."

The room erupted then into stunned surprise and even outrage. Ian had to physically restrain Brogan, to keep him from killing Aymer with his bare hands. Mairghread stood on shaking legs as her worry piled on top of dread.

"Ye married yer own niece off to *him?*" David asked in wide-eyed disbelief.

"By proxy, yer grace," Aymer said, as he tried to hide a smile.

"That be a bloody lie!" Brogan shouted.

David had to call for quiet three times before everyone finally settled down. He'd turned red with anger and frustration. "One more outburst and I will have ye all removed," he called out to the crowd of onlookers.

Once the room quieted, he looked upon Aymer with a stern countenance before taking his seat again. "When did this marriage by proxy take place?" he asked.

"More than a year ago," he replied drolly.

David turned to gauge Mairghread's reaction, but was speaking to Aymer. "And when did ye let yer niece know of this marriage by proxy?"

"The very day it happened, yer grace. But she might no' remember, fer she was verra drunk."

Mairghread stepped forward to face her uncle. "Ye lie," she told him.

"Nay, lass, I do no' lie."

"So ye told me? Only once?" she said, challenging his accusation. "When did this supposedly take place? And where be this proxy now? Was it too, destroyed, along with me father's will?"

"After Claude visited our keep nearly two years ago," Aymer told her.

Tired of being held back and quiet, Brogan shook himself from Ian's grip. "Ye had more than one occasion in that time to tell Mairghread what ye did," he said through gritted teeth. "But ye claim ye only told her once, whilst she was too drunk to remember?" He looked to David then. "Yer grace, ye can no' believe such lies."

David was growing angrier with each passing moment. "Do no' tell me what I can or can no' believe," he said.

For the first time, Brogan was worried. Worried that Aymer had paid David off, and that no matter what evidence they laid before him, he was going to side with Aymer. A shiver of fear tickled the back of his neck, making his hair stand on end.

"Again, I ask to see the proxy," Mairghread demanded.

Aymer smiled, as if he'd just won a great battle. "Claude has it," he said.

The crowd parted as Claude Courtemanche made his way from the back of the room to stand before the King of Scotland.

TERROR ALL BUT SEIZED HER HEART. BROGAN, SEEING THE FEAR IN her eyes, pulled her behind him and took a protective stance. He'd kill Courtemanche and Aymer before he let either one of them lay so much as a finger on her.

Bowing with a flourish, Courtemanche smiled. "It is a pleasure to finally meet you, your grace."

David was not impressed. "Ye have the proxy?" he asked, refusing to return the man's smile.

"I do," he replied as he pulled a small scroll from his purple jacket. Bowing again, he handed the scroll to the man who had read the charges.

He read it before handing it off to David. Reading it thoroughly, he looked up only once, before handing it back to his man.

Peering around Brogan to look at Mairghread, he said, "And ye claim ye were unaware of this marriage?"

"I knew nothin' of it, yer grace, I swear it," she replied nervously.

"Again, she was too drunk to remember," Aymer said.

Consternation was etched in David's face. "And ye only thought to tell her once?" he asked. "Ye claim she drank heavily, why would ye no' tell her again?"

Sneering at Mairghread, he replied, "'Tis difficult to find her in a sober moment."

"She has no' had so much as a drop of strong drink in more than six months," Brogan countered. "And why did ye no' mention this when ye last visited the keep last *Samhain?*"

"I was so surprised to learn she had married ye, that it must have slipped me mind," Aymer replied, sounding bored with Brogan's questions.

Brogan raised a dubious brow. "Be it yer contention that ye did no' ken of our marriage until last Samhain?"

"Of course I did no' ken about it until last Samhain," Aymer responded angrily. "I did no' ken about it until I returned with Claude."

Brogan smiled at him, then to David. "He be lyin', and I can prove it."

IAN LEFT AT BROGAN'S BARELY PERCEPTIBLE NOD. BROGAN TURNED his attention back to David and Aymer. "Yer grace, I tell ye the proxy presented to ye this day is false. I also tell ye that Aymer has lied to ye when he says he had no knowledge of me marriage to Mairghread until he returned to our keep last *Samhain,* and I can prove it."

Aymer laughed at Brogan's declaration. "Prove it? How?"

"Do ye remember the messengers Mairghread sent to ye, the day after we wed?"

Still believing he was going to win this day, Aymer offered a shrug of indifference. "I remember no such messengers."

Lifting a brow, Brogan said, "Archibald and Drayton? Ye do no' remember them?"

"Archibald? Be he the lad who hanged himself?" Aymer replied, still feeling quite in charge. "And Drayton, did ye no' die recently during a drunken brawl in Inverness?"

"Archibald did die, but no' by his own hand," he said before turning his attention back to David. "The day after Mairghread and I were wed, she sent two messengers to find Aymer and to tell him of our marriage. Aymer, ye see, was on his way to France, to collect Claude Courtemanche. With him, were a dozen Mactavish men, as well as the dowry. They were to be married upon their return to the Mactavish keep. No' once did he ever mention a marriage by proxy. No' even to the messengers."

David's patience was growing thin. "Get to yer point, Mackintosh."

"Less than a week after he visited our keep, Archibald Mactavish was found hangin' in our armory. 'Twas meant to look like a suicide. Supposedly, he hanged himself. But there was somethin' missin': A chair or a stool with which to lift himself off the floor. The lad was far too short to wrap the belt around his neck twice, then somehow manage to get it across the beam, lift himself several inches off the floor, and tie the belt around the beam twice, without the aid of chair, stool, or ladder. Unless, of course, he knew how to fly."

Light laughter broke out amongst the crowd. They were silenced immediately by a scowl from David.

A quick glance at Aymer proved his theory. He had paled visibly.

"As fer Drayton Mactavish, he be no' dead, yer grace."

"That be impossible!" Aymer shouted. "The lad died naught more than three weeks ago, in a drunken brawl!"

Cocking his head to one side, Brogan asked, "And how did ye come to this knowledge afore anyone else?"

Aymer looked fit to be tied, his face purple with rage. "Since I be the chief of clan Mactavish, it behooves me to ken such things."

"Afore anyone else kens it?" Brogan asked again. "And how did ye come by this information?"

Gritting his teeth, Aymer said, "I still have ties to the clan, Mackintosh."

"Ties or spies?" he asked with a sneer of his own.

The crowd parted for a second time, as Ian, three of their guards, and one very afraid looking young lad, made their way through. Brogan watched as Aymer's eyes grew wide with astonishment.

"Yer grace, this be Drayton Mactavish of clan Mactavish," Brogan said.

The young man looked positively terrified as he bowed before his king.

David ordered him to rise, and studied him closely for a long moment. "Aymer, be this the young man ye claimed was dead?"

Swallowing hard, he could only nod his head as he stared at the young man in question.

Brogan looked at David. "If I may, yer grace, have the lad tell ye about the day he and Archibald met with Aymer Mactavish."

"Ye may," David replied.

"Drayton, please tell yer king about yer mission to find Aymer last summer," Brogan said.

The lad's adam's apple bobbed up and down before he could find the words to speak. "Well, our lady, lady Mairghread, she asked Archibald to go in search of her uncle. Archibald asked me to go with him, fer God only kent how long it would take, ye ken."

"And did ye find Aymer?" Brogan asked.

"Aye, m'laird, we did. Just outside of London. Aymer and them had made camp, ye ken. Though we was both right scared about tellin' him and givin' him our lady's letter."

"That is a lie!" Aymer cried out. "I never met with this *boy* or the one named Archibald."

"Ye had yer chance, Aymer," David told him. "I want to hear what this lad has to say."

A light sheen of sweat broke out on Drayton's forehead and upper lip. Brogan imagined the poor young man was terrified of being dragged before the king. "Please, tell us what happened when ye met with Aymer."

"Like I says, we found them encamped just outside London. I was already as nervous as a sinner in church, because we was in England. I had never been so far from home before, yer grace."

"How did ye find England?" David asked with a playful twinkle in his eye.

Confused, the lad said, "Well, we just rode south, yer grace, until the people started talkin' funny."

David found the boy's confusion and honesty refreshing and laughed heartily at his reply. Everyone in the room, save for Aymer and Courtemanche, laughed.

Not understanding why they found it all so humorous, the boy looked up to Brogan. Brogan offered him a comforting smile. "And ye were able to meet with Aymer?" he asked, prodding the lad to continue.

"Aye, we did, m'laird," he said with a rapid nod of his head. Turning to David, he said, "So Archibald gave Aymer our lady's letter and message. Told him, he did, that she had married Brogan Mackintosh."

"And what did Aymer say or do?"

"He was right angry, he was. Punched Archibald in the face twice, before turnin' his anger on me. Cracked one of me ribs, he did." Absentmindedly, he rubbed his left rib with his fingertips, as if he could still feel the pain.

"Did Aymer say or do anything after that?" Brogan asked.

"Well, after screamin' that our lady was ungrateful, and callin' her names I will no' repeat in front of her, he wrote a letter back to her. I never saw him that angry, and we had seen him angry plenty of times. All the while he was writin', he kept sayin' she had ruined everythin', meanin' our lady. That he did no' ken how he would explain it to the Frenchman."

Brogan was pleased that thus far, Drayton's story matched everything that Archibald had recounted last fall.

"And did anythin' else happen?" Brogan asked, growing more and more pleased by the moment.

Drayton went pale, uncertainty awash in his eyes. "Do I have to tell him that?"

Brogan had listened to the lad's tale earlier that morn, after Ian had taken him to him. "Aye, ye do."

"But he be the king," the lad pleaded.

David sat up straighter in his chair. "Tell me."

Looking David straight in the eye, he stammered for a moment. "He said he did no' care if he had to lie or bribe ye or even the pope, he was goin' to get the marriage to Brogan set aside, so that he could marry our lady off to Courtemanche. He said there was too much at stake."

The entire room drew their breaths at once. David was furious. "Be that true?" he asked Aymer.

Aymer looked as though he had seen a ghost. "N-nay, yer grace!" he exclaimed.

Looking at Courtemanche, David said, "And what part do ye play in all this?"

The Frenchman looked no better than Aymer. "I-I did not know she had married the Scot until we arrived at their keep last autumn. 'Twas Aymer's idea to forge the proxy. I went along with it, because he promised her to me."

Bolting to his feet, David called for his guards. "Take him away," he ordered. While Aymer protested vociferously about the injustice being shown him, David looked at Brogan and Mairghread. "I find ye both innocent of all charges. Yer marriage stands." With a wave of his hand, he bid them good day before quitting the room.

Mairghread all but collapsed into Brogan's arms. A few people in the crowd cheered as Ian and the rest of their men put up a protective wall around them.

"Thank, God!" Mairghread cried against Brogan's chest.

He kissed the top of her head. "'Tis all over now, lass."

Hugging him tightly, she said, "Brogan, I want to away this place at once. I want to go home."

There would not be a request he would deny her for a very long while.

They did not wait to find out what punishment David would bestow upon Aymer. Within an hour of the proceedings they were on their way back to Mactavish lands.

Chapter Twenty-Seven

Brogan and Mairghread returned to their keep three short weeks after leaving Stirling. David had ordered Aymer put to death, by beheading. Knowing he was no longer a threat left them feeling safer than they had in a very long while.

Reginald had met them at the steps with news that Hargatha had died — of natural causes they assumed — just a week before their return. Only two people had attended her funeral: Reginald and auld Seamus. None were apparently mourning her loss.

They had been home less than two days when Mairghread's birthing pains started. Because this was not her first time giving birth, she was not at all worried or nervous. She had experienced false pains three times before actually giving birth to Connell. With two weeks left until she was due, she decided she would wait before telling Brogan. Besides, he'd not left her side in weeks. Although she was quite glad for his attention, and loved him dearly, she was in desperate need of a respite.

She enlisted Reginald's help later in the afternoon. "I love him, I truly do," she told him. "But I would like to be able to use the chamber pot without him askin' me if all be well."

Unable to deny his lady anything, and believing all was well, Reginald agreed. "I shall take him to count horses."

Knowing that could take most of the afternoon, she breathed a sigh of relief. "Thank ye, Reginald," she exclaimed with a hug.

Convincing Reginald to aid her was significantly easier than getting Brogan to agree to leave her side for more than a moment.

"I am well, love," she told him with a smile. "We have two weeks before our babe is due. I promise, I'll do naught but sit here with Gertie and Tilda and sew."

Eying her closely, he finally relented. "But if aught changes, ye will send fer me at once."

The urge to roll her eyes was great. "Why? So that ye can pace up and down the hallway for hours and hours until our babe is here?"

"Who says I will no' be right beside ye the entire time?" he asked with a raised brow.

"Och!" she said with a giggle. "'Twould be the death of Gertie and Tilda, fer certain, to have ye there at the birth."

"I was there at the makin' of this babe," he teased playfully. "I do no' see why I can't be there for the birth."

She could not help herself. Rolling her eyes, she said, "There are some things a man is no' meant to see and the birthin' of his bairn be one of them."

PAYING OFF THREE GUARDS TO HELP EFFECT HIS ESCAPE WAS FAR easier than bribing the king. And far less expensive. Within two days of being tossed into the dungeon, he was free, and meeting with Courtemanche in a small forest a few miles outside of Sterling.

A bag of gold and the promise that he could do whatever he wished with Mairghread was all it took to convince the Frenchman to help him. In short order, Aymer Mactavish was soon heading back to Mactavish lands with his eager French friend. And twenty well-paid, well-trained mercenaries.

Because they were not travelling with a woman heavy with child, they were able to reach the keep long before Mairghread and Brogan.

For more than a week, they camped away from the border, in a dense forest. The mercenaries were used to living in harsh elements. Courtemanche however, was not. He complained incessantly. Aymer ignored the man's protests for there was far too much at stake. He needed the Frenchman's resources if he were to succeed at someday overthrowing David.

Aye, the Mactavish seat had been his primary goal for a very long while. But 'twas just a stepping stone to what he truly wanted: the kingdom of Scotland.

For years now, he'd been forging allegiances with other clans who were opposed to David. With the Frenchman's backing and coin, they would be able to move forward with his plan within two short years. He could almost feel the weight of the crown resting on his head when he thought of it.

But in order to gain Courtemanche's loyalty, he had to give him Mairghread. She was a small sacrifice in his grander scheme. He cared not what plans Courtemanche had for her. But they had to get her out of Scotland first.

'Twas a bright and sunny afternoon when they finally set their plan into motion.

Because of their false sense of safety, the gate was left open during the day to make it more accessible for clan members to come and go as needed. Additionally, Aymer still had loyal friends inside the Mactavish keep. Donning monks robes, he and one of his mercenaries walked through the open gate without anyone questioning their presence.

Soon, ye will have all ye have worked for, he mused silently as he walked through the gates. His heart beat against his chest with excitement. They would be taking Mairghread from here today, allow her to birth the child along the way back to France. He'd simply leave the babe to the elements, and leave the world to think she had died. With her death he could then take his rightful and God-given place as chief, which would in turn lead him to the throne of all of Scotia.

For decades now, he'd been working diligently to rest the Mactavish seat from his brother and his direct descendants. Killing them off had been easy and he possessed no regrets, for he was doing God's work.

His path was righteous.

❧

With Brogan away for the afternoon, Mairghread tried to enjoy a nap. But the pains in her back were persistent. They'd been plaguing her off an on for several hours since morning. But now, as they day drew on, they became steadier and gradually more intense and moved to her abdomen.

Mayhap these were not the same false pains she'd experienced with her first bairn. Deciding 'twas best to err on the side of caution, she called for Gertie and Tilda. They were hovering over her like mother hens in short order.

"Now, do no' panic or cry out," Mairghread warned them when they came bustling into her room.

Gertie's eyes turned to slits. "Ye can no' begin with 'do no' panic or cry out', fer that is sure what we will do!"

Of course she could not expect calm at a time like this. "Why did I even bother to call fer ye?" she murmured under her breath. *Because no matter how frustratin' they be, ye love them.*

Another pain came, twisting and intense. She waited until it passed before speaking again. "Quietly, and as calmly as ye can, I need one of ye to fetch Martha."

Almost instantly, they realized what was happening. Tears filled both their eyes as they each beamed happy smiles. "Och! It be yer time!" Gertie shouted.

Rolling her eyes, Mairghread was already exasperated with them. "I said *quietly and calmly*," she reminded them. "'Twill likely be hours before this babe is here."

Moving into action, Tilda went to the cupboard and removed the birthing basket. "How often are ye having pains?"

"I'd say two every quarter of an hour," Mairghread replied as she pressed a hand to her back. "Like I say, 'twill be hours before this babe is here."

Gertie was too busy crying to help. "It be a glorious day," she murmured. "A glorious day indeed!"

"How bad be the pain?" Tilda asked, taking charge.

"No' too bad, but we all ken that will change," Mairghread said with a light giggle.

Tilda pulled the small table closer to the bed and set the basket on top. "Gertie, I think ye should go below stairs and have someone fetch Martha."

Gertie wiped her eyes on the sleeve of her dress. "'Tis a glorious day," she repeated.

Tilda and Mairghread exchanged knowing glances. "Never mind," Tilda said. "I shall fetch her. More likely than no', Gertie will be tellin' one and all that yer time draws near. We'll no' get a moments peace if Brogan finds out just yet."

Mairghread had to smile at Tilda's insight. "Ye be right. He says he wants to be with me durin' the birth."

Tilda froze in place. Gertie was aghast. "Nay!" Gertie exclaimed. "Be he more tetched than we realized?"

Laughing at their horrified expressions, Mairghread said, "I have been wonderin' that meself."

"Then we shall make certain he does no' find out just yet," Tilda told her. "I shall go get Martha meself."

It seemed to Mairghread that much time had passed since Tilda left. Of course, that could be attributed to the fact that her pains were growing more intense and closer together, as well as the fact that Gertie couldn't seem to pull herself together. The poor woman kept bursting into tears of joy.

"Gertie, will ye please stop yer cryin'?" Mairghread asked as she held onto the back of a chair for support.

"I can no' help it," she said with a smile. "I be just so happy!"

Yer happiness is goin' to drive me to madness, Mairghread thought as another pain came.

"'Tis a girl," Gertie told her. "I can feel it in me bones. A right bonny wee lass she will be, as well."

At the moment, Mairghread did not care if it were a boy or girl. All

427

she wanted was for the child to be healthy and to live a long, happy life. "What do ye think is keepin' Tilda and Martha?" she asked.

"Mayhap Martha be helpin' Joanne, wife of Phillip," Gertie said. "I think she was due to have her bairn any day now."

The thought of not having Martha at her side nearly sent her into a fit of panic. Only because she knew Brogan would be fit to be tied and that would leave her alone with Gertie and Tilda. Taking in deep, steadying breaths, she refused to think of the *what ifs*. Worrying over all the things that could go wrong would serve no purpose.

Gertie was ringing her fingers together, no doubt lost in worrying. "Gertie, please, do no' fash yerself. With or without Martha, this babe will be born." She tried to sound cheerful.

"I ken ye be right, lass," Gertie replied in a soft voice.

"But that still does no' stop ye from worryin', does it?" Mairghread said with a smile.

"I fear it does no'," Gertie said.

Wanting to lighten her somber mood, Mairghread giggled. "Mayhap ye should go fetch Brogan."

That was enough to bring her out of her current state of dread. "Och! Do no' say such things!"

"Then stop yer worryin'," Mairghread told her. "Else I will go fetch him meself."

An hour had passed and Tilda had yet to return with Martha. Mairghread refused to worry. Instead, she would rejoice in the fact that soon, she would be holding Brogan's bairn in her arms. He had confessed to her once that he had thought he'd never be a father. And although he was overjoyed with the prospect of impending fatherhood, he was secretly quite worried. She had refused, however, to allow him to be consumed with self doubt. He was, she reassured him, going to be a wonderful father.

Her pains had not changed much since Tilda had left. They were still steady, coming at regular intervals. Although she wished for it all to be over soon so that she could hold this precious bairn who had been kicking her ribs for weeks now, there was a small part of her who wanted to keep him safely ensconced in her womb. 'Twas silly, she knew, but no harm could come to him whilst he was still tucked away within her.

Gertie had quit worrying and set to work finishing what Tilda had started. She tied lengths of heavy yet soft rope at the edge of the bed. When the time came to push, Mairghread could grab hold of the rope for strength and balance.

Next, she stripped the blankets from the bed and replaced the linens with older, worn ones. "No sense in ruin' perfectly good sheets, aye?" she said as she tucked the corners in.

Mairghread was not listening to her. Another pain hit, stronger than the last few. The tall backed chair was quickly becoming her friend. Each time a birthing pain hit, she would lean over, with her head down, whilst she grasped the back.

While working through her pain, a knock came at the door.

"Well it be about time!" Gertie exclaimed as she went to the door.

Mairghread was too busy trying to keep from breaking the chair in half to greet the midwife properly.

An eery silence fell over the room. Gertie wasn't chastising Tilda or Martha for taking so long. Instinct warned that something was amiss, but what, she could not say. Slowly, she stood straighter, still clutching the chair, and turned to see what had stunned Gertie into muteness.

Standing just inside the door was Aymer Mactavish and a man she'd not ever seen before. Aymer was sneering at her, while the man held a large blade to Gertie's neck.

"Scream and she dies."

HER WORLD BEGAN TO SPIN AS SHEER TERROR ENVELOPED Mairghread. *Nay! This can no' be!*

Too stunned to speak, all she could do was watch in horror as Aymer Mactavish walked into her room.

"Did ye miss me?" he asked sarcastically.

Bile rose in her throat. She could make no sense of how the man who was supposed to have been beheaded weeks ago, was standing in her bedchamber.

"Me thinks she be surprised to see me," he said, speaking over his shoulder to the large, menacing man.

"What do ye want?" she stammered with wide, horrified eyes.

"What do I want?" he asked, feigning surprise. "I thought ye already knew what I wanted."

Swallowing back the bile, she tried to sound stronger than she actually felt. "Leave now, Aymer, and I will make certain Brogan does no' kill ye."

"Brogan?" he asked with a raised brow. "He will no' be back fer hours. I be told he is off with Reginald and Seamus, countin' horses."

It felt as though the floor beneath her feet had suddenly disappeared. She had to grab the chair again, to keep from falling over.

"Ye are comin' with me, Mairghread," Aymer said as he grabbed her arm. "Claude has missed ye."

Claude? Nay, nay, nay! She wanted to scream, to lash out, to fight. But there was no doubt in her mind that the strange, dark man would kill Gertie in the blink of an eye. Before she could tell him there was no way on God's earth she was leaving with him, Gertie spoke up.

"She can no' go anywhere, ye fool! It be her time!"

Aymer spun to look at her. "What are ye rambling' on about ye old bat?"

"Her pains started this morn. Martha has been sent for," Gertie explained, using a harsh tone.

Aymer studied each woman for a short moment. "It matters no'," he said. "She be comin' with me."

"I can no' leave!" Mairghread cried. "I am goin' to have me bairn soon."

Aymer grabbed her arm more forcefully. "I do no' care how soon," he hissed. "We leave now."

Gertie squeaked when the man twisted her arm and pressed the knife even harder against her neck. "Please, laird," she begged Aymer. "Please, do no' harm our lady or her babe."

Aymer sneered at her. "Shut up, auld woman! Or I shall kill her now and let ye watch her die!"

Tears streamed down Gertie's wrinkled cheeks. Closing her eyes tightly, she could not bear to watch as Aymer pulled Mairghread from the room.

☙

BROGAN FELT HE'D BEEN AWAY FROM HIS WIFE LONG ENOUGH. BUT Reginald and Seamus were insistent that they needed his help.

"Just one more cottage," Reginald promised. "It be less than an hour away."

"An hour?" he exclaimed. They had already been gone for hours. Hours that seemed like days to a man much in love with his wife. "Nay," he said. "Ye may go on without me. I am returnin' to me wife."

Some might call it naught more than jitters attributed to impending fatherhood. No matter the reason, he'd begun to feel uneasy about being away so long. He thought back to his sister-by-law Rose and how she had conspired with the women of their clan to keep Ian away for an hour or two when her time drew near. His brother loved her, of that, there was no doubt. But even Brogan thought he had hovered too much over Rose during those last few days before she gave birth to John. Back then, he believed his brother was naught more than a besotted fool.

But now he understood what Ian felt, with vivid clarity. He loved his wife. He knew without equivocation he could not survive losing his wife or their babe. *Let them call me a besotted fool,* he told himself. *I care no'. I love Mairghread and it be perfectly reasonable to be concerned.*

"But Brogan," Reginald began to argue.

"Nay," he said with a shake of his head. "I have been gone long enough."

With a light tap to his horse's flanks, he steered the beast back toward the keep.

In less than an hour, he was handing his horse off to one of the stable boys and racing up the steps. An uneasiness had crept in to his heart. He barely understood it himself, let alone could he make any attempt to explain it to someone should they ask. Something, an inner voice or feeling, was telling him that Mairghread needed him.

Eager to see his wife, he did not stop to speak to anyone, or otherwise dawdle or delay. He did not care if his presence annoyed her. He *needed* to see her, to see that she was in fact quite well. Mayhap 'twas fatherly instincts that propelled him forward. Or perhaps 'twas naught more than unjustified worry. Either way, he raced above stairs and flung open the door to their room.

His heart fell to his feet when he saw Gertie, tied to a chair, a wad of cloth stuffed into her mouth, and panic stricken eyes.

"What in the bloody hell happened?" he yelled, reaching her in naught but a few short strides.

Her eyes were wide with horror as she struggled against the ropes. 'Twas then he realized she was screaming but not looking directly at him. Her eyes were pinned on something behind him.

In one fluid motion, he removed the dirk from his waist and spun around. A man he did not recognize was coming at him with a dirk raised over his head.

Ducking low, he was able to miss the blade by a few inches. Lunging forward, he tackled the man about his waist, hurling them both to the floor. There was no time to wonder who this man was, or why Gertie was bound to a chair. He could only *act*.

Pinning the man to the floor with his knees, Brogan tossed his dirk into his left hand, balled his right into a fist and plunged it into the man's face. Blood began to spurt from his nose, but the stranger was not ready yet to give up the fight.

"Who the bloody hell are ye?" Brogan asked through gritted teeth.

He replied by planting his feet firmly on the floor and pushing Brogan up and off.

Caught off guard, Brogan rolled over, and crouched on one knee, ready for the man's next move. A moment later, he crouched low and lunged once again. Slicing in a wide arc, aiming for Brogan's neck, the blade whistled through the air. Brogan had anticipated the move, and fell onto his back, knocking a chair over in the process. A moment later, he was on his feet again.

Just as he was about to tackle the man again, Martha and Tilda appeared at the door.

"Brogan!" Martha called out.

The man spun around at the sound of her voice, just the distraction Brogan needed. Lunging forward, he tackled him once again, this time sending him crashing to the floor on his stomach. The dirk fell from his hand and slid across the floor.

Wrapping a strong arm around his attacker's neck, Brogan pulled his head up and back by his hair. "Who the bloody hell are ye, and what have ye done with me wife!"

Chapter 28

I will find the traitor and kill them with me bare hands, Mairghread thought angrily as another wave of pain shot through her lower belly. Tight, twisting, 'twas near agony.

They had left the keep an hour ago. Had walked right through the gate without anyone inquiring as to where she was going. The entire courtyard had been eerily quiet. *No matter who is to blame, I will find them.*

They had walked a good distance in a north-easterly direction, before several men stepped out of the woods. Much to her vexation, Aymer insisted she mount a horse brought to her.

"I can no' possibly ride!" she had argued. "I be about to have this babe, ye ignorant fool!"

Furious with the disrespect she was showing him, Aymer slapped her hard across the cheek. Blood filled her mouth and trickled from her lips, her cheek burning as white dots blurred her vision. 'Twas the first time in her life she had ever been hit.

"Ye will mount this horse and ye will mount it now!" Aymer shouted.

His voice was still ringing in her ears when they finally reached their destination.

'Twas an old, decrepit mud and daub hut, nestled deep in the woods. She had forgotten all about the place and could not remember who had once lived here. Not that it mattered in the least at the moment. A blend of fear and anger roiled in her stomach.

Her pains were coming closer and closer together, and lasting far longer. Intense, deep pain that made it next to impossible to walk. Aymer pulled her from her mount without warning or ceremony. She fell to the ground, racked with pain.

Frustrated with her, he yanked her by the hair. "Up!"

Unable to move or speak, she could only swallow back the tears. "Hurt," she finally managed to mutter.

Not so much as an inkling of compassion could she find in his eyes. He all but dragged her into the ancient structure. 'Twas all she could do to breathe.

The small space was void of any furniture. Just a small room with part of the crumbling roof lying on the dirt floor. Decades worth of weeds and vines sprouted from the corners and hung down from the ceiling. It smelled damp, musty.

Aymer pulled her inside, leaving her where she collapsed in a corner near the entrance. On her hands and knees, she rocked back and forth, the pain nearly unbearable. *Please, God, watch over me babe!* She cried silently. *Please, send Brogan to me before it be too late.*

The next voice she heard made her want to retch.

"What is wrong with her?" Courtemanche asked. He sounded far more concerned than Aymer.

"It be her time," Aymer told him. "She is about to give birth."

Although she could not see him, she heard the worry in Courtemanche's voice. "Why did you bring her here?" he demanded to know. "Why not wait until she had her babe?"

The frustration in Aymer's voice was undeniable. "Because we must get to France as soon as possible, ye fool! I told ye, I will need to seek refuge in your castle until I can regain the seat. I can no' do that with *her* still sittin' in it!"

"But it could have waited!" Courtemanche argued. "What will we do with a babe?"

"*We* are no' goin' to do anything with the babe but leave it here.

Leave it to the wolves and scavengers. As long as that babe lives, I will no' be able to take what is rightfully mine."

Mairghread had heard enough. "Brogan will *never* allow ye to lead clan Mactavish!" she cried out. "He will see ye dead first."

His hand swung out once again, just as sharply as before. This time, it landed on her right eye. Bile rose from the pain, from the horror of the moment. "Brogan will kill ye fer that," she all but spat at him.

"Stop!" Courtemanche shouted, grabbing Aymer's arm to keep him from hitting her again. "I do no' want her face harmed."

Me face? She thought. *He cares naught about anything but me face.*

Aymer was furious, but backed away. "How much longer?" he snapped at her.

There was no need to ask to what he was referring. "Hours," she told him. But if the pains were any indication, 'twould be far sooner than she wanted. 'Twas growing more and more difficult to keep from screaming out, to keep from crying from the pains as well fear. She thought of Brogan and cursed herself for wanting a few hours to herself. It had been a selfish decision to send him away with Reginald and Seamus. 'Twas a selfish act that would lead to the death of her babe as well as herself. *Please fergive me, Brogan,* she cried silently.

"We can not have her giving birth here," Courtemanche said. His voice was filled with panic and worry. "We do not know the first thing about births. You should not have brought her here."

Rolling his eyes, Aymer said, "Would *ye* like to take her back to the keep?"

He paled visibly at the notion. "Of course not. But she could die, you fool. I swear to you, if she dies, Aymer, you will not get one red cent from me. Nor will I give you refuge."

Clenching his jaw, Aymer growled angrily. She watched him pace back and forth like a cornered wild beast. Undoubtedly, he was trying to think of his next course of action.

Her own mind was racing for a way out, a way to, at the very least, save her unborn child. She cared not what Aymer or Courtemanche did to her. The only thing she cared about was Brogan and their child. She had to do something and quickly.

Desperate, she was not above bargaining. "If ye fetch Martha to help me have this babe, and if ye let my babe live, I will give the seat of chief to ye."

Aymer studied her dubiously for a long moment. "Ye lie."

Shaking her head she choked back tears. "I care no' what ye do to me, Aymer. Just let me babe live. I swear to ye, I will go with ye to France." Nodding her head at Courtemanche, she said, "I care no' what *he* does to me either. I am too tired to fight ye anymore." Most of what she said was a lie. There was no way in hell she was going to go anywhere with these men.

From his pursed lips and furrowed brow she could see he was giving some weight to the idea.

"Please, Aymer, I beg of ye, let me babe live," she said, her voice filled with undeniable fear. Pleading, begging, she would do what she must to see that her babe lived.

Breathing out through his nose, he crouched low, to look her in the eyes. "And let him someday try to rest the seat from me?"

"Nay, he will no'! Brogan will return to his family." If she did in fact die, 'twas her fervent wish that he do just that. Take their babe back to Mackintosh lands, where he could grow up in peace, surrounded by people who would love him and protect him. Tears pooled in her eyes when she thought of not being able to watch her child grow. *'Tis better I die than me babe.* Nothing was worth this babe's life.

Another pain formed, growing, building, twisting, taking her breath and good senses away. No longer able to think clearly, she cried out. Screaming from the intensity, she rocked back and forth again, on her hands and knees. Sweat covered her face, her back and hands, her dress clung to her skin.

Aymer's voice sounded far away, barely audible over her own screaming. But she could not focus on what he was saying. She only knew he was angry.

Unable to hold herself up, she collapsed to the floor, writhing in agony. Tears blended with sweat as she grew uncomfortably hot.

Aymer and Courtemanche were arguing again, but she cared not and paid no attention to it. Gradually, the pain let up, but did not go away completely. *God, please bring Brogan to me.*

IT TOOK SOME VIGOROUS CONVINCING. REGINALD, HENRY, LIAM, and Comnall, had helped to get the man to see things their way. Eventually, he got tired of the blows to his face, gut, and groin and began to disclose what he knew in earnest.

"'Twas Aymer Mactavish," he said as he spit a glob of blood on the floor.

Brogan had already suspected that at the least, Aymer had ordered something be done before he was put to death. "But who carried out his order?"

The man laughed. "Think ye he is dead?"

"David ordered his execution," Henry said harshly.

The man smiled lopsidedly. "Aye, that he did. But Aymer paid much to gain his freedom. He bribed the guards."

The room fell silent as a fissure of fear raked Brogan's spine. He knew the man was telling him the truth. The news should have surprised him but didn't. Instead, he became furious. There were many questions to be asked, such as *how* they had gotten into the keep, *who* were the traitors who allowed them access. But he asked the most important one first. Grabbing him by his tunic, Brogan leaned in. "Where is me wife?" His words were harsh, clipped, and filled with rage.

The man took no time at all in telling him the whereabouts of Mairghread.

"But good luck with gettin' out of the keep," he added with a sloppy and pained smile.

Brogan's brow knotted into a fine line as he asked him what he meant.

"Yer keep," he chuckled, sounding like a madman. "It be surrounded."

He HAD NOT LIED.

Brogan stood along the walkway of the wooden wall, looking out at the sight before him. Surrounding the keep were some one hundred armed men. Aymer's mercenaries.

"Bloody hell!" he ground out angrily.

Henry, Reginald, and Comnall were standing with him. They were almost as furious as he. *Almost,* for none of them had a wife being held captive by dark, sinister, insane men. A wife who was about to give birth.

Liam came racing up the ladder to join them. He took one look at all the armed men below and gave a low whistle. "Shall I give the order for Iarainn to begin handin' out weapons?"

As much as he wanted to ride through the gate and kill every last one of them, he knew such thoughts were useless. The Mactavish men were not trained in the fine art of battle.

"Have ye interrogated the traitors yet?" he asked, gritting his teeth. The mercenary hadn't known the names of the men who had given entry to Aymer. But he was able to describe them well enough. They were two young men, neither of which Brogan could recall even talking to. Their parents were amongst those who had left months ago, when Mairghread had taken her rightful position as chief.

"Aye," Comnall nodded. "They swear there be no others who aided Aymer."

"Ye be certain of that?" he asked, his brow furrowed, his face growing darker and darker with fury.

Comnall smiled as he gave his right fist a good shake. Brogan took note of the bloodied knuckles. "Aye, I be certain."

WITH THE TRAITORS IN THE GAOL, BROGAN GAVE THE ORDER FOR every one within the keep to be armed. What they truly needed, however, were more men. More well-trained men, as Henry pointed out.

"We need more than just a handful of cooks," Henry said. "'Tis a death sentence to be certain."

"Thank ye fer pointin' out the most obvious," Brogan ground out as he climbed down the ladder.

Iarainn was waiting for him at the bottom. "Be it true?" she asked breathlessly. "Be we surrounded?"

"Aye, 'tis true. Have ye armed everyone?"

She swallowed hard before answering. "Much to me consternation, aye, I have. But I warn ye, I have armed Tilda and Gertie as well."

The thought of Gertie and Tilda armed sent a shiver of dread up and down his spine. Gertie was fighting mad when he had first discovered her tied to the chair.

"The order *was* fer everyone," Iarainn politely reminded him. "And no' even I be brave enough to tell those two 'nay' on anythin'. Especially this day."

The image of Gertie and Tilda leading the charge to slay the men responsible for taking their lady was an amusing one. It almost brought a smile to his face.

To Liam and Comnall he said, "Bring everyone to the yard at once."

THE MERCENARIES WERE ALL THAT STOOD BETWIXT BROGAN Mackintosh and the rescuing of his wife. He now stood in the courtyard, looking out at his people with a most heavy heart. Cooks, sculleries and maids, plus his own men.

'Twas a certainty they would be defeated.

Before he could utter any encouraging words, Reginald and Henry pulled him aside. "We have a plan," Reginald told him.

"If the plan involves our people suddenly gainin' the experience and heart of a thousand highland warriors," he began.

Reginald cut him off. "Nay," he said, sounding most serious. "We need to get to Mairghread. And quickly."

Gertie and Tilda appeared at Reginald's side, each of them holding a broadsword nearly as long as they were tall. "And how do ye intend to do that?" Gertie asked angrily. "Sprout wings and fly?"

"Of course no'!" Reginald growled. Turning his attention back to Brogan, he said, "Ye ferget, there be more than one way out of this keep."

It took a moment for Brogan to realize what Reginald was speaking of. *The secret door!*

Reginald smiled knowingly when he saw clarity dawning in Brogan's eyes. "I have already checked, Brogan. They have no one set below."

Brogan was so relieved he could have kissed the man.

"Ye can take a few of the men with ye," Reginald said. "Michael Mactavish and his family live no' far from here. Ye can get to them, get horses, and be on yer way to Mairghread without the men surroundin' us even knowin'."

"What be ye goin' on about?" Henry asked, his brow furrowed in confusion.

Brogan quickly explained about the secret passage out of the keep. His relief faded instantly when he remembered the lack of stairs. "But we have no stairs built yet," he all but growled.

"Nay, but we have ropes," Reginald said. He was far more hopeful than Brogan.

"Ropes would work," Henry agreed after thinking on it for a long moment. "I fear it be our only hope."

Brogan knew there was no other choice. Looking out at the people in the yard – less than forty in all – he was reluctant to leave them behind to face the mercenaries beyond the wall.

Tilda pursed her lips and shook her head. "'Tis too bad those ten thousand horse thieves Henry spoke of are no' here. We could let them fight those men outside whilst we waited for reinforcements."

Each of them stared at her as if she were daft. "Och! Are ye mad?" Gertie asked. "'Twould be easier to fight the men beyond the walls than ten thousand thieves and murderers!"

'Twas then that Henry began to smile. A most devious smile that made his eyes twinkle. "I think we could manage to scare up a few of them," he said.

Brogan was almost afraid to ask what he meant.

In the end, he was quite glad that Henry Mackintosh was on his side.

❦

With Henry's plan set in place, Brogan, Henry, and Reginald were soon making their way through the secret passage. Moments later, they were scaling down ropes along the side of the cliff.

In less than a half an hour, they were beating down the door of Michael Mactavish's home. The puzzled, brown-haired man stepped outside, leaving his frightened wife huddled near the hearth with their three children.

Reginald quickly explained their quandary. By the time he finished, Michael was fighting mad. "I ne'er did trust Aymer!" he said, spitting the ground at his feet. "I have fifteen horses and ye be welcome to all," he said as he started walking toward the corral.

"We only need three," Brogan pointed out. "For that is all we have with us."

Michael chuckled low and deep. "Knowin' Aymer as I do, three men will be all ye need to go against that coward."

"He has at least ten men with him," Brogan told him as he pulled himself atop a grand, black stallion.

"Then I suggest we stop at me brother's home along the way. He has three grown sons who will be glad to help us."

In no time at all, they were mounted and heading north to gather Marcus Mactavish and his sons. They rode bareback for the man didn't own enough saddles for everyone.

All the while, Brogan prayed silently for God to watch over his sweet Mairghread.

In between her pains — which were coming in great waves now — she prayed frantically. Prayed for Brogan to find her, prayed she would not have to give birth in this filthy, abandoned place. She prayed for her child, for his future, and that God would somehow find it in His heart to see her babe live.

Aymer and Courtemanche continued to argue. Courtemanche was frantic with worry that someone would hear her screams. Aymer was worried they would not make it to France if she did not hurry and have this child. Courtemanche continued to threaten to abandon Aymer if she died. They talked about plots and alliances and the future.

But neither of them made any attempt to help her.

Each time she cried out in agony, they stepped farther away until they were huddled in the far corner of the hut.

Soaked with sweat, twisting and turning in tormenting pain, she lay on the floor, praying, hoping, wishing with all her heart for relief and for Brogan. How much time passed, she didn't know. Doubt crept in. *He should have been here by now.*

Chances were he was still out counting horses with Reginald and Seamus. And what of Gertie? Was she still bound to a chair in her room? Had the dark stranger killed her? Her only hope was that Tilda had found Martha, which would have led to the discovery of Gertie. Unless Aymer's man killed each of them, one by one.

And even if it was soon discovered she was missing, how on earth would they find her? Doomed. She felt doomed to give birth on this filthy floor, alone, with no help, while two deranged men argued over seats of power and gold.

Another wave of pain washed over her. Cursing the madmen to hell, she screamed. Low and guttural and loud with suffering. Her screams drowned out the sounds of her tormentors, the men she prayed would die slow, horrible, painful deaths.

BROGAN LEAPT FROM HIS HORSE BEFORE IT EVEN STOPPED. HENRY, Reginald and the rest of their men took care of the guards posted along the perimeter of the hut as Brogan thundered across the clearing to the small structure. He paused only once when he heard his wife's guttural screams. But his pause was brief as fury coursed through his veins, turning his blood hot. When he stepped inside and saw his wife writhing in pain while Aymer and Courtemanche huddled in the far corner, 'twas all he could do to breathe.

He made no inquiries as to what they were doing. He gave them no time to defend themselves or plead for mercy. With his sword in one hand, his dirk in the other, all the rage and fury he had bottled up came rushing out in his own low, guttural growl. In span of a few furious heartbeats, he was thrusting his sword into Aymer Mactavish's heart, tearing through bone and flesh as it pinned him to the dirt wall. What he might have said, Brogan did not hear, nor did he care.

Whilst thrusting his sword into Aymer, he took the dirk and sliced it across Courtemanche's throat. Their deaths were in tandem, like a macabre, morbid dance. Blood drained from Aymer's belly, it spurt from Courtemanche's throat.

Clutching his wound with both hands, a look of horrific surprise was permanently etched on the Frenchman's face. Just like Aymer's.

Over the sound of his own blood rushing in his ears, Brogan heard his wife cry out. He went to her and knelt down beside her. "Mairghread, I be here!" he exclaimed. 'Twas then his hands began to shake.

Lying on her back, wracked with sobs and tears, she finally opened her eyes. "Brogan!" she cried out.

He did not know what to do for her. Lost, terrified he would lose her, he quickly removed his plaid, then his tunic. Using the tunic, he wiped the dirt, grime and sweat from her face. "I know not what to do," he said, his voice filled with worry.

Grabbing his arm, she looked up at him with pain-filled eyes. "Get me the bloody hell out of here!"

"But ye're havin' the babe," he said, at a loss to what he should or shouldn't do.

She was taking in deep breaths of air into her lungs. "I ken that! But I will no' have this babe in this filthy hut whilst two dead men stare at me!"

Henry and Reginald came rushing inside then. Each were covered in blood. "We killed half of them," Henry said.

"The other half ran off," Reginald informed him.

"Get me out of here!" Mairghread cried out.

Henry and Reginald stared down at her, their eyes wide with horror. Brogan, not wanting to cause his wife any further distress, scooped her up in his arms. "I do no' think we can get ye back to the keep," he stammered out.

"Just get me outside," she pleaded with him.

❧

Wracked with another wave of pain as Brogan carried her outside, the urge to push came over her. There was nothing to grab on to for purchase or strength, save his shirtless chest and arms.

As quickly as he could, he took her to the nearest tree and gently set her on the ground. Immediately, she rolled to her hands and knees. "Help me," she ground out as she continued to sweat.

"God's teeth!" Henry cried out. "She be havin' her babe?" Panic stricken, he knew had no more an idea what to do than Brogan.

Reginald stepped forward, looking just as terrified as Brogan and Henry. "It can no' be much different than a horse givin' birth, can it?"

Knowing that if he did not take charge of the situation, Brogan took in a deep breath and squatted down on his knees in front of Mairghread. "Give me yer plaids," he ordered both men. Without questioning his order, they both removed their plaids and tossed them to Brogan.

Mairghread grabbed each of his arms. "I need to push," she told him through gritted teeth.

Suddenly, he wished he hadn't left the room whenever the women in his life began to talk about birthing babes. But he did know enough that when pushing was mentioned, it meant only one thing; the babe would soon be here.

Helping her into a squatting position, Mairghread clutched his arms and held on for balance. "Henry, put one of the plaids under her."

From his scandalized expression, one would have thought he'd just asked the poor man to strip naked and run through he streets of Edinburgh wearing flowers in his hair. "Henry!" he barked out.

With his eyes half closed, he tried to do Brogan's bidding. "I swear I'll no' look," Henry muttered nervously.

"For the sake of Christ," Brogan ground out while his wife was bearing down. "Just put it under her to catch the babe!"

"I can no' catch a babe!" Henry said, appalled at the idea.

Panting harshly, Mairghread said, "Just put the bloody plaid *under* me!"

Quickly, he did her bidding and stepped away as if he were afraid he'd catch fire.

Reginald knelt beside her and began to rub her back. "I fear none of us know what to do, lass."

There was no way to reply, for the urge to push was too great. Closing her eyes, she groaned and bore down. Exhausted and worried, she pushed with all her might.

Brogan could not see a thing from his current vantage point. "Be it out?" he asked.

"Nay," she said through heavy panting breaths.

It went on like that for what seemed to all an eternity. Several more attempts to push went unfulfilled. Dread settled deep in his gut. Mairghread collapsed against his chest. "I can no'," she said, sounding exhausted beyond hope. "I can no' do it."

Brogan knew she must. Letting go of one arm long enough to lift her chin, he said, "Ye can and ye will." His voice was firm yet kind. "Just lean on me, love. Do no' give up."

❧

SHE WANTED TO CLOSE HER EYES AND SLEEP FOR A SENNIGHT. SHE wanted to scream that he did not have any bloody idea what she was going through. She wanted to slap the warm smile from his face. Yet at the same time, she wanted to hold on to him for dear life.

"'Tis a good thing I love ye," she said harshly.

Brogan could not resist the urge to chuckle. "And I love ye." He kissed her forehead and smiled warmly at her. But there was no mistaking the worry in his eyes. "Now, ye keep pushin', aye?"

Truly, she felt she did not have any strength left. But the warmth and love in the eyes staring into hers was what she needed to see. Weakly, she began to push again when the urge came.

"Come, Mairghread," he said. "Push now. Ye can do this, I know ye can!"

She knew exactly where her newfound strength came from. It came from the love in his eyes as well as his encouraging words. Laying her head against his chest, she clung to his arms as she pushed and pushed and pushed.

Finally, she felt the squish of her babe beginning to leave her body. "Someone catch him!" she cried out.

'Twas Reginald who kept the babe's head from hitting the ground.

One strong push later, and the babe was out.

Relief consumed Mairghread when she heard her babe's strong cries for the first time.

"'Tis a boy!" Reginald shouted happily.

Clinging to her husband, she sobbed uncontrollably. Using the laces from her dress, Reginald tied off the cord. Poor Henry had to step away then, for he had no desire to learn what happens *after* a babe is born.

BROGAN LEANED AGAINST THE TREE, HOLDING HIS WIFE AGAINST HIS chest, his arms wrapped protectively around her and their babe. In her arms, she held their son, a strong lad, with a head full of dark red, curly hair, and strong lungs. Overcome with joy and relief and a heart bursting with love and pride, Brogan's eyes grew damp. He cared not who saw them, for 'twas the happiest moment of his life. He had a son.

The sun had begun its late afternoon descent. A peacefulness had fallen over the little yard. While some of his men took their prisoners back to the keep, the others had left them alone to go build a makeshift litter. There would be no way for Mairghread to ride just yet. As far as Brogan was concerned, they could take their time. He wanted to make this special moment last as long as he could.

"He is so beautiful, aye?" Mairghread asked as she caressed their babe's cheek with her fingertip.

Now was not the time to argue over whether or not a man or lad could be considered beautiful. "Aye, he be a right handsome lad."

Mairghread sighed contentedly then placed a sweet kiss on the tip of her son's nose. "What shall we call ye?" she whispered, unable yet to take her eyes off him.

"Would ye like to name him after yer father?" Brogan asked softly.

Tearing her gaze from her son, she looked into Brogan's eyes. "Me da?" she asked. "Why no' yer da?"

Brogan chuckled. "Do ye ken how many of his grandson's carry his name? Six, at last count." He kissed her forehead and gave her a gentle squeeze. "Nay, I think Gavin suits him better." *Besides, 'twould be one more thing to haunt Aymer while he rots in hell.*

"Brogan, do ye have any idea how much I love ye?" she asked as tears pooled in her eyes.

He chuckled before answering. "If it be at least half as much as I love ye, then we have more love than could fill the entire world."

Chapter 29

While Brogan had been off rescuing his wife, Comnall and Liam were left behind to deal with the mercenaries. Comnall was not nearly as confident in Henry's plan as Brogan had been.

Each of the womenfolk had been dressed in tunic, trews, and hooded cloaks. Gertie and Tilda, though reluctant at first, agreed to dress as men.

"I have to admit," Gertie said as she adjusted the hood of her cloak, "that it feels downright empowerin' to be wearin' trews."

Tilda giggled in agreement. "I be three and seventy and never thought I would see the day where I was dressed as a man *and* given a quiver and bow."

They took to the upper wall with the rest of the women, and took up spaces between Liam and Comnall. "I think we be as ready as we ever will be," Gertie told the men.

Comnall rolled his eyes and sent a prayer heavenward. "Where the bloody hell be Seamus?" he asked Liam.

"Iarainn went to fetch him."

"Why do ye suppose they have no' attacked yet?" Comnall asked as he peered over the wall.

Liam shrugged his shoulders. "I imagine they be waitin' fer Aymer."

Gertie spat on the floor at the mention of Aymer's name. "I imagine he be burnin' in hell right about now."

Tilda nodded in agreement. "And the Frenchman right along with him."

Each of those lining the upper wall had all the faith and confidence in their laird, Brogan. None doubted that he was at this very moment, attacking Aymer and the Frenchman and rescuing their lady.

A moment later, they heard Seamus grousing loudly as he made his way up the ladder. "Did no one think to build stairs fer the wall?" he shouted. "I be an auld man, fer the sake of Christ!"

Urging him upward was Iariann. "Stop yer bellyachin'," she yelled at his back. "Or I swear I'll toss ye over the wall and let the murderin' bastards below have at ye."

He growled deep and low as he made his way upward. Liam and Comnall each grabbed an arm to pull him up the rest of the way. Seeing he was balanced on his own two feet, Comnall helped Iariann next.

Once everyone was in place, Comnall and Liam took their positions. "Be ye ready?" Liam asked Seamus.

Thankfully, the man did not shout. Instead, he gave a nod of his white-haired noggin.

"There be no way this is going to work," Comnall muttered under his breath.

"Have faith," Gertie said, nudging him in his ribs with a hard elbow.

Liam took a deep breath and looked at the men below. "I recommend ye men be on yer way!" he shouted. His deep voice echoed off the walls and across the glen.

Three of the mounted men urged their horses closer. "We recommend ye give up yer keep now," the man in the middle shouted up. "Surrender now and Aymer will let ye live!"

Liam glanced at Comnall and smiled before turning his attention back to the men below. "We have some three thousand men headin' toward the keep as we speak! They be Mackintoshes, father and brothers and kin to our laird, Brogan Mackintosh. And they be right mad that ye be attemptin' to lay siege to this keep!"

The three men below looked to each other before bursting out with laughter. After catching his breath, the one in the middle spoke again. "Think ye we are to believe such a lie?"

"Believe it or nay," Liam shouted back. "Ye'll find out soon enough."

He pulled Seamus to the wall and gave a nod of his head. Seamus took a deep breath and let out a long, shrill whistle.

COMNALL WOULD NEVER HAVE BELIEVED IT IF HE HADN'T SEEN IT with his own eyes. Long moments after Seamus whistled, they could hear the low rumble of countless horses pounding their way across the land.

Comnall and Liam had heard the tale almost as soon as they had arrived last summer. The tale that Seamus could let out but one whistle and all the Mactavish horses would come running to him. But they had believed 'twas naught but an exaggerated tale. Until now.

"Archers!" Liam called out excitedly. "Ready yer arrows!"

The women, who had had only one lesson on how to nock and aim their bows, stepped forward excitedly. It mattered not where they aimed or even if they hit anyone. What mattered was how the men below would react to both the sound of the horses fast approaching and the arrows flying in their direction.

The sound of hooves pounding against the terrain was like rumbling thunder in the distance. Soon, the three men who had come forward were looking quite surprised. Their mounts began to whinny and fret with anticipation, knowing a battle was about to ensue.

As the sound of the horses grew louder, Liam called out to the women. "Archers!"

One of the women lost an arrow in her excitement. Quickly, she scooped it up and nocked it again. "So verra sorry," she said, sounding embarrassed.

"Och!" the woman standing next to her said. "Do no' fash yerself over it, Mildred."

Comnall and Liam rolled their eyes but remained quiet.

The crowd of gathered men below began nervously scanning the horizon. Uncertainty and doubt began to fall over them as the sound of horses grew nearer and louder.

When it sounded as though hell was about to rain down on them, Liam looked at the women. "Archers!" he called out. "Ready! Aim! Fire!"

Caught off guard by what sounded like thousands of mounted soldiers heading their way, the mercenaries were not ready for the hail of arrows. Dozens of arrows flew through the sky. Only two hit anything; a log in front of the three men and a rock near the others.

"Archers!" Liam called out once again. "Ready yer arrows!"

Quickly, albeit a bit haphazardly, the women nocked more arrows. He gave the order once again. "Ready! Aim! Fire!"

More arrows flew through the air. This time, three of them hit, all of them landing in the same man. He fell from his horse, arrows sticking out of each of his arms, and his thigh.

"Oh, dear!" One of the women called out. She went as pale as a sheet. "I did no' mean to hit him!"

"Och!" Gertie yelled. "Ye're *supposed* to hit them! The bloody bastards want our keep!"

The thunder of hoof beats grew louder and louder. Liam called for the archers to ready themselves again.

"I wager ye I can hit the one closest to the front of the line," Gertie challenged Tilda.

"Which one?" Tilda asked. "The one in the red tunic?"

"Nay, the one next to him who looks ready to shite his trews!"

"Ready! Aim! Fire!" Liam called out.

Gertie missed her intended target, but Tilda's aim was true. Dead center in the chest of the man in red.

"That be some right good shootin'!" Gertie exclaimed happily.

Before Liam realized it, he no longer had to give the order to shoot. The women were doing it of their own volition.

BEFORE THE MACTAVISH HORSES COULD BE SEEN, THE WOMEN HAD killed or maimed at least a dozen of the mercenaries. Even as the hired men began to flee, heading northeast, the women continued to shoot arrows through the air.

They took great pleasure in their work. "I hit one!" Evelyn called out happily. "I hit one!"

It took several attempts to get the women to stop. "They have fled!" Liam shouted. "Ye can stop shootin' now!"

They looked positively disheartened to hear his call. "But they have no' shot back!" Tilda said, nocking another arrow.

"Because they have fled," Liam ground out.

"But what if they come back?" she asked, her brow furrowed with determination.

Liam chuckled. "Then ye can shoot them."

Pleased with his answer, she un-nocked her arrow and put it back in her quiver. "Ye promise?"

"Aye," he laughed. "I promise."

HOURS LATER, AFTER BROGAN AND MAIRGHREAD RETURNED TO THE keep, he listened intently while Liam and Comnall recounted the afternoon. They were in Mairghread and Brogan's chamber. The hour was quite late, but the excitement in the air did not lend itself to a restful sleep just yet.

Mairghread had bathed and changed into a clean nightdress. Sitting up in the bed, she cradled her son in her arms as she listened.

Henry was sad to have missed the sight of the mercenaries fleeing, as well as the women archers happily defending their keep.

Mairghread declared that they should celebrate this day each year. "We should never forget the day our womenfolk defended the keep so gallantly."

Liam and Comnall would not necessarily call them *gallant*, but brave they had been.

Gertie was sad to learn that Mairghread had ordered the traitors banned from the clan. "Are ye certain we can no' line them up and let our archers at them?" she asked hopefully.

Liam nearly choked at the image. 'Twould be torture for certain, for he was convinced 'twould be a slow, painful death. Who knew how long it would take before their arrows either hit their targets or did any damage.

"Nay," Mairghread said as she kissed the tip of her son's nose for what seemed the hundredth time since he had been born. "I think we have had enough killin' fer one day."

Brogan readily agreed. "I think it be time we celebrate *livin'*."

Gertie and Tilda glanced at once another. "We have called fer a priest to come and christen yer son."

"I hope ye do no' mind," Tilda added. "But 'tis a most joyous occasion. One that must be celebrated, aye?"

Mairghread knew where they were trying so delicately to go. Rolling her eyes, she gave a slight shake of her head. "Aye, 'tis to be celebrated. I suppose ye already have somethin' planned?"

The two old women smiled sheepishly. "We might have an idea or two," Gertie admitted.

"I suppose it be nothin' simple," she replied as she handed the babe off to Brogan.

"Simple?" Tilda asked, unable to look her lady in the eye.

"Aye, simple," Mairghread said with a yawn.

"Twill no' be too extravagant," Gertie said.

Mairghread knew she was lying.

THREE WEEKS LATER, A CELEBRATION TO RIVAL THE CORONATION OF a king was held in honor of Gavin Mactavish. There was not a spot in the keep that had not been scrubbed clean or that did not hold a flower or candle.

A grand feast was held after Gavin's christening that made the celebration of Mairghread and Brogan's wedding pale in comparison.

The affair was attended by Ian and Rose and half their clan, as well as Arline and Rowan Graham and Leona and Alec Bowie. Hundreds upon hundreds of people came to help celebrate the momentous occasion.

No expense was spared.

They sat at the high table as one person after another approached and offered their well wishes. When Mairghread complained of the cost, Brogan simply smiled. "Ye would have me ignore me first son's christening?" he asked as he held the babe in his arms.

Her eyes grew wide in astonishment. "Ye mean this be all yer doin'?"

Smiling at his son, he said, "I might have helped Gertie and Tilda just a bit."

Unable to keep from smiling, she rested her head on his shoulder. "Will ye never cease to surprise me, Brogan Mackintosh?"

"I hope no'," he said. "Elst ye might get bored with me."

"Bored? With ye?" she asked with a good measure of disbelief. "That will never happen."

"Do ye promise?" he asked playfully as he kissed her forehead.

"I do so promise."

Epilogue

FIFTEEN YEARS LATER

In the tall summer grass, on the northwestern shores of Scotland, the seventh annual meeting of the clans Mactavish, Mackintosh, McLaren, Bowie, and Graham was in full swing. Hundreds of people had made camp in a clearing betwixt loch and woods. Banners from each clan fluttered in the warm afternoon breeze. Cooking fires blazed while small groups of people huddled together.

Sitting on blankets in the warm sunshine were Mairghread Mactavish and her friends, Rose and Aggie Mackintosh — sisters-by-law but more importantly by heart — Arline Graham, and Leona Macdowall-Bowie.

"Did ye ever think?" Arline Graham asked as she handed her youngest child, son Liam, an apple before sending him on his way to play with the rest of the children.

"Ever think what?" Mairghread asked as she looked out at the group of children playing not far away. Doing a quick headcount for all her own children, she breathed a sigh of relief. Seven in all, and every one of them with either dark auburn locks like hers, or Brogan's ginger coloring. Five strong sons and two beautiful daughters she and Brogan were blessed with.

"That we would be sittin' here, watchin' all these children play?"

Arline replied. She and her husband Rowan had seven children of their own, four daughters and three sons.

"Of course I did," Leona answered. Though in truth there had been a time in her life where she thought she would never have children of her own. But that time was short-lived. Four daughters and a son she had given Alec Bowie. He blamed his white hair on the fact he has so many beautiful daughters. 'Twas worry, not age, or so he proclaimed.

"Be that young Rowan who just fell down?" Leona asked as she looks out at the crowd of people.

"Which Rowan?" Arline and Aggie asked in unison as each of them craned their necks to get a better look.

"Aggie's lad," she replied, craning her neck to get a better look. "Och! Never mind. 'Tis Nora MacDougall's grandson, Angus." Aggie and Frederick had five children of their own — two daughters and three sons — including her oldest son Ailrig. Knowing their relationship had been strained of late, no one inquired as to where he might be.

To an outsider, or someone who was not yet a mother, it might have appeared there were too many children to keep track of. But not to these mothers.

"Och!" Arline cried out as she struggled to get to her feet. "Me Aiden and Leona's Grace are fightin' again."

Leona let loose a frustrated sigh as she got to her feet. "I swear that girl will be the death of me someday."

Mairghread watched as Leona's daughter Grace had Aiden pinned to the ground. She was amazed at the strength the seven-year-old girl possessed. She was also surprised at nine-year-old Aiden's restraint. He refused to give her a taste of her own medicine.

Lost in her own thoughts, she did not hear her husband approach. Still, she knew he was there. She could feel his presence without him uttering a sound.

"How be the most beautiful woman in all of Scotia?" he asked in a whisper as he sat down behind her.

Mairghread smiled warmly at his compliment as she continued to scan the area, keeping a keen eye on her children.

"Ye best go talk to Gavin," she told Brogan.

"What has he done now?" he asked with a heavy sigh.

"He be takin' Arline's daughter, Grace, into the woods.

Rolling his eyes, he got to his feet. "I swear he acts like Ian more and more each day."

Rose sat taller at hearing her husband's name. "Och! Ye best cut *that* behavior now, Brogan. Elst ye will be a grandfather afore ye want to be. And Rowan will kill him."

Brogan waved off her comment as he hurried toward the woods.

"I feel sorry fer ye," Rose said to Mairghread.

"Do no' feel sorry fer me," she replied with a giggle. "*Ye* be the one married to Ian."

Rose smiled. "Aye, and happily so."

"I declare here and now, that I have married the *best* of the Mackintosh men," Aggie said with a smile. "He be the most handsome and easiest to get along with."

Rose and Mairghread could not argue on the latter part of her statement. Out of all the Mackintosh men, Frederick *was* the most patient. Until he was provoked, that is.

They watched and giggled as Leona walked back with a very angry daughter in tow. Sitting her down on the ground, Leona stood over her young daughter, with hands on her hips. "Now tell me, what on earth possessed ye to be so mean to Aiden?"

Little Grace crossed her arms over her chest and glowered across the lawn at the object of her consternation. Her blonde locks shone brightly in the afternoon sun. But her dark brown eyes were filled with anger. "He said he was going to marry me."

Leona hung her head low and rubbed her forehead as if a headache was coming on. "That be no reason to tackle him and pin him to the ground. Need I remind ye that ye are a lady?"

"I be no lady! I be a Bowie!" she argued. "And I will no' marry Aiden Graham. I will no' marry anyone."

"Use that tone with me one more time and I will paddle yer behind," Leona warned her.

'Twas all Mairghread and Rose could do not to laugh at the little girl's declaration or Leona's consternation.

Tears filled Grace's eyes. "But I do no' want to marry anyone, mum. Men be eejits."

"No' all men are eejits," Leona told her.

"Da says they are."

Letting out a frustrated sigh, Leona looked done in. "Yer da only says that because he does no' want *any* of his daughters to marry. Were it up to him, ye'd all be sent to convents."

Grace looked appalled at that idea. "But they will no' let me be a warrior at a convent!"

Before she could voice her reply, Arline and young Aiden returned. "Aiden has somethin' he wants to say to ye, Grace," she told the teary-eyed little girl.

Aiden smiled brightly down at Grace. There was a twinkle in his green eyes. Mairghread thought he looked very much like his father, but with Arline's auburn hair and bright green eyes.

"Mum says I have to apologize to ye fer what I said."

Arline quirked a brow and thumped the back of his head with her finger. "Aiden," she said, her tone warning him to tread lightly.

Begrudgingly, he poked at the ground with his toe. "I be sorry I said I was goin' to marry ye."

Grace was not quite ready to accept his apology. But when she looked up at him, he winked.

Before she could pummel him again, Leona was scooping her up. "*Ye* need a nap and a bit of time to think."

With her head over her mother's shoulder, Grace stuck her tongue out at Aiden.

Aiden chuckled openly. At which his mother thumped his head once again. "Go and find yer father," she scolded. "And tell him what ye have done."

"I do no' ken what I did wrong," he said as he rubbed the back of his head. "All I did was tell her we'd be married."

Arline rolled her eyes and counted to ten. "Did ye ask her or tell her?"

Flummoxed, he looked aghast. "I told her. Why would I ask?"

"Ask yer father *why*," she told him.

With his head hung low, he walked away. Slowly. As if he were a man heading to the gallows.

Exasperated, Arline said, "Why can no' *one* of me children possess me good-natured disposition?"

Her friends did their best to contain their amusement. But 'twas all too much. Soon, they were rolling on the ground, consumed with laughter.

"What?" she asked, her brow drawn into a line of confusion. "I happen to have a very good natured spirit."

"Aye," laughed Rose. "Good natured, until ye be vexed or have yer mind set upon a thing."

She didn't know what one thing had to do with another and told them thus.

"Ye and Rowan be made fer one another," Rose said, wiping away tears from laughing so hard.

"Aye," agreed Leona. "Ye both be as stubborn as an ox. No wonder yer children are just as stubborn."

Unamused, Arline said, "I am no' stubborn. Determined, aye, but no' stubborn."

"And ye wonder where Lily gets it from," Aggie said, trying to get her giggles under control.

Arline's face burned red. "*She* acts just like her father. Though she is no' mine by blood, she is still me daughter. I would like ye to remember that."

"How many potential husbands has she turned down?" Aggie asked, knowing full well the answer to that question.

"Four," she replied indignantly. After a long moment, her anger faded. "Though they were broken-hearted, 'twas all I could do no' to tell them how lucky they were."

"She be a handful, that one," Leona said. "Be she still set on marryin' Liam McKenna?"

Arline rolled her eyes. "Liam McKenna. I swear to ye, if I never hear that name again, 'twill be too soon."

Lily had fallen in love with the lad when she was four years old. One would have thought after seventeen years, she would have given up and changed her mind. But not Lily Graham. Her *determination* to marry the boy was legendary. He, however, had no intention of marrying her. Mairghread felt sorry for the beautiful young woman. Unrequited love could be a very painful thing.

It soon became apparent that the younger children were in dire need of naps. One by one, the mothers ushered their babes into tents, under protest of course.

Mairghread found her husband standing with his brothers, near the edge of the woods. Their conversation seemed serious. But these were Mackintosh men. They had the same countenance when discussing the weather as they did the current political atmosphere.

He glanced up from his conversation and smiled warmly at her. Giving his brothers a nod, he stepped away. Drawing her in, he kissed her sweetly.

"So, what did Gavin have to say for himself?" she asked.

Brogan's smile faded rapidly. "While he is quite fond of the lass, he has no thoughts of marriage."

"I should hope not!" Mairghread exclaimed. "He is far too young."

"On that, we can agree," he replied.

"What will we do with that boy?" she asked.

"I told him that if I caught him trying to lift the skirts of any more lasses before he is one and twenty years old, that *we* would send him to a monastery in Germany until he was forty."

"And did he believe ye?" she asked with a quirked brow.

"Nay, but he did believe Rowan."

"Rowan?" she asked, her brow now etched with more worry.

Brogan chuckled. "Rowan explained that his daughter was far too young at three and ten to be escorted into the woods by a lad who could no' yet shave. He also explained that if ever he caught him near any of his daughters again, he would kill him."

"And what did ye say?" she asked in wide-eyed astonishment.

"I told him I'd let him."

There was very little doubt that each man meant every word they said. She supposed, however, 'twas just the thing her son needed to keep him away from innocent lasses. Resting her head against his chest, she held him tightly. "I love ye, Brogan Mackintosh."

"And I love ye," he replied. She loved the way his voice still sent shivers of excitement coursing through her body.

"I have put the younger children down for naps," she said as she looked up and into his eyes. "I think I should like a nap as well."

After all these years, he knew what kind of *nap* she was referring to. There would be very little actual sleeping taking place.

"Brogan," Frederick called out to him. "We need to finish discussin'—"

Brogan shook his head. "No' now, lads. Me wife and I need a nap."

Prologue to Black Richard's Heart

THE HIGHLANDS, 1356

Death could not come fast enough for Black Richard MacCullough.

'Twas difficult to distinguish his blood from the countless others who lay dead or dying on the cold spring grass. Grass he had played in as a child. Now, 'twas painted in blood.

It had been a long, hard-fought battle between the MacCulloughs and the Chisholms. A battle that had lasted for three long, bloody days. The MacCulloughs were laying siege to their own keep; a keep that had been stolen from then five years ago by the ruthless Maitland Chisholm.

The first two days had been spent trying to get beyond the massive, well-fortified walls. Knowing how well built they were, for he'd built the damn things with his own hands, a decision was made. On this, the third day, Galen MacCullough decided to burn the bastards out. Thick, black smoke billowed from the roof of the keep. The early spring breeze picked up sparks and carried them from the keep to the granary. Before they knew it, several fires burned. The Chisholms came pouring out of the gate like rats leaving a sinking ship. Apparently, their ill-gotten gains were not worth fighting for.

Through the pounding rain and relentless wind, they fought. They fought for revenge. They fought for honor. And they fought to regain their home and lands.

Black Richard had watched his father die first, cut down by Maitland's own blade. Unable to aid him for he was too busy in a fight for his own life, all he could do was watch his father fall to his knees. A moment later, Maitland was using his battle axe to chop Galen's head off.

Then, one by one, four of his six brothers fell.

All the while he fought ferociously and bravely, until he could no longer lift up his own sword. His last and final act, before being cut nearly in half, was sending Maitland Chisholm to hell.

Now Black Richard lay dying, his face flayed open by Maitland, his gut sliced open by a nameless Chisholm.

The MacCulloughs had fought bravely, and none who had died or were about to, would die in vain or in shame. He was certain just as many Chisholms - may the greedy bastards all now be burning in hell — had been killed as his own clansmen.

Knowing death was inevitable, he did not bother with plotting revenge. He would have to leave that up to his two younger brothers, Raibeart and Colyn. Far too young to fight but, hopefully, with time and guidance by anyone left standing, the two young boys would rise and seek revenge in the name of their father and brothers. There was one Chisholm left to be dealt with; Randall. The son of the Chisholm chief responsible for the hell on earth they had been living all these years.

Through the fog of pain, the blood rushing in his ears, the pounding in his skull, he thought he heard the call of victory. Whether it be real or his imagination, he neither knew nor cared. All he wished for was the pain to cease and for the sweet release of death. Mayhap someone would take mercy on him and slice his throat to speed up the process of dying.

Which hurt the worst, his face — flayed open from skull to neck — or the gaping, bleeding wound on his side — he did not know. 'Twas agony either way.

It seemed an eternity passed before silence filled the air. The rain stopped as suddenly as it had arrived. A strong breeze blew in, chasing away any remnants of the clouds. Soon, the sun was shining so brightly it pained his eyes to look upon it.

This must be the end, he told himself. *Death has finally come for me.*

ARRIVING IN 2017

BookBub

BookBub is a free service that helps millions of readers discover great deals on acclaimed ebooks. It's free and easy to join! Tap the image above to follow me and BookBub will notify you directly whenever I have a new release or a special price on one of my existing novels.

Also by Suzan Tisdale

Forever Her Champion

The Edge of Forever

Arriving in 2018:

Black Richard's Heart

The Brides of the Clan MacDougall

(A Sweet Series)

Aishlinn

Maggy (arriving 2018)

Nora (arriving 2018)

Coming Soon:

The MacAllens and Randalls

About the Author

USA Today Bestselling Author, storyteller and cheeky wench, SUZAN TISDALE lives in the Midwest with her verra handsome carpenter husband. All but one of her children have left the nest. Her pets consist of dust bunnies and a dozen poodle-sized, backyard-dwelling groundhogs – all of which run as free and unrestrained as the voices in her head. And she doesn't own a single pair of yoga pants, much to the shock and horror of her fellow authors. She prefers to write in her pajamas.

Suzan writes Scottish historical romance/fiction, with honorable and perfectly imperfect heroes and strong, feisty heroines. And bad guys she kills off in delightfully wicked ways.

She published her first novel, Laiden's Daughter, in December, 2011, as a gift for her mother. That one book started a journey which has led to fifteen published titles, with two more being released in the spring of 2017. To date, she has sold more than 350,000 copies of her books around the world. They have been translated into four foreign languages (Italian, French, German, and Spanish.)

You will find her books in digital, paperback, and audiobook formats.

Stay up to date with Suzan's App for Readers! Available for iOS, Android, and other smart devices.

Apple Store
GooglePlay

www.suzantisdale.com
Email: suzan@suzantisdale.com
Tap any of the icons below to follow me at Facebook, BookBub, Instagram, Twitter, Goodreads, and Amazon.

Made in the USA
Middletown, DE
27 August 2018